AN INDEPENDENT
WOMAN

Visit us at www.boldstrokesbooks.com

AN INDEPENDENT WOMAN

by

Kit Meredith

2023

AN INDEPENDENT WOMAN

ISBN 13: 978-1-63679-553-9

This Trade Paperback Original Is Published By
Bold Strokes Books, Inc.
P.O. Box 249
Valley Falls, NY 12185

First Edition: September 2023

CREDITS
EDITOR: RUTH STERNGLANTZ
PRODUCTION DESIGN: STACIA SEAMAN
COVER DESIGN BY INKSPIRAL DESIGN

Acknowledgments

Thank you to all at BSB for the warm welcome. Thank you especially to Rad and Sandy for listening to my pitch and encouraging me to finally get this book finished. Thank you to my editor, Ruth, for the kind words and helpful feedback.

Thanks to my writing buddy, Holly, for putting up with me talking about this project for so long and helping me keep going. Thanks also to Liz, Antony, Jodie, and all the rest of our awesome writing crew for being the best alpha/beta readers and support system. I'm so glad we formed our little writing group, and I'd encourage any budding writers out there without one to find or create a writing group in their area.

Thanks to all in the poly community who've taken the time to share their experiences and support others to find their way outside the usual boundaries of love. Especially to those who shared their mistakes so I didn't have to repeat them (or could at least try not to). I was fortunate to find a wonderful partner and metamour who have stuck by me through the years and who I hope to spend many more years with yet. Here's to more adventures and limitless love.

Thank you to all who work within our precious National Health Service. You are not superheroes or monsters, but underappreciated workers doing your best in difficult circumstances. Support our nurses and save our NHS!

Finally, a heartfelt thank you to the friends who helped me through the darkest of days: to Helen, Zoe, Beckie, Emma, Alison, Julia, and all who walked that path with me. I will never forget you. And to all those people lost in our under-resourced health and social care system: You matter. You all matter. You deserve a life full of love, laughter, and kindness. There is a whole world out there, and it is better for having you in it.

To Liz,
for gifting me the words to unveil different kinds of love
and staying by my side as I found my way

In memory of Zoe,
a brilliant rainbow who lit up every room
and had so much love to give, if only she'd had the chance

CHAPTER ONE

Nobody warned her about the sister. Not that it would've made much difference, given that the decision to dump them on her had been made behind closed doors. But still, a warning would've been nice. Unfortunately for Rebecca, Marie was in charge that day.

"So, our new resident is moving in today. In fact, they got here an hour ago," Marie announced.

A few glances were exchanged between the morning shift that made Rebecca uneasy. Had something gone wrong with the move?

"We've left her settling into her room. I've allocated a key worker and told them she'll be there soon to answer any questions and help her settle in."

Her colleague sitting opposite rolled her eyes not at all discreetly. Marie acted like she hadn't seen it. Maybe she hadn't, but Rebecca suspected it was more she knew what it was about. Rebecca, however, had nothing else to go on. She'd arrived at Avebrook House just in time for handover, via the kitchen for a much-needed cup of tea. By the time she'd sat down, Marie was already waiting to start, impatiently shuffling paperwork and checking the clock. On the days Marie was in charge, handover started at two p.m. on the dot, whether everyone was there or not.

"She had been assigned a key worker, but after meeting with her we decided someone else would be a better fit."

Rebecca stiffened. That was not how things were done. It wasn't like it was the first time anyone had met or found out anything about the new addition. The key worker system was carefully balanced—you shouldn't make changes on a whim. What were they up to?

"We've had a bit of a shuffle round, so she's now with…" Marie paused to look down at the papers in front of her, making a show of studying them. "Rebecca." She looked straight at her, a crocodile smile spreading her painted lips.

The announcement was greeted with a mixture of faux surprise and suppressed relief. Rebecca stayed silent, her hands tightening until her knuckles whitened and the heat radiating through the mug she clasped became almost unbearable. She was clearly being set up; there was no way she was next in line, and Marie knew it.

"I trust that's okay with you, Rebecca?" Marie kept her lips stretched thin as she waited for her to accept the ruling.

No. "Yes, of course." It wasn't like she had a choice, and she was clearly outnumbered. If only Patience, their manager, was there to put a stop to whatever game they were playing. "But…I'm not prepared at all—I've not even seen her file. Maybe whoever had her originally could carry on today, or at least introduce me…" She trailed off as across the table her colleague's eyes narrowed.

"No, it'd be best if she's with the same person from the start, to avoid confusion, don't you agree?" Marie dismissed her attempt at compromise with no sign of consideration other than a mild twitch of her lips.

"Yes." The tightness in Rebecca's chest and throat made it difficult to get the word out. There was no point arguing, even if she could think of what to say. The only thing she could do was try to keep a panic attack at bay.

"Excellent. You can introduce yourself as soon as we're finished here."

Marie slid a thin file across the table to her and moved onto a general review of the last eighteen hours. The blue cardboard cover had a new label, stuck haphazardly over the remains of an older one. Rebecca picked at the torn edges that peeked out as she attempted to listen to the rest of the handover and fought the urge to start scanning the paperwork underneath. There was no further mention of the new resident, though she didn't follow everything that was discussed so might have missed it if they'd circled back round to her. The sticky remains gathered under her short nails, messing them up and failing to improve the neatness of the file. Paler board was revealed underneath the removed pieces. She'd have to find a larger label to cover it before heading to meet…She blanked their name.

No one appeared to be paying her any attention since she'd accepted her assignment, but she still tried to be discreet as she focused her gaze on the writing on the label instead of the mess around it.

Phoebe Jennings.

There was no other information on the outside, and she daren't flip it open and make it too obvious she wasn't listening. Besides, she really should be, as Phoebe wasn't her only responsibility. She tried to tune back in to Marie's narrative, but her shirt was throttling her where it was pulled too tight around the collar. If she could release the top button and let it hang open, then she could breathe, but it wouldn't look professional. The enclosed room had no windows and a dozen exhaling bodies in it, filling it with their warm breath. She needed to get out of there.

She saw rather than heard the meeting end. Everyone abruptly started shuffling and stood up, heading for fresh air and, in a lot of cases, the opposite. Out back would soon be dominated by the smokers, so instead she headed to the small office and opened the window, sticking her head out like a dog in a car and swallowing the air in large gulps. A deliciously cool breeze greeted her clammy face, cooler than her skin despite the summer sun that was attempting to peek through the rain clouds, and she stayed there a few minutes.

Refreshed and breathing easier, she sat down at the desk by the window and finally opened the file. As she'd suspected, there wasn't much there. Only very basic information had been provided, and the care plans were a simple cut-and-paste job she'd seen dozens of times before. She sighed. It seemed she'd be starting from scratch. The social services assessment report wasn't much better. Phoebe had missed out on being allocated a flat in supported accommodation apparently due to needing more support than they offered, but it could be at least partly down to the lack of options in the area. The reality was that personal choice and needs were only part of these decisions—placement also depended on where there was room. The report didn't contain much about what Phoebe's support needs were apart from some basic tick box questions that could be interpreted a number of ways.

The glow of the computer screen was tempting, but Rebecca knew it'd be a waste of time to seek further information on the system. A lot of her colleagues were old school, and there was always more information in the paper files than on the computer. The only advantage would be not needing to decode any handwriting.

Before she headed out, she memorised one piece of information. The emergency contact was recorded as Alexandra Jennings. It was a good start to at least be able to greet the resident's mother by name. Hopefully she wasn't as fierce as the name implied. The contact form had been completed in a tight, controlled hand that she didn't recognise—presumably the hand of Alexandra.

Rebecca scooped up the documents and slotted the folder back in the creaking filing cabinet in the corner of the office. There was no point taking it with her. A pen and paper would be much more useful, and less obtrusive. She'd noted the nervous glances clients would give their files, and the curiosity in their relatives' eyes. She needed to have more to show for it before she risked them asking to see.

They had put Phoebe in one of the upstairs rooms, the downstairs being kept for those with mobility issues or higher care needs, so that told her something. Rebecca headed for the stairs, focusing straight ahead and walking with purpose. It was important to walk with purpose at the home, otherwise you'd be grabbed to assist with something else, or stopped by a resident for a general chat, which she always felt in two minds about, as she liked to give them that human interaction but stopping to talk to everyone could put her way behind schedule. They'd got used to the way she said hello and kept moving, only returning their own greeting and sometimes agreeing to their request to come see them after she'd done whatever she'd set out to do.

As she climbed the stairs, the clamour of the home receded. It was calmer away from the communal living areas. Usually. As she reached the top, a piercing wail drifted down the corridor to greet her. She picked up her pace—she couldn't make out any words until she got closer.

"I don't want to!" someone whined.

"I know, Bee, I know. But we don't have much choice right now," a lower voice said, filled with urgent reassurance.

"But I don't want to stay here." The voice rose at the end, threatening to break.

Rebecca froze, a few steps away from Phoebe's door, her fears confirmed. Something had gone wrong, and she'd been left to fix it. Her nails bit into her palms. She just hoped too much damage hadn't been done for her to stand a chance.

"It won't be for long, I promise."

Were they already trying to find a way to move her on? Surely nothing that awful could've happened in an hour. Maybe they were just trying to calm Phoebe and had no other plans. Rebecca hoped that was the case. Avebrook House wasn't a short-stay respite centre, it was a home.

A fresh wail escaped from under the door. "Don't leave me here." Phoebe—it must have been her—wasn't letting up.

"Listen, it's going to be okay. I'll hang around and visit every day."

Rebecca shifted and tugged at her shirt, trying to loosen its tight grip on her throat. The parents coming that often would not make her job easy.

"Promise?" Phoebe sniffed loudly.

"Promise. As long as you need me. I won't abandon you."

It went quiet, and Rebecca imagined them wrapping Phoebe in a loving hug.

"This is a good thing, remember? It's exciting, finally moving out."

"Yeah." Phoebe's sniffs grew quieter.

"Think about all the things you can do now!" The enthusiasm injected into their voice sounded fake, but at least they were trying to move the conversation in a positive direction.

Rebecca figured this was a good time to make her entrance and knocked quickly before she could change her mind. There was movement in the room and whispering she couldn't interpret.

Eventually, there was a just audible, "Come in."

When she tried the door handle, she found it was locked, and there was more shuffling behind it before someone turned the catch. Rebecca plastered an attempt at a relaxed smile on her face as the door swung open.

She was greeted by a fierce scowl, emanating from an alternative-looking young white woman who she assumed was her charge, based on the distinct facial characteristics that indicated Down's syndrome. Other than that, she didn't look like their average resident, with jet-black hair ending in purple tips and an outfit that belonged at a rock concert.

They stared at each other until Rebecca remembered where she was and why she was there. "Hi, I'm Rebecca, your key worker here." She held out her hand, but the woman showed no signs of wanting to take it.

After a moment's silence, she replied, "I'm Phoebe," with obvious reluctance. Her scowl hadn't lifted, and she stood blocking the doorway.

Rebecca forced herself to keep smiling and plough on. "May I come in? I just wanted to introduce myself to you and your family, and answer any questions you may have."

She tried to peek around Phoebe to see how many people she had to contend with. She'd only heard two voices, but no one had even told her the mother was still there, so it could be crammed with relatives as far as she knew.

Phoebe turned and looked behind her, as if seeking an answer there. Rebecca waited while she supposed a silent exchange took place. After a few beats, Phoebe moved aside with a simple, "Okay," and without making eye contact.

It was becoming clearer why this case had been dropped on her. She took a few steps into the room, then paused to locate the other speaker she'd heard. A wiry figure lounged against the back wall next to a giant poster of a sparkling vampire.

The sight threw her. Not all parents of people with Down's syndrome were elderly as was assumed, but this person was surely too young to have birthed Phoebe. Unlike Phoebe, they were dressed not to be noticed, in a slouch T-shirt and jeans. Their amber hair was short, a standard non-fuss barber cut, and the light copper streaks highlighting it looked natural. Sea-green eyes stared back at her out of a pale pixie face. They had an androgynous vibe or perhaps butch lesbian, but Rebecca didn't want to make any assumptions. Maybe it was wishful thinking—despite their unassuming appearance, Rebecca couldn't stop staring. Those eyes, you could swim in them.

The eyes narrowed. "Can I help you?" Their voice rose in a way that made it sound more like an accusation than a question.

Rebecca shook herself and moved forward, "Sorry, I wasn't expecting you." The wrong thing to say, given she'd entered their space. But it was true, she hadn't been expecting…She discreetly wiped her sweaty palms against her trousers and tried again, "I'm Rebecca."

This time her hand was delivered a short, sharp shake. "Alex."

Rebecca was drawn back into their gaze, clutching their strong hand, until Alex pulled forcefully away. Alex looked around her, and Rebecca realised she had her back to the person she'd come to see. As they didn't seem set to offer any further information about themself, Rebecca tore herself away. They probably thought she was an unexperienced slacker, with all the staring she was doing. *Get a grip, you know how to do this.*

Phoebe had sat down on the single bed on the other side of the poster. Apart from that, there was nothing personal about the room, and her bags and boxes were still firmly closed. Her black- and red-rimmed eyes, shadowed with smeared eyeliner, provided the explanation for why.

The only seat was by the desk next to Alex, but Rebecca didn't think she could concentrate in such close proximity to the enigmatic stranger. As she looked from Phoebe to Alex and back again, she could pick out a familial resemblance in the set of their jaws and the curve of their eyebrows. Maybe she'd been too quick to judge. Alex could've had her as a teenager, at a stretch. Or maybe she wasn't the birth parent and had an older partner. Or Phoebe was adopted. Either way, if Phoebe's parents were queer, that could explain why she was matched with Rebecca.

"Okay if I sit with you?" She moved towards Phoebe, who shuffled further towards the head of the bed in response. It was as much of an invitation as she was going to get, so she sat down, perched on the edge. "I know this is a big move for you, so I'll give you time to settle in. I won't ask you lots of questions now."

Phoebe's shoulders relaxed slightly, and she puffed out a sigh. Had Rebecca's colleagues been pushier in their initial approach?

"For now, I just want you to know who I am, in case you need anything. Okay?" Phoebe was clearly overwhelmed, and there was no point trying to force her to understand anything more.

After a few moments Phoebe muttered, "Okay." It was something.

"Do you have any questions?" Rebecca looked from Phoebe to Alex, trying not to linger on the latter. "Either of you?"

"We're fine," Alex answered for both of them, shifting away from the wall to stand closer to Phoebe. "If she needs anything, we'll call you."

It was a clear dismissal. Rebecca reluctantly rose to her feet. Phoebe looked so small and lost in the bare room that she wanted to give her a squeeze but knew it wouldn't be appropriate. Hopefully she'd have better luck trying to talk to her once she'd settled in.

"Thank you. Just knock on the office door downstairs or you can press this button in an emergency." She walked over to the red block on the wall, ensuring she had Phoebe's attention. "If you need help, if something's wrong, press this and someone will come."

The buttons were a contentious addition in recent years, with many staff fed up with their overuse by residents who'd discovered they got a quicker response by using them than hanging around the office. Plus, sometimes it seemed they just didn't want to leave their rooms, something many of her colleagues regarded as pure laziness. Rebecca didn't blame the residents, though—the bustling home could get a bit much, and there were times she wished she could stay shut in a quiet room. The only-for-use-in-an-emergency part wasn't important as far as she was concerned. If they needed help, they needed help.

"I press it if I need help," Phoebe repeated, verifying she'd understood.

"Exactly." Rebecca smiled properly for the first time.

Then she looked over to find Alex staring at the button like she'd seen a ghost, or as if it was a suspicious piece of tech someone had left in an airport. It was just a simple button, set in a square plastic box attached to the wall. Normally relatives found its presence reassuring, if anything. Rebecca was tempted to ask what was going through Alex's mind but doubted her enquiry would be welcomed.

Instead, she ended up leaving with an overly casual, "See you later."

Despite her cold reception, she hoped she would. She wished certain people would be more patient with the residents, rather than labelling them as difficult over the slightest bump in the road like she suspected they had with Phoebe. You couldn't expect someone to be happy and settled straight away, especially someone with a learning disability who'd left home for the first time.

She kept an ear out for Phoebe's buzzer for the rest of the day, but it never sounded.

❖

It had that smell, the sickly-sweet stench of certain institutions that lingered around, covering something rancid underneath. It filled Alex's nostrils and caught in the back of her throat and wouldn't let go, along with the memories that crept in with it. She tried not to retch. She'd been right about the place.

Avebrook House looked like a centuries-old town house from the outside, but the inside had been refurbished to the point of stripping out all its personality. The pastel walls and generic landscapes lent it a sterile air. It did not feel like a home, though it claimed to be one for adults with learning disabilities. At least it was clean, on the surface anyway.

Thankfully the smell didn't follow her upstairs as she headed back to Phoebe's room. She managed to avoid any staff, besides the one who answered the door. She'd asked for Phoebe to have a key of her own, but apparently it was "out of the question for security reasons." At least they got a key to her room. She'd told Phoebe to keep it locked at all times. It wouldn't keep the staff out, of course. She'd have to check through the heap of paperwork they'd dumped on them for the exact rules. They had a procedure for everything in these places, and it was best to know it so they couldn't take advantage. She'd learned a lot of lessons from her own time in care.

Alex tapped on the door. She'd left Phoebe asleep, exhausted by the emotions of her big move. She hadn't wanted to leave her little sister alone like that but couldn't afford to miss her meeting at the warehouse.

A sleep-filled voice called out, "Who is it?"

Good, Phoebe had got the message to check before inviting anyone in.

"Just Alex."

Heavy footsteps rushed towards her, and the key ground in the lock. Phoebe swung the door open, a relieved smile lighting up her creased face. "Hey, sis."

"Hey, duck." Alex kissed her on the forehead as she walked past.

Phoebe had managed to unpack one box at some point while she was out. A full CD rack now sat on the desk. Alex had offered to buy her an MP3 player for Christmas to replace her vast CD collection, but she'd acted mortally offended. The spinning silver discs were a love of hers and had been for as long as Alex could remember, back to when she was a little kid and used to spend hours taking them on and off their parents' hi-fi. They'd eventually given in and bought Phoebe her own, desperate to listen to a whole album without her toying with it. Alex was grateful too—as a teenager she'd not been happy about her little sister sneaking into her bedroom to play with her own sacred collection.

"Glad you've got the important bit done." She smirked. "Want me to hang around and help with the rest?"

Phoebe nodded. She was unusually quiet but had just woken up.

"How about I sneak us in a takeaway to help us along?"

That seemed to perk her up. "Yes, please. We can't do it all anyway—there's nowhere to put stuff." Phoebe waved her arms around the bare room.

She had a point. Apart from the desk and bed, the only other furniture was the wardrobe and an inbuilt unit under the sink. The furniture was basic, and the walls were painted beige—the bedroom was as featureless as the rest of the house. It seemed unlikely they'd get away with repainting it—besides, they weren't planning on Phoebe staying long enough to justify it—but they could get some bits to brighten it up while she was stuck there.

"We'll have to make a trip to get you some more furniture. I don't start work for a couple of days, so we could go tomorrow."

"Can I get a big CD stand? They don't fit just in there." She paused for a moment, and Alex could almost see the cogs turning. "You got the job!" She ran over and gave Alex a big hug.

"It's only temping, just for now. It'll mean I can stick around for a while." She wrapped her arms around Phoebe, feeling more relieved than she'd admit. Without any money coming in, it wouldn't have been possible no matter how much she wanted to be there for her.

"I knew you'd get it," Phoebe mumbled into her shirt.

Alex held her tight. "I'll be here, as long as you need me," she repeated, a promise she was determined to see through. She looked over Phoebe's head, around the impersonal room, and at the stark red button standing to attention against the pale walls. She planned to keep her word but also didn't plan for either of them to stay there for long.

"Can we get Chinese?"

"Huh?" She'd started to slip in time, and it took a second to realise what Phoebe was referring to. The place was already doing her head in.

"And the hug's finished now." Phoebe tried to remove herself.

Alex laughed and released her from her tight hold.

"And chocolate cake. To celebrate."

Alex arched an eyebrow.

"Your new job. And my moving out." There was a seemingly genuine smile on Phoebe's face, and her eyes had lost some of their redness from earlier.

"Yeah, yeah. Any excuse." Alex couldn't help smiling back.

They shared a love of baked goods, something their mother had disapproved of, but as it got Phoebe in the kitchen, it'd been allowed. Sundays had been baking day for years. She wondered if they'd carried on after she left but bit back the question. She didn't want to make Phoebe think of their family home and set her off again. Dwelling on the past didn't do anyone any good.

It was time to look ahead. Knowing Chinese was Phoebe's favourite, she'd already scoped out a decent-looking takeaway nearby that had good reviews. It was only ten minutes' walk from the home, so she didn't bother with the van. Plus, summer had finally arrived, and she'd enjoy a gentle stroll. Phoebe didn't feel up to going, so she headed out alone.

The neighbourhood seemed to have come to life since they'd arrived. Car doors slammed as adults returned from work, and kids whizzed past on their bikes. As she paused at the end of one cul-de-sac, she saw a group playing football in the road, a chalk outline etched onto the tarmac for the goals. A car turned into the street. Before she could yell a warning, it slowed right down and the kids grabbed their ball and moved aside to the pavement. They actually smiled and waved at the driver as the car rolled past. Alex let out a long breath. She was definitely not in the city any more. Maybe it was a safer place to raise kids, but she'd never fancied living in a small place where everyone knew each other and each other's personal business. The anonymity of city life meant you had much more freedom to live your *own* life. It was a freedom she had no plans to give up. As soon as Phoebe was sorted, she'd be heading back to Leicester.

There were some advantages to being out in the sticks. Despite the shouts from the neighbourhood children, it was peaceful. Instead of a constant roar of traffic, there was just the odd unhurried driver. The air tasted different too, purer, cleaner. When you went out for fresh air, it was actually fresh.

There was only a short queue at the Chinese, so she took a seat on one of the hard plastic chairs lining the wall and pulled her mobile out to check for messages, having felt it buzz in her pocket at Phoebe's. There were a couple of texts from Willow asking how the big day was going and telling Alex to give Bee a big squeeze from her. She'd been the first to suggest Phoebe look at getting her own place and had stayed involved through the whole saga.

Alex tapped out a quick reply, without letting on how upset Phoebe had got as neither of them would want to worry her. Phoebe had always worshipped Willow and tried to impress her, even though it was obvious the feeling was mutual and there was no need. Not having any siblings of her own, Willow had been devoted to Phoebe right back to their schooldays and was like another sister to her. When Willow and Alex had transitioned from friends to lovers, Phoebe was the first family they'd told. The kid had accepted the news without hesitation, though with plenty of questions, and they'd not regretted letting her in. It helped that Phoebe's assumed innocence made her an excellent alibi.

There was also a text from an unknown number. She clicked on it.

A short message popped up on the screen, and she groaned when she guessed who it was from.

How's Phoebe settling in? She's not called us.

How had their parents got her number? Alex was sure she'd not given it, backed up by the fact her phone hadn't been able to warn her who it was. *I bet they snuck if off Phoebe.* The thought of them looking through her sister's phone made her fume. They had no respect for privacy, or for Phoebe. She was definitely better off out of there.

It was tempting to flat out ask them, or act ignorant with a *Who is this?* She started to tap out a pointed reply, then changed her mind just before sending and deleted it. That would just drag it out, and she did not want to engage with them.

She's fine, just tired after a big day. I'm sure she'll call you soon.
Okay.

No *and how are you* then. Alex slipped the phone back in her pocket. Their parents had given up trying with her years ago, despite everything that had happened since, and that suited her fine. Still, they could at least pretend they cared a little given they'd contacted her. Knowing them, they were probably busy sulking about Phoebe not calling. And possibly scared that texting would tie up the phone and stop a call coming through. Just teaching them to use a mobile had been a lesson in patience, which had never been Alex's strong point. They'd not got round to the finer details.

As she strolled back, the smell of takeaway trailed her through the streets, pushing her into a quicker pace. Phoebe was right—this was a celebration. It was a big change for her, but Alex knew she'd manage it, with support. She just hoped it wasn't a case of *Out of the frying pan...* She wasn't sure what to think about the key worker. The way she'd just stared at them, Alex'd had to bite back a *What are you looking at?* Though she had to admit, she'd done a little staring herself at the cute brunette. Was it so bad that she was glad they'd sent someone nice to look at, and even better with a whiff of queer about her—there was something about the way Rebecca'd checked her out that didn't feel entirely professional. Even if she was useless—better useless than controlling.

Distracted by her image, she walked past the shop and had to turn back. Phoebe would not be happy if she came back without pudding. She chose something properly gooey and chocolatey, and far too big for the two of them. It could keep Phoebe going for a while and maybe even help her make some friends there. Whenever Alex had moved, Phoebe had sent her off with a big box of freshly baked cakes to share with her new housemates. She usually ate most of them herself, although a couple of times she'd taken them into work where they'd gone down very well. Then afterwards they'd kept asking after her baker sister, which had made her miss Phoebe more, a yawning hole that no amount of cake could fill.

The staff member who let her in gave the bags a look and a sniff but didn't say anything. She headed straight up to Phoebe's room. Just as she knocked, footsteps hurried towards her. She didn't turn around, hoping Phoebe would open the door before whoever it was reached her.

"Hi there. I was hoping to catch you before I went home."

Alex turned reluctantly towards the speaker, ignoring the slight quickening in her chest as she saw it was the key worker, whose name slipped her mind. "Hi."

They stood looking at each other for a moment, the key worker apparently as lost as she was for what to say next.

"Hey, sis." Phoebe finally opened the door and broke the tension. She eyed the bulging bags. "Good, I'm starving."

Rebecca, that was it. Rebecca's eyes widened as if something had dawned on her and a soft *oh* slipped out.

Phoebe didn't seem to notice and grabbed for the takeaway bag. "What are we going to eat with? I didn't bring any kitchen stuff."

Good point. Maybe it was handy Rebecca had appeared. Alex turned back to her. "Where can we get plates and cutlery?"

"I'll get them." Rebecca gulped and stopped mid-turn. "Um, residents aren't supposed to eat in their rooms, for hygiene reasons. Snacks are okay…"

Alex folded her arms, ready for a fight. Phoebe should be able to eat what and where she pleased in her own home. Wasn't that what this claimed to be?

"But as it's her first night, I'm sure we can make an exception." Rebecca backed away, colour rising on her cheeks.

"Wow, that's a big cake." Phoebe had taken the other bag while they squared off.

"As you said, we're celebrating." Alex reached over and tousled Phoebe's hair, earning a dark scowl.

Rebecca returned moments later with everything they needed. Then she lingered in the doorway.

"Do you want some cake?" Phoebe offered.

Alex glared at her, and Rebecca caught the look.

"No, I'm okay. Thank you, though, that's kind of you."

"You could have some another day—there'll be plenty left," Alex added.

Alex wasn't sure why she made the offer, but she was glad to see Rebecca's tight lips spread into a warm smile, lighting up her pale face. Despite her slim frame, she had dimples. Alex's fingers tingled with the desire to touch them and run across the soft mounds of her lips. *What is wrong with you?*

"I might take you up on that." They smiled at each other and then Rebecca seemed to remember why she was there and turned to Phoebe. "How about we have tea and cake tomorrow afternoon, and we can have a chat and get to know each other."

"Deal," Phoebe said.

"Great, I'll see you tomorrow."

Maybe Alex shouldn't have made the offer after all. Rebecca could be one of those professional carers that try too hard, encouraging the people they care for to become reliant on them and even consider them a friend. Just because she was cute didn't mean she could be trusted any more than the rest of them.

Alex would have to keep an eye on her.

Chapter Two

The next time, Rebecca was prepared. Or that's what she thought after she'd studied Phoebe's file fully and managed to fill in some gaps. The initial report was ambiguous in places, just like the assessment, but hinted at some kind of trouble in the family. Phoebe had been living with her parents, but then Alex had taken over and been the one to assist in finding her a new place to live. Why was unclear. Rebecca hoped Alex would be there again so she could get some more information from her.

Not because she wanted to see Alex again. It was important she understand Phoebe's background in order to support her moving forward. Officially everyone worked to a person-centred care approach, but there were vast differences in how seriously they took it—the state of Phoebe's file indicated no real interest in her as an individual or in finding out what she wanted. She'd had to grit her teeth to stop herself tracking down whoever put it together and asking why they hadn't bothered to do their job properly. Not that she would've dared do that outside of her daydreams.

The printer had decided to cooperate and whirred into life, spitting out her extra templates to fill in with Phoebe and expand on her records. She'd ended up creating her own person-centred planning tools, adapted from various sources that were at the forefront of disability rights. These focused on what the individual wanted from life, instead of what staff assumed they needed—their basic needs were already assessed and catered for, so their goals could be more meaningful and properly personal. Her versions were a lot more user-friendly too, not constructed of professional jargon and set up to suit the staff or tick the inspector's boxes. The generic templates never made much sense to anyone, let alone someone with a learning disability like all their residents. It was a bugbear of hers that often led to long rants, though it was her nesting partner Ishani that usually ended up on the end of them after she'd bit her tongue all day at work. Taking matters into her own hands meant at least her key residents could get the care they deserved. With Phoebe being her first new resident since she'd spent the last year honing the templates, this was her opportunity to put them into practice.

If Phoebe agreed to work with her. Both women had seemed reticent yesterday, but it had been an emotional step and it was understandable they might be overwhelmed. She hadn't pushed them for that reason. Hopefully after a good night's sleep, Phoebe would be feeling more settled. She tried not to overthink it or take it as a personal rejection, always easier said than done.

At the start of the shift, she'd popped up to arrange a time to see Phoebe but there was no sign of her. The only information she could get from the other staff was that she'd gone out with her sister. Rebecca had felt her stomach flip at the mention of Alex. She was glad to hear she was around as a source of information, she told herself; it was only professional curiosity.

"Hello in there!"

Rebecca looked up from the desk and from her thoughts, to see her favourite colleague standing by her side. "Hi, Luisa."

"So, you are still with us." Luisa folded herself into the chair next to Rebecca.

"I was just looking up some background information on the new resident." She didn't want Luisa thinking she'd been slacking off, hiding in the office. Did they all think that? Rebecca placed her hand on top of Phoebe's file, ready to show it as evidence if needed.

"Yes, I heard about how they stuck her on you."

Rebecca bit back a laugh and a correction. Luisa's English was excellent, but her grasp of English phrases wasn't perfect, and her clipped accent compounded her unusual choices. She shouldn't judge— languages had never been her strong point—and Luisa was one of the more decent workers there. And the only one she considered a friend. "What exactly did you hear?"

"That they thought she could be trouble, and that they would prefer trouble was with you. Her and her sister."

Rebecca sighed. Just what she'd suspected but had hoped was more paranoia than reality. She considered asking for more details, even though she probably wouldn't like the answers, but was distracted by a glinting on Luisa's left hand.

"Looks like you've had a more fun weekend!" She took Luisa's hand to study the shining rock newly positioned on her ring finger.

"Yes, he *finally* proposed." Luisa held her hand up, giving Rebecca a closer look.

"Congratulations, I'm really happy for you both. I hope you're very happy together." Despite her own misgivings about marriage after growing up with bitterly divorcing parents, her congratulations were genuine—Luisa had wanted this forever.

"Thank you." Luisa leaned over and pulled her into a tight half hug. "You know, you could always join us. We could become bridezillas together. All three of us."

Rebecca laughed off the suggestion. The idea of Ishani ever becoming a bridezilla was an amusing and terrifying thought, but it was not on the cards. "How about we stick with helping you out. I know you don't want to share the spotlight really."

Luisa laughed. "Correct." Her smile waned for a moment, and she squeezed Rebecca's hand. "I realise it may not be so simple for you two."

"Yes. But it's not what I want anyway." For a number of reasons.

It was more complicated, but not in the way Luisa might have imagined. The situation for queer people was a lot worse in Poland, which might be why she'd jumped to that conclusion, or maybe it was Ishani's heritage. Either way, it wasn't the point, though she was sure Luisa was trying to be supportive. The fact was that Ishani's parents had come round to the extent that they'd even started asking when Rebecca was going to make an honest woman of her. Luisa knew Rebecca better than anyone else at work and had managed to wriggle past some of her home–work boundaries, but there was still plenty she didn't know. It was best kept that way.

Luisa's smile returned but not completely. There was a hint of pity in her eyes that Rebecca didn't appreciate. Maybe she should tell her that there were good reasons to not go down the traditional path, including her fantastic other lover. But it was probably not the time or place to raise the topic of polyamory.

"Have you made any plans yet?"

That brought Luisa's smile back fully, and the excitement in her voice as she described her dream wedding was infectious. Rebecca got so drawn in that she lost track of time, and when she glanced at the clock realised it had snuck past four.

"Crap. I said I'd visit Phoebe this afternoon, and I've not even arranged a time yet."

"I let them in before I came over to see you, so she has not been back for long. Relax."

Rebecca started pulling her paperwork back together. "I better pop up and at least make a time." The longer she left it, the more chance Phoebe would be alone by the time she got up there. "See you later."

Luisa rolled her eyes but held an amused smile as Rebecca rushed towards the door. "Sure."

"I really am happy for you. Let me know if you need any help." She didn't look back as she fumbled her way out.

As she climbed the stairs, a steady thumping got louder and her heart started to pound with it. She paused at the top, trying to ascertain where it was coming from. The banging rang out again. Oh God. Alex and Phoebe would have to wait.

Rebecca crept along with her ear close to the wall as she attempted to track down the source of the sound. Depending on whose room it was coming from, she might need backup. She inched forward, dread building in the pit of her stomach. It was coming from Phoebe's.

When she reached it she paused, hand on the doorknob, and put her ear right to the door. It was quiet.

Then the banging started up again, even more forcefully than before. Should she just burst in? Rebecca had no idea how Phoebe would react, so it was risky. Instead, she knocked firmly. The sound stopped again. "Everything okay in there?" she called, in a deliberately clear and calm voice.

No response.

She knocked again. "Phoebe, are you okay? It's Rebecca. May I come in?"

This time there were footsteps. The door swung open, to reveal Alex. She had stripped down to a tank top which pulled taut over her breasts, and her muscular arms were on display. They were adorned with ink, the tattoos on her right mainly hidden from view as she held the door open, but on her left Rebecca could make out what looked like a winged wheel with flames running paths down towards her wrist. Rebecca had the urge to reach out and trace the lines of fire.

She bit her lip. She was staring again but needed to get her thoughts under some semblance of control before she dared open her mouth. They were definitely not professional in that moment.

Alex gestured behind her to where Phoebe was curled on her bed with a serious pair of headphones wrapped around her skull. She looked like she would struggle to lift her head up with them on. "A bomb could go off and she wouldn't bat an eyelid when she's plugged in."

Rebecca giggled, then wondered whether that counted for smoke alarms too. Was it safe for her to be so unreachable? She let her gaze drift back to Alex and realised what she had missed in her initial awe: a hammer dangled from her right hand, and in the corner of the room a half-constructed set of shelves lay in wait. The dread lurking in her stomach dissolved and gave way to the butterflies.

"Did you need her for something?" Alex raised an eyebrow and a half-smile.

Rebecca hoped there was no outside sign as her insides fluttered. "Um no, I was just checking...I heard banging and wanted to make sure she was okay."

"Oh yeah, sorry about that. Just knocking together a few extra bits of furniture. Bee needed more storage space. Hope it didn't upset anyone." She seemed genuinely concerned. Maybe she wouldn't be such a tough nut to crack.

"No, no, it's okay. Most of the residents are out anyway at this time, so you shouldn't be disturbing anyone. I just needed to check that you're okay." Rebecca swallowed. That should have been if *Phoebe* was okay.

"We're good."

"Good."

They stood smiling at each other, Rebecca making every effort to keep her eyes up and not let them roam over Alex's exposed body. Did her tattoos only cover her arms or did they creep under her clothes? Jesus, what was the matter with her? Alex wasn't there for her to perve over, and she was at work.

"*Sooo*, do you need to speak to her?" Alex broke eye contact first, shifting to remind them of Phoebe's presence. Though Phoebe herself appeared oblivious to them.

"No, not necessarily. I don't want to disturb y—her." Rebecca was tempted to leave it there, before she made an even bigger fool of herself, but remembered her initial intention. "I just wanted to check when would be a good time for us to have tea and our introductory chat."

"Sure." Alex moved out of the doorway and loped over to the bed. She nudged Phoebe's foot so she looked up and noticed Rebecca's presence.

Phoebe pulled down her headphones and sat up slightly. "Hi."

"Hi, Phoebe. How are you today?" Rebecca stayed behind the threshold, waiting until she was invited, like the vampire staring back at her from the wall. She wanted Phoebe to understand it was her space, and within reason, it was up to her who she let in.

"All right. We got some stuff for my room, so it's better." She did seem brighter than the day before. Hopefully getting her room how she wanted had made it feel more like home.

"Would you still like to have tea, and cake if there's any left?"

Alex laughed and nudged Phoebe again. "There may be a little bit."

"There's lots!" Phoebe protested.

Rebecca twiddled the door handle. "Is that a yes?" The sisterly banter was cute, but she needed to be sure.

"Yes," Phoebe said.

"What time shall I come back? I could do about half four, or if you're free now…" Rebecca trailed off, glancing back at Alex. She'd been resisting looking at her, but they couldn't really talk if she was going to be hammering away. Among other distractions.

"I'll be done with this in about twenty minutes, so you'll have some peace and quiet then."

Rebecca felt her professional smile waver. She didn't want Alex to leave, but maybe it'd be for the best. It was better to get any information from Phoebe directly. Even the most supportive family were influenced by their own biases.

"Okay if I join you?" Alex continued.

"Of course," Rebecca gushed before she realised Alex had actually been asking Phoebe. She felt her cheeks burning.

Alex smirked, seeming pleased with her enthusiastic response. "What about you, Bee?"

"Yes, stay." Phoebe's eyes fluttered towards Rebecca nervously as she instructed her sister to stay by her side. Alex clearly had Phoebe's trust, which was good to know. That wasn't always the case with family members.

"All right. We'll see you in half an hour. Give me a chance to clean up a bit." Alex turned towards the shelves, set to get back to work.

Once again, Rebecca was dismissed. She watched Alex bend over, her top riding up her back. She might need to spend the next half hour having a cold shower. She tore her gaze away and headed off to find something sufficiently uninspiring to do in order to bring her heart rate back down.

❖

Alex hammered in the last nail, then sat back and wiped a light sheen of sweat from her forehead. She'd managed to construct a large chest of drawers, shelves, and an oversized CD rack, which Phoebe was already lovingly filling. They'd also picked up some wall-art stickers that Phoebe had arranged artistically around the room. She pushed herself to her feet and looked around with a satisfied smile. It was already looking a lot cosier.

"All finished," she declared. "Right on time, as she's due back in five."

Alex had found herself repeatedly checking her watch as she'd worked and trying to ignore the rising anticipation that'd made her unsteady on her feet. It was a good thing she'd been able to finish building on the floor, as going flying with a hammer in her hand would not be good, especially as she'd already pushed her body enough that day.

The cute key worker was throwing her. Alex automatically distrusted her, given her position and enthusiasm, yet couldn't deny she was drawn to her. At least the feeling seemed to be mutual, or else Rebecca was not completely with the plot. She physically shook off the bitchy thought.

"What are you doing?"

She turned to find Phoebe looking at her with a confused expression that matched the confusion in her own mind.

"Nothing, just relaxing. You've been working me hard."

She stretched and shook out her limbs, realising as she did so how true that was. It felt good to stretch, but the movement revealed damp patches under her arms. She needed to wash and change before Rebecca got there. It sucked that Phoebe didn't have her own bathroom, given the number of strangers she was forced to share her new quote-unquote *home* with. At least there was a sink in her room.

"Do you want more cake?" Phoebe fiddled with the tin, clearly struggling to wait for their guest.

"Definitely. But first I gotta clean up." Alex dragged her T-shirt over her head and went to the sink. The cool water was bliss as she splashed her face, then armpits and chest. In doing so her bra got drenched. Damn, she'd have to take that off too. She undid the clasp and slung it on the floor with her top.

At which point there was a knock at the door.

"Coming," Phoebe called as she headed over to open it.

"Shit. Bee, chuck me a T-shirt or something." Alex looked around for something she could use to cover herself.

Phoebe paused, a mischievous grin spreading. She reached for the door key. "Help yourself."

"Don't you dare!" Alex caught her foot in a bra strap as she rushed to the wardrobe, nearly tripping as it shackled her.

Phoebe burst out laughing, turning right back around to enjoy the spectacle.

"Piss off," Alex grumbled, but without venom.

It was good to hear her sister laugh again, even if it was at her own expense. She reached into the wardrobe and grabbed one of the many black band tees and wrestled it over her head. It was only just long enough to graze the top of her jeans, but at least it wasn't too tight.

A click signalled Phoebe had unlocked the door just as she pulled it down. At least she'd waited until then, Alex wouldn't have put it past her to cross the line and open it while she was still topless.

"Hello again. Are you ready for me?"

Alex turned to see Rebecca standing in the doorway, beaming. She attempted to shake off the bra that was still attached to her ankle without attracting attention, but it didn't budge. And it did get Rebecca's attention, who turned pink and pursed her lips either in silent judgement or trying to hold back a burst of laughter.

"Almost," Alex replied, giving in and removing the offending item by hand. Which was when she realised another thing Phoebe didn't have was a laundry basket. She chucked the bra under the bed.

"How about I go get the drinks and give you a minute to get sorted." Rebecca's gaze seemed to be settled on Alex's chest, and her voice was a little shaky.

The scratch of her bare nipples against the T-shirt made Alex very aware of her lack of underwear. She wrapped her arms around herself, creating a makeshift support for her free-swinging breasts. At least the thick black material should prevent indecent exposure, though the way Rebecca was looking at her, you would've thought she had nothing on. "I'll have a builder's brew."

"Seems appropriate." Rebecca finally stopped staring at her and took in the additions to the room. "You've got it looking great in here already."

"I have it black," Phoebe piped up.

"Of course you do, gotta keep on style."

Phoebe's late teenage alternative phase was amusing, though Alex always stopped short of laughing at her. At least she was wearing what she wanted and no longer let their parents squeeze her into the cutesy kid's clothes they'd bought her well into adulthood. She might be a short-arse still, but she wasn't a child.

Rebecca's gaze had somehow made it back to Alex's chest. Alex crossed her arms more firmly.

"Two sugars in mine and do you wanna grab some plates for the cake too."

"Yes, I'll go now." Rebecca stepped backwards out of the room, almost tripping over her own feet. "See you in a minute."

As soon as she left, Alex relaxed her grip on herself and looked down to see what Rebecca had been staring at. She snorted back a laugh. She was right—it wasn't see-through. However, there were two skulls with their tongues hanging out positioned right over her breasts, over a nearly naked woman stretched out below them. No wonder Rebecca had been staring. She should change it before she got back, she didn't want her thinking—she stopped herself there. What did it matter what Rebecca thought of her? She was there to support Phoebe, and the tee was Phoebe's, so she'd have to get used to it. She smoothed down the T-shirt. It covered her, it was fine.

"Mum hates that one."

"I was wondering how you got it past her." Which was what she was thinking, now Phoebe had brought it up.

"Dad got me it, at a gig. He said I could have whatever I wanted." There was a hint of sadness to her voice as she recalled that past happier time.

Of course he did. Alex was tempted to ask if she missed them, wondered if she *should* ask. But the truth was she didn't want to know the answer. It wouldn't make any difference anyway—neither of them could go back.

Another sharp knock at the door signalled Rebecca's return. Alex strode over to answer it, this time making no effort to cover herself.

Rebecca was holding a large tray which contained not only tea and plates, but scones filled to bursting with cream and jam. "I thought we could make it a proper afternoon tea." Her eyes seemed to seek permission as they met Alex's.

"Looks tasty." Alex wanted to give her permission to do anything she liked. She broke eye contact abruptly, struck by the danger of her desire. She didn't know this woman, didn't know what she would try to take. She did know she had power over her. Over Phoebe. She must remember who Rebecca was there to see and who she was there to look out for.

"Yum." She turned to see Phoebe's face lit up and her eyes firmly fixed on the piled tray.

"Where shall I put it?"

Alex rushed over to the desk to clear a space, glad of the excuse to turn her back. She took long, slow breaths as she worked, in a vain attempt to bring herself back to reality. But Rebecca joined her, so close Alex could feel the heat that radiated from her slender frame despite the long-sleeved blouse she wore. The hair on Alex's arms stood on end as if attempting to bridge the tiny gap between them. She moved away to safety and perched on the bed next to Phoebe.

"Here you go." Rebecca brought their tea to them, and Alex took hers carefully to ensure their fingers didn't accidentally touch. She needed to keep her wits about her.

"Thank you," said Phoebe.

"Thanks," Alex mumbled a beat later when she realised she hadn't said anything.

Rebecca brought over the scones. "We better eat these first while the cream's fresh." She retreated back to the desk and took the seat there.

The tea Alex held was a rich, dark colour, properly brewed. She took a sip, and the hot liquid scorched her mouth. It was just right. She glanced over to see Rebecca's drink matched her own.

They all tucked into their scones in silence, or at least without words. Phoebe slurped her tea and chewed with her mouth open. It had driven their mother nuts. Alex didn't care, she was used to it, and who was to say what was the right way to eat? So Phoebe breathed through her mouth, what did it matter? Their parents never were fans of showing your differences, though. Pride wasn't something they understood, not in the way Alex did.

Rebecca turned round in her chair to face Phoebe. "It's looking nice in here. I'm glad to see you're making yourself at home."

Home. Alex stiffened, and her mouthful of scone suddenly seemed very dry.

"Alex took me to Ikea, so I could choose furniture to put my stuff in. We built it all ourselves."

Phoebe made it sound like she'd done it, and Alex nearly jumped in to point out it was her who'd done all the building. Instead, she choked on some crumbs as she tried to swallow. Both of them looked at her as if they wondered if they should help, so she waved to tell them to carry on and ignore her coughing.

"I love Ikea. I can spend all day there. I could take you if you need anything else."

"Okay, I'll—"

"I'll take her—you don't need to." Alex did jump in then before they could get too carried away.

Rebecca turned to her, seeming surprised by her interruption. Alex held her gaze. Boundaries were needed, and Rebecca was just the type to skip over them with a smile. Alex would have to keep her back.

"Of course." Rebecca pulled at the neck of her blouse. "You're lucky to have such a supportive sister."

"She's the best," Phoebe agreed.

Now Alex looked down, in an attempt not to react to the blatant flattery that was meant to disarm her. She wasn't that easy. And it wasn't true.

"That does raise the question: What do you need my help with? It'd be good to write down some plans and figure out how I can support you in them."

Phoebe hesitated and looked over to Alex. She deliberately didn't say anything—she didn't want to tell Phoebe what to do, she just wanted to make sure no one else did.

"We should think about timing too. Some things we might aim to do in a month, some a year. We can take things one step at a time." Rebecca smiled at Phoebe in what was obviously supposed to be a caring, reassuring way.

Okay, it was time for Alex to step in. "Look, let's not get carried away. She's not going to stay here for that long, so there's no point making any big plans." She crossed her arms under the leering skulls.

Rebecca didn't reply. Alex could see her chest rising and falling quickly, maybe too quickly. She bit back the urge to ask if she was okay.

"I want my own flat. I want to be an independent woman."

At other times, this declaration by Phoebe had led to them bursting into song. Not this time. The reality of her new set-up was sinking in. She wasn't anywhere near that yet.

"That's a goal we can work towards." Rebecca's reply was hesitant, either due to fear of saying the wrong thing again or because she didn't agree with it.

It didn't matter which—it wasn't up to her. "Coming here's a practice for that, isn't it, Bee. Starting straight away."

We mustn't get attached to you. Phoebe *mustn't get too attached.* There was no reason Alex would get too close anyway. Apart from the obvious, and she wasn't a slave to her hormones.

"Of course." Rebecca's smile was looking faker by the second. "As we have a duty of care for her, we'll do what we can to enable her—"

"Your *duty of care*"—Alex added quote marks around the gross phrase that was a handy excuse to control people—"is a basic one. Keep her safe but let her live her life. Got it?"

She had to break her glare as Rebecca's eyes became translucent with a film of tears. She knew if she kept looking she wouldn't be able to stay tough. It wasn't personal, but Rebecca needed to know her place. She was just there in case anything went wrong while Phoebe learned to stand on her own two feet.

The room was truly silent now. And too small. Phoebe was staring at her, mouth wide open, a part-demolished scone on her lap. So much for a civilised afternoon tea. Alex stood up, unable to stay still with all the raw energy pulsing through her. She needed to run or, better yet, dive back into the swimming pool and let the heat dissolve in the cool water.

Out of the corner of her eye, she saw Rebecca lean over and squeeze Phoebe's hand. She pretended not to hear their whispered exchange and Rebecca's promise to return at "a better time," which obviously meant when Alex wasn't there. Which she couldn't always be. Alex balled her fists. She didn't want to leave Phoebe there, within the broken care system's grasp, but she had no choice. Not yet.

CHAPTER THREE

Rebecca did not cry. At least, not until she was safely home. *Don't give them the satisfaction of knowing they've got to you.* It was a mantra she repeated to herself often, whenever she felt that prickly heat in the corner of her eyes.

When she got home late that night, she cocooned herself in a soft blanket on the sofa with a large chunk of chocolate and let the tears flow. They stained the chocolate, adding a salty tang she was all too familiar with.

"Hi, honey. I didn't hear you get in." Ishani had been nowhere in sight when she'd returned, and Rebecca hadn't sought her out.

"Hey," she mumbled into the fleece.

Ishani took in her nest and tear tracks, her eyes narrowing with obvious concern as she rolled closer. "Tough day?"

Rebecca nodded and inched forward so Ishani could squeeze in behind her. Ishani took the hint and transferred herself from her wheelchair onto the sofa. Warm arms wrapped round Rebecca, and Ishani's silky hair stroked her neck as she snuggled in.

"Do you want to talk about it?"

"I can't." In more ways than one. Even when Rebecca felt like offloading about work troubles, she had to be careful not to let slip any private information. Most of her colleagues seemed less worried about it and could be heard bad-mouthing their residents and anyone else who'd irritated them as they hung around outside for their very regular cigarette breaks. It was how Luisa got all the gossip and information Rebecca wasn't privy to. God knew what they were like at home. Despite that, maybe because of it, she couldn't let her own professional boundaries slip.

"Work stuff?"

It helped that Ishani knew how seriously Rebecca took her oath of confidentiality, and so could figure that out without Rebecca having to say any more.

She nodded again and let a last few tears flow as she sank into Ishani's embrace.

"Oh, honey, I'm sorry." Ishani stroked her hair soothingly. "They need to start appreciating you properly."

"It's not my colleagues." She remembered Marie's smile at the meeting and the knowing looks exchanged. "Well, not just them."

"I see. Was there an incident with one of the residents? Did something happen to one of them?"

Ishani held her close, the concern in her voice reassuring. Rebecca wasn't the only one who really cared, even though sometimes it felt that way. No, that wasn't fair on Luisa. And Patience. She had to remind herself she wasn't some lone hero, doomed to battle alone for what was right and good.

"No."

"So"—Ishani paused, seeming to consider the other possibilities—"a family member, then?"

Rebecca nodded. That much wasn't breaking confidentiality—she hadn't *told* her anything.

"I know you can't give me any details, but as long as you don't say anything that identifies them, you've got the right to let it out."

It wasn't the first time they'd been in that situation, and Ishani worried about Rebecca taking too much on without support. They'd often debated it, Ishani generally coming out on top with her professor's experience in presenting an argument.

Maybe Ishani was right, but Rebecca didn't have the words to describe how Alex had made her feel and why it had hit her so hard. She was used to pushy relatives and knew they usually calmed down once everyone was settled in. Why was this any different? She shook her head, trying to clear the image of the steel in Alex's eyes.

"I'm sure you'll get them onside, and they'll realise how much you genuinely care for your residents and do for them. They'll be glad they got you."

Rebecca wasn't so sure. Alex had given the distinct impression she'd prefer Rebecca not be involved. It felt personal, though, maybe it wasn't. She likely wasn't the first one to be on the receiving end of Alex's fierce tongue, or they wouldn't have been dropped on her.

"You've just got to do what you can and remember who you're

there for." Ishani dropped a kiss in the crook of her neck, as if attempting to eliminate all the tension there with her soft lips.

"Yes." This time, Rebecca fully agreed. That was what she needed to focus on: Phoebe. She was there for Phoebe, not Alex. "Thank you."

"You know I'm here, sweetie, if you do ever need to—"

Rebecca twisted round and cut her off with a kiss. That was enough talking—she'd said all she could, and she didn't want to think about work any more. Ishani returned her kiss, revitalising Rebecca, the heat of her body and their passion melting away the stress of the day.

❖

A night in her loving partner's arms was just what Rebecca had needed. She woke with a smile on her lips, their tender puffiness no doubt matching her eyes' but with a much more pleasant cause. Ishani must have already left for work, and though Rebecca didn't remember her leaving, she knew she wouldn't have left without a goodbye.

Early on in their relationship she'd thought Ishani slipped out unnoticed while she slept on, which was not the way she liked to end a night in a lover's bed. When she'd plucked up the courage to raise the issue, Ishani had laughed and pointed out that Rebecca was usually just half-asleep still so didn't remember their dreamy embraces. For months after she'd requested a morning cup of tea to ensure she fully experienced waking up next to Ishani, but the reality of her late shifts and their differing schedules meant she went back to getting the sleep she needed, content with Ishani's promise that she would never leave without saying goodbye.

It also helped that it was her last shift of the week, only one more day before she could enjoy a whole three days off. Even better, they fell over the weekend, so Ishani would be around to enjoy them with her. The last weekend she'd had off, Ishani had already booked to stay with another partner, and there'd been no room for manoeuvre in their overpopulated shared calendar. She checked it briefly to reassure herself—yes, this weekend was clearly booked for them to relax at home together, with just one joint social engagement. Maybe Ishani would be up for a box set marathon, some cheesy sci-fi that would sweep away the real world, where good and compassion always triumphed over evil and indifference.

Her musings were interrupted by her second alarm, shrill and insistent and out of reach of the bed. Rebecca sighed and dragged herself up and through her morning routine. The promise of the weekend ahead fuelled her for a cleaning spree that kept her occupied all morning. When her house was in order, her mind felt clearer too. By the time she got to lunch, both appeared significantly improved from the night before, and she was able to get ready for work with only the occasional mild twinge in her chest. Her anxiety was much more under control than it had been in her younger years, but mild symptoms still popped up regularly and reminded her of the risk that a primal fear could overwhelm her at the slightest provocation.

The lightness lasted until she got to Phoebe's door, where she found herself bracing for a confrontation she'd much rather avoid. Her knock went unanswered, drowned out by the music blasting loud enough that she could feel the vibrations through the handle as soon as she laid her hand on it, sending the beat right to her bones. She took a deep breath and pushed down. It was locked. Now what should she do?

"Is everything okay?"

Rebecca jumped at the voice, realising she had been standing there for too long with her outstretched hand resting on the unmoving handle. She turned to find Luisa beside her, eyeing the pulsating door with what seemed to be a mix of amusement and suspicion.

"Do you need backup?"

"No, it's fine." Rebecca managed a smile for her workmate, then remembered who she might be bursting in on. "Actually, maybe. They can't hear me. I don't want to scare them."

"Do we know how she might react?" Luisa continued to study the door as if it might hold a clue.

"No." There really was little of use in Phoebe's file, including whether she had any tendency towards behaviour that they might find challenging. From what she'd seen of Phoebe so far, Rebecca suspected she was much more likely to go into a moody sulk and give her the silent treatment than anything violent. It was Alex that seemed more likely to lash out, verbally if not physically, and Rebecca couldn't be sure she wasn't there. She'd checked the visitor book beforehand, but there was no guarantee she just hadn't been signed in properly. "I'll try knocking again first." She tapped uselessly against the wood.

"She can never hear that," Luisa said, reaching over her to rap sharply on the door. They waited. Still no answer. "What do we do now?"

"We open the door." Rebecca could hear the slight waver in her voice but hoped Luisa didn't. She was the senior and Phoebe was her responsibility—it was her call.

The master key was slippery in her hand, the metal cold and sticky. The door unlocked with a click that she felt rather than heard, the music still drowning out everything else. She pushed it open.

Rebecca didn't know what she'd expected, but it wasn't to find Phoebe sitting in the middle of the floor with clothes strewn all around her and tears streaming down her face.

A soft *oh* fell from Luisa's lips and she turned to Rebecca as if for an explanation. It was clearly not what she'd been expecting from the rock chick either.

"It's okay, I'll take it from here."

Rebecca waited for Luisa to leave and shut the door before she turned back to Phoebe. At least she didn't have her guardian standing over them, ready to jump on her if Rebecca said the wrong thing. Or the wrong thing as far as Alex was concerned. With her clearer head, she doubted the validity of Alex's intervention. Phoebe still hadn't looked up from her heap on the floor, and Rebecca wasn't certain she was aware of her presence. She crouched down directly in front of her.

"Hi, Phoebe."

Phoebe glanced up briefly to meet Rebecca's gaze, and the look of complete helplessness in her eyes almost made Rebecca break down and join her in her tears.

"What's wrong?" she asked, though she doubted Phoebe would open up to her that easily.

She was correct. Phoebe hunched down further and continued to bawl.

Rebecca tried a different tack. "Do you want a hug?"

A deep nod.

Rebecca shuffled closer and wrapped an arm around Phoebe's quivering shoulders. Even she knew sometimes professional boundaries needed to flex. She'd discovered years ago that no number of supportive words could replace the comfort of physical affection when someone needed it. It was best done in a public space of course, with plenty of witnesses and no risk of misinterpretation. Not a private bedroom with the door shut. She should've told Luisa to stay.

"I can't do it," Phoebe mumbled, chin still on her chest.

Rebecca gave her an extra squeeze. She clearly needed it and it was too late to call Luisa back. It was unlikely Phoebe would make any complaint, and Alex had appeared more queer than homophobic, though you never could be sure. She tried not to get distracted by contemplating Alex's sexuality.

"Hey, it's only your third day here. It takes time to settle in. You'll do great." She made herself sound more sure than she was, but it wasn't hard to convince herself of her own words. Surely Phoebe could manage living there and would be better off away from her overprotective family, who surely wouldn't keep hanging around so much forever. There was a clenching in her gut at this thought.

"No. I know. That's not it." Phoebe straightened up, shrugging off Rebecca's arm as she gestured to the clothes strewn around them. "They said I have to do my laundry today."

"And you can't do laundry?" Rebecca held back a relieved laugh. Laundry was not an insurmountable issue.

"I don't know how."

And no one offered to help you? Rebecca bit back the question, not wanting to draw Phoebe's attention to her colleagues' possibly malicious failing. And Alex's. How could she seriously expect Phoebe to live independently without even teaching her how to do basic chores? Rebecca took a deep breath. "No problem, that's what I'm here for. To show you how, and then you *will* be able to do it."

Phoebe took a minute to take this on-board, then smiled and met Rebecca's eyes for the first time since she'd joined her. "Okay."

"Okay." Rebecca smiled back. "Let's do it. To start with we have to sort the clothes into colours and whites and delicates."

She pulled over the nearest item and showed Phoebe the care label. "They should all have symbols like this to tell you how to wash them."

Rebecca paused, unsure of Phoebe's ability to understand. She seemed to be able to but could just be good at hiding her confusion and following other people's lead. "I've got some instructions with pictures and symbols I can give you."

"I can write it down myself." Phoebe seemed to perk up as she stumbled over to her desk to get something. "In my new notebook."

The pad was a deep black with threads of gold running through the cover.

"That's pretty."

"Alex got me it as a moving present. To write important things in, and if anything happens that upsets me." Phoebe held it out for Rebecca to see.

Rebecca froze, fingers outstretched to stroke the textured cover.

Alex had instructed her to keep an incident log. What the hell? A cold slice of dread shivered down her spine at the realisation that Alex didn't just not trust her, she actively distrusted them and was looking for evidence to back that up.

"What's wrong?"

"Nothing." Rebecca drew her hand back. "Nothing at all. That sounds like a good idea. You can write all the things you learn in there to help you remember." *And she can see all the things I'm doing to help you, and why you need us.*

No, this wasn't about Alex. This was about teaching Phoebe the skills she clearly hadn't been taught before, so she had a chance of living the independent life she wanted. Rebecca doubted it was just laundry Phoebe was clueless about. "Also, you could make a list of anything else, like the laundry, that you want me to show you how to do."

"Okay." Phoebe took a few moments to consider this. "But I don't know what else."

"That's fine. One step at a time, remember? Every time something like this comes up, you just write it down and then we'll make a plan." Rebecca could make an educated guess at what those things might be, but it was better if Phoebe came up with them herself. It was her first time in professional care, as far as Rebecca knew anyway, so she might not be experienced at identifying her needs. It was all likely to be a steep learning curve.

"Deal." Phoebe sat back on the floor opposite her.

"Great. So, page one, laundry."

Phoebe dutifully opened her notebook and started to write in a slow, careful hand.

❖

Cool water enveloped Alex, a welcome shock to her tired body. She pulled long strokes down the pool, focused on the freedom of movement as she glided through the water, which supported her limbs. Her muscles were cramped after another night in the van and the tension she held in whenever she visited that place. If she wasn't careful, she could end up in serious trouble. She ducked her head under in a somersault as she reached the end of the pool, drowning out the sights and smells that even in memory were overwhelming. She hadn't anticipated how much Phoebe's placement would bring back the past that she'd worked so hard to leave behind her. She was lucky to have clawed her independence back after all that time in hospital and so-called supported living. Phoebe hadn't even had the chance yet to live her own life and know what she could miss out on if she was swallowed by the system.

At least Alex had a job to keep her busy and stop her spending too much time at Avebrook. She should give Phoebe space to settle in, but at the same time she couldn't ignore the threat of malevolent eyes on them whenever she stepped outside Phoebe's bedroom, and the zombielike presence of the other residents who hung around the corridors. She pummelled the water, pushing herself faster and harder than she ought to, as if she could outswim it all.

The evening before, she'd dropped in to say hi to Phoebe about eight o'clock. It had taken several knocks to lure anyone to the front door, and when a member of staff had finally answered they'd snapped at her for arriving at a bad time, as if she should know their schedule. They were probably as institutionalised as the residents they watched over. Alex had walked past a queue of people, most already in their PJs, taking their turns to throw small pots of pills down their throats in casual obedience. Did they even know what they were taking? Or why? She'd have to keep an eye out to ensure they didn't start dosing Phoebe too.

Her fingers brushed the wall, and she almost cracked her head on the edge of the pool, her mind not on her movement. She'd hoped not to have to stick around for long or hang around Avebrook much, but her fears kept being confirmed. She might be there for a good while yet, whether she liked it or not. Phoebe needed her.

While she was stuck there, she should check out the local community to help her pass the time and find her people. There must be some other queer nonconforming folk even in a small country town like Wynbury. Apart from the guys at the warehouse and Phoebe, she didn't see anyone who offered her more than a polite *How are you?* without any interest in her answer. The Avebrook staff didn't count, and they had other motivations.

She pushed off from the side, this time gliding away on her back. The cool water lapped around her face and cushioned her as she drifted away, letting her strained body rest. Yes, she needed to put herself out there, meet some people who were more her scene. There was likely to be some kind of local meetup at least, and if not she could easily drive somewhere bigger. As the water stroked her arms and chest, she realised she didn't just need a mental connection, she needed physical touch too.

Willow was in the middle of an intense tour of her new stand-up show, so unlikely to drop by anytime soon, and with everything that had been going on Alex hadn't been dating. In fact, she hadn't been seeing anyone other than Willow since her latest romantic relationship ended years before, since her hospitalisation and slow recovery had taken her out of action. Her comets who she used to connect with from time to time hadn't crossed her orbit in a long while, which she knew was mostly down to her staying away, but still…Having one relationship felt weirdly monogamous, given she'd been poly pretty much all her adult life. It was handy in some ways, as it had meant she could move easily and focus on supporting Phoebe. But as much as she loved Willow and Phoebe, she wanted more. Nothing too major or time-consuming, or with any expectation she would stay. Not just casual sex either—she needed a richer connection. Maybe it was time to put herself back out there.

This time she did bump her head. Her slower pace meant it didn't make her see stars, but it sent a sharp jolt through her body that threatened to awaken other pains. The lifeguard looked over and eyed her up in a way that seemed more suspicious than worried. *Probably thinks I'm hung-over. Or still drunk.* She lifted her hand to indicate she was okay, and they turned away. That was her cue to go before she did herself any real damage.

Alex paddled over to the steps as the ache in her head receded. She gripped the slippery handrail firmly as she hauled herself out, giving her legs time to adjust to bearing her weight again and checking they would hold, the cool metal biting into her hands. Her towel and flip-flops were just where she'd left them, the pool still almost empty. It was too late for most people to have a pre-work swim, and too early for the classes of splashing kids and aerobicizing pensioners. Shift work had its advantages.

The changing room was also quiet, with only a couple of gym bunnies gossiping in one corner. They stopped when they clocked Alex. She pretended not to notice their silent judgement as she walked past and retrieved her bag from a locker, even when she heard them giggle as she struggled to open the misshapen door. She strolled over to the opposite side of the room, aware their eyes were still on her. It was a pleasure to release her body from the tight fabric of her swimsuit, and the women restarted their conversation once they'd registered her swinging breasts, which to people like them confirmed she was in the right place.

Alex draped her towel back round her and plonked herself down on the slatted bench. There was only one short text waiting for her, a *Good Morning* from Willow, the yawning smiley showing her grumpiness at being up to see it. Willow's job encouraged her natural nocturnalness as most of her stand-up gigs were late-night. When they spent the night together, Willow struggled to settle before the early hours of the morning and would happily sleep until noon. Alex's attempts to serenade her with the joys of the still morning air and quiet streets always failed to tempt her out.

Given her regular touring, Willow had a good working knowledge of the queer and poly scenes all around the country and was the perfect person to ask. A social media sweep might give some idea, but most groups would be closed or even secret. She got that need for some people, the type who worried about unsuspecting family members stumbling across more info about their personal lives than they wanted them to, but it made it hard to know what you were getting into before joining. She didn't want to accidentally turn up at a small, closed group ruled by cishet dudes desperate for more women to attempt to seduce.

She tapped a fake cheery reply to Willow.

Gooood morning sunshine! Fancy seeing you *winky kiss* Looks like I may be stuck here for a while, so I'm thinking of checking out the local scene. Any pointers?

Willow immediately replied with one smiley, a stuck-out tongue. Alex laughed, earning her another curious look from the gym bunnies as they sidled past and out the door. She took the chance to stand up and give herself a thorough towelling, without having to worry about revealing parts of her body she'd rather weren't inspected. She'd never been body-conscious before, but the scars that events had left were cruel reminders and could draw morbid curiosity from others. It wasn't that she cared what strangers would think—she couldn't give a shit— more she'd prefer they just let her be.

By the time she was dry, Willow had come through. She'd sent an invite to the county Polyamory/Ethical Non-Monogamy group, which included links to various smaller meetups. A quick scan revealed one in a larger town that was only twenty minutes away. Bingo.

Alex clicked the link, which took her to a closed group. There wasn't much she could see as a non-member except the date of the next meetup. It was that weekend, another win. She requested to join, and after answering a few questions that hinted it wasn't cishet run, she was let in almost immediately. A few group photos showed what seemed like a good mix of genders and queerness. A scroll through the posts revealed the organiser was a *they*, not a *he*, with liberal views that went way beyond their relationship style. Willow had steered her right, as usual.

One face caught her eye, familiar somehow. She spread her fingers over the brunette sitting next to someone in a wheelchair. *Could it really be her?* She paused to rub her eyes. It seemed so unlikely. Yet when she looked again, she was certain. She'd studied that same profile as they'd sat together drinking tea and had stared into those sparkling brown eyes.

Alex leaned back against the wall, her bare back sticking to the tiles. What was someone like Rebecca doing there? To be fair, she didn't know anything about her. Maybe she wasn't as strait-laced and uptight as she looked. Alex knew plenty of poly people and kinksters who you would never guess to look at. She had that hint of queerness after all. Of course, she might not be there for herself. She was sitting with a wheelchair user so probably was just there as a carer.

Even so, she wouldn't have expected a professional carer to support someone to attend a group like that. Maybe she had misjudged her and that place.

CHAPTER FOUR

Rebecca nearly left on time. She'd spent a good hour with Phoebe, chatting and getting to know her as they sorted her laundry. Once Phoebe had calmed down, she'd started to open up, though she'd mainly talked about her musical influences and Rebecca hadn't known half the band names. Maybe she should look them up, but how much rock music could she tolerate even if it was for work? It'd never been her scene—she was always more of a geek than a mosher and was out of her depth when conversations went into that territory.

Luckily Phoebe hadn't wanted anything more from her than to nod along and let her talk as much as she liked. How much of a chance had she got to do that at home? Was she able to speak her mind, or was it like at Rebecca's childhood home, where you had to compete with more forceful and quicker-witted family members? It had been nice to spend quality time with her while her guardian wasn't watching over them, and Rebecca had found herself listening out for her with dread. Alex might be attractive, but Rebecca wasn't one for courting trouble.

It was as she was heading to the office to prepare for handover that Faye caught her, calling out, "Hello, stranger!"

Rebecca smiled and stopped midstride, turning to greet her. "Hello. Has it been so long that you've forgotten me already?"

"I thought you'd forgotten me." Faye brought her hands out from behind her back to wave a battered book at Rebecca. She must've been listening out for Rebecca to pass by and then grabbed it to confront her with when she did. "I can't handle the suspense. You left me on a knife's edge."

It was true the last time she'd read to Faye they'd stopped at a pivotal moment, but the number of times they'd read that series meant any suspense had gone long ago. But she played along, careful not to inject too much sarcasm into her voice. "And you're dying to know how it ends?"

"I don't think I can sleep another night without knowing." Faye didn't hold back on the sarcasm—her tone dripped with it.

Rebecca laughed. "In that case, I better see what I can do."

She paused and checked her watch. She didn't have time before handover, but it was true she'd not sat with Faye for too long. She usually made sure to at least twice a week, especially as Faye was reluctant to bathe otherwise, but she'd been so caught up with Phoebe that she hadn't at all that week. It wasn't good enough.

"I'll just go check in, then meet you at your room."

Faye grinned and practically bounced away. Rebecca always hoped she'd have at least half her energy and enthusiasm when she got to Faye's age. Not that she had it to begin with. She checked her watch again and hurried to the handover room.

When Rebecca pushed open the heavy door, she found only Patience there. A relieved sigh escaped her lips—she wouldn't have to engage in a public debate.

"Good to see you too," Patience said, obviously having heard her reaction.

"It's always good to see you're in charge," Rebecca said, meaning it. Although she'd won the debate about whether it was age appropriate to read to a resident, especially books for children—books consumed by plenty of neurotypical adults, as she always pointed out—some of her colleagues were still snotty about it.

"I've not managed to supervise Faye's bath-time all week, and she's just caught me now. Is it okay if I skip handover?" She hated to skip out on her responsibilities, but there was no real need for her to be there, and it was the only way she'd get home anywhere near on time. Which she'd promised Ishani she'd try to do.

"As long as you've done your notes, that's fine. We wouldn't want to let Faye go too long without your…guidance." Patience crinkled her nose.

"Thanks. I've already completed them, except to update some of Phoebe's plans." She'd not wanted to push her during their first real opportunity to bond, especially given the state she'd found her in, but had got a few more ideas about Phoebe's interests and capabilities.

"How is our new resident doing?"

"Still getting used to it." Rebecca paused and chewed her lip. She wasn't sure how much to say, but as it was only the manager there it was a good opportunity to speak up. "She's not lived away from home before and it shows. Her sister's pushing for her to be one hundred percent independent, but she's not got the skills or experience." Guilt gnawed at her stomach, as if she'd betrayed the sisters, but it was the truth.

"*Tsk.* I suspected as much. Do you think she'll pick things up?"

"I think…I think she's got a chance. She's young and seems pretty driven. She's literate too, which helps enormously. With the right support, yes. Maybe."

Patience stared at her thoughtfully. "I'm aware she wasn't initially assigned to you, and I still haven't got to the bottom of why that was changed."

Rebecca had a good idea why, but she held her tongue. She didn't want to seem like she was bitching about her colleagues, or a resident and their family, and couldn't think how to put it nicely.

They remained in silence until Patience accepted she wouldn't get anything out of Rebecca and let it drop.

"Are you able to give her that support? Considering her lack of experience, it's likely to mean extra work to fit into an already busy shift. I could see if I can move one or two of your other residents to someone else—"

"No! I mean, that won't be necessary, I can handle it." It wasn't that she distrusted her colleagues exactly, but she couldn't be sure they'd follow through on the personalised plans she'd made. Plus she didn't want to drop them for someone new—Faye's teasing admonishment was still ringing in her ears.

"If you're sure. Just don't overdo it, and let me know if you need any help. Remember, there is such a thing as delegation."

"I can do it," Rebecca said, with more confidence than she felt. She had to at least try.

By the time she knocked on Faye's door, Faye was ready and waiting. She answered straight away, her bathrobe on and towel draped over her arm, book crammed into the stretched pocket. "Let's go!"

They traipsed to the bathroom to the hum of Faye recapping where they'd got up to. Rebecca was never sure whose benefit this was for, but it was part of their routine, and Faye seemed to enjoy it. She felt her shoulders drop and her mind become less tight as she let Faye's chatter wash over her. Faye was easy company, and it never felt like work to care for her.

When they reached the bathroom, Rebecca realised she hadn't checked it beforehand like she usually would. It was cleaned daily by the night shift, but a lot could happen in a day. Her pulse quickened as she pushed open the door.

Faye strode past her before she could even give the room a cursory inspection. It'd have to do. Faye was unlikely to notice or care what state it was in. But still, it was part of her job to check everything was safe and as it should be.

She went straight to the bath before Faye could beat her. Officially she was supposed to draw it, but Faye was perfectly capable and it was difficult to justify not letting her. Rebecca was only there in case she had a seizure. Faye's love of a bubble bath had led to no end of debates and protests, especially as Faye was initially reluctant to have anyone watch over her. She would rather not wash than be supervised, which was understandable. Rebecca shuddered at the thought of someone standing over her as she bathed, naked and vulnerable.

The bath was passable, but she gave it a quick swish out with the shower head just in case, being careful to keep her back to Faye to give the older woman some privacy while she undressed.

"You've been spending a lot of time with the new girl?"

Rebecca was pretty sure the question was rhetorical. Faye liked to be in the know and knew more than Rebecca did about the goings on in the home half the time. She was never sure how, considering Faye didn't like to hang around in the communal areas much.

"I'm her key worker," Rebecca stated, the minimal response she could get away with. Maybe she should correct Faye on calling Phoebe a girl, but they were all just girls compared to her. Faye was old enough to be Rebecca's mother, let alone Phoebe's.

"I heard she's been stirring things up already, her and her sister." Faye's tone wasn't malicious, just keen to hear about any drama. She didn't get out much, so you couldn't blame her, and the home could be better than a soap opera.

For some reason Rebecca felt heat rising in her cheeks at the mention of Phoebe's sister, matching the warm water she swirled her hand in as she mixed in the soap. "Maybe you two will get on well."

"Maybe. I've not talked to her yet. She doesn't come out of her room much, except when they make her for meals."

"You know it takes time to settle in when you've moved home."

If she remembered. Faye had been there long before Rebecca started working at the home seven years earlier. Joking aside, having

Faye as a housemate might be what Phoebe needed. There was a big difference in age between the two women, but they both had a spark and a mildly rebellious attitude that could make them good company for each other. "She might like it if you did talk to her and hang out with her a bit. She doesn't know anyone here."

"Long as you don't accuse me of being a bad influence."

"How could I ever do that?" Rebecca smiled and picked up the book Faye had left next to her. "Now, where were we…"

❖

The meetup was held in a pub tucked down a side street, which Alex managed to hunt down after a couple of false starts. Her phone's satnav didn't quite match the twisty streets or show which you could get a van down. One of the organisers, Drew, was meeting her so she didn't have to worry about identifying the group. She'd probably give the small-town countryfolk a heart attack if she sat down at the wrong table and started talking about her queer, poly life.

Drew had sent her a picture, and Alex checked the grinning profile one last time before pushing open the pub door. They shouldn't be hard to spot, with short stylishly messy hair sporting red highlights and multiple ear piercings, and about her age or at least somewhere in their thirties, possibly their forties—after all she was nearing them herself. As soon as she was inside, Alex saw them at the bar, chatting away to the bartender, their red highlights gleaming like a beacon in the dull interior. They turned when she let the door swing shut with a too-loud bang and waved her over.

"Hi—Alex, right? Good to see you." Drew clasped her outstretched hand in both of theirs, giving it more of a hug than a shake. "Jo, this is Alex—she's new in town."

The bartender dipped his head in a silent greeting.

"Thanks for offering to meet me. I don't really know anyone around here yet." Alex took the stool next to them at the bar.

"We'll soon fix that. There's plenty going on around here when you know where to look."

"Glad to hear it." She got the impression Drew might be just the person she needed to be her guide.

"So, what brings you to our neck of the woods?"

It was the obvious question, but Alex had still hoped to dodge it.

"Family needed me." She kept her reply short and trusted they'd get the hint. As much as she loved her sister, she needed an afternoon off and didn't want to get into all the messy details.

"Always the way." The bartender gave her a look that seemed to be approval and didn't add any questions.

She smiled back gratefully. He had the classic bartender vibe—knew when you needed to talk, and when you needed not to.

"Whereabouts are you living?"

Before Alex had the time to answer, or dodge, they stood up and beamed at someone over her shoulder.

"Excuse me a minute." Drew gave her shoulder a friendly squeeze as they strode past.

It really had been too long since someone showed her even friendly affection. Her shoulder glowed from the touch, along with the warmth of Drew's reception and the small comfy pub. Alex took the chance to look around. It was all wood panels and exposed brick, and she was half surprised there weren't any hunting trophies hanging off the walls.

A voice with a hint of a South Asian accent drifted over to her. "I'll let you two get reacquainted and go get the drinks in."

"Thanks, sweetheart." The second speaker sounded familiar. Really?

She was joined at the bar by someone she was almost certain she'd seen before. Her black hair and brown skin were unusual in those parts, from what Alex had seen so far, and the wheelchair she was sitting in was another giveaway. Which meant it really could be…She couldn't contain her curiosity, or at least that's what she told herself it was.

But she still wasn't expecting the sight that greeted her when she turned to the door. Drew was embracing Rebecca, their lips locked in a tender kiss. Alex felt a hot flush of…what? Embarrassment at the PDA? Joy at the sight of queer love? Envy?

Behind her the bartender coughed. "At least move out of the doorway, will you."

Everyone laughed and they broke apart, which gave Alex a chance to shrug off her excessive response. It also gave Rebecca the chance to notice her. She turned towards the bartender, flushed and smiling, but when her gaze fell on Alex her smile wavered. There was no way Alex could interpret the look in her eyes as happy to see her. She felt her jaw stiffen. She had as much right to be there as Rebecca and…She deliberately breathed out the tension and unflexed her hands. She had stepped into Rebecca's safe family space. She tried a reassuring smile. *I'm not here to hurt you.*

"This is Alex—she's new in town." Drew took Rebecca's hand and brought her over, Rebecca staying a couple of steps behind, like a reluctant child being forced to greet a strange relative.

"We've already met." Alex meant to break the tension, but as soon as the words left her mouth, she realised how blunt they sounded. "But not socially. Hi, Rebecca, good to see you again."

Rebecca narrowed her eyes as if she suspected sarcasm. Alex's hand itched with sweat. This was not going well.

Now Drew was looking at her funny too, giving the distinct impression that if she hurt Rebecca she would not be welcome there. They turned back to Rebecca. "Would you like a drink, my love?"

"Yes. I mean, it's okay, I'll get it." Rebecca opened her handbag and started to root around in it, seeming glad of having something to focus on other than Alex.

"Allow me." Alex managed to catch her gaze. "Please?"

After a few seconds' pause and looking like she really wanted to say no, Rebecca nodded. "Okay. Just a Coke please."

Alex realised she'd turned her back on Rebecca's companion from the photograph. Why was she being such an ass? Making a good first impression was not something she excelled at.

"I'll get a round." She hadn't been planning on buying a load of drinks, in fact she'd only budgeted for one to nurse through the afternoon, but what else could she do. She couldn't just offer Rebecca, especially after her partner had welcomed her so warmly, and she needed to smooth things over before she messed up her chance at a social life.

"Thank you. In which case, I'll go get a table. I'm Ishani, she/her." Ishani tilted her head and studied Alex. She must've noticed Rebecca's reaction too.

Crap. "Alex, she/her." She shook her outstretched hand, surprised by the strength of her grip.

"That okay, honey?" Ishani addressed Rebecca over Alex's shoulder. Behind her, Rebecca must've nodded her consent as Ishani unstopped her brakes and started to roll away. "I'll have one of the local ales. Are you coming, Drew? I don't fancy playing host."

"Hey, you'd be great, but I'll spare you the labour." Drew placed their hand on Alex's shoulder again, but this time it felt more like a warning, albeit a friendly one. "I'll have the same. See you in a minute."

They strolled after Ishani, and Alex couldn't help noticing the gentle squeeze they gave Rebecca's hand as they went.

Rebecca stayed standing where they'd left her. Alex swung out the stool on her right, with another attempt at an I-won't-eat-you smile. The wood creaked as Rebecca perched on the edge.

She needed to do something to reset things. There was only one thing for it—she'd have to apologise or at least explain why things went down like they did at Avebrook. She took a deep breath.

"I know we've not got off to a great start. It's nothing personal—Phoebe's my little sister. I get a bit overprotective sometimes." She attempted to make light of her reactions, although inside she stood by them. But it really wasn't personal.

"Yes, some families can be like that." Rebecca's tone was cold, and it was clear Alex would have to offer more to make peace.

She fiddled with a drinks mat from the bar, twirling it between her fingers, then let slip in a quieter, less assured voice, "I…I wasn't there when she needed me before. I won't let her down again."

She glanced up to find Rebecca gazing at her, her lips moving as if she was trying to form a question.

"So, what kind of ale do they like? Looks like there's a good selection." She stared at the cards on the wall, marking a clear end to her disclosure before Rebecca could ask any questions. She wasn't about to spill more than she had to.

A soft hand lightly pressed hers, stopping the spinning mat. And her breath. "What do you recommend, Jo?"

The bartender seemed happy for the chance to wax lyrical about his stock, and Alex tried to concentrate and respond appropriately. But Rebecca's hand had felt so cold and delicate that she had the urge to clasp it to her and breathe warmth into it, to share the heat Rebecca's close presence gave rise to in her, which she tried to shrug off as embarrassment, but that didn't fully explain it.

By the time they'd collected their drinks, Rebecca had found her voice and even managed a smile. Alex found herself walking extra slowly over to the back room, not wanting her time with Rebecca to herself to end, with the pretence of not wanting to spill the drinks. Truth be told, she'd done enough waitressing and bar jobs to be able to march right over with a far bigger burden to balance. Or at least she had been able to.

They were welcomed into the group, which included about a dozen folk who all seemed to know Rebecca. Drew rose to relieve Alex of the pint glasses, and of Rebecca. The couple embraced again, Drew planting another kiss before asking her in a whisper—that Alex pretended not to hear—if she was okay. Out of the corner of her eye, Alex caught Rebecca's nodded reply. As Rebecca leaned forward for another kiss, Alex's lips tingled, and she lifted her fingers to her mouth, gently pressing the eager flesh to satiate it, as in a flash she imagined what it would be like to be on the receiving end.

When she looked away, she was met by Ishani's studious gaze. This time there seemed to be a smile tugging at the corners of her mouth, as if she could guess what Alex was thinking. Alex was exposed and not in a good way.

"Everyone, this is Alex. She's new in town." Drew introduced her to the group en masse, then let her make her own individual introductions.

Apart from Drew, Ishani, and Rebecca, most people appeared older than her, in some cases significantly older. Which was fine. She'd always hung out with older people and didn't know if she had the energy for a load of lively young 'uns any more. She ended up on a well-worn sofa between Drew and a woman who was possibly called Nancy—it was too much to remember everyone's names.

Possibly-Nancy kept leaning over onto her, partly to speak to Drew and, Alex suspected, partly because she'd had a few too many.

"Sorry, love, I'm not usually like this. I don't usually get like this on an afternoon," she said, after nearly spilling her drink over Alex for the third time.

"Special circumstances, we understand," Drew jumped in, adding weight to her claim.

"I'm celebrating my divorce finally going through today!"

"Congratulations," Alex said and raised her glass to toast her. "To your freedom!"

Nancy hooted and sank back into the sofa, shoulder to shoulder with Alex. "Not everyone agrees it's something to celebrate, of course, but even the kids know it's right for us. And when I say kids, they must be about your age. Old enough to know better than to believe it has to be happily ever after."

"This could be the start of your happily ever after." Drew joined the toast, chinking glasses with both of them.

Alex's gaze landed back on Rebecca, sitting opposite them by Ishani's side, their hands gently linked in her lap. The initial surprise at realising Rebecca was poly had faded, leaving a thrumming in her chest. Could this be the start of something for her too? She couldn't deny she was drawn to her, and she could've sworn Rebecca had been checking her out. But she was still Phoebe's carer, something it was easy to forget in the outside world, but it wouldn't be when they went back inside.

"I gotta admit, I'm loving living on my own, the peace and quiet. Anna and George did offer for me to stay with them, and I considered it, but I reckon I made the right decision for now especially while I'm still medically transitioning as well. Maybe one day." Whether it was the drink or her comfort in the group, Nancy wasn't holding back.

"It sounds like you did. Living with another married couple right away might have been too much and put a strain on you and Anna, considering it's still early days," Ishani added.

Alex might not know Nancy's situ, but she couldn't imagine ever moving in with a couple. Or a single partner. There was no way it wouldn't limit her. It was good to hear they weren't guiding Nancy down that path.

"Exactly. And to be honest, we're still doped on NRE, and I don't know how much George could handle." Nancy winked at her.

They laughed at that, including Alex. She might have no idea who they were talking about, but she knew what she was like in the early days of New Relationship Energy, no matter how many times she went through it. Rebecca also sported a knowing smile. The thrumming in Alex's chest moved to her stomach, where the butterflies hatched.

"It's lovely to see you both so happy," said Rebecca.

"They are sickeningly cute together," Drew confirmed in a stage whisper.

"You're just jealous!" Nancy whispered back.

"What have I got to be jealous of?"

At that moment, another small group walked over to join them. Drew took the opportunity to invite Rebecca over to the sofa and onto their lap, making room for the newcomers. And proving their point.

"Nothing at all," Rebecca murmured, as she leaned back against them. Her knees pressed against Alex, who couldn't pull away even if she'd wanted to within the confines of the couch.

"So, what about you?"

Nancy turned her attention to Alex, which was a relief as she didn't know how to dampen the fire inside her when she looked at the cute woman she was pressed up against. It was strange seeing Rebecca so relaxed and happy, and it made Alex aware how unrelaxed she usually was around her. This was the Rebecca she wanted to get to know.

"What about me?" Alex replied in her best husky voice.

Nancy chuckled and nudged her again, nearly causing her to lose her drink over Rebecca's lap. Rebecca broke her gaze away from Drew. A smile still played on her lips, which made Alex smile too. Compersion had never been difficult for her—she didn't have to be the one making someone happy to be glad of it.

"I mean, how's your love life?"

"Nancy! She doesn't have to tell you that. Let the poor woman get to know us first."

It was surprising that Rebecca jumped in to defend her privacy as if she was worried Alex would be scared away. Did that mean Rebecca wanted to get to know her? Something stirred in Alex at the thought. She made herself refocus on Nancy. She didn't actually mind the question. She had nothing to hide.

"Good, but not exactly full right now. My current only partner is touring the country, and I don't see much of her."

"So you're looking for someone to fill it?"

Alex nearly choked on her drink.

"*Nancy!*" Both Rebecca and Drew jumped in this time, mock outrage colouring their voices.

"I'm not hitting on her." Nancy held up her hands in a protest of innocence.

"Glad to hear it. We don't jump new people as soon as they come through the door." Rebecca aimed this last remark at Alex, as if to reassure her.

"And here I was hoping you would jump me," Alex shot back before she could think whether it was a good idea.

Nancy roared with laughter at that, but Rebecca blushed crimson and didn't seem to know how to take it. She leaned back into Drew, who kissed her flushed cheek while keeping an eye on Alex. They didn't seem the possessive type and their look seemed more amused curiosity than a challenge, but she'd better not push it. Hitting on people's partners right in front of them wasn't usually the way to make friends.

"Just kidding. I'm not here on the hunt."

"Good to know." Drew leaned in. "This isn't a dating event, but if you are on the lookout, we're not above a bit of matchmaking."

"Just tell us what you're looking for, and we'll get to work," Nancy added.

"Cheers, but I can manage myself, and I'm not looking to rush into anything. Especially as I don't know how long I'll be sticking around."

"I thought…" Rebecca trailed off, seemingly remembering where she was and where her knowledge of Alex came from.

"It depends how long she needs me to stay. And how long she stays."

"Of course." Rebecca chewed on her lip and seemed on the verge of saying more.

"So you two do know each other." Drew was the one to address the elephant in the room.

"Yes," Rebecca said. "Well, not exactly know each other, we've met…"

"Through work. She's my sister's carer." Alex put Rebecca out of her misery, guessing she shouldn't be the one to say it.

"Ah, that explains it."

"And why I couldn't say…" Rebecca twisted to face Drew.

"I know, sweetie, I get it. No worries." Drew planted another reassuring kiss.

Alex sat silently watching them, trying not to notice how her stomach flipped every time they kissed.

"Excuse us, we've not seen each other for a while."

"It's all right—I know what it's like." When she finally saw Willow again, Alex knew she wouldn't be able to keep her hands or lips off her, either.

"Yeah, it's been a whole ten days," Rebecca added, in a mildly mocking tone.

"In which case, you've got no excuse!" a newcomer heckled.

"Hey, it's a long time to be apart from this wonderful woman." Drew nuzzled Rebecca.

"Fair enough." If it was her…Alex deliberately stopped her mind running away with that image.

"But," Drew said, "I had better leave you alone for a bit and check in with everyone else."

They slid out from under Rebecca, almost depositing her on Alex's lap. Alex moved back to give them room and only realised then that Nancy had left.

"You two behave yourselves." They gave Rebecca a final light kiss, then reached over and ruffled Alex's hair.

From someone else, their level of familiarity might have been unwelcome, but somehow it didn't feel like she'd only just met them. Alex tried not to read too much into their parting remark. Were they leaving them alone together on purpose? Was it some gesture of permission? She didn't know how she felt about that.

"By the way, they don't know. At work. I mean, they know I'm gay, that I live with Ishani, but…that's enough." Rebecca stuttered out this confession in a low voice that Alex had to lean forward to hear. "They don't know we're poly, or about Drew, or…They don't need to know."

"Sure." Alex didn't make any attempt to hide her relationships, but she also didn't shout about her private life. "It's none of their business what you get up to outside work."

"Exactly." Rebecca shifted in her seat, relaxing back into the arm so she was facing Alex. "So I'd appreciate it if you'd be…discreet."

Alex laughed, she couldn't help it. As much as she tried to be inconspicuous, her queerness always seemed to come through.

Rebecca shrank back.

"Sorry, it's just people tend to make their own assumptions about me, no matter how much I try to fade into the background."

"I'm not asking you to hide your sexuality—"

"Good, but don't worry, it's not like poly's likely to come up. I don't exactly hang out gossiping with the staff." She remembered their last meeting, how blunt she'd been in her attempt to get Rebecca to back off from Phoebe, and flinched.

"I know." Rebecca caught her eye, seeming to remember too.

"I didn't mean—"

"I know, you already explained, it's okay." Rebecca rested her hand on Alex's again with the gentlest of squeezes.

Was it okay? Could she protect Phoebe *and* get close to Rebecca? A lump formed in her throat with the acidic taste of betrayal. The urge to snatch her hand away, to run away, took over. *This is exactly the kind of complication you don't need.*

"Phoebe…" Rebecca started, and withdrew her hand. Was she thinking the same thing? "Does she know? About you being non-monogamous?"

Apparently not. She was still fixated on the privacy side of things.

"Of course she knows about me." Why would she not? She paused and took a breath. Rebecca was just trying to protect herself. "But it's okay—she understands the need to keep things quiet sometimes."

Like her, Phoebe had learned that the hard way.

"You won't tell her about me?" Rebecca twisted the hem of her top.

"Course not."

"Thank you." Rebecca smiled, a smile that brought out the dimples Alex longed to kiss.

Control yourself.

They were interrupted by the raucous entrance of another bunch of people, clearly part of their party, who shouted over to Rebecca. She rose to greet them, spelling the end of their private chat. She didn't introduce Alex, which gave her the chance to stop and consider what the hell she was doing flirting with her.

Because she couldn't deny she had been and that she wanted to do more.

CHAPTER FIVE

S o, who is she?"

The question was asked in a casual manner, but clearly had layers. Rebecca stifled a groan. The weekend had not turned out as relaxing as she'd been counting on.

"If she's popping up outside work too, then you've got the right to talk about her," Ishani added, as if that was the issue.

So Drew had passed that on. Or she'd used her people-watching skills. Ishani had a way of studying people without them realising, taking advantage of the way she was so often overlooked. Except, no— she'd been around when they were chatting and probably just heard them mention it. It didn't matter anyway, it was no big deal. Rebecca had nothing to hide.

"There's not much to talk about. That was the first time we met outside."

"I could see you clearly weren't expecting her."

At least that was obvious too, and she didn't think it was some underhanded plan. Ishani took a sip of her tea, leaving space for Rebecca to disclose any further relevant information.

"You can say that again." Rebecca gave a nervous laugh, letting some of the tension from her unexpected predicament seep out. What were the odds of Alex showing up there? How could she have anticipated that?

"Will you be seeing her again?"

"I don't know." The idea made her chest flutter. They'd spent most of the afternoon in each other's company, moving from group to group as well as occasional moments alone, but parted with nothing more than a *See you around*.

Ishani put down her mug in order to manually shift her legs into a more comfortable position on the sofa, settling in against Rebecca's side. "She didn't take your number then?"

"No." Rebecca flapped her with a cushion. "We work together, kind of. It would be unprofessional."

"I doubt there's an explicit rule about dating the family member of a resident."

Trust her to be the pragmatist. She was right too, there wasn't. Rebecca had already checked, not with any intentions, but after she'd caught herself drooling over Alex, she had wondered whether it was explicitly forbidden and if she needed to be careful not to draw any attention to her unprofessional crushing.

"That's not the point—that doesn't make it right. Besides, I'm not looking for another relationship, you know that. Everything's good as it is." It was. Ishani and Drew filled her life with love and joy, and what with her job and need for quiet time, she was officially polysaturated.

"But if someone happens to come along without you looking…?" Ishani instantly pointed out the weakness in her position.

"I'm not interested," Rebecca said, as if she was certain, ignoring the increase in the fluttering in her chest. Sometimes she wished Ishani was less open and set more boundaries as her primary partner, then there would be no question. Rebecca had suggested they set a limit on other partners when they'd first started dating other people, but Ishani considered that unnecessarily restrictive. And unrealistic.

"I was only asking. You know I'm fine with you seeing whoever you want, as long as you let me know." Ishani gave her thigh an affectionate squeeze.

"I know." Rebecca gave her another playful bat with the cushion in return before burying her face in it. "Anyway, what makes you think she'd even be interested in me."

Ishani scoffed. "I saw the way she looked at you. My legs might not work, but my eyesight is perfect."

"Maybe she was just happy to see someone she recognised." And to get the chance to apologise. She hadn't explained that Alex was the one who'd upset her the other day and hoped Ishani hadn't figured that out.

"Maybe she was." Ishani stroked Rebecca's hair in a soothing motion. "Or maybe she's completely into you. Or at least open to the possibility that you could be into each other."

Rebecca hugged the cushion tightly. "Well, I'm not. Open."

"And did you tell her that?"

Did she think she'd been leading her on? Oh God, had she made a complete show of herself in front of everyone? No, not necessarily. *No need to spiral, it's just a question.* Rebecca bit her lip, then shook her head. "It didn't come up."

"Hmm. Well, we'll have to see what happens next time." Ishani sank back on the sofa, as if getting ready to watch that show.

"There might not be a next time." There was no guarantee Alex would come along again. She might not even still be there by the time the next meet rolled around.

"I think there will."

Ishani smiled as she wrapped Rebecca in her arms. Trust and patience were among her strengths, something Rebecca was often grateful for. She didn't push her to rush into anything or give a definitive answer where there wasn't one. Though the push to talk was pressure enough.

"Can we leave it now? I've been looking forward to a peaceful weekend on the sofa all week."

"Of course, honey. Which reminds me, I have a present for you." Ishani let go of her and reached over to grab the rucksack off the back of her wheelchair. "Close your eyes."

Rebecca obeyed and held out her hands, resisting the urge to help. After a little rustling, a hard rectangular object was placed in them.

"You can open them now."

She gasped when she saw what it was. "Where did you find it?"

"Charity shop. I've been on the lookout since you mentioned it."

"That was ages ago, I can't believe you remembered." Rebecca turned the slightly battered case over. It was *Azura*, an old sci-fi series she'd not seen or heard of in years but remembered fondly. "This is exactly what I'm in the mood for."

"Glad to be of service. Now, as I provided the entertainment, you can provide the munchies." She kissed Rebecca on the lips. "As much as it's tempting just to enjoy you, I need some nutritional sustenance."

"As long as I don't have to actually cook," Rebecca moaned, already getting comfy curled up against her.

"Your call. I won't judge." Ishani wrapped her arms back around Rebecca, true to her word.

Eventually they ordered a takeaway, then when it arrived they got started on the new box set. It was indeed exactly what Rebecca needed after a roller coaster week. Ishani, never a big fan of TV, had picked up a book after the first couple of episodes. Rebecca lay down with her head resting on a cushion in Ishani's lap, where she wouldn't get in the way of her page and could carry on watching. It was their habitual position. She didn't know how Ishani could read with the TV blaring—Rebecca struggled if anyone even talked in the same room—yet she claimed to be undisturbed.

As a carefully choreographed fight scene filled the screen, Rebecca looked away and studied the box again. How had she never noticed it before? Max, the lead character, who she'd remembered as a kick-ass lesbian, might in fact be non-binary. Okay, so it didn't explicitly say anything about them being genderqueer, but considering it was from the eighties, it wouldn't, would it?

In the show Max was referred to as *they* if anything, which, once she'd noticed it, she couldn't help being hyper aware of. She itched to text Drew to tell them, but they were on a date, and she should resist interrupting them even with such an interesting titbit. Which reminded her of said date. A twinge in her chest indicated the start of an anxious turn, and she googled the show instead to distract herself. It led her to a forum where the show's queerness was being hotly debated in retrospect by fans. Evidently, she wasn't the first person to question Max's gender as well as their sexuality.

The internet hadn't existed when it was first created and aired, so there wasn't much out there. Maybe that was a good thing. At the time it'd slipped under most people's radars and avoided any mass controversy. There were definitely sapphic vibes all over it and not just in the androgynous Max—the way they and one of the other leads flirted, there could surely be no doubt a queer relationship was being hinted at.

Surely their suggestive smile would be enough to make anyone do their bidding, and yet the show had steered clear of having them use this to their advantage, except in their personal relationships. It was one of the other things she liked about it—she was always turned off by those stories where the heroines just flirted their way out of any sticky situations. If she ever had kids, this was the kind of show she'd want them to watch. Once they were old enough for the faux violence.

Not that she had any desire to have children. There'd be no more quiet evenings if they added kids. Thankfully Ishani was on the same page; it'd been one of the pivotal factors in them deciding to move in together. Rebecca loved her chosen family and didn't need any of them to be blood relations.

Would she ever want to add anyone else to it? She'd told Ishani she wasn't interested in another partner and that had always been true. But it didn't stop her being interested in Alex, particularly the charming, open, funny Alex from the pub, who made her forget there was any reason they couldn't enjoy each other's company.

❖

Alex woke with a smile and answered her phone before she remembered that no one she wanted to talk to would ring her at that time in the morning.

"We've still not heard from her!" a gruff voice barked.

Alex stifled a groan and stretched as best as she could in the back of the van. "Good morning, Father, how are you?"

"Your mother's worried. It's been a week. How are we supposed to know if she's okay?"

"Have you tried calling her?" Alex rolled her neck in a vain attempt to release the strain of another night sleeping on a mattress on the floor, and the phone call.

A pause. "She said not to, and we're respecting that."

Sure you are, by harassing me instead. "Well she's fine, just settling in. She'll call you when she's ready."

An exaggerated huff carried down the line, which made Alex roll her eyes.

"We've not even seen where she's living. Maybe we should drop by, to check everything is okay."

How would the staff react to their parents turning up? They'd probably take one look and decide they were preferable to Phoebe's queer sister and welcome them with open arms. Would Rebecca see through their nice act? Their time together in the real world was still playing through her mind, but she couldn't be sure Rebecca would risk taking her side. Rebecca's career seemed very important to her, and there was no reason Alex should be.

"Everything is okay, I can tell you that."

There was a longer pause while no one admitted out loud that Alex's word meant nothing as far as their family was concerned.

"I would really want to hear that from Phoebe herself."

"I know." Alex resisted the urge to just tell him to fuck off. She didn't want to fight with him; she didn't want anything to do with him. She tried to breathe deeply through her gritted teeth. "Look, maybe you could text her and get something that way."

If they hadn't tried that already: it was unlikely they'd left her alone completely. Maybe she would have to grit her teeth and talk to Phoebe about them, so she was at least prepared to field their accusations. In the meantime, a text would be a lot less invasive than them rocking up at the home.

"I suppose. And you can tell her to call us."

Alex clenched her phone hard enough it felt like the plastic cover might give way. "If it comes up. I'm not gonna force her."

"I am her father. I have a right—"

"To what?" Alex nearly pointed out he was her father too, but that would not lead anywhere either of them wanted to go. "Phoebe's a grown woman now. She's got rights of her own."

"I've a right to care about my child and ask after her."

Child, not children. He didn't even seem to remember who he was talking to. "And I answered, didn't I?"

More silent seething. Alex almost expected smoke to start seeping through the handset.

"Well, if we don't hear from her in another week, I'll call back. And maybe we will have to just go there." His words had the bitter edge of a threat.

This time, Alex managed not to rise to meet it with a threat of her own. "Text her, see what she says."

"I will."

She grabbed at the chance to end the conversation. "I've gotta get ready for work now. Bye."

"Bye." The line went dead.

Why had she answered the phone? As much as she hated to give in, she would have to talk to Phoebe and soon. Their father couldn't be trusted not to follow through on his threat. She sat up and shuffled to the edge of the mattress, and grabbed her socks and shoes. Now that she was awake and unlikely to get any more rest after that call, she might as well take advantage of the extra time to take a dip and drop in on Phoebe before work.

Maybe Rebecca would be there. Something had shifted between them, and it was intriguing. She couldn't deny, at least to herself, how watching Rebecca with her partners had sparked a little envy in her. How she'd wished she too could draw Rebecca close and feel her melt in her arms. Even though in reality she knew nothing should happen—Rebecca was still Phoebe's carer.

What if she explained to Rebecca about their parents in case they contacted the home. They couldn't be trusted to be patient enough to wait another week to try to get to Phoebe, especially now she'd stood up to their father. Competing voices at the back of her head wanted to know if she should trust Rebecca, and if there wasn't a way they could get to know each other more.

She pulled on a hoodie and jumped out the back of the van into a cool summer breeze. It was delicious on her clammy morning skin. A swim would give her the chance to process and ensure she didn't stink when she met Rebecca, or at least wouldn't smell unclean—even after showering the chorine sting seemed to hang around her for hours. It was best not to think about how much they pumped into that pool, and what they were trying to kill.

By the time she got to Phoebe's, she was less sure of bringing Rebecca onside. Their father might just text Phoebe and wait, as he'd said he would. To drag Phoebe's key worker into it could be a mistake. Memories of their outside meet had faded and were overshadowed by those of Rebecca's enthusiasm for getting involved in Phoebe's life. They did not need her sticking her nose into their family and trying to help. Alex mustn't let whatever there was between them mess with her head. It was simple chemistry and would probably fizzle out all by itself if she let it.

"I'm afraid she's not home." The door was answered by a bored-looking member of staff with bleached-blond hair almost as light as her skin, or its natural tone anyway. She looked like she'd been out in the sun too long. Her skin had a dodgy glow, her sharp nose reddened and starting to peel.

"Where is she?" Alex stood on the step like a child calling on a friend to come out to play and being stopped by a grown-up who didn't approve of her.

"I can't give you that information."

"Seriously?" Alex's fists clenched by her sides. "I'm not a random, I'm her sister."

The staff member stared down her nose at Alex and folded her arms before letting her eyes flick over her figure. Had they met before? Who knew and it might not have made any difference to either of them.

"Hmm, then don't you know?"

Enough already. Alex managed to push the door open and pass

her without barging her out of the way as much as she wanted to. "I'll wait."

"You'll be waiting awhile."

"Is there a problem, Marie?"

Another member of staff came up behind Alex. She was dressed more formally than the others, in smart black trousers and a crisp blouse. Gold glasses frames glinted against her rich black complexion.

Marie dropped her arms and adopted a less hostile impression. "Phoebe's sister was insistent she come in to see her. I did try to explain she's not here right now."

"And I was trying to find out where she is," Alex shot back before Marie could pretend she had told her. She unfolded her own arms, in a mirror of Marie.

"I believe she's at the day centre, isn't that right? As I'm sure Marie was about to explain, Phoebe will be back this afternoon." She had the calm, authoritative voice of someone used to dealing with hostile parties.

"I wasn't told about any day centre." Alex turned to face the newcomer instead of Marie. It seemed likely she would provide more sense, and from the way Marie changed her tune, it appeared she was in charge. "When was this all arranged?"

Phoebe had only been there a week, and they were already packing her off to another facility she hadn't had the chance to check out.

"We usually explore options with new residents to help them settle in, particularly when they're new to the area, like your sister."

"And why wasn't I involved?" Alex could sense Marie smirking next to her but didn't break eye contact with the apparent boss.

"If your sister wants you to be, we could arrange a meeting to discuss everything, or the best thing may be to have a chat with her key worker."

It was hard to argue with that, and it doused some of the fire coursing through her veins. "Fine, I'll talk to Rebecca. Is she here?"

"Not yet, but she'll be in later. Maybe you'd best return when Phoebe's back and see them both then. Or if you prefer, we can have a chat now. I'm Patience, the manager here." Patience held out her hand, challenging Alex to play nice.

"Alex." She gave it a short, sharp shake, and Patience returned her firm grip. "I'll come back after work when they're both here."

"Thank you. We'll see you later."

Patience guided her to the front door, past Marie who stood against the wall with a gloating expression. Alex was certain Rebecca would be prewarned for her return.

❖

Phoebe was full of beans when she got home. Rebecca had worried it might be too soon to send her to the day centre, but she seemed like someone who'd appreciate the stimulation and the chance to get out. There were groups and activities aimed at people with milder learning disabilities like Phoebe, and she might make some friends. She'd jumped at the opportunity when Rebecca suggested it.

"Guess what?"

Phoebe bounced on her heels, like she might take off into the air at any moment. It was great to see her happy, and her joy was contagious.

"What?" Rebecca said, failing to come up with any idea of what she could be so excited about.

"They've got a karaoke machine!"

"Oh yes. Do you like to sing?" Although she'd heard plenty of Phoebe's music already, she'd not heard Phoebe herself and had no clue if she was any good at it.

"I love singing, and not just rock stuff. Everything." Phoebe walked over to her CD rack, which was as tall as she was, and stroked the line of cases.

"I'll have to come and hear you sometime—though, I can't sing myself, so don't ask me to join in."

Standing up and singing in front of a group of people was not her idea of fun, quite the opposite, but if karaoke made Phoebe this happy, then she'd support it. From a distance.

"No, if you come, you have to sing. No hiding at the back like Alex." Phoebe crossed her arms in mock seriousness.

Rebecca's breath hitched at the name, and she hugged her paperwork to her chest. After the weekend she'd been secretly looking forward to seeing Alex again, but Patience's—and Marie's even more dramatic—account of her visit that morning had left her no longer sure she wanted to. "In that case, I'll leave you to it."

"Spoilsport."

"So you want to go there again?" Phoebe's enjoyment would be hard for anyone to mistake, but Rebecca still had to check with her before making any more plans. It was too easy to make assumptions, and she tried to avoid falling into that trap by checking everything with the residents themselves. And double-checking.

"Defo."

"Great. I'll get you the timetable, and we can have a look at what days to go. They have different groups on different days." She actually had it already in the file under her fingertips, but she needed to check where there were free slots first. She didn't want to get Phoebe's hopes up, then tell her she couldn't go because it was full.

"Karaoke days."

"You might get bored if you only do karaoke."

"Never!" Phoebe turned her hi-fi on, as if to prove the point that she could never get tired of music.

"I'll bring it anyway, so you can see when they do karaoke. And something else might take your fancy."

"*Okaaay*, I'll look." Phoebe reached for her headphones.

That was Rebecca's cue to go. She promised to come back later that afternoon and left to see to her other residents. And make sure everything was in order before Alex returned.

The afternoon passed quickly, and she only just managed to squeeze in updating the timetable, then leaving it with Phoebe for her to look over. She'd wanted to discuss it with her and help her decide—there were a lot of options, which could be overwhelming—but there was just too much else to do. Phoebe could read, and it was only reasonable to give her time to think it over.

And if Alex saw what they were offering, maybe she'd feel better about Phoebe going there. It might help smooth things over if she felt she had a say in what Phoebe signed up to, as well as seeing Phoebe was making the choice herself. *As long as she doesn't talk her out of it.*

Would Alex do that? Surely she'd see how happy Phoebe was about going there and step down off her high horse. She clearly cared about her sister's happiness. Who knew what Marie might have said to set her off that morning? They were all putting it down to Alex being spiky as if Marie couldn't possibly be at fault, but Rebecca knew how difficult Marie could be. And even though they'd only just met, she felt she knew Alex better than that too.

It was almost the end of Rebecca's shift when the doorbell rang and she was summoned to the office. Alex had returned and had asked for her. Her skin tingled with anticipation as she approached the closed door.

When she entered, Alex was studying the certificates on the wall with her hunched back to the door. Rebecca stood there for a moment, not knowing how to greet her, alone together, at work. She didn't usually mix her work and social lives, which was deliberate when it came to colleagues, let alone her residents' families. Or her crushes. Was that what she should call the feelings bubbling inside her?

She settled on an ambiguous, "Hi."

"Hi." Alex kept her back to her. "I came to see Phoebe earlier, but she wasn't there. They said to come back later and talk to you." There was no warmth to her voice, no apparent pleasure at seeing Rebecca. Not that she looked at her.

Business it was. Rebecca could almost forget the Alex she had hung out with at the weekend, faced with this cold, hard presence.

"Apparently she'd been shipped off to some day centre." Alex spat out the last words as if they left a bitter taste in her mouth, but gave no clue why.

Rebecca remained silent, only moving to tug at the neck of her shirt, while running through her options and trying to decide the best approach to broker peace. Why was Alex making such a big deal of Phoebe going out?

"I didn't know anything about it. Why didn't I know anything about it?" There was steel in her voice, and it pierced Rebecca's chest.

What did she want her to say? Was it a rhetorical question? Maybe she should've taken Patience up on her offer to accompany her. She shifted her weight, trying to find a place of balance.

Alex glanced over her shoulder, as if to merely ensure Rebecca was still there and listening, her eyes narrowed and unreadable. "When was it decided?"

"We discussed the possibility on Friday, Phoebe and me. We…" Rebecca licked her lips to wet them. She tried again. "Phoebe wanted to go. It was her choice. She was getting bored just staying here."

"Why wasn't I in on this discussion?"

"You weren't here. And it wasn't about you," Rebecca shot back, then pursed her lips too late. She shouldn't have said it, but Alex's accusatory tone was needling her. What was her problem? You'd have thought she'd packed Phoebe off to join the army without telling her. "It was Phoebe's choice. Today she was just checking it out as an option."

"So, there are other options? Other places to offload her?" This last part was delivered with a definite sneer.

"We're not..." Rebecca bit her lip, bit back her anger. She mustn't let Alex get under her skin. Her prickly palms reminded her she already had. She tried to forget the other Alex she'd met and treat her the same as any other family member resistant to change. *Emphasise the positives, let her see this is about what's best for her sister.* "Phoebe's a dynamic young woman. She needs stimulation, to be out in the world. Isn't that why she moved here?"

"Hmph. I wouldn't call some old day centre *out in the world.* Sounds like the opposite." Alex remained steadfast in her objection, her defensive posture—back stiff, arms crossed—mirroring her tone.

Could Rebecca handle her, or was it time to give up? *Remember, you've done this before.* Alex wasn't the first person to have qualms about their family member's treatment, Rebecca just needed to find a way to get through to her. "And where would you have her go instead? Where would you start?"

Silence. Thick, heavy silence. Rebecca wanted to open the window, let some air in, but Alex was standing by it. At least she didn't jump in and pretend there was an easy answer.

"Have you talked to Phoebe about it? She seemed to really like the place. It could be a good first step for her as she gets to know the area and settles in."

If this was about Phoebe, then surely that's what Alex would do. However, she was getting the impression it might be more about Alex's own control issues. Some families struggled to let go.

Alex seemed to consider this, and her limbs loosened. "Just as long as she doesn't get too settled. This isn't where we want to stay. Where she wants to stay."

Where we want to stay. Alex really did have no intention of hanging around. Maybe that was for the best—the others seemed like they had been right when they assumed she'd be difficult to handle. Not that she'd tell them that. They did not need encouragement to jump to conclusions.

But there was something that still didn't add up. Rebecca used her frustration as fuel to summon the courage to ask the question that had been on her mind since they first butted heads. It didn't seem like she could make things worse.

"If you're so against her being here, why didn't you take her to live with you?" She kept her voice calm, low, trying not to sound like she was accusing her of anything.

Alex stiffened again anyway.

"It's not that simple," she eventually said, barely audible, turning back away from Rebecca.

"No, it's not."

She should leave it there, but for once she wanted to grab the chance to say her piece. "It's not that simple or easy, especially when no one's even taught her how to do basic things for herself, like wash her clothes. Independence requires work."

The sisters might not understand why Phoebe couldn't live alone yet, but it was becoming clear to Rebecca. No wonder her application for her own flat was turned down, even in supported accommodation, given her evident lack of independent living skills. It was a nice idea, but Phoebe wasn't prepared for the reality of it. Not yet.

"You think I don't know that?" Alex's voice was softer. She sounded…sad.

"I don't know. I don't know you." *And I'm not sure I want to.* The thought rushed into Rebecca's head, shoving aside anything else.

Alex slumped, staying facing out of the window and away from Rebecca. She seemed to have turned in on herself and gave no smart comeback.

For the briefest of moments, Rebecca had the urge to rush over and comfort her. But she didn't. Who knew whether it would be welcome, and she had to keep in mind where she was. She had her job to do, people who needed and wanted her care. She walked off without another word, closing the door quietly behind her.

CHAPTER SIX

M um texted me."

"Huh?" It took a moment for Alex to process what Phoebe had said. When she did, she still had no better reply. "Huh."

"She wants to visit. See what it's like." Phoebe was staring at her phone.

"And what do you want?" Alex put away her own phone, focusing on her sister and trying to ignore the clenching in her gut.

It was Phoebe's turn to pause and process. A slight frown furrowed her forehead, and she chewed her lip. "I guess that would be okay."

"You don't have to let her—it's up to you. You can take your time to decide." *And don't let her push you into it.* Alex shouldn't have been surprised they'd jumped right in and invited themselves over.

"I said I don't know." Phoebe dropped her phone back onto the bed beside her.

Alex let out a trapped sigh. "Good." She leaned over to ruffle Phoebe's hair. Light roots were starting to show at the base of her jet-black strands. She grabbed the chance to change to a safer subject. "Want me to do your roots? Your goth is growing out."

"I'm not a goth, I'm a rock chick. I told you, it's different!"

"Sure." She did know that really, but it had become a habit to wind Phoebe up. "Do you want me to do your rock roots?"

Phoebe glowered at her, then drew her fringe down in front of her face to inspect it and made herself cross-eyed. "Rebecca said she'll help me do it."

The smile that had briefly relaxed Alex's face slipped and she gritted her teeth. So much for safer. "Did she now."

"Yes. I like her. She's teaching me to do lots of stuff. So I can be an independent woman." She sang the last part, and as always her voice made Alex's heart expand.

As much as Alex hated to admit it after the way Rebecca had spoken to her, maybe it was for the best. The sooner Phoebe got the skills she needed, the sooner they could go. And Rebecca would be out of their lives. She ignored the tightening in her chest at this last thought. It was for the best.

She'd managed to avoid Rebecca for the last week, since they'd had it out in the staffroom. Then just as she'd got to Phoebe's, she had got a text from Drew.

Hey, how are you settling in? Sorry I didn't get to chat to you much at the meet. Fancy a cuppa at some point? Not hitting on you, don't worry ;)

It was tempting to say no because of their link to Rebecca, but she smiled at how they'd reached out. They seemed like her kind of people, and it would be good to make friends. Plus, Drew was a gatekeeper, her way into the local scene. It didn't have anything to do with their partner. Her mind kept drifting back to it. Phoebe was focused back on her own screen, so she decided to take the plunge.

Sure, that'd be nice. Still don't know many people round here. When were you thinking?

As she pressed send, she felt herself relax. It would be good to see a friendly face. Thankfully, Drew replied straight away before any niggling doubts could creep back in.

Great :) *My hours are flexible—I'm self-employed—so I can fit in with you.*

The ball was in her court. Alex pictured the empty weekend ahead and decided the sooner, the better.

I'm guessing you're booked up at the weekend? How about Friday, before I start work.

It also gave her not too long to start doubting Drew's intentions. They'd said they weren't hitting on her but had mentioned enjoying matchmaking. What if they had plans for her? Would that be so bad?

What if it was about Rebecca? Alex cringed when she remembered how focused she'd been on her at the meetup. What if Drew planned to warn her off? But they hadn't seemed possessive—in fact they'd seemed almost keen to leave the two of them to get to know each other. Was this some kind of vetting process? It better not be. Anyone who used their existing partners to vet potentials was not someone she wanted to get with.

Despite not being in the habit of overthinking things, it was a struggle not to question it.

Not that she wanted to get with Rebecca. She looked over at her little sister, curled up next to her. She was there for Phoebe, and that meant keeping an eye on the staff charged with her care. And not in the way she tended to when it came to Rebecca. Phoebe might not remember that Rebecca wasn't her friend, so Alex had to.

The question of Drew's intentions kept springing to mind over the next few days. Whenever she got to the Rebecca part, though, she remembered their last meeting and how it was clear she wasn't interested in knowing Alex better. Alex had watched her reflection in the window, her frustration clear in her tight body. This wasn't about Rebecca. But if she was going to be able to face Rebecca's partner, she might need to make peace first.

And maybe if Rebecca spent some time getting to know her, she'd realise Alex wasn't so bad to have around and was only trying to do the right thing.

❖

When Rebecca stepped out of the meeting room after handover, she was surprised to find Alex lurking in the corridor. She stopped in her tracks and let her colleagues flow past her as they said their goodbyes and headed home after an uneventful shift. Or what she had thought was uneventful. It seemed Alex had something to say about it—she hadn't moved as the others went by and seemed to have her sights set on Rebecca.

What now? It had looked like Rebecca might actually leave work on time, but as Alex met her eyes that went out the window. She should tell her she'd clocked off already and to make an appointment for another day. But the slump to Alex's shoulders and the way she'd tucked her hands in her pockets made it seem like she wasn't getting ready for a fight this time. Maybe she wanted to apologise. It would be good to clear the air. Rebecca had been trying to avoid her since their fraught last meeting, but that wasn't a long-term solution. They needed to be able to be in the same room together. For Phoebe's sake.

Or that's what she told herself as Alex gave her a sheepish lopsided smile and moved towards her in the rapidly emptying corridor. Maybe an apology was too much to hope for, and she'd get a charm offensive instead like at the pub. Would that be such a bad thing? She'd take that charismatic Alex over the cold, defensive minder any day. Except she shouldn't be hanging out with that Alex at work. It had been hard not to be drawn in by her magnetism—not that she'd really tried to resist—and she could be in danger of letting her professionalism slide.

"Are you rushing off home, or do you have a minute?"

Alex clearly knew she was supposed to be leaving and was giving her an out.

Yet for some reason she didn't take it. "My shift's finished now, but I'm not in a rush if you needed something quickly."

"Cool."

They stood staring at each other for a moment, as if they were both waiting for the other to make their intentions clear. She must stay strong and not blurt out something just to relieve the tension. Her hands curled into claws.

"Is there somewhere we can chat? Privately." Alex's voice dipped at the added request.

Rebecca felt her cheeks start to flush. *She doesn't mean it like that.* It was best they go somewhere in case Alex said something to hint at their outside connection. She chewed her lip as she considered the options. "The upstairs kitchen might be free, as it's usually just used for breaks. We can try there." She'd also have the benefit of the option to busy herself making tea.

"Good plan. After you." Alex held out an arm, pointing towards the stairs.

Should she tell anyone she was staying on and where they were going? Maybe she should, but she hadn't signed out yet and she was intrigued to hear what Alex had to say to her that required a private space. If she said anything, someone else might offer to take over or question their intentions. It was best no one looked too hard at those, including her. She took Alex's cue and headed up.

The kitchen was, thankfully, empty. Even the most casual workers didn't head for a tea break straight after handover, though there would be a group of them hanging out on the smokers' stoop, no doubt. Alex followed her in and stood by the round table as if waiting for permission to sit.

"Tea," Rebecca offered. Now that they were in the room alone together, she definitely needed something to distract her from the full draw of Alex's presence.

"If you're having one. I don't want to keep you too long," Alex said but seemed to take it as a cue to get settled and took a seat.

"So, what was it you wanted to speak to me about?" Rebecca had to move towards her, in order to be able to hear her response over the boiling kettle, but stayed standing.

"I just…" Alex paused, seemingly unsure what she wanted to say despite being the one to initiate their meeting. "I wanted to let you know that I spoke to Phoebe, and she seems to really like the day centre. Maybe it was a good idea, at least for now while she finds her feet."

Was that her admitting she'd been wrong? It wasn't an apology exactly, but it might be the best Rebecca could hope for, and with her professional hat on she couldn't push for anything more. "I'm glad it's turned out well for her."

"Me too."

The kettle clicked off, and Rebecca took the opportunity to move away from the awkward silence that had fallen. "Milk, two sugars?"

"Well remembered." There was a hint of teasing to Alex's voice.

Should she have remembered after only making it once before?

"We're realising it may not be so bad here after all," Alex moved on, "though she still wants to move out to her own place as soon as she's ready."

Rebecca smiled to herself and tried not to overthink the *we*. "I'm glad to hear that."

Did this mean Alex would be content sticking around for the foreseeable future too? Maybe if they took the chance to get to know each other, Alex would see Rebecca wasn't so bad either and her initial defensiveness would fade away, leaving Rebecca with the version of Alex she would like to get to know.

She finished making the teas and carried them over to the table. It was true that she was in no rush to go anywhere that evening and it might be best to take advantage of Alex's unguarded state. She pulled out a chair opposite Alex and sat down to nurse her drink. "How are you finding the area? Have you had a chance to explore much?"

"Not much. That meetup was the first social group I've tried. They seem like a nice bunch. It would be good to hang out more and get to know the local community."

Rebecca couldn't help glancing at the door in case anyone was listening or about to walk in on them. It wasn't like Alex had said anything too telling anyway. She seemed to have taken on board Rebecca's request to not mention their poly lifestyles at work. That was good to know. But what she really wanted to know was if she was included in that collective compliment. "They are. I'm glad we've got something like that round here. It helps knowing you're not the only ones."

"It sure does. I'm glad I found you. It." A visible flush crept over Alex's cheeks as she stumbled over her phrasing. She didn't seem the blushing type, so it was particularly cute.

You're at work. Rebecca pulled herself back from following that thread and raised her cup to hide her smile. "Community is important."

"One hundred percent. Not being close to my family, except Bee of course, it's always been something I look for."

"Me too. Everyone needs somewhere to belong."

They smiled at each other over the small table, finally on the same page. Surely there was no harm in them getting to know each other a bit more and in her welcoming Alex into the local community. She could even pretend to herself that it was for Phoebe's sake. If Alex was happy there too, she wouldn't try to rush her sister out before she was ready. It was the right thing to do.

❖

Friday arrived, and Alex got to the cafe in time to find a good spot, a couple of armchairs tucked in a corner, to wait for Drew. The coffee shop was a cute independent place with old-fashioned china painted in a variety of floral motifs that belonged in someone's grandmother's house. Alex lifted the cup with care, afraid of breaking the delicate stem of the handle with her boorish hands. It reminded her of the feel of Rebecca's hand on hers, so delicate in comparison. She let out a sigh. She really needed to stop thinking about her. Maybe she should ask Drew to set her up with someone and redirect her daydreaming. Her interest in Rebecca must be at least partly just loneliness plus sexual frustration.

"Hey, sorry I'm late. Got caught up in some…drama." Drew waved away the end of their statement as too much trouble to get into.

"No worries." Alex stood up and clasped their outstretched hand. "Hope everything's okay."

"It's fine. Nothing to do with me, I just end up getting called in to help sort out other people's messes." They shrugged off their jacket. "So, how about you, how are you doing?"

"Okay. Still getting ourselves sorted."

"Yourselves? So, who did you drag with you to our idyllic country town?" Drew settled in the seat opposite her, their knees almost touching the table the armchairs were angled around.

Alex laughed. "No one. My sister was the one who dragged me."

"That's the sister at Becca's home, right?"

Alex flinched. She tried not to think of the place that way. "Yes, she's in that care home. As much as you can call that kinda place a *home*."

"Some people call it that." Drew paused to blow on their coffee. "If you don't mind me asking, how come it's you that traipsed along with her?"

"It was time for her to leave our parents. They still see her as a child, which she's not. She's a grown woman who wants to live her life. She needed someone who got that." It was a question she had prepared for and as much of the truth as they needed to know.

"Which is you. That explains it. I've met folk like that, think they're protecting their children from the big, bad world, but they're suffocating them." Drew wrapped both hands around their mug.

"You got it." Alex smiled, a real, relaxed smile, and felt her guard start to slip. "Not everyone does."

"Lucky she's got you. And Becca."

Alex tried to stop herself tensing right back up again. What if *Becca* was no better than their folks in that respect?

"She's been fighting that sorta thing for years." Drew leaned in. "She may seem timid, but trust me, when it comes to the people she cares for, there's a real fire in her."

"I might've seen that." Was that what it had been? Was Rebecca just standing up for Phoebe? But that was what *she* was there for. She wasn't the one Phoebe needing defending against.

"Did she tell you about her ongoing fight to get them to do sex ed? Or at least take the residents' sexuality seriously."

Alex shook her head. She wanted to change the subject, but Drew's openness was revealing some interesting new information.

"God knows how long she's been raising that. Like you said, some people treat them like kids, and they're not. They've got the same drive and right to love as the rest of us." Drew's tone was firm with conviction.

"They do." Alex liked to think even without Phoebe, she'd get that. After all, she wasn't someone who believed there was only one way to love.

"Of course, she has to be careful around those kinds of things. Can't risk looking like us queers are trying to recruit." Drew's eyes twinkled with mischief.

"You mean we're not all trying to campaign for the homosexual agenda?"

"You missed that memo too, huh? Personally, my battalion's coming along nicely."

"You should see our numbers. Willow's touring means she covers plenty of ground." It was only partially a joke, given Willow's tendency to pick up new love interests wherever she went. Alex didn't know exactly how many women she'd left pining in her wake, and she didn't need to, but she knew her style.

Drew laughed, a rough barking sound. They were clearly also pleased to find someone who shared their sense of humour.

See, making friends. You got this.

"What does she do, aside from campaigning for our cause? What's her cover story?" Drew skipped the classic mono reply about how difficult it must be for them being apart so much. It was a great advantage of poly friends and why most of Alex's were—they didn't question the basics like that you could be happy living like that. Not that everyone agreed all the time. There were plenty of clashes inside the community, not helped by the small scene that meant it was more like two degrees of separation. At best. Drew was a case in point.

"She's a stand-up. Comedy. She's built herself a decent following around the UK, though the big mainstream venues don't get her of course." Willow made out like it was her choice and she'd rejected them, not the other way round, but it wasn't hard to see how narrow-minded the hotspots were. Maybe one day poly would come in vogue, and then she'd get her shot. Not that it was all there was to her or her act, but that seemed to be how it worked if you weren't a cishet white man.

"Of course." Drew rolled their eyes. "Screw them anyway, we gotta keep some good things for ourselves. You'll have to let me know when she's performing round here, and I'll check her out. I love a bit of stand-up."

"I will. Don't think she'll be around anytime soon, though."

"That's a shame."

"Yeah." It had already been too long since Alex had been able to hold her. She liked the freedom of their connection, and neither of them had any desire to build a nest, but still. With all the stress of the last few months, it would've been nice to have her closer. "She might manage to drop in on her way past at some point, as I'm stuck here for the time being and she's not seen Phoebe in ages."

"Your sister?" Drew put their empty cup down in front of them, then leaned back as if in no hurry to head off.

"Yep. We've known each other since we were teenagers. Willow's like another sister to her." A better one. Alex closed her eyes as she took a slug of her lukewarm tea to wash down the memories that had crept up. It hadn't been her choice to neglect Phoebe in a moment of need, she'd have come running if she hadn't been laid up herself, but that didn't stop her feeling guilty.

"That's cute. Quite the modern family."

"Ha. You could say that."

"Family doesn't have to be blood—I'm a great believer in that," they said, their sincerity clear in their soft tone.

"Ditto." Alex finished her cup of tea and attempted to drain the last dregs out of the teapot. She agreed, she just didn't want to get into the whole story of how they ended up that way.

"Wanna refill or have you got to shoot?"

There was still another hour or so before she had to clock in, but she'd been planning to drop in on Phoebe first. She could go later—it'd be a shame to leave when they were getting on so well. That way she might get to see someone else too. Rebecca seemed to always work late. Since she'd cleared the air, the only feeling that arose at the thought was a tingle of excitement. There was more to Rebecca than the dedicated professional she'd first met, and she was enjoying discovering the woman behind the role.

"I'll get it. I need another caffeine fix myself. It's been a long week." Drew stood.

They seemed to have misread Alex's hesitation. To be fair, she hadn't planned to fork out for more than one drink. It wasn't quite Starbucks prices in there, but it wasn't cheap.

"I do owe you a round from the other day." Drew's voice rose gently, enticing her.

"True." She gave in and put her empty cup on the tray. "Thanks. I've not got to run yet."

They accepted her order with enthusiasm and sauntered over to the counter where they appeared to engage the barista in easy conversation.

They seemed to know everyone. Alex watched them chatting away and wondered if everyone in this town was welcoming of their open queerness.

"*Sooo*," Drew began, as they placed the tray between them, "if you're not going to be seeing Willow, will you be looking for someone else to pass your time with?"

"I may have my eyes open." Alex smiled. So she'd been right that this wasn't just about making friends.

"Good to know." A light glittered in Drew's eyes.

"But," Alex said, before they could get carried away, "not anything too committed. As I said, I'm not planning on staying here and building a nest. Not that that's something I'd want anyway. I like my Solo life."

"I was gonna ask about your flavour. You're Solo Poly?"

"Yep. Part of why me and Willow work—neither of us is looking for someone to mesh our life with." They'd figured that out early on, before they had the language to explain it or knew anyone who did relationships the same way. It wasn't that she didn't care deeply about her partners, she just never needed anyone to complete her or her life.

"That adds up." Drew paused for a moment then looked at Alex thoughtfully. "I may know a couple of women looking for secondaries. No commitment required."

"Ugh. No thanks. Been there, got the scars. No human should be secondary to another." Maybe she should've put that less harshly. But it would be hard to hide her conviction, even if she wanted to.

"I hear you, and in general life I agree. But when it's consensual and suits everyone…" Drew held up their hands, as if no harm, no foul.

But there was harm in it, and Alex had fallen foul. "Hierarchies leave too much room for misuse of power. Secondaries' feelings, their needs, are dismissed. They get hurt."

It was the brutal reality when you labelled someone as automatically less important than someone else. She glared into her fresh teacup. This one was plainer. They must've run out of the fancier stuff.

"I'm sorry that's your experience." Drew reached over, just missing the steaming fresh teapot, to squeeze Alex's knee. "It works for some of us, though."

"So you're…" Of course. Rebecca would be in favour of that kind of controlling setup. She held in a sigh. She should've guessed. It was a surprise from Drew, though—they'd seemed on the same wavelength.

"Becca's secondary and she's mine. My nesting partner's monogamous, so it's easier on her. Though I'll admit I don't take it as far as Becca—I'm still open to other partnerships and less…rule-bound." Their mouth twitched at the corners.

Alex was tempted to question them about that relationship in particular but didn't want to risk offending her new friend. It wasn't like Drew was some innocent newbie being taken advantage of, so she had no good reason to ask. Or no reason she wanted to share with Drew.

"If it works for you." She repeated Drew's hands-up gesture in resignation. "I need my freedom. I gotta know we can do, we can be, whatever we want, whatever's right for us. You know?"

"I get you. Some flexibility is good for all of us."

"Agreed." Alex was relieved they'd managed to sidestep the thorny issue and find common ground. She wasn't interested in getting with Drew in a sexual/romantic way, so what did it matter. "I just want someone I can have a genuine connection with and have fun, without worrying about labelling it."

"I'll keep an eye out for you. Leastways, I reckon you'll be a good influence on Becca." Drew eyed her with the same amused curiosity they'd displayed when seeing Alex with Rebecca at the meet. "She fights for others but isn't so good at embracing her own freedom."

Alex raised her eyebrows. In what role was Drew picturing her doing this influencing? Were they imagining Rebecca embracing her? It wasn't like she hadn't imagined it herself in off-guard moments, but… "I thought you said she wasn't open?"

"Hmm. Exactly." Drew sat back and took a slow sip of their dark coffee, looking suspiciously like they were hatching a plot. "I'm gonna need some more pointers, mind. What's your type? Just women? Men too? Those of us beyond the binary? Age? Politics? Kinky?"

Alex spluttered a mouthful of tea. "Whoa, slow down. I didn't say I was hiring you."

"Yeah, yeah. But I need to know the basics, to field enquiries." Drew had that twinkle back. At least they'd moved on from focusing on Rebecca. That could've got awkward very quickly. If they'd asked how Alex felt about her, she didn't know how she'd answer. She didn't even know herself yet.

It was clear Drew was someone with connections. They'd be a good person to have in her court as long as she could stop them getting too carried away.

❖

"Deal!" Phoebe held out an upturned pinkie.

Rebecca was momentarily taken back, back to her childhood best friend who had secured every agreement in that way. Until it had turned out she didn't take her side of their bargains as seriously as Rebecca. Especially that last promise of secrecy, which had been cast aside when someone better, cooler, had come along. She'd been sure they were in it together, especially when in private they started to seal each deal with a kiss. Rebecca's chest tightened at the memory of the betrayal and her lost innocence.

"Pinkie promise?" Phoebe stretched further towards her, her smile faltering slightly.

"I don't know." Rebecca tried to shake off the cold weight it brought back. It was unnerving to think of her. She hardly ever did, it had been so long ago.

"That's okay. I'll teach you!"

That made Rebecca smile, and she was happy to not correct Phoebe's misunderstanding of her hesitation. Phoebe seemed keen on being the teacher instead of the student for once. It would be mean to deny her. "Do I need to take notes?"

Phoebe shook her head, then laughed when she got the joke. "No, it's simple. You hold fingers, like this." She took Rebecca's proffered hand and curled their fingers around each other. "See?"

"I think I got it. And what does it mean?" Rebecca held her position, her little finger wrapped around Phoebe's, while her other fingers curled into a fist.

"It means it's a sacred promise, and you have to keep your word."

"And if I don't?" Rebecca jiggled their joined hands.

"You burn in hell," Phoebe said, in a matter-of-fact tone, although a smile tugged at the corner of her lips.

"Isn't that a little…overdramatic?"

"Alex does always say I'm a drama queen." Phoebe spun around, arms outstretched as if basking in front of an adoring audience.

"I'm not sure I'd go that far." She couldn't help smiling at Phoebe's joyful flamboyance. And the mention of her sister.

"I don't mind. I love drama."

"I am starting to get that impression." Her new charge was really starting to come out of herself, and the spark she'd spotted at the start was shining through. Rebecca hoped she wouldn't let her down. So far, she was managing to find the time to support her, though Ishani had started to grumble about how late she was getting home. But Ishani understood how important her job was. Still, she should probably do something to make it up to her. She was booked in to see Drew at the weekend, but maybe they could change it into polycule time instead? Drew wouldn't mind—they liked family time.

Phoebe grabbed a battered leather jacket from the back of the door and slipped it on. The sleeves went way past the tips of her fingers, and it was the length of some dresses on her, though not the kind Rebecca would wear. Maybe it was an old one of her father's? Rebecca still hadn't heard anything from her about the parents she'd left behind, and it could be a gentle way in.

"Cool jacket. Is it yours?"

"Yes," Phoebe said, slipping her phone in the pocket and heading out the door. "But it used to be Alex's."

She should've guessed. She didn't seem to be able to avoid bringing Alex up, even though she was trying not to focus on her. There was no denying Alex was central in Phoebe's world and wouldn't want to be distracted from her protective older sibling role.

The jacket looked more practical than pretty, though that could just be Alex's style. Rebecca had only ever seen her in simple clothing and with her hair clipped short. She didn't need fancy clothes or accessories to draw the eye. "Is she a biker?"

Phoebe stopped walking and looked down at it. "No. Not after the accident." She looked back up at Rebecca, her jaw set. "I won't let her ride any more."

The electric buzz of the doorbell made them both jump. The minibus must be there already. If Rebecca was going to join them and keep her promise to Phoebe, she needed to get moving. An image of Alex in the jacket, being knocked from her bike and tossed across the road, made a shiver slice through her. She tried to shake it. Maybe Phoebe was being dramatic again and it wasn't serious. Alex seemed to have recovered okay even if she had been injured. She took a few deep breaths, calmly blowing away the horrific vision, and marched on to her next duty.

❖

It wasn't quite as excruciating as she'd imagined, but it was getting there. At least no one had asked her to sing. There were plenty of volunteers among the service users, Phoebe included.

Unfortunately, they'd arranged for her to sing last as the big finale, which meant Rebecca had to smile her way through the best part of an hour of mostly tuneless crooning too close to the sputtering microphone. Karaoke was definitely best enjoyed with a few drinks inside you and even more if she was going to sing. Not that you would ever get her up there. She had to admire these singers' confidence in getting up to the mic, even if their performances lacked precision. She gritted her teeth and tried to keep smiling encouragingly as someone mumbled their way through a well-known track that they obviously didn't know the words to. Phoebe would hopefully do a bit better, but Rebecca was still dreading having to face her after and pretend she'd enjoyed it.

"It's nearly over, don't worry," someone whispered in her ear.

She turned to see she'd been joined at the back by a few of the day centre staff and blushed. They must have spotted her displeasure— she'd never had a good poker face.

"This one'll make up for it." They nudged her with an elbow. "Genuine talent, she is. I reckon we'll be seeing her on *BGT* one day."

Rebecca turned back to see the next person taking to the makeshift stage. Phoebe's black-and-purple hair and matching clothing were unmistakable. "I'm looking forward to hearing her," she murmured in reply.

She suddenly was, their words having started a buzz inside her. But what if they were joking, and Phoebe was actually awful, and everyone was going to laugh at her. Oh God. Maybe she shouldn't have encouraged her.

A tinkling intro she recognised wafted from the speakers. It wasn't what she'd expect, given Phoebe's image and musical tastes. Maybe she hadn't had the options she wanted and had been lumped with the stage musical number. As she stood waiting for her cue, Phoebe closed her eyes, and the whole room seemed to still with her.

Her first note was timed perfectly, her tone mellow and mature, the voice of a woman who knew too well the heartache she sang. Rebecca watched, mesmerised, drawn into the swelling notes and Phoebe's emotional performance. They were right: she had real talent and belonged on a better stage than this. Rebecca drifted into a daydream with Phoebe's voice as the soundtrack, imagining finding a place for her where she could truly shine and share her song with the world. She floated back as Phoebe launched into the final refrain.

Through tear-filled eyes, she spotted a young man crouched at the side of the room. He was staring at Phoebe with a look of pure adoration, beyond the overflowing admiration of the rest of the audience.

As everyone applauded the star performer, she leaned towards the person next to her and whispered, "Who's that? In the red T-shirt." She pointed discreetly at the man in question, though he was clearly oblivious, still gazing at Phoebe.

"Callum? He's been coming for years, though you may not have met him, he still lives with his parents. Nice lad, quiet though, tends to keep himself to himself. Why?" They divulged the information with no apparent consideration for whether it was anything they should give.

Usually that would bug Rebecca, but it was to her advantage as it meant she didn't have to reveal any good reason. "Just wondering, I didn't recognise him, that's all."

She kept an eye on them and noted Phoebe was now returning his gaze with a shy smile. There was something more guarded about the way she was looking at him, but there was still clear interest there. Rebecca would have to ask her about him. She didn't want to intrude, and at the same time, the situation would need to be monitored.

Maybe she needed to step up her campaign for sex and relationship education. The last thing she wanted was for Phoebe to end up in a compromising situation. Given her general state of cultured ignorance, God knew if she'd had access to any before. Phoebe was vulnerable, and she could only imagine the backlash from the other staff if she ended up in trouble, and Patience's disappointment in her. Not to mention the fury of a certain guardian, who she had definitely not been daydreaming about getting to know better. Not at all.

CHAPTER SEVEN

The voices stopped her. Alex stood by the door, knuckles raised, heart suddenly beating faster. She'd wanted to come by earlier, but with Phoebe out most days it made sense to see her in the evenings. The summer heat made the pool much more tempting than the stuffy care home, and she'd been going regularly before work. By the time she finished her shift, it was more bearable to hang out there, at least as far as the outside temperature was concerned. It did mean she arrived during the late shift and had to manage the rising heat between her and Rebecca.

She shook herself. She wasn't doing anything wrong. She shouldn't avoid Rebecca and she didn't want to. Maybe Rebecca wouldn't want her to either. Drew's suggestive words were still playing on her mind, though she deliberately avoided reading too much into them. Or tried to, anyway. She knocked.

"Come in!" Phoebe yelled.

Alex opened the door, slow and steady, determined to act casual. "Hey, Bee, hope I'm not inter—"

The person sitting across from her sister stole her attention. Their profile was unfamiliar. They were too broad, their hair too short, to be her. Alex blinked.

"We're nearly finished with this game."

Phoebe was focused on the cards in her hand so hadn't clocked her reaction. The stranger also held a fan of cards, and the rest of the deck was balanced on a box between them.

"No rush." Alex tried not to let any disappointment in the company show.

"Cool." Phoebe drew another playing card and swapped it with one in her hand.

"Yes! Just what I needed." The stranger grabbed the discarded card, then threw down her hand, triumphant. "Rummy!"

"Oh man, I was so close." Phoebe laid her own cards down with a sigh. Her mouth didn't stay downturned for long, though. "Let's play again."

"What about...?" Her companion gestured towards Alex, who continued to stand in the doorway, waiting for a cue from Phoebe about whether to stay.

"Alex likes cards—she can play too."

"Sure, if you like." She walked over to join them and nudged Phoebe to introduce her. The newbie didn't seem like a member of staff. "Who's this?"

"Faye. She lives here too. She's my friend." Phoebe smiled with pride at her new friend, and Faye returned her grin.

"Hi, Faye. I'm Alex, Phoebe's sister."

It was good to see Phoebe had made at least one friend. It would help her remember the staff weren't her friends. Hanging out with the other residents instead was a step in the right direction, as long as it didn't make her want to stay there too long.

"Hi, Alex, Phoebe's told me *all* about you." Faye's eyes twinkled with a touch of mischief. She looked a lot older than Phoebe, but with plenty of spirit.

"I have not."

"You better not have." Alex sat down next to Phoebe on the bed as there was nowhere else to. "We need to get you some more chairs in here."

"They like us to hang out together in the main rooms, not our bedrooms, so they don't put them in. There's more chairs downstairs. They like to keep an eye on us," Faye said.

Phoebe had made a good choice of ally. Faye seemed to know how things worked there, but to still be doing what she wanted. Maybe she could be a future flatmate—living independently didn't have to mean living alone. Alex didn't usually, mostly for financial reasons, despite being committed to Solo Poly, which was all about keeping her independence. You could have important people in your life without being unhealthily co-dependent, though she still couldn't imagine living with a partner by choice. It was too easy for your lives and selfhoods to merge until you forgot who you were by yourself. She and Willow had experimented with living together at one point, several years before, but it nearly broke them. They both needed space to flourish, as did their love.

"But then everyone can hear us and try to join in," Phoebe grumbled.

"I hear ya, I wouldn't want to be down there either. I'm sure you've got space for at least one extra seat in here."

"Ooh and we could get one of those proper fold-out card tables." Faye picked up the deck and started to shuffle haphazardly. "One of the guys has one to do his jigsaws on, but he doesn't like to share."

"Good idea. Alex can help us get one."

Alex quirked an eyebrow at this assumption, but who was she kidding—she wasn't going to deny her. "I'm sure I can find one somewhere."

"Thank you," said Faye. She turned back to Phoebe. "So, are we gonna play, or are you scared I'll thrash you again in front of your sister?"

"I'm not scared!" Phoebe stuck out her tongue, and Faye copied her, pulling a contorted face that caused Phoebe to cackle.

"Let's play then. Who's dealing?" Alex looked around the room as Faye finished her shuffle. They could definitely fit another chair, maybe even a couple of comfy ones so Phoebe could hang out with her friends as much as she liked away from the watchful eyes of the staff. It wasn't like she needed constant supervision.

"You can." Faye passed her the deck.

"Okay." She shuffled the well-worn cards between her hands too, out of habit, a memory surfacing of when they had got the garish pack. It had been on holiday, the last holiday they'd spent together as a family. She'd spent hours on the beach teaching Phoebe a new game and chasing after escapees when the sea breeze caught them, Phoebe running across the sand, clapping her hands in vain as she attempted to capture one, their parents lying back, smiles on their faces, laughing even. A long time ago.

She stopped shuffling and refocused on the grown-up version in front of her. "So, have you got anything planned for tonight, Bee? I was wondering if you fancied a trip to the cinema? There's a few films out that look decent."

The thought of sitting in the cinema alone on a Friday night was depressing. And it would be good for Phoebe to get out of the small town for an evening.

Phoebe looked at Faye, then back at Alex. "Can Faye come too?"

"I don't see why not, if she wants to." She'd taken Phoebe's friends out with them plenty of times before, though she was still a kid at the time. Who were her friends these days? Had she left any behind? Alex frowned—she should know that. She knew she missed her own, though she hadn't been seeing so much of them even before the move, having become a bit of a recluse after the accident. She'd been busy getting back on her feet and getting her life back on track, then helping Phoebe do the same.

"Can I? I've not been to the cinema in *ages*."

The excitement in Faye's eyes made Alex wonder just how long it had been since she'd been let out. Poor woman. Maybe Phoebe would be a good influence on her in return.

"Sure. We'll have a look and see what we all fancy." Alex started to deal out the cards into three piles.

"Awesome. I want to—" Phoebe was interrupted by another knock at the door. "Come in!"

"Shouldn't you check who it is first?" Alex hissed.

"It's probably just Becca. She said she'd join us if she had time," Faye informed her.

She was right. A second later Rebecca's face peeped round the door. When she saw Alex, she didn't show any reaction. Which was fine. At least she wasn't annoyed with her any more. But Alex couldn't help feeling deflated at Rebecca's complete lack of interest in her presence.

"How's it going in here? Just thought I'd check in quickly as you've already found another player."

Maybe Alex being there *had* made an impact. She'd just been prewarned so had time to glue her professional mask in place. Or was that just wishful thinking?

"There's room for more," Phoebe replied before Rebecca could escape. "We were starting a new game."

Rebecca hovered in the doorway. She chewed her lower lip and finally let her eyes meet Alex's.

"Budge up, sis." Phoebe grabbed her arm to pull her closer. Alex reluctantly broke eye contact with Rebecca and shuffled along, creating space for her on the bed.

Though she appeared to try, there was no way Rebecca could sit down without them getting close. She folded herself up as small as possible, but their elbows still touched and generated a spark that made Alex jump. They really needed to get more chairs.

"Becca?" Faye's tone was less confident than before Rebecca entered. Maybe she didn't welcome her being there. Maybe Phoebe had found someone who could give them a clearer idea of how good Rebecca really was at her job.

"Yes?"

"Alex and Phoebe are going to the cinema, and they invited me to go with them." She rushed the statement out, then looked to Alex as if for backup.

"She's welcome to tag along with Phoebe." Alex hoped Rebecca also recognised the importance of Phoebe making friends and wouldn't get in the way.

"So, can I go?" Faye wiggled in her seat opposite them, waiting for Rebecca's judgement. That did not bode well.

Had Alex let her guard down too soon and let her budding feelings for Rebecca skew her own judgement? Before she could jump in and tell Faye she didn't need to ask permission, she felt Rebecca tense against her side and draw in a long breath.

"Faye, you know I'd let you if it was safe." She paused and seemed to take in Alex's narrowed eyes. "Let's go talk about it."

As Rebecca stood up and attempted to guide her outside, Faye caught her wrist and stopped her leaving. "I won't be by myself!"

Rebecca sighed audibly.

"I haven't been in so long. No one ever has the time to take me where I want to go." Her voice rose, pleading.

Rebecca rubbed her forehead. "You're right. We'll have to book an outing, make sure you get to go out somewhere fun soon."

"It's not a problem. I can keep an eye and I'm sure there won't be any trouble. It's just a movie." Alex managed to bite back the rest of what she wanted to say, for Faye's sake. Why was Rebecca treating her like a little kid who couldn't be trusted? She was clearly older than all of them, and it wasn't like they were taking her out on the lash.

"I wish it were that easy. Really." Rebecca kept her back to Alex, giving the brief reply over her shoulder. "You know why, Faye."

"I know." Faye sank down in her chair.

"Why?" Phoebe asked.

It wasn't really their business, but Alex wanted to make sure Rebecca's stance was legit. It was a good thing Phoebe asked—it likely came across as more innocent from her, and Alex couldn't match her non-aggressive curiosity.

"In case I have a seizure," Faye explained in a sing-song voice, as if repeating a well-worn script. "There has to be someone with me."

"Me and Alex will be with you," Phoebe pointed out.

Alex put her hand over her mouth to hide her smirk. Phoebe still didn't take anything lying down—the system hadn't got her yet.

"Shall I explain to them?" Rebecca asked Faye.

Faye nodded but crossed her arms.

"Sometimes Faye has epileptic seizures, bad ones, and someone has to give her special medication and look after her." Rebecca directed this to Phoebe.

"Can I not?" Alex jumped in. What, did Rebecca think she was completely irresponsible?

Rebecca shot her a *You're not helping* glare. "You need to be trained and certified. It's not just handing her a pill. She can't take it herself in that state."

"Oh." At least that meant Rebecca wasn't restricting Faye's movements for no good reason. Alex made herself stand down—they couldn't risk the woman's health. "You're right. We can't do that, Bee."

"Sorry guys, another time. I'll make it up to you." Rebecca squeezed Faye's shoulder.

Both Faye and Phoebe had slumped, and the atmosphere had turned bleak. Maybe they should postpone the trip. It seemed cruel to leave Faye behind. She could text Bee later and arrange it for a time when her friend wouldn't be left alone disappointed.

"I know!" Phoebe sat up straighter, commanding attention. "You can come too. You can give Faye her medicine if she needs it."

Faye sat up too, looking hopeful.

Alex saw the hesitation on Rebecca's face. "It's already getting late—Rebecca will be off home soon. I'm sure she's got better things to do than keep us company."

She'd meant it in a nice way, to make it easier on Rebecca to say no, but Rebecca visibly stiffened and gave her a wounded look. *Crap.* How could she turn this around?

"It is late, but I may be able to swing it for you," Rebecca said after a few beats. She obviously hadn't been too put off by Alex's clumsy intervention.

"Really?" Faye jumped up and gave Rebecca a hug. "Thank you."

"I'll try, but no promises." Rebecca extricated herself from Faye's arms and headed for the door. She paused when she reached it, gazing at her hand curled around the handle. Then she turned back and looked directly at Alex. "If it's okay with you? I don't want to ruin your evening by gatecrashing."

A lump formed in Alex's throat. It was tempting to reply that going to see a movie with a cute woman like her was Alex's idea of a perfect Friday night, but she checked herself in time. It was just practical, and Phoebe's idea. Who would also be there. It was not a date, however much she might want it to be. "Whatever Phoebe wants."

Rebecca gave a tight smile and nod, then left without another word, leaving Alex staring at the closed door. It was hard to know what was behind that smile, but it seemed like her answer was not what Rebecca wanted to hear. Whether that was because she wanted Alex to say no or wanted some hint that she would like her to come was anyone's guess. Surely she wouldn't want Alex to give any sign of how much she really wanted her, at least not while she was at work. She had been clear about keeping her polyamory quiet there, so openly flirting with her wasn't on the cards. At least until they got out of the building.

❖

It had seemed like the right thing to do. Faye had looked so downcast when told she couldn't go, and it had been Phoebe's idea. It definitely wasn't Alex's, so no one could accuse Rebecca of agreeing for the wrong reasons. Patience hadn't required much persuading but had insisted Rebecca go home early next shift to make up for it.

And make it up to Ishani, who had seemed less impressed, though it was hard to tell from a text message. Rebecca had stared at her short reply, trying to figure out if she really was okay with it or whether it should be read with a more passive-aggressive tone. No, that wasn't Ishani's style. More likely she was just disappointed. The realisation made Rebecca's heart constrict. If only she could please everyone at the same time, but it never seemed to work out that way.

The feeling faded as she was swept up in Faye's excitement. You'd think she was going on an exotic cruise, not to the local cinema, which only amplified her needling guilt over not ensuring Faye could go on trips out more regularly. It must've confirmed Alex's apparent view that they were more jailers than carers. Not that it mattered what Alex thought. It just didn't give a good impression of the home, and her. She really did care about the residents.

Which was how she ended up staying late on a Friday night to fulfil Faye's wish.

"Are we getting the bus?" Faye paused in the midst of selecting her outfit, having insisted on getting changed before they went out.

Usually they would, but that was during the day. By this time on a Friday, it'd be full of people on a night out, drinking ill-disguised cheap spirits from their water bottles and discreetly smoking on the upper deck.

"No, it's too late. I'll drive." Rebecca's car was insured to take residents out and hopefully in a decent state.

When did she last hoover it? Maybe she should've checked before offering, but it wasn't like there were other options. She was not about to ask another member of staff to give them a lift. She could imagine how well that would go down. They'd say it was unfair on the other residents, while really meaning it would mess with their own routines and set a precedent to go above their usual duties. It was lucky she'd been able to get Patience alone to get permission for the unplanned trip without anyone else having the chance to raise objections.

"Cool, I don't want to wait for the bus. I'm ready." Faye selected a denim jacket to go with her fresh T-shirt and strode out the door still putting it on.

Phoebe was waiting for them in her room. There was no sign of Alex. Maybe she'd found an excuse to not come with them. She hadn't seemed keen on Rebecca joining the party so could well have decided to duck out and let Rebecca take them instead, which she should be happy about, if anything. She could handle Phoebe and Faye—Alex was the loose cannon. She tugged at her tight collar, wishing she'd worn something more comfortable given she was going to be spending several more hours in her work clothes.

"Good, you're ready. Let's go." Phoebe gave Faye a quick hug and threw Rebecca a beaming smile. "Thanks for coming with us so Faye can come."

"You're welcome." Rebecca fiddled with the clasp of her watch as she checked the time. They would need to leave ASAP to catch the next showings. "Where's Alex?"

"She's just getting her stuff from the van. She said she'll meet us in the car park." Phoebe led the way out of the home.

So she hadn't dropped out. The release of pressure in Rebecca's chest and its replacement with a light fluttering confirmed that she was happier with that outcome, which she shouldn't be if all she cared about was doing her job. She took some deep breaths in an attempt to disperse the butterflies and tried to refocus as she trailed Phoebe outside.

Phoebe and Faye wanted to share the back seat so they could finish their debate over the choice of film, which meant Alex was directed to sit in the passenger seat next to her.

Alex didn't argue about the arrangements. "Thanks for driving us—it would've been a real squeeze to fit us all in my van. We'd have to stick Bee in the back and hope she didn't bounce around too much."

Rebecca laughed, more out of relief than at her turn of phrase. It looked like she might get the sociable Alex for their trip. It was bizarre how she seemed a totally different person as soon as they stepped outside the home. Rebecca was different too, she knew, but it wasn't like Alex was acting professional inside—it was more like she was wearing a suit of armour that kept her rigidly on guard.

"I'm insured. It was the obvious solution." She couldn't switch modes quite so quickly even if she wanted to. She was still on duty after all.

"Obviously." Alex's tone didn't give anything away, and Rebecca couldn't look at her as she navigated her way out of the full car park. Alex waited until they were safely on the main road before continuing, "So, have you got any exciting plans for the weekend?"

Rebecca glanced in her rear-view mirror at the women in the back. They seemed focused on Phoebe's phone, which by the sounds of it was playing trailers, and oblivious to their conversation. "I'm looking forward to seeing Drew and hopefully having some family time."

"As in your chosen family? Or the flesh-and-blood type?"

"God, no," Rebecca said. Before remembering who she was speaking to and where she was. *There goes my professionalism.*

Alex snorted with laughter at her offhand response.

"We can't all be as close as you two are." As soon as she said it, she regretted it. She hadn't got to the bottom yet of why Alex had taken guardianship of her sister but knew it was unlikely to be a happy story, and Alex had said she didn't get along with the rest of her family. Why was she suddenly turning into a blabbermouth? "I mean, definitely chosen, which for me means no direct relation."

"Can't blame you. Drew's cool—it was good to get to know them a bit over coffee."

When had Alex and Drew had coffee together? Rebecca clutched the steering wheel. Why hadn't she known about it? Did this mean they were interested in each other? Was Drew—

"It was nice of them to reach out"—Alex cut through her thoughts—"knowing I don't have any friends yet around here. Though I think I might be in danger of being set up by them. They have that matchmaker vibe."

That explained it. As the meet organiser Drew often took new people under their wing. It didn't mean anything. Rebecca shoved the image of Alex and Drew together out of her mind. It elicited far too many inappropriate feelings she did not want to risk delving into. It wasn't up to her who Drew hung out with when she wasn't around.

Alex also had a point about potential matchmaking. The thought of Drew setting Alex up with someone else didn't make her feel any better.

"They do enjoy helping people get together. Just be clear if you don't want that. We wouldn't want to make you uncomfortable." Drew did sometimes get swept up in it and not necessarily wait to get everyone's permission. They always meant well—they just got a bit carried away.

"You're all right. Maybe it's what I need, someone in the know to pave the way for me."

Rebecca pulled up at some traffic lights and took the opportunity to face Alex. There was something dancing in her eyes, and she sported a lopsided smile that managed to be both cocky and shy at the same time. A horn honked, and Rebecca realised the lights had turned green. Maybe she'd been wrong in her first impression—she couldn't swim in those eyes. She could drown in them.

She focused back on the road, trying and simultaneously trying not to figure out what Alex meant by that last comment. Pave the way with who? With her? She flushed at the self-obsessed thought. Alex's interest in her at the meet was surely just that of someone glad to see a familiar face in an unfamiliar place. And since then, well, it was hard to keep up with Alex's fluctuating attitude.

It was time to steer them away to less risky subjects. "I saw Phoebe sing today. She was amazing."

"Yeah, she always has been." Alex sounded wistful. "She loves being on stage, a right drama queen."

Rebecca smiled. So that's what Alex meant when she called Phoebe that—she wasn't just making fun of her. "You can see she's at home there."

"She used to make me act in her plays when she was a kid and perform them for our family and neighbours." Alex gave a shudder, exaggerated enough for Rebecca to catch it in her peripheral version. "I wasn't sad when she joined a drama group instead. I do *not* share that gene."

"She was in a group before she came here?" Interesting. That brought up a possibility.

Alex took a moment before she replied, "I'm not sure if she still was. She wasn't getting out much any more."

Before Rebecca could ask why, Phoebe piped up from the back.

"Okay, we've decided. We want to see the romcom."

Rebecca and Alex groaned in unison.

At least we agree on something.

"You said we could choose!" Phoebe didn't sound like she was about to take notice of any protests from them.

"Yeah, yeah. But it's definitely my choice next time, and I'll be sure to pick something you don't want to see. Ow!"

From the thump that accompanied this exclamation, Rebecca guessed Phoebe had given Alex's seat a good wallop.

"Hey! Please resist beating up my car, it doesn't deserve it." Not that it was in pristine condition, but she hoped it would last her a good few years yet if she took care of it.

"Sorry, Becca." Phoebe didn't sound particularly sorry.

"Oh, but I do?" Alex mused.

"I didn't mean…" Rebecca belatedly noted the mocking tone in Alex's question.

"I know. You'd not wish anything bad on anyone."

There were worse assumptions she could make. Another warm flush ran up her neck. It could even be a compliment, or the nearest she'd get from Alex.

"I'll book the tickets." Alex turned her attention to her phone, and Rebecca felt just a little disappointed that it was no longer on her.

By the time they arrived, Alex had secured their seats so headed straight to the machine to print their tickets. Phoebe and Faye were more interested in the refreshments. Rebecca hung back, not wanting to be too obvious in her role, especially as she really was only there in case Faye had a seizure. She reminded herself of this as she gazed at the short wisps of hair on the back of Alex's exposed neck, the bright lights illuminating them. Would they be as soft as they looked if she reached out and stroked them…

"I'll get the snacks. You want anything, sis?"

Phoebe almost made her jump, startling her out of her reverie.

"In that case, I'll have a massive bag of popcorn." Alex kept her eyes on the machine as it whirred to life, printing out their tickets.

"No problem. Becca?"

"No. Nothing for me. Thanks." It would be wrong to let Phoebe pay for any extortionately priced confectionary for her. Though popcorn sounded good. Maybe Alex would let her share.

"Okay. I need my card, I forgot my wallet." Phoebe held out her hand to Alex.

"Don't you mean *my* card." Alex tilted her head slightly in Rebecca's direction.

"Um yeah, of course." Phoebe looked between the two of them, her smile suddenly tense.

"You can pay me back later." A look was exchanged between the sisters that seemed to convey another agreement.

Something was off. Could she find a way to catch a glimpse of the name on the card and see if they were telling the truth? Though it couldn't be Phoebe's, could it? She didn't have a job, and her parents hadn't bothered to support her to apply for state benefits—for herself, anyway, they may well have claimed some for themselves as her carers—which had left her entirely financially dependent on them. Rebecca cringed as she realised that during the last-minute planning, she'd forgotten to draw any money for Phoebe to pay for the trip. It looked like they would have to rely on Alex.

"I'm gonna get some pic 'n' mix. I'll meet you back here," Faye piped up behind her.

Which reminded her who she was supposed to be keeping an eye on. At least Faye kept hold of her own spending money so wouldn't miss out from her disorganisation.

"I'll come with you." She followed Faye over to the rows of plastic tubs. She wasn't going to stoop to spying on Phoebe, like a mother rummaging through her daughter's drawers for a hidden diary or cigarettes. If she needed to know anything, she would just ask her. But a feeling of unease had settled on her at the way Alex had seemed to be covering up in front of her. The sisters hadn't acted like it was just a slip of the tongue. They acted like they had something to hide.

In order to distract herself, she selected a few sweets and tried not to think about how long they might have been sitting there in the transparent cubes. She was working late after all, which warranted a treat. Not that a cinema trip could be classed as hard work, but she was on duty.

What was Ishani doing without her home to cuddle in front of their own movie with a Friday night takeaway? *She's fine.* Ishani could find someone else to keep her company if she wanted, even at that short notice. Unlike Rebecca, Ishani managed to navigate a wide social circle. Both her partners had always been a lot more sociable than she was. It was one of the advantages of their relationship style for Rebecca—she wasn't expected to do everything with them.

"Come on, Becca, it'll be starting soon."

Faye guided her towards the till, then back to the others, clearly anxious to not miss the start despite their reassurances that there'd be at least twenty minutes of previews before the film. She even relieved Alex of the tickets and presented them to the staff member at the entrance to the screens, giving them no choice but to follow her in already. Phoebe was nearly as enthusiastic and stuck close to her, leaving Alex and Rebecca to bring up the rear.

"It's good to see she's making friends," Rebecca said. She had to keep reminding herself she was still at work, which seemed to slip her mind around Alex. It was an uncomfortable collision of different worlds. She'd never been in the situation before of meeting someone attractive at work. Or anyone queer, poly, and attractive who might be interested in her too.

"Yeah, it is, glad you agree."

It was an odd thing to say because why wouldn't she see it that way? Was this the start of another disagreement about Phoebe's care? Rebecca slowed her stride, not wanting Phoebe or Faye to overhear it if it was.

"Though, you know, I wish she'd chosen someone with better taste in films." Alex turned to her with a smile, waiting for her to catch up.

When Rebecca came up next to her, Alex opened her mouth as if to add something, then seemed to think better of it and shut it. Instead, she just looked at her for a moment, another smile teasing her lips, until Rebecca looked away. Out of the corner of her eye, it looked like Alex shook herself before she walked on. Rebecca didn't know what she'd been going to say, but she had the feeling it wasn't anything to do with her sister. It seemed she might not be the only one struggling with distracting feelings.

She trailed behind, trying not to overthink that look, leaving it to Faye to select their seats. Too late, she realised that meant she was left on the end next to Alex. She should point out that she should be next to Faye. But she could easily see or get to her from a few seats away, and Faye obviously wanted to enjoy the night out with her friend, not her carer. She willed herself to relax and took her seat next to Alex.

"I hope you like sweet 'n' salted," Alex said, tilting her box of popcorn towards Rebecca. She definitely seemed in a better mood recently.

Maybe she was just having a bad day when they'd had their big argument about Phoebe. Rebecca conveniently forgot how Alex had behaved at all their earlier meetings at the home too. She settled into the plush seat. There were worse ways to spend a Friday night, especially when being paid for it. She accepted a handful of popcorn with a smile. "Yes, thanks."

"Just help yourself whenever you want." Alex smiled back, then slouched in her own seat, her knees almost touching the row in front. "Excuse my lanky legs." She spread them slightly, allowing herself more room to stretch out.

If Rebecca did the same, they would easily make contact. She forced herself to sit up straighter.

But when the film finally got going, she started to relax, shifting in her seat to more easily give Alex her ear. Her companion's sarcastic reflections on the characters' motives were more entertaining than the actual film. Their limbs pressed together as Alex leaned on the armrest between them, and Rebecca felt warmed by the close contact in the large, air-conditioned room. Alex seemed to take delight in pulling the—only loosely plotted—film apart, and nearly making Rebecca choke on her popcorn.

Halfway through, a piece of popcorn bounced off Alex's head and into her lap, as Rebecca recovered from a particularly cutting remark.

"Will you two behave," Phoebe hissed.

Thankfully the lights were down and no one would have been able to spot Rebecca's cheeks and ears turning the bright pink Rebecca feared.

"Where's the fun in that?" Alex said.

With a particularly mischievous grin, she reached over to pluck the piece from where it had landed between Rebecca's thighs. Rebecca could have sworn that Alex's fingers brushed her legs, leaving the trace of a tingle, despite the fact she could see they didn't.

A shiver ran up her legs to somewhere her blood should not be flowing during work. It was hard not to be charmed by Alex's wit and devilish smile. Did she know the effect she had? Probably. And if she didn't, Rebecca doubted she would be unhappy about it.

Perhaps Ishani was right. Perhaps she did need to make it clear she wasn't looking for another relationship. But as they sat close together in the darkened room, whispering their shared judgements of the trope-filled hetero-mono romance, it was the last thing she wanted to do.

Chapter Eight

The voicemail symbol flashed up as soon as Alex turned her phone back on. She frowned at it. Who needed to call her rather than just texting? She checked the entry for the missed call.

"Excuse me a sec," she said to Rebecca and pressed redial.

Willow's voice blasted from the handset, as loud in her ear as if she was being projected over the surround sound speakers. "*Hey babe, guess what? I've managed to swing it so with only a slight detour I can come by on Monday and stay with you for a couple of nights. I know it's last minute, but I couldn't pass up the chance, so please tell me you're free! Anyway, hope you're out having fun, just couldn't wait to tell you. Love ya!*"

Alex stared at the phone in her hand for a moment while she let it sink in. Willow was coming, and soon.

"Good news?" Rebecca's voice cut through, quiet and unsteady.

"You bet. Willow's coming to stay next week." She beamed at Rebecca, who still seemed unsure whether this was good news. "My partner of many, many years. She's on tour, and we didn't think we'd get to see each other for a while."

"That is good news." Rebecca smiled back, but the twisting of her hands undermined it.

"It is. I've not seen her in ages. For Phoebe it's been even longer." How long had it been? With the move and everything, it was hard to keep track of time.

"What about me?" Phoebe said, as she caught up with them.

"You'll be happy to hear Willow is coming to see us." Alex reached out an arm, ready for Phoebe to bounce into a hug.

Which she did, acting out the excitement Alex felt. "When's she coming? How long for? Can she come see my place?"

"Hey, slow down, I don't know much yet. I need to call her back. But Monday, she's coming Monday." Alex's own mind was buzzing with questions, but there was no point trying to plan anything until they'd spoken.

"She can come visit me, can't she, Becca?"

"Of course, if you want her to," Rebecca said. Her eyes kept darting towards Alex and never settled.

"I'm sure you'll get a chance to say hi too, if you like," Alex told her, then regretted it. That could get weird and seemed like a bigger deal than she meant it to, especially with Rebecca being so closeted at work.

"If I'm on shift, I'll try to say hello," Rebecca said, in a way that made it sound like she'd do the opposite.

Yep, it had been a mistake. There was no mistaking that cold professional tone back in Rebecca's voice, as well as her words. But why wouldn't it be? She was Phoebe's professional carer. She was with them for work, something they both seemed to have forgotten while they'd been wrapped up in the film and their physical closeness. A closeness that was long gone.

The journey back was quiet, in the front of the car anyway. Phoebe and Faye chatted away about the film and their favourite actors. They seemed to have some debate going about the casting. Phoebe's theatre background shone through as she argued, seeming to take it much more seriously than her friend. Alex didn't feel any need to join in. At moments she found herself studying Rebecca's profile as she drove, tight-lipped and hands wrapped firmly round the steering wheel. It was late, and she was probably eager to get home. Unlike Alex, she did have a home to go to and someone waiting for her.

It was a good thing Willow was nocturnal, so there was no real rush and Alex could call her after she got back. She picked up on the second ring.

"Hey you!" Willow sounded slightly breathless, and there were voices in the background.

"Hey you. Are you busy?" Alex said.

"Nope, good timing, I've just come offstage. Gonna chill back here while the others finish up, then we might head out for a drink or seven after."

"Cool. How'd it go?" Alex asked the question, pretty sure of the answer. She was practised at reading Willow's moods after a gig, even over the phone, and could feel out whether it was a good idea to ask.

"Awesome. There was a real buzz out there tonight. Though they may have been picking up on my excitement over seeing you soon."

"Smooth." Alex smiled at Willow's way of turning the conversation. She never had a problem knowing what she was feeling. "Bet you're not as excited as me, stuck out here in the sticks all by myself."

"Hang on, let me grab my tiny violin." Willow made pathetic string sounds to make up for Alex not being able to see her mime.

"Thanks for the support." Alex flopped back on the mattress, stretching out her aching limbs. By the end of the ride home, she'd been dying to get out of her seat and had quickly made her excuses and left, trying not to limp. The cinema might not have been the greatest idea—sitting still for that long could be torture, but she used to go a lot and didn't want to give it up altogether. At least she'd had Rebecca to distract her from the pain, from her legs and the crap film.

"You're welcome. So where were you earlier, all on your lonesome?"

"I took Bee to the cinema." Alex bent her legs gently towards her and rolled her hips, suppressing a groan.

"Ah, that explains your phone being off."

Had she'd imagined it was for a more exciting reason? Fat chance.

"See anything good?" There was a crash in the background, followed by a cheer.

"No." There wasn't much to say about the film itself, and she didn't want to admit she hadn't been entirely focused on it.

Willow cackled at her blunt honesty. "She talk you into something terrible or was it a promising let-down?"

"The first one. We took a friend of hers from the home too, and they picked it together." Alex started to massage her thighs and ignore the shooting pains. She could take some of her decent painkillers, but she didn't know when she'd be able to get another prescription so needed to make them last as long as possible. She didn't fancy having to go over her medical history with a new doctor and try to persuade them she wasn't an addict. At least she didn't need to worry about the sedative effects—it wasn't like she needed to be up to doing anything at night.

"We?"

"One of the staff had to come because of her friend's epilepsy."

"Mm-hmm. And this staff member wouldn't happen to be a cute poly lesbian whose name begins with R?" Willow called it, without skipping a beat.

"Maybe." Alex drew out the two syllables. She couldn't really object to Willow's ribbing as it did sound suspicious, but it really was just about Faye.

"I knew it." Willow sounded delighted, as if it was a deliberate ploy of theirs to get to spend a Friday night together.

"How? There's plenty of others who work there." Alex bristled slightly though couldn't get seriously angry. It was Willow—she had a pass nearly as complete as Phoebe's.

"Because you wouldn't have let anyone else. Are you telling me you would've been happy for just any carer to tag along while you took Bee out?"

She had a point.

"Okay, you win." Alex hadn't consciously thought of it that way, but she never would have agreed to the compromise if it wasn't Rebecca. "She was only there as a carer, though."

"I'm sure you both kept it completely professional." There was a definite teasing tone to Willow's voice.

"Totally." Alex recalled how she'd spent the film leaning in to Rebecca, distracting them both with her commentary and determined Rebecca should enjoy herself. Which she did seem to, despite the awful film. If she hadn't responded, Alex would have left her alone. But she had, repeatedly, with the cutest stifled laugh and bitten lip.

"Uh-huh." Willow paused and Alex could only hear the strains of a shared joke in the background. "Just be careful, okay."

"I always am. Fully tested and packing." Alex teased her back.

"I don't mean it like that, and you know it." Some of the lightness left Willow's voice.

"So you're not bothered about safer sex any more?" Alex deliberately continued the joke in a desperate attempt to steer Willow away from bringing up anything deeper. She wished she'd never mentioned Rebecca before. There had been so little to say about her life, and she thought Willow would like to know that Phoebe's carer was one of them. She hadn't counted on Willow picking up on her mixed feelings.

"I trust you to do that without my checking up on you. That's not how you usually get hurt."

Alex sighed. Looked like they were going to go there. "I know."

"You said this woman isn't open, right? And not just closed but in a full-on hierarchy, right?"

"Right." Why had Alex told her that? She'd wanted someone to agree with her after Drew had waved off her views, but Willow maybe wasn't the right choice. Especially as she had an excellent memory.

"Which means she's clearly not a path to happiness for you." Her voice took on a more compassionate tone, a reminder not an order.

"I know, I know. Don't worry, I'm not getting invested—I just have no choice but to have some friendly contact with her as she's Bee's key worker." Alex tried to shrug it off.

"I get that. You've gotta stay on good terms for Bee's sake."

"Exactly." It would make Phoebe's life easier if they could work together. And if everyone got that.

"Just be careful. You're not as tough as you think you are, remember."

Alex rolled her eyes. "I can look after myself. It's all under control."

"Mm-hmm. Sure it is." Willow paused and let her disbelief sink in. "So, tell me what you plan to do with me when I come visit next week." Alex heard a couple of wolf whistles and an *oi, oi* from Willow's backstage audience.

She gladly shifted onto the happier, less complicated subject. "To start with, I better book us a nice hotel room. I'm assuming you don't want to spend it in the back of my van." It had occurred to her seconds after getting Willow's message that she would need to find somewhere with an actual bed for them to sleep together.

"If I'm with you, my love, you know it doesn't matter where we are."

Alex grinned at the line and called her bluff. "So no to the hotel room?"

"Well, if you're offering…"

"I'll get right on it." She'd need to check in beforehand to make use of the en suite before Willow got there. The thought of a clean hotel bathroom was almost as thrilling as seeing Willow.

After they hung up, she started browsing possible places for them to stay. But something was niggling her from what Willow had said. She'd been right that Rebecca was the only staff she'd have let come with them, but the option of someone else hadn't even come up, despite Rebecca being near the end of her shift. Surely it would've made sense, if it was only about caring for Faye, for someone from the next shift to go instead so Rebecca could be home on time. Why had no one thought of that? Why hadn't Rebecca? She was clearly dedicated to her job, but even for her it was suspicious. Maybe she'd wanted to spend her Friday night snuggled up with Alex, as much as Alex had wanted to spend it with her.

❖

All was in darkness when Rebecca got home. She slipped off her shoes by the glow of the outside security light and padded through to the kitchen for a drink. The salted popcorn had left her mouth dry.

Rather than turn on the harsh strip lighting, she opened the blinds so the kitchen was illuminated by the streetlights. She stood at the sink, staring out into the night, taking large gulps of cold water. The evening had left her fazed and she felt like she was floating, cast adrift and not knowing where the current was taking her. She couldn't pretend she hadn't enjoyed her time with Alex, but that didn't mean it had to lead to anything. She didn't have to let it lead to anything. It could just be one nice not-date. The circumstances were unlikely to reoccur. Now that Phoebe and Alex knew Faye couldn't just tag along with them without support, they'd hopefully make plans ahead of time. Or just not invite Faye on unplanned nights out.

She gazed out, past the streetlights into the darkness beyond. She'd have to put something in place to ensure Faye didn't miss out, but so she wasn't expected to drop everything and go wherever they wanted. That night had been doable only as a one-off—it couldn't become a pattern. It would be better to block out some time to take Faye out to places of her choosing, and Phoebe could come too if they wanted. The two women seemed to have bonded quickly and to be good for each other. Rebecca couldn't remember the last time Faye had asked to go anywhere. That's why she couldn't say no.

It hadn't been about Alex. In fact, she hadn't even thought Alex had wanted her there at first. Rebecca had seen her face when Phoebe suggested Rebecca join them, and she had not looked impressed. She'd even made excuses for why Rebecca shouldn't come, which for some reason had made Rebecca more sure she should. It shouldn't be about what Alex wanted. Or what she wanted. Though once they'd got there, it seemed very much like Alex wanted her.

What did she want? She finished her glass and refilled it before wandering through the lounge and down the corridor to the bedroom. There was no sound coming from anywhere, not even a gentle buzz— everything had been turned off and shut down. There were no lamps outside the small window at the end of the corridor, so she had to turn on the light. She stopped for a moment while her eyes adjusted to the brightness, like a rabbit in the headlights, except they didn't blink and she couldn't stop. She rubbed her eyes with the back of her empty hand. She needed to get some sleep. It had been a long, weird day.

She pushed open the bedroom door as quietly as possible. Ishani was sound asleep, her dark hair fanned out across the pillow. Or pretending to be. No, she wouldn't do that, even if she was cross. It wasn't unusual for her to be out by ten p.m. after an early start, and it was almost eleven.

She stood and gazed at Ishani in the beam that followed her through the open doorway. She was so fortunate to have such a lovely, gorgeous, nurturing partner. She never wanted to do anything to risk losing her and what they had. Rebecca had never been someone who wanted total independence—she liked the give and take of their relationship, having someone to come home to who she knew would always be there when she needed her. And she liked being that someone for Ishani. Neither of them were close to their families of origin, they had never entirely fit, so creating their own chosen family had meant creating a home where they could finally be just that—at home.

They'd bought the bungalow twelve years ago. She had been unsure about making that level of commitment, but her rental wasn't accessible for Ishani and Ishani's wasn't in great condition. They didn't have somewhere they could enjoy being together for long, except when they went on holiday and it had been hard to say goodbye after. Every time, it got harder. Ishani was already looking at purchasing a place and together they could get somewhere nicer, and sooner. Neither of them had lived with a partner before, so it was a big step and had taken some adjustment, but it had been the right move.

That was back when it had just been the two of them. When Ishani had first suggested they try polyamory, it hadn't been a big surprise, as Ishani had always been open about her history of consensual non-monogamy and been honest about not seeing herself wanting to stay monogamous long-term. It was still terrifying. When they'd first got together, it had just been an abstract concept and she hadn't known that their relationship would last long enough for it to matter. Ishani having sex with other people was one thing, but falling in love? Rebecca had no idea what it would mean for them and where they'd end up. It had taken a lot of consideration, a lot of research, a lot of learning from painful mistakes, for them to get to this point. She leaned on the door and watched Ishani doze on, her face relaxed and peaceful. It had all been worth it.

When they'd first discussed poly, they'd imagined having very separate relationships and not much to do with each other's partners. The important thing was that they didn't let anyone get between them and weaken their bond. Rebecca had agreed, on the condition she could say *stop* if things were going in a direction she didn't like. And she'd been tempted to once or twice, but even when it was tough, she'd seen the advantages. She liked that they could live together and not live in each other's pockets. And it gave her the chance to experiment in a way that felt safe, with Ishani there to come home to. She'd been young when they met and didn't have much experience with relationships. She knew she didn't believe in The One, but she wasn't sure what she did believe in.

Then she fell for Drew, and there was no turning back.

It had been Drew who suggested KTP—Kitchen Table Poly. Rebecca was struggling to balance two romantic relationships, with only so much time and social energy to spare. She wanted to be with them both, and though they'd both respected that, it was hard to find space for everyone and everything in her life. When Drew had pointed out that they could all hang together sometimes, rather than always having to split their time between different partners, it had been the obvious solution. Ishani and Drew already knew each other from the local poly meets and had always got on well. Why shouldn't they enjoy hanging together by design and talk together about things that affected them all, rather than relying on several parallel conversations? The change in dynamic had taken pressure off and had lessened Rebecca's insecurities around Ishani's other relationships, as she got to know her metamours and saw they meant her no harm. It turned out there was no competition for her to lose.

So here they were. They were happy, they were fulfilled, they had grown their family in their own way and lived by their own rules. And though she hadn't known it beforehand, it turned out to be just what Rebecca had always wanted.

She got ready for bed quickly and curled around her lover, gentle enough not to wake her but so that Ishani snuggled in subconsciously, taking her place, held against Rebecca's heart. She had closed the door on further relationships for a reason—having come that far, having gained that much, why would she do anything to risk shaking things up? But as she drifted off to sleep, she had a vision of Alex beside them, a part of their family, slipping into a space she hadn't realised still existed.

❖

When Rebecca woke, she was alone. The familiar unease struck momentarily before she intervened and reasoned this was how it normally was. She padded out to the living room to find Ishani curled up with a book.

"Morning, darling." Rebecca leaned over and kissed her forehead.

"Morning." Ishani tilted her head back so Rebecca could plant another kiss on her lips.

"Not working, I hope?" Rebecca indicated the book.

"Nope. Pure trash, I promise." Ishani flipped it over to reveal a bright cover featuring two brooding female models.

Rebecca laughed. "Excellent. Mind if I join you after I freshen up?"

"I think I can cope with the distraction. And I could do with another coffee." Ishani held out her drained mug.

"I'm sure I'll pass by the kettle." Rebecca took it and a final kiss, then headed through the kitchen to put the kettle on before she dived into the shower.

Twenty minutes later, she settled herself on the sofa and lifted Ishani's legs into her lap, turning her to face her. She chewed her lip, wondering whether to say anything or just let it go. She didn't want to ruin their chilled Saturday morning vibe.

"I'm sorry," she blurted out before she could talk herself out of it. She owed Ishani that, at least. "It was a last-minute thing and the residents were counting on me."

Ishani let her book fall into her lap. "I understand, honey. I know your work's important to you—just remember there's more to life." She squeezed Rebecca's hand, then left their hands entwined, stroking Rebecca's palm with her fingertips.

The light touch sent a pleasant shiver down her arm, their connection immediately reignited. "I've been neglecting you for it, haven't I?" Rebecca mumbled her confession into her chest, not meeting Ishani's eyes, not wanting to see the disappointment in them.

"I've got my own life to lead—I can cope. I just miss you when we don't get our evenings together."

"I miss you too." It wasn't the first time Rebecca had got wrapped up in work and let it take over. She needed to redraw her boundaries, again. "Next week, I'll manage it better. I get to leave early one day to make up for last night, so maybe we can do something together."

"That sounds perfect." Ishani leaned forward to kiss her, and Rebecca met her halfway. Their lips brushed tenderly. Ishani broke off first, shifting back and leaving Rebecca with parted lips. "Was there anything else you wanted to talk about?"

"No." Nothing she wanted to, but was there anything she should? She was drawn back to the night before and Alex's whispers in the dark. No, it was just some mild flirting to get them through the terrible movie. Nothing to report, nothing to worry about. "Was there anything you needed to?"

"Nothing that I'm aware of," Ishani said, head tilted and studying Rebecca as if wondering whether there was something she wasn't.

"Good. I don't think my brain's up to much. It's been a long week." She willed her not to push. Ishani was quick to pick up on any change in her mood, which wasn't always a good thing. Not everything benefited from being discussed.

"It has." Ishani opened her arms, shifting her book to the side so Rebecca could climb into them.

Rebecca rested her head on Ishani's chest and breathed deeply. She was home, time to rest and to reconnect. "I was thinking maybe we could have some family time tomorrow. I'm booked to see Drew, but as I've not really seen you all week…"

"That sounds lovely." Ishani dropped a kiss onto her forehead. "What were you thinking?"

"I don't know yet—I need to talk to Drew." She did, and not just about that. Bringing them up brought a certain someone else to mind again.

When and why had Drew been hanging out with Alex? Could they have something to do with Alex's change in behaviour towards Rebecca, or could it really just be a matter of getting her away from the home? She trusted Drew, but she also knew their penchant for *helping* in others' relationships. They never meant any harm, but she worried sometimes they might still do some when wrapped up in a mission.

She returned to her first notion: maybe they were interested in Alex for themself? That was the alternative explanation for Alex being extra nice to her. What if Alex wanted Drew, not her? Again, a tangle of emotions surfaced at the idea, Alex and Drew. She didn't need to get her head around it yet as it was just in her imagination, but maybe she was on to something. She needed to talk to Drew. Not yet, though, the weekend was for resting and enjoying being together. Any serious discussions would have to wait until she had the spoons to manage them.

CHAPTER NINE

She'd had to dip into her savings, but it was worth it. Alex let out a groan of pleasure as she stretched out on the crisp bedsheets, naked and still wet from the shower. After so many nights cramped in the back of the van, the large hotel bed was paradise.

Her phone buzzed on the nightstand, and she reached over to read the message. It was Willow, with a screenshot of her train ticket, confirming she would be with her early the next day—early by Willow's standards, which meant early afternoon. As well as booking the hotel room, Alex had managed to swap shifts, so she could be there to greet her and make the most of the next couple of days. It meant working the weekend, but it wasn't like she had any other plans.

Somehow, an hour had passed since she'd checked into the hotel. Had she really spent that long in the shower? At least she wasn't paying the water bill. It had been blissful standing under the steady stream of hot water, with total privacy and without the need to ram a button every minute to release another trickle, as she'd got used to doing at the pool. The mirror was fogged up, and a waft of steam had followed her out of the bathroom when she'd finally stepped out.

She couldn't spend all day bathing and lying around. Alex forced herself to sit up. Except the truth was, she could. There was nowhere she needed to be. It was a not entirely comfortable feeling for her. She would've liked to have some plans. She pulled the towel up around her, then let it drop and grabbed her phone again. Willow would surely enjoy a preview of the hotel room and all it had to offer.

Lying back down, she held it close, fitting her outstretched naked body into the shot as well as the view from the bed. She attached it to a short message:

All ready for you x

It was tempting to send more, but she'd have Willow there for real soon enough that she didn't need to imagine it. So much of their sex life was virtual, something neither of them had any hang-ups about, but having Willow there in the flesh was always worth waiting for. And Alex wanted to make sure Willow was anticipating their reunion with the same craving.

Yeah you are. Stay right there gorgeous, can't wait to get my hands on you x

Alex groaned again, this time a mix of desire and frustration. Okay, so she couldn't wait that long.

Good, cos I need you baby, I need you right now x

She let her hands run down her body, her left pausing to stroke her nipple while her right ventured further down.

I wish I could be there right now gorgeous. But I'm out and I'm not alone. Soon, so soon xxx

Alex sighed. So Willow wouldn't be joining in, even online. She continued teasing her nipple as she tapped a final reply.

You'll just have to make it up to me then xxx

She threw the phone to the far corner of the bed, in case of temptation. Even she had some lines, and the idea of one of Willow's workmates getting a look at her was a definite turn-off. Most of them were straight cis men, or at least that's what they loudly claimed. Willow had her suspicions that wasn't one hundred percent true, and there had been the odd drunken confession to her to back them up. But Alex still did not want them getting the full picture of their relationship. She tried to stay out of Willow's material, let alone her fellow comics'.

That didn't mean she couldn't enjoy herself alone. She felt truly clean for the first time in weeks and was in no rush to put her sweaty clothes back on. That was something she still needed to sort, unless she was planning on staying naked the whole time Willow was there. It was an option—Willow wasn't likely to complain.

Either way, the laundromat could wait. She let her hand drift back over her belly, running it firmly over the soft skin. Her legs parted automatically as she reached between them. She teased herself, trailing her fingers over her lips as she squeezed her nipple harder. No rush.

When she finally parted her lips, her fingers were met with slick juices, so different to the water cooling on her skin. She gasped as she slid up to her clit, allowing herself a firm jolt of pleasure.

An image filled her mind, dark hair spread on the pillow next to her, pale fingers reaching down.

"Can I help?"

The voice was familiar, but huskier in tone and more sure than she'd ever heard it.

The unexpected guest made her tense and open her eyes. What was Rebecca doing there, she shouldn't...But it was okay, it wasn't real. Maybe Willow was right about her, but she couldn't hurt Alex there. Fantasies were the place where she could enjoy things that would never happen in real life, that she might not even want to happen. It was safe. Here she could let her in. She closed her eyes again.

Rebecca's hand joined hers over her breast as she waited for Alex's permission. Alex nodded, whispered, "Yes." Rebecca leaned over and captured her nipple between her lips, sucking gently, rolling it with her tongue. Alex moaned, letting herself relax and give herself over to the woman who would never dare touch her in real life.

The hand between her thighs became Rebecca's, stroking her with urgency. She wanted to slow down, to not let it end too quickly. She imagined laying her hand over hers, taming her fast rhythm, begging her to make it last. Rebecca raised her head from Alex's breast and kissed her on the mouth, hard. She broke off and left Alex gasping, desperate, knowing she couldn't hold off much longer. Rebecca smiled, her delicious dimples framing her curved lips. She licked them, staring Alex straight in the eyes. Then she dived down between Alex's thighs before she could protest, not that she would, not that she could. She wrapped her hands in Rebecca's hair, keeping her clasped tightly to her, rocking as she sucked her, as she slipped her fingers inside her.

Alex held her there as her breathing grew faster and she neared her climax. Rebecca pressed her down with her other hand, trying to keep some control as Alex thrashed beneath her.

She cried out as she came, not bothering to restrain herself in the private, anonymous room. Opening her eyes, Alex took in her own hand on her stomach, her other resting between her legs cupping her swollen flesh, and the towel twisted beneath her.

"Damn." She grabbed a pillow and pulled it to her, wishing it was the body of the woman who had seemed so close a moment before. Maybe it was a good thing she'd got that out of her system and could move on from the doomed fantasy.

Why did she have to reassure herself of that? And why did her chest feel quite so heavy when she did? Rebecca wasn't even a friend. Willow was right—there was no future with someone like her. It was just a fantasy, born of too much pent-up desire.

But as she closed her eyes again and let herself drift off into a gentle post-orgasm snooze, it was still Rebecca she pictured in her arms, her body warmed against her own, finally relaxed in her arms. In her dreams.

❖

The hotel was in the centre of Ampchester, the larger town where Alex had attended the poly meet. They would still be close enough to drop in on Phoebe but would have more options of places to go if they wanted to head out. Not that Alex had any big plans on that front, except for finding places to eat. She'd got a room with a small fridge so they could keep some supplies and wouldn't have to head out every time they got hungry. Before heading to the shop, she'd carefully removed the overpriced minibar contents and stashed them out of sight so they wouldn't get tempted. She'd have to remember to put them back before she checked out to avoid any ridiculous charges. Why would she pay that much for a chocolate bar when she could get a pack for less by walking five minutes down the road?

After locating the laundry room and sticking a wash on, she set out to stock up on snacks and drinks. Willow would get there way before dinner time and would probably want to crash for a bit in the room. Alex wanted to have it all ready for her and not have to waste time trawling round a supermarket together.

The street was humming with shoppers and bored-looking teenagers killing time on a quiet Sunday. She was in no rush, so she took it steady and peered into each of the restaurants as she passed, studying the menus to find somewhere Willow might like. Alex wasn't adventurous in that department, but Willow liked to root out hidden gems on her travels. As she carried on down the street, the bright flash of a comic shop caught her eye. She was about to walk on past, it wasn't like she had the spare cash to buy anything, when she spotted a vaguely familiar poster in the window. It showed an androgynous figure in the centre of a gang of misfits, in front of a floating city, reminding her of a favourite old TV show she hadn't come across in years. On closer inspection, she saw it was exactly that.

There was no harm in having a look. She pushed open the door and it clanged above her head. Crap. She'd been hoping to quickly check it out then leave, but now she would have the attention of the owner. There was something about comic shop owners which meant they tended to make genuine attempts to strike up a conversation with anyone who wandered in and could spot a new face as soon as you set foot in their door. Hopefully there was some kind of Sunday crowd to get lost in. Or at least someone who actually wanted to chat to them. She did a quick scan of the store: there were a few student types in a corner, having a heated debate about a new series, and an older dude with them who, at a guess, worked there. Maybe she was safe.

There was only one other person standing at the other side of the shop, long brown hair tied back in a loose ponytail. She had turned to the door and was staring right at Alex, with as much intensity but less pleasure than she had been earlier in her dreams. If it wasn't for that and the way she was chewing on her lip, Alex would've thought she was hallucinating.

Was it too late to pretend she hadn't been planning to come in? Probably, given she had already taken a few paces inside before spotting Rebecca and stopping still. She desperately tried to wipe thoughts of her earlier fantasy from her brain and hoped it didn't show on her face.

"Hi." Rebecca spoke first.

"Hey." Alex shoved her hands in her pockets and tried to look casual. "Fancy seeing you here."

"I usually pop in when we're in town—there's nowhere that really sells graphic novels in ours."

"Fair dos." She tried to think of something else to say but was distracted by a flash of memory of Rebecca's lips on her body, except it wasn't memory because *it didn't actually happen*. She squeezed her eyes shut and reopened them to reality.

Rebecca was still standing there. "Um, what about you? What brings you here? Is this where you live?"

"No, just dropping by." No need to explain the hotel or why she'd booked it. They stared at each other, the silence thrumming. She broke first. "I saw a poster in the window that I wanted to check out, an old TV series I used to like."

"You mean this one?" Rebecca gave a shy smile and held up a thick volume with the image from the poster on the front.

Now Alex had no choice but to close the distance between them. "Yep, that's the one."

She took the tall paperback from Rebecca's outstretched hand and let her fingers graze the tips of Rebecca's, not being able to resist the chance to make contact. Rebecca seemed to hold on to the book a moment longer than necessary, holding them together. After the cinema she'd seemed keen to get away, but she wasn't trying to escape Alex's company this time.

This could be Alex's chance to extend the connection that had started to build between them. She scanned the back of the book. *Azura*, that was it.

"Have you read it before?" Rebecca stayed close, watching Alex as she studied the book.

"Nope, just seen it on TV. Not in years but I remember loving it. It was the first thing I watched with a lead I could relate to, you know?" Alex ran her fingers over the volume, bringing back warm memories.

"I know, I was the same."

When Alex looked back up, Rebecca was still smiling, and it had reached her eyes. Maybe they had more in common than she would've guessed. She couldn't resist probing deeper. "I remember there being queer vibes all over it, but not just that. She was a proper independent badass who played the game but never let anyone talk down to her. I hate it when the supposedly strong female leads go all pouty and flirt their way out of trouble."

"Yes, I can't stand all that simpering and the unnecessary romances with sullen guys."

"Hell, yeah." Alex grinned back, holding Rebecca's gaze until she looked down.

There seemed to be something suddenly fascinating to her on the floor by Alex's feet. "By the way, I don't think…I mean it doesn't say for sure, but I don't think they are a woman." Rebecca spoke fast. "I didn't register at the time, but I watched it back the other day, and they're always referred to as *them*, not *her*. They don't say they're non-binary, but I don't think we had that word yet or not that most of us knew, so maybe they were."

"Huh, I didn't click." Alex looked back at the book in her hands. Rebecca was right—there was no mention of Max being a woman. She'd always read them as a butch-ish lesbian, but maybe not. "Cool."

"I thought so." Rebecca let out a breath, as if she'd been braced for a bad reaction. "I'll be interested to see how they're written in the books, if it's the same. When I looked it up, there were some complaints about the lack of focus on their queerness and love life, but I like that. It's not the point of the story from what I remember. They love all the crew, whether they're sleeping with them or involved romantically or not."

There was a spark in her eyes, and it seemed like she could happily talk about the series for hours. Alex hadn't had her down as a sci-fi geek, but who knew what she got up to outside of work. Maybe she spent her weekends cosplaying, dressed up in a flashy rubber…Best she didn't let that thought go any further. She cleared her throat.

"Totally. Though I reckon it had some poly vibes as well as queer ones—a lot of them seemed closer than was shown on TV. Or maybe that was just my fantasy." Another flash from earlier struck Alex. Why did she have to mention fantasies?

Rebecca laughed, but lightly, seeming unsure of Alex's strained expression. "I didn't spot it at the time, but maybe I will now."

"Happy to help, you'll have to let me know what you think." Alex handed the book back to Rebecca and started to back up before she said anything else accidentally suggestive, making sure their hands didn't meet this time and send sparks flying.

"I will. Did you not want a copy?"

"Nah, I'm okay for now, I was just checking it out." She turned to walk away, intending to say a quick goodbye over her shoulder, but something else popped out instead. "Maybe you can lend me yours after you've finished, and then we can see what we both think."

"Maybe." Rebecca hugged the volume to her chest.

Alex tried not to look. "Anyway, I gotta go." She really should go, before she ended up saying anything she'd kick herself for later. But she didn't want to make it seem she was running out because of Rebecca. "It was good to see you."

"It was nice to see you too."

They stood there, neither of them seeming keen to part.

"Are you a hugger?" Alex held out her arms, ready to shrug it off if Rebecca said no, taking her chance while they were somewhere that it was possible to lean in.

She had meant a quick goodbye hug, but when Rebecca moved forward and wrapped herself in Alex's arms, it was hard to let go. Rebecca nestled her head into the crook of Alex's neck like she would happily stay there for as long as Alex wanted. And she wanted.

But she had other plans for the day, and there was only so long they could hold that position in the middle of a shop before they started attracting attention. She reluctantly gave Rebecca a final squeeze and backed out of her embrace. "See ya."

"Bye."

Alex headed out, not pausing to look at anything else. Damn, Rebecca was distracting, with those bloody dimples and deep brown eyes that seemed to be constantly brimming with all kinds of feelings. And what had she meant by that *maybe*?

❖

Rebecca checked her messages again. She couldn't wait to tell Phoebe, despite some niggling doubts about whether she'd be too disappointed if it didn't work out. It was a risk, but it was up to Phoebe whether to take it. She'd clearly been shielded more than enough.

Before she could find a moment to go see Phoebe, Luisa caught up with her.

"I heard you had an interesting night on Friday."

It was the first time they'd seen each other since. Rebecca had hoped it might have slipped Luisa's attention and she could avoid any questions. Fat chance.

"I'm not sure I'd say that." She ignored the wave of guilt that rose up at the white lie. "The film wasn't my cup of tea and it was a long day, but Phoebe and Faye seemed to enjoy it."

"And what about the sister? I bet she wasn't happy to go out with you."

It was a punch to her chest that made Rebecca hold her breath. *It's okay, she didn't mean it that way.* A quieter internal voice whispered *And she's wrong.*

Luisa looked horrified as it seemed to dawn on her how Rebecca had taken it. "Not that any woman would not like to go out with you, if she has good taste." She put a reassuring arm around Rebecca's shoulders.

Rebecca attempted a smile. "Thanks."

"I mean, she would not be happy to have *staff* go out with them."

"I know that's what you meant." She did know, really. There was just a gap between knowing and feeling, where her anxiety took the opportunity to seize control of her frazzled brain. "Actually, she was fine while we were out. She didn't seem to mind."

It was a deliberate understatement. Alex hadn't just not minded, she'd seemed glad of her company. But Luisa did not need to know that. She didn't want Luisa reading anything into it. Or to let herself get carried away. She'd brought it back and said a professional goodbye at the end of the night, prompted by the change of focus to Alex's partner's visit, but when they'd bumped into each other in town, their goodbye had been something else. She could use the excuse of the bad film for their behaviour in the cinema, but there was no excuse for how right it had felt to be nestled in Alex's arms. That one hug had passed through friendship to another level of intimacy, and she hadn't wanted it to end.

"Good. She should understand we are doing our jobs and that you are doing extra to help her sister."

Rebecca wasn't sure Alex did understand that still, but it was a less complicated explanation for Alex's behaviour. "Yes, hopefully she's realising that and will come to trust us."

"And stop checking up so much, now that Phoebe is settling in." Luisa removed her arm and clapped her hands, as if this was good news.

It was the logical conclusion, and Rebecca remembered Alex's own words: *I'm only sticking around while Phoebe gets settled.* Which meant she might be on her way soon. She tried to reason her way out of the deflating feeling that realisation brought. It would be for the best, for everyone. Goodbye, complications.

"She definitely seems happier here now. I need to go see her, actually, to tell her something. See you later." Rebecca rushed out of the office before Luisa could say any more.

She paused round the corner, with no one in sight, and took a few long breaths, willing the tension in her chest to go away. It was for the best. Phoebe didn't need Alex hanging around all the time—she needed to build her own life. Rebecca was helping her do that and should not allow herself to be sidetracked from her mission. An image of Alex's fluffy hair and unusually shy smile, from when they'd met at the weekend, blossomed in her mind. She'd longed to reach over and run her hand through the disordered strands. *No.*

Bringing herself back to the task at hand, she headed upstairs to Phoebe's room. There was no sound coming through the door, which was unusual. Maybe she wasn't home after all. Rebecca gave the door a gentle knock. No answer.

"She's probably got her headphones on. I told her, her music's too loud and I can't hear my TV."

"Thanks, Faye." It was a conversation she'd been meaning to have with Phoebe herself, once she was sure Phoebe wouldn't take it the wrong way. She wiped away a trickle of guilt. It was probably better coming from her housemate.

"Haven't you got a key?" Faye had stopped half out of her own door and stood watching Rebecca as she tried to figure out what to do.

The audience did not help. Rebecca twisted her keys in her hands. "Yes, but I wouldn't want to barge in on her."

"She won't mind. It's not like she's got a man in there." Faye grinned, then ducked back into her room.

Why would she say that? Was there a man in Phoebe's life that she'd like to have over? No, it was just a joke. Though there had been that man who'd been staring at Phoebe as she sang. They should have a talk at some point, just in case.

She gave the door another knock, louder this time, despite knowing that if Phoebe was blasting music through her high-tech headphones, there was no way she'd hear, no matter how hard Rebecca knocked. She could come back later. This wasn't just a random visit, though— she had something important to say. Before she could get herself too tied up in knots, she put her key in the door and slowly pushed it open.

Faye was right. Phoebe was sitting on her bed, plugged in and oblivious to the world. Rebecca wished she could switch off so easily. She disliked wearing headphones. There was a primal part of her brain that worried someone or something would be able to sneak up on her unnoticed. A doctor had once explained her clinical anxiety as her amygdala, the part of her brain that processed threats, being permanently switched on instead of just activated when there was something concrete to fear. It made sense, but her brain had a point about there always being some threat. Evidenced by Phoebe, who didn't even know someone was there. If Rebecca didn't move into her eyeline, how long would it take her to notice?

At least she kept her door locked. Rebecca shook off the morbid line of thought and stepped forward. When she reached the foot of the bed, Phoebe looked up. A bright smile welcomed her, and she removed the headphones immediately. They were definitely making progress.

"Hey, Becca."

She noted the shortened version of her name, another sign Phoebe was warming to her. Or had just copied it from Faye. "Hi, Phoebe, how are you today?"

"I'm good, just chilling. Guess who's coming over later?" Phoebe leaned forward, bracing herself on the mattress with her fists.

It must be someone different from usual. Rebecca recalled something discussed in handover, another potentially sensitive topic she needed to raise. "Is it your parents?"

"No." Phoebe's face fell, her full eyebrows knitting together. "Not today. They might come soon. I don't know."

"Okay." Rebecca winced, having misjudged it entirely. "You know it's up to you when and if they come. They can't come in without you saying it's okay." She bit back the string of questions that entered her mind. Phoebe did not look like she was up for being quizzed about her relationship with her parents, and she didn't want to completely wreck her good mood.

"I know." Phoebe's expression didn't match her words. She looked torn.

"So, who is it? Who is coming?" Rebecca perched on the edge of the bed and gave her hand a squeeze, trying to bring back the initial good vibe from before she'd put her foot in it.

"Willow." As soon as she said the name, she broke out in a smile again. "She wants to see where I'm living, and then she's going to take us out for dinner."

"That sounds great." Rebecca tried to ignore the slight twist in her gut and focus on Phoebe's renewed enthusiasm.

"I've not seen her in ages, months and months."

"You get on well with her?" It wasn't really a question—the answer was clear in Phoebe's demeaner, but it was something to say.

"Yes. I've known her since I was really little. She's like an extra sister. She's really cool. She goes all around the country doing comedy, sometimes even to other countries. She says I'm a natural onstage like her."

Rebecca's gut twisted tighter. How could she compete with someone like that? *You're not competing!* She gave herself a mental slap. *Focus.* "Talking of the stage, I've got some news for you."

"What?"

"After hearing you sing so wonderfully and hearing you like drama, I thought you might like to join a musical theatre group." She held back from saying any more, in order to give Phoebe time to process.

Phoebe pushed back off the bed with such force she nearly toppled over backwards. "Yes! I want to. When can I go?"

It was what Rebecca had expected, and she hastened to make sure they didn't get too carried away. "You will have to audition. Not everyone can have a part. I spoke to the director, who's a friend of mine. There are auditions in two weeks for their next show, which is going to be *Sister Act*."

"Oh my God, I love that film! I can do auditions. Is there a script to look at?"

It was a relief she already understood how it worked. Rebecca didn't want her thinking she'd automatically get in and being too upset if she didn't. "Yes. He said he'd email me the part for the audition if you were interested. And there's a few songs to choose from, which you can listen to before, but you'll learn them there together."

"Cool. I'll practise it lots. Ooh, if you give me it now, I can show Willow and she can help me practise!" Phoebe beamed.

"Of course." That made sense. Willow was a performer—she would know what she was doing. *It's not a rejection of you.*

"If you come back later, you can meet her too."

"I'll...I'll see if I have time. I might not be able to today." She did have a lot to do, and she wasn't sure she was up to facing Alex's glamourous girlfriend and being on the outside while they played happy families. Even if it was her choice to stay at that distance.

"Oh, okay. She's going away again tomorrow, so it's your only chance."

Phoebe clearly didn't understand why Rebecca might not be so keen to see her, and there was no way Rebecca could explain. She couldn't even explain it fully to herself, without opening floodgates that were best kept shut.

"I'll see."

She was careful not to make any false promises. It was doubtful they'd be bothered either way when it came to it. Phoebe would most likely forget all about her once Willow was there. As would Alex.

CHAPTER TEN

They had managed to spend some time dressed, though it was only their promise to Phoebe that made them drag themselves out of the hotel room for the evening. Being with Willow always made Alex feel like she'd come home. Home wasn't a place for her, but there were people, a few people, who housed the feeling.

"We should shower before we go." Alex reached over and attempted to comb Willow's hair with her fingers. Her waves were in turmoil, like she'd passed through a storm. They hadn't spent much time talking. They did plenty of that when they were apart.

"Hmm, it may be very evident what we've been up to. However, Phoebe won't mind, and she knows we haven't been able to get our hands on each other for a while. And we both know she's not half as innocent as some might like to believe." Willow rolled back on top of Alex, pinning her down. "Besides, time in the shower means less time in bed."

"Good point." Alex captured Willow's lips with hers and felt her body melting into hers, their limbs winding back together. It would be so easy to stay. She broke off the kiss, then took a moment to get her breath back before continuing. "But we are going to be out in public."

"Since when did you care what people think?" Willow wriggled on top of her, stroking Alex's bare chest with hers, snaking her thigh back between Alex's legs, parting them…

Alex squeezed her legs shut, blocking Willow's move. "You may enjoy being the centre of attention, but I prefer the shadows."

"Ah yes, my woman of mystery. Can't have everyone knowing what you get up to."

"It's no one else's business." Especially not the staff at the home. Alex didn't plan to give them another reason to gossip and stare. She already felt watched when she moved though those halls and didn't need to spark more of an interest in herself, or Phoebe.

"Long as you're not making me a dirty secret."

"Never." Alex wrapped her arms around her tightly. It wasn't that. She was proud to be with Willow and had no reason to deny it. "I just don't need anyone else picturing us like this."

"Like this?" Willow trailed her lips across Alex's collarbone and down to her right nipple.

Alex moaned and wrapped her fingers in Willow's hair, in no attempt to tame it this time, but to urge her on. She relaxed her legs and let Willow take her place between them.

"I thought you wanted us to clean up." Willow ran a hand over Alex's hip and inwards towards her gently twitching thigh.

"If…we shower together"—Alex managed to make some sense between gasps as she let her hips start to roll in rhythm with Willow's stroking fingers—"we can save time."

"That is an excellent compromise." She moved her lips to Alex's ear to whisper, "And you may need help standing up."

She was right. In the end, Willow had to drive. She kept a satisfied smile on her face as Alex lounged in the passenger seat, enjoying the afterglow.

"Worth the wait?"

"Huh?" Alex tried to get her head together, which was crowded with images from the last twenty-four hours.

"Me. Us. Still worth the wait?" Willow kept facing the road ahead, but her eyes darted over to assess Alex's face.

"Always."

"Good. I know it's been even longer than usual. I've missed having you join me on the road. Maybe I got a little too used to it. Can't expect you to follow me around forever." There was humour in Willow's voice and something else too.

Alex reached over and squeezed her knee. "Hey, that's not over. I won't be stuck around here forever." She missed it too. When she'd been off work, she'd tagged along with Willow as she toured around the country. It'd been a good distraction from her demons while she healed. She might not be free to do it as much any more, but she still planned to join her on some trips. It'd been fun, being a roadie, and if Willow could afford to pay her, she'd have been tempted to carry on. It was probably best she couldn't. Being together all the time wasn't what either of them enjoyed long-term. Working and as-good-as living together, it was bound to break them eventually.

"What if you meet someone and decide you want to stick around. Permanently." Willow didn't seem to have many insecurities, but that was the big one—that their lifestyles might become incompatible one day.

"Not gonna happen." It wasn't down to a career choice, but she didn't want to stop in one place forever any more than Willow.

"Uh-huh. So there's no one around here you'd like to get to know better?"

So that was what had sparked the question. "If there is, I'll tell them that from the start. That's not the point, anyway. You know me. I don't want to get tied down anywhere."

"Except literally." The smile returned to Willow's face.

And Alex's, as she pictured her holding the rope.

"Behave, we're nearly there." Alex sat up straighter as they passed the too familiar streets, the blissful calm seeping from her. "Bee's missed you too."

"And I've missed her. It'll be weird seeing her in her own place. Our little sister, all grown up."

"I know." Alex still had to check herself when she thought about Phoebe and remember she wasn't her kid sister any more. "It's not her own place yet, but she'll get there."

"I'm sure she will. She's got you by her side and her share of the Jennings stubbornness."

"We're not stubborn, we're strong-willed." It was Alex's standard retort when anyone threw that accusation their way, joking or otherwise.

"You are definitely strong women." They pulled up at some traffic lights, and Willow took her hand. "I know you've both been through shit, but you find your way. And you don't have to do it alone."

No, they weren't alone. That was part of the problem. As they drew closer to the home, the claustrophobic feel of the place grew more palpable. It was like driving into a gathering storm. She could feel it in the air, surrounding her. Could Willow feel it too? She did know what they'd been through, better than anyone, but she hadn't been through it herself. She was far enough away to not feel the full force, which Alex was glad of. She hadn't taken Willow down with her.

"I love you," Willow said, bringing her back to the moment with a tug of affection.

"Love you too." Despite how many times they'd said those words, they still gave Alex a buzz, as if she was still that brooding teenager who couldn't believe that Willow Valentine would want to be with her. Willow had always been the more popular one, the louder one, the brighter one, the hotter one. Alex didn't mind—she really did prefer it in the background. While the spotlight was on Willow, she was free to do what she liked. She wouldn't trade that.

❖

Phoebe was waiting for them. As soon as Alex knocked on her door, it opened and she flung herself into Willow's arms.

"I missed you." Phoebe never held back in saying how she felt. That was a big difference between her and Alex.

"I missed you too." Willow eventually released herself from their tight embrace and peered past her into the room. "Hey, look at this. You've got it looking like your place already."

"Yeah. Alex helped."

"I bet she did. Did she choose this gorgeous vamp?" Willow walked up to the poster that still dominated the opposite wall and stroked his bare chest.

Phoebe laughed. "No, she hates it."

"I don't *hate* it. I just don't get it."

"So he's still not your type? Good to know." Willow came back towards Alex and slipped her arm around her waist.

Alex draped her arm around her shoulders and pulled her closer. Phoebe stood beaming at them.

"What?" said Alex.

"It's nice you're happy." She turned to Willow. "She's been *sooo* grumpy."

"I have not." Somehow being around Phoebe could turn her back into a surly teenager in an instant.

"You have too." Phoebe folded her arms in mock sullenness and scowled, earning a laugh from Willow. "Especially with Becca."

At this, Willow turned to her, arching an eyebrow. "I hope you're not being mean to the staff." She leaned in and whispered, "Especially the hot, queer staff."

Thankfully Phoebe's hearing wasn't great, and probably getting worse from the way she blasted her eardrums.

"I'm the model of professionalism." Alex puffed out her chest and straightened her spine.

Phoebe snorted.

"So, where are we going to eat? I'm starving." The topic needed changing, but it was also true. After the last twenty-four hours, she needed some serious refuelling.

"Bee can choose."

"Chinese. Faye said there's one in town that's good and you can eat in." Phoebe had clearly already done her homework.

"Sounds good to me. Do you wanna give me the tour first?"

Alex groaned. "I need to eat." She also needed to get out of there without Willow bumping into Rebecca and things getting even more awkward. Rebecca had made it clear she liked to keep her private life separate from work, but Willow had no such boundaries.

"Poor baby." Willow patted her cheek, then turned back to Phoebe. "We better get your sister fed before she gets hangry. You can show me round when we get back."

"Oh, wait." Phoebe stopped halfway across the room. "Becca was going to bring the script and say hello."

"Script? What script?" Alex held the door open.

"This one."

The voice behind her made her jump. Rebecca had come up so quietly she hadn't known she was there.

"Yes! Thanks, Becca."

Phoebe strode over and took the papers from her outstretched hand. Rebecca stayed hovering in the doorway as Phoebe studied them, flicking her eyes over Willow and Alex.

"Hi, I'm Willow." Willow uncurled from Alex and reached out to Rebecca.

"Rebecca, Phoebe's key worker." She shook hands with Willow in a stiff, formal gesture.

"It's a pleasure to meet you, Rebecca. I've heard so much about you."

This was why she hadn't wanted them to meet.

"Um. Phoebe's told me all about you too. She's been looking forward to your visit." Rebecca stuttered slightly and seemed even quieter than usual but kept a cool professionalism. She turned to Alex. "Sorry to interrupt, I didn't realise you were here—I didn't see your van."

"I drove. And it's not a problem. I wanted to meet you." Willow smiled at Rebecca with a hint of warm curiosity.

"Okay." Rebecca looked at Alex still, as if seeking reassurance she felt the same.

"It's fine." Alex turned to Phoebe and away from the others' searching looks. "So, what's this script?"

Phoebe was still fixed on the printed pages. Alex nudged her with her foot.

"I've got an audition!"

"For what?" Alex heard the sharp edge to her voice but didn't try to temper it. Where had this suddenly come from? It wasn't like Phoebe not to say anything if she'd been thinking of auditioning for something. She was more likely to not shut up about it.

"It's for the local musical theatre production. The director's a friend of mine—they're a nice group," Rebecca answered for her.

"That's fabulous, Bee. You can get back onstage, where you belong." Willow's enthusiastic response made Phoebe smile harder, but Alex couldn't bring herself to join in.

"When was this arranged?" Alex rounded on Rebecca. It sounded suspiciously like it wasn't Phoebe's choice, again, but hers. *Did she just roll her eyes?*

"Phoebe and I talked about it this afternoon. Auditions are in a couple of weeks." Rebecca kept her voice quiet and calm, as if trying not to enrage a spooked animal.

"Sounds perfect. Doesn't it, Alex?" Willow squeezed her hand, a warning to play nice. "Want me to run some lines with you after dinner, Bee? Start getting you prepped?"

"Yes, please!"

"Great, it'll be fun. I've not acted in years. It'll brush off my cobwebs too." Willow turned back to Rebecca. "Thanks for sorting it. I'm sure Bee's been missing performing and her old troupe."

Was that what Alex should've said? Why couldn't she accept it as a good move quite so easily?

"You're welcome. She's welcome. After I saw her sing, I just knew—"

"That she belonged onstage?" Willow finished Rebecca's sentence for her. "She's definitely got the star gene, takes after me in that way, not her skulking sister."

Alex attempted to smile, knowing Willow was just trying to break the ice, but she was still rigid with suspicion. It seemed like a big step and a potentially dangerous one given they knew nothing about the company. Audiences, and other performers, weren't always kind. Willow knew that even better than she did. Just because Rebecca had an in, it didn't mean it was right for Phoebe. She'd said herself, she picked it because her friend ran it, not because it was the best option. Plus, it was bound to carry some kind of commitment. Was this their way of tricking Phoebe into staying longer than she'd planned? Alex lowered her gaze and clenched her jaw, not wanting to get drawn into another clash with Rebecca, not with Willow there.

"She must do." Rebecca's voice carried a mix of warmth and steel.

Alex got the feeling the steel was to match hers.

"Anyway, it was nice to meet you, but this one's starving and we were heading out to eat." Willow said goodbye for both of them and practically dragged her outside by the hand, Phoebe trailing behind.

"Shotgun!" Phoebe called, as soon as the car was in sight, and rushed in front.

"Are you gonna tell me what that was all about?" Willow spoke quietly, this time being careful Phoebe definitely wouldn't hear.

Alex sighed. "It just came out of the blue. She keeps making these big decisions for Bee, without checking it's all right."

"You mean checking it's all right with you? What, does Bee need your permission now?"

"No." Alex stopped halfway across the car park. "Checking it's safe. We don't know this group, what it's like."

"She said her friend runs it, so she obviously knows them."

"Yeah, exactly. She decided on it with her friend, not Phoebe. Shouldn't it be up to her what she joins? And why's Rebecca talking about Phoebe to her friends?"

"It's not like there's gonna be lots of options around a small town like this, especially groups that are welcoming of newbies. You have to take these kinds of chances. I'm sure she was just trying to help and wouldn't put Bee in a dodgy situation." Willow rested her hand on Alex's shoulder, gently rubbing the tense muscles in an obvious attempt to try to get her to relax.

"How can you be sure? How do you know we can trust her and that it isn't some trick to make her feel she has to stay?" Willow didn't seem to have picked up on the smothering vibe of the place, but Alex couldn't ignore it.

"I don't. But Bee trusts her, and she seems to be doing right by her. You know how much she loves performing—do you really want to hold her back?"

"I want to keep her safe."

"Isn't that what your parents wanted?"

Alex flinched as if she'd been slapped. "I'm not like them!"

"No, you're not. You want Bee to be free to live her life and be herself. And this is who she is. She's not like you, you know that. She thrives in the spotlight."

"I do. I just…" Alex hung her head so it butted against Willow's shoulder.

"I know, darling. I know it's hard for you to trust." Willow drew her into a warm embrace. "The world's a scary place, but Bee wants to be out there too. It's why we're doing all this."

Alex sank into her arms and let the tension start to melt away. She did want Phoebe to be free and to enjoy her life, but she couldn't be sure who they could trust. She looked up at the home over Willow's shoulder. A pale, slender figure stood at an upstairs window. She couldn't make out their face, but she knew who it was. Rebecca was watching over them. The question was, why?

❖

A haze of chatter wafted over them as soon as they walked through the door. The printed signs and bright arrows weren't needed, Rebecca could've just followed the noise.

The community centre sounded fuller than it was, with all the voices bouncing around the large hall. There were maybe three dozen people there, milling around, grouping and regrouping. They appeared to all know each other. Phoebe stayed by her side, seeming much less confident than she had when she'd been practising at home.

"There's Sebastian, the director. Let's go introduce you," Rebecca told her.

It was easy to spot him, commanding attention in the middle of the loudest cluster.

"Okay," said Phoebe.

"Are you sure you want to do this? You don't have to, you could wait for next time and—"

"I want to." Phoebe lifted her chin up. "Let's go."

She strode off without waiting for Rebecca, as if afraid she might be the one to change her mind and take them back home.

Sebastian met them halfway, walking over to greet Rebecca with a wide smile and outstretched hands. "Darling, it's wonderful to see you. And this must be your protégé."

It was hard to resist rolling her eyes at his affectations. Outside the theatre crowd, he wasn't half as camp. He was just playing his part like everyone else.

"I'm Phoebe." Phoebe held out her hand.

Sebastian took it and pulled her into a brief hug. "Hi Phoebe, I'm Sebastian. Thank you for coming along. It's always exciting to find new local talent." He kept an arm around her shoulders and added in a stage whisper, "We're in danger of getting a bit old and saggy around the middle."

"Who are you calling old and saggy? I assure you, I'm as young and pert as I've ever been." An older woman appeared behind him, giving him a playful tap on the cheek. "But it is nice to get some new blood in here to liven things up. I'm Estelle."

"Drinking it is what keeps you young, after all," Sebastian added.

"Behave, Seb, don't scare the new girl off. What's your name, sweetheart?"

Around them, Rebecca noticed others drawing near. Had they also caught the scent of new blood? Sebastian had assured her Phoebe would be welcome, and Rebecca had taken his word for it. Maybe she should've come along and seen for herself first.

"I'm Phoebe." Phoebe seemed to be studying Estelle, perhaps also unsure of the warmth of her welcome.

"Pleased to meet you, Phoebe. Don't mind him—he just enjoys a flair for the dramatic. We're a friendly bunch. A family."

Phoebe smiled and let herself be pulled into another embrace.

"Now, let me introduce you to everyone." Estelle kept one arm around Phoebe and steered her away.

As Estelle and Phoebe moved off, Rebecca took the chance to have a good look around at the others. Sebastian was right—they were mainly much older than Phoebe, possibly even older than they looked, judging by the care some of them appeared to take of their appearances. There were a few younger people dotted around, including a couple she recognized as friends of Sebastian's who were more her age.

"They really are, a friendly bunch that is. She'll be fine." He gave her a hug, less affected and more intimate than the one he'd given Phoebe.

"I'm sure she will," Rebecca said, watching as Phoebe was welcomed by the rest of the group. Was there even any need for her to stick around now that Estelle had taken Phoebe under her wing?

"And on the plus side, not much competition for the younger roles. Though I try not to let things like age and gender get in the way of my casting. It's talent and passion that matter."

"Phoebe's definitely got both of those."

The only question was whether it'd show through in the unfamiliar setting. Rebecca remembered what Phoebe had been like when she'd first come to the home. Hopefully she wouldn't need the same settling-in time. Maybe she should've arranged for her to meet everyone beforehand and get a feel for the place. Sebastian had said they were holding auditions over a couple of evenings, so she could delay taking her turn and treat this as a warm-up.

"Then she'll fit in just fine. There'll be no special treatment, of course, just because she's a friend of yours. She'll have to earn a part."

"Of course."

He wasn't just talking about Phoebe being a friend of hers. Sebastian had made it clear when they spoke before that, although he would do his best to support any additional needs of his actors, no one got a free pass. Which was as it should be. Phoebe didn't need anything handed to her—she would earn it. It was impressive how seriously Phoebe had taken her preparations, rehearsing every day, even pushing Rebecca into practicing with her. She clearly wasn't taking anything for granted either.

"Do you want to hang around? You can be my honorary assistant." Sebastian bumped her shoulder with his, having moved to stand by her side for a better view of the group.

Rebecca chewed her lip. The offer was tempting, in case Phoebe needed support and so she could spend some time with Sebastian, who she hadn't seen much of in a while. With the extra hours she'd been working and her desire to just relax with Ishani or Drew when she was free, she'd not been seeing much of any of her friends. She tried not to be one of those poly people who only hung with their partners and metamours, but it tended to work out that way.

Besides, she might not have an option. Questions would be asked if she just left Phoebe there. There'd been a muttering from certain colleagues about whether it was a good idea for Phoebe to join an unknown organisation, and she needed to be able to defend it with all the evidence she could. Not to mention Alex, whose peeved reaction surprised her. Wasn't this what she wanted, for Phoebe to be out enjoying herself in mainstream society? And yet—

"*Sooo* are you staying or going? I need to get this show on the road if we're not gonna be here all night."

Rebecca looked up from her thoughts to find him staring at her, a slight frown beginning to furrow his brow.

"Hey, everything okay? You don't seem quite…with it."

"I'm okay, just got a lot on my mind," Rebecca mumbled. "I'll stay, if you're sure I won't be in the way. And if Phoebe doesn't mind."

"Great." Sebastian squeezed her hand. "It'll give us a chance to catch up on all the goss while they practice. I don't think I've had the chance to tell you about the new man in my life."

"No, you've not. You can tell me all about him." Some light gossip and a chance to bask in his happiness might be just what she needed.

While Sebastian rounded everyone up, Rebecca quickly sought out Phoebe. She'd managed to integrate herself into the younger crowd and seemed happy there. Rebecca discreetly pulled her to one side, being careful not to appear too carer-y. She didn't want to make Phoebe seem any more different than she already did.

"I might stay and take the opportunity to have a catch-up with Sebastian, if you don't mind me hanging around."

"I don't mind. I want you to see my audition." Phoebe seemed more excited than nervous again.

It was difficult to understand. Rebecca couldn't imagine anything worse than getting up on stage in front of everyone, let alone doing so voluntarily.

"Break a leg!" she said, then regretted her choice of phrase in case Phoebe thought she meant it literally. "That's what they say in the theatre, isn't it?"

"Yep." Phoebe turned away. "It's starting—I gotta go."

"Good luck. Not that you'll need it." Rebecca gave her a quick squeeze and moved to the sidelines where she prayed nothing went wrong and the pressure wouldn't suddenly get to her. Phoebe seemed so confident and carefree at times, but she had a vulnerable side too. Rebecca didn't want to be responsible for setting her up for a fall.

Sebastian explained to the assembled crowd how the evening would work. It wouldn't just be scripted auditions they'd practised— there were group improv exercises too. Phoebe seemed unfazed, despite the disadvantage she might have without extra processing time, and even eager to jump right in.

Rather you than me. Improvisation was even worse, with no script to instruct you who to be and what to say. How did people do that, just act on the spot? At school she'd hung back during drama class, desperately trying to avoid being pushed into the ring and happy to let her more boisterous classmates run the show.

"Not tempted to join in?" Sebastian nudged her.

"God, no." She had nearly been persuaded to join the drama club at one point as a backstage worker, helping organise the props and direct the actors. Only she'd feared being dragged out front to fill in. The stagehands seemed to often double as the chorus.

"Shame. You'll just have to entertain me with tales of real life." He winked, not putting up any real fight, knowing from experience that she wasn't going to say yes.

Rebecca stiffened. Talking about her own life was not what she had in mind. Sebastian was not known for his discretion, and he would want to know *everything*. "I thought you were the one who was going to regale me with tales of your new love?"

"Oh, I will, don't you worry." He sauntered back to the group and handed out sheet music, then introduced the musical director.

As they took over, he slipped back to Rebecca's side.

"*Sooo...*"

"So tell me all about him," Rebecca said, before he could start asking questions. Not that she had anything to hide—she just didn't have anything she wanted to talk about either. "I want to know who's put that glint in your eyes."

"Okay, but I want to know who's put the one in yours," he shot back with a mischievous grin.

Rebecca felt herself blush hot, probably making Sebastian even more suspicious. "No one! No one new."

"Whatever you say, sweetheart, but I know when someone's holding back, and there's definitely something you're not saying."

"Maybe because there's nothing I can say. Or do." What was the point in saying more? Maybe there was someone new who she sparked with, but not always in a good way, and there was no future there.

"Okay, okay. I won't push you." Sebastian held his hands up, then took hold of hers. "But you know where I am if you ever do want to talk about it. Seriously, I'm here for you."

There was a tug of temptation. Would it help to share her frustration with Sebastian and have him reassure her that she was right in not making any moves? But what if he didn't agree, what if he persuaded her to go for it instead? And what if Phoebe overheard and realised they were referring to her sister? No, it was too risky. Better she kept quiet and let it all wash over her. Alex would be gone soon.

Over the next twenty minutes, Sebastian entertained her with a full breakdown of his new relationship, from first glance to meeting the family. Occasionally she found herself envying him, the simplicity of his monogamous life. It was already all scripted and being rehearsed everywhere you looked. Of course, it wasn't that easy in reality. There was little room for error or manoeuvre. You had to play the part you were assigned, together. She thought of Drew, who could never stand in line. If Rebecca had stuck to the script, she would never have chanced it with them. They'd been worth waiving the rules for. Another face swam to mind, less familiar and proven. Could Alex be worth taking a risk on too? She shook her head and focused back on Sebastian's monologue. She'd made her choices and it had all worked out. The end.

"We're ready to start now, Sebastian." The music man beckoned Sebastian to come join him as the actors clustered at the far end of the hall.

"Come on, you can help me get through this." He linked arms and pulled Rebecca along behind him, then guided her into a seat at the long table that had been set in one corner. "I'm afraid they're not all superstars, especially when it comes to singing. Just because you can act doesn't mean you can sing. Think *Mamma Mia!*"

Rebecca groaned softly. Was this going to be a repeat of the karaoke session, where her face would hurt by the end of it from forcing a smile? At least Phoebe's performance had made it worth it. Hopefully it would again. She tugged at the neck of her shirt, nervous for her.

"We'll start you off gently," Sebastian said, as Estelle stepped forward.

She was competent and more once she warmed up. Clearly experienced and possibly professionally trained, she glided through the song without skipping a beat. Everyone applauded when she finished, and she bowed graciously. Rebecca breathed a sigh of relief. It wasn't going to be so bad.

The next few auditionees were also competent, but nothing more. They could hold a tune, but Rebecca wasn't convinced they'd hold an audience's attention. They were missing something. *Phoebe* had that something. Rebecca could see her at the back of the hall, bouncing on her heels and quietly watching the others. It seemed some nerves might be starting to rise. She wished she could go over and give her some reassurance, tell her how she compared.

Sebastian seemed to have clocked her growing tension too and declared they should let the new girl go next and put her out of her misery. Rebecca only winced slightly at his use of the term. He probably called them all girls—his lack of interest and insight into women was obvious. Not that straight men were generally better.

The other auditionees gave Phoebe what looked like words and pats of encouragement as she walked over, though they were too far away for Rebecca to be sure. The long hall seemed even longer as Phoebe shuffled towards them. *Head up, Phoebe, let them see who you are.* She stopped a few metres away, and Sebastian beckoned her closer.

"I'm afraid there's no mic tonight, so make sure I can hear you."

"I don't need one. I can project." Phoebe stood up straighter and pulled her shoulders back, giving off a professional air.

You've got this. Rebecca's nails dug into her palms.

When the pianist banged out the first notes, Phoebe closed her eyes. She'd been listening to the music all fortnight and must've memorised the words. She opened her eyes as she let the first note glide out.

And nailed it. Rebecca felt Sebastian and the musical director sit up to attention beside her. There was a change at the back of the room too, the murmuring dying away as everyone turned to watch. Phoebe easily filled the hall with her song, even without a mic, and enraptured all its occupants. Rebecca could concede that she lacked Estelle's polish, but the raw emotion and talent she exuded was more powerful.

Rebecca glanced over at Sebastian. His mouth hung slightly open, and his eyes sparkled as he drank in her performance. The musical director was visible next to him, having moved slowly forward, leaning over the desk towards Phoebe as if itching to join her. His expression was more subtle but hinted he was no less overjoyed. The song ended with a burst of applause and even a few hollers of approval. She hadn't known anyone actually still shouted *Bravo!*

Sebastian leaned in to her. "I thought I was doing you a favour, but you were doing me one! You're right, she's the real thing."

"We will have to make sure she can act too, before we get too carried away," a voice piped up behind him.

"That won't be a problem," Rebecca said. Nerves hadn't beaten her for her solo, so surely she'd breeze through the group acting scenes. "I bet it won't."

It hadn't been a mistake. Rebecca couldn't stop smiling. She had been right to take the risk, and soon everyone would know it. As long as no one interfered or tried to stop Phoebe again.

Chapter Eleven

Alex had to admit it: she was happy. She also had to admit who was helping Phoebe feel that way.

They'd called Phoebe the very next day to ask her to come back in to read for one of the biggest parts. Alex had tried to stop her getting carried away, but it was hard not to get caught up in her excitement. Even if she didn't get the part, it was like she was fully alive again. Willow was right—it was what Phoebe needed. Rebecca had done right by her...and Alex had been an arse about it.

"Run my lines with me again?"

"Surely you've done enough—you've been practising all week. You'll nail it." Alex leaned back in the newly built armchair, enjoying her handiwork. They'd made another trip to flatpack heaven and come back laden with everything they could fit in Phoebe's room. She'd also treated herself to a fancy mattress that had been on offer. She couldn't wait to sink into it later and chuck out the old one that even she had to admit had served its time.

"Just one more time. *Pleeease.*" Phoebe drew out the last word so pathetically that there was no way Alex could say no.

"Can I at least get a cuppa first?" She rocked lightly in the springy chair, soothing her worn-out frame. It was a good excuse to stay sitting down and give her legs a break, without having to admit they needed one. She knew Phoebe still worried about her and tried not to give her any reason to fuss.

"Deal."

"Cheers." Alex closed her eyes and continued rocking. She'd been avoiding asking something, but it wasn't going away. She tried to keep her tone casual as she finally addressed the elephant in the room. "So, have you heard any more from Mum? Is she coming to visit?"

There was no reply, and when she opened her eyes Phoebe was sitting frozen in her new chair looking like all the rebuilt confidence had drained out of her. *Damn, should've left it.*

"It's okay, she doesn't have to. You know I'm not gonna push for that."

"I know." Phoebe paused. "They're coming this weekend," she continued, quieter, her voice betraying her with a slight shakiness.

Alex raised an eyebrow but didn't say anything. It was Phoebe's choice.

"I didn't want to upset you. You don't have to see them." Phoebe gave a slow shrug, rolling her shoulders right up with the air of a tortoise withdrawing into its shell.

"It doesn't upset me—you can tell me. Don't make it some big secret." Alex realised it had come out too loud and gritted her teeth. The idea of their parents sneaking back into Phoebe's life without anyone knowing sent a shiver down her spine. "I'll stay out of the way, if you tell me when they're here."

"Okay."

"Okay."

They sat in silence, not meeting each other's eyes.

"So…how are you feeling about it?" She'd brought it up now, so she might as well plough on.

"I want to see them. But I'm a bit scared." Phoebe gazed down into her lap and knitted her fingers together.

Alex nodded slowly. "That figures, you're gonna feel nervous seeing them again after your big move."

"Yeah. I don't know if they understand."

"Understand what?" There was a hell of a lot their parents couldn't seem to get their bigoted heads around. She really couldn't be sure what part Phoebe was talking about.

"Why I left."

"Maybe they don't. Maybe they never will get it." Alex leaned forward and squeezed her hand. "Get *us*. But they don't have to totally understand to accept it."

"I suppose." Phoebe didn't sound convinced, but she might've just needed time to process.

Alex gave her a minute before continuing. Or tried to anyway, it might've been more like ten seconds. "Look, maybe they don't understand why you had to move out, but maybe they don't have to, they just need to know that you have and that's that. You're moving on and they need to let you. They don't have a say in it any more—it's your life."

"Yeah." A half smile lit up Phoebe's face. "It's my life, not theirs."

"Exactly. Just remember that if they say anything you don't like." She knew it wasn't so easy for Phoebe. She had gone her own way so many years ago and they'd not put up a fight, at least partly because they'd been focused on Phoebe, smothering her with all the love they could give. "So, where's that cuppa? I'm parched after all the labour you've had me do."

"I helped!"

"I must've missed that moment."

Phoebe grabbed the pillow lying next to her and batted Alex with it.

"Oi!" Alex grabbed the pillow off her.

At least Phoebe was smiling fully again. Before Alex could get her back, she jumped up and left to get their drinks.

When she returned, she wasn't alone. Alex heard her chatting away to someone as she shuffled back down the corridor, someone with a sharper, faster step. The door opened while she was halfway out of her chair, having paused, unsure whether to run over to open it if Phoebe wasn't alone. Rebecca held it open as Phoebe balanced their drinks.

"Hi," Alex said.

"Good afternoon." Rebecca's reply seemed stilted, over-professional. The tension of their last conversation was still hanging in the air.

Once again, Alex would have to do something to break it. It was her own doing. She really needed to start thinking before she spoke and not assume the worst of everyone. Especially the only person she'd met in a long time who made her want to let someone new close.

"Thanks, Becca." Phoebe moved past her, over to the desk, where she placed their steaming mugs. "Ooh, you can help us rehearse!"

"Isn't Alex doing it?" Rebecca glanced at Alex briefly as she said her name. Alex realised she was still in an awkward half crouch, which would explain the smile that played on Rebecca's lips at the sight of her.

"She is, but there's more than two parts. It'll be better with both of you."

"Fair enough. If you're not too busy…" Alex didn't want to push her, but the thought of Rebecca acting was intriguing. Did she have a hidden diva inside?

"I can spare twenty minutes." Rebecca closed the door and walked over to her. "I see you made another big shopping trip. It's looking very cosy in here."

They'd got it looking less like a care home and more like student digs. Not that Alex had gone to uni—she'd got a job and her independence as soon as possible—but she'd spent plenty of time in Willow's run-down shared houses. They'd managed to fit two comfy wooden armchairs in, and Phoebe had found a deep purple rug to cover most of the dull carpet. It was the kind you could sink your feet into, making it look like your toes were under attack from alien tendrils.

Rebecca took the other chair, drawing it towards her and away from Alex before sitting down. Phoebe picked up the script from the desk.

"Don't you know it off by heart by now, after all your practise?" The teasing tone in Rebecca's voice was a surprise, so much less formal than how she'd spoken to Alex.

"Nearly. I don't have to for the audition, do I?" Phoebe's eyes widened.

"No, no. I was joking. They won't be expecting you to—no one else will have." Rebecca spoke with a calm authority that made it sound like she knew what she was talking about.

Did she actually know, or was she just trying to calm Phoebe? Alex didn't ask. It wouldn't help. And she was trying not to get in the way of Rebecca helping.

"Okay, phew." Phoebe dropped onto the bed with a dramatic sigh. "Oh wait, you haven't got a drink. I'll get you one."

"It's okay, I can get one myself later."

"No, you should drink. You have to keep your voice box lubricated so you don't damage it rehearsing."

Rebecca smiled and relented, seemingly taken in by Phoebe's professional approach. Which she would be—Alex couldn't imagine her ever doing anything half-arsed. She held in her own snigger at the mention of lubrication.

Once Phoebe had gone to get her drink, they were left in awkward silence. Rebecca's eyes darted around the room.

There was no easy way to lead in, so Alex decided to get straight to the point. She stood up and walked over to Rebecca. "I just wanted to say thanks."

Rebecca blinked at her, deadpan, as if suspecting a trap.

"Thanks for everything you're doing for Phoebe. She's a lot happier here and more…*her* again." If she was Willow, she'd have found a more lyrical way of putting it, but Alex didn't have her way with words.

This earned a nod and a smile, but Rebecca still didn't say anything.

Alex took a deep breath. "I know I've not always seen it that way, I didn't know if we could trust you to do right by her, but you obviously are. So, thanks." She could feel heat rising as she stumbled over her speech. If only Rebecca would say something and give her a sign she could shut up.

"Just doing my job," she finally said, with a shrug which failed to look casual.

"No, you're not."

Rebecca met her gaze. She looked like she wanted to deny it but was biting her tongue.

"I'm sorry I've made it difficult. Not all carers are like you." Alex shrugged this time, not wanting to go any deeper.

"It's okay, I know," Rebecca said, so quiet Alex wasn't sure if she'd imagined it.

"Lucky for us, we got you. Maybe not so lucky for you!"

She was grateful when Rebecca laughed, and she joined her, dispelling the memories that had started to crowd in. They definitely weren't all like her. If Alex'd had someone like Rebecca there for her, maybe she wouldn't have ended up in as bad a state. But would she have made it easier to move on?

"Well, you wouldn't be my first choice if I wanted a quiet life."

"Who wants that?"

"I do." Rebecca was suddenly quietly serious again.

It burst the bubble their laughter had created. Alex sighed. "I gotta admit, I've had enough drama over the years, so I'm with you there. Sometimes."

Except when it came down to it, some drama still crept into her relationships, and she wasn't sure she'd want it to be different. That spark, that passion, was that the feeling of being alive that Willow and Phoebe felt onstage? She didn't want to settle for a life without sparks. She stretched out her hand towards Rebecca without thinking, and Rebecca took it, the flashes of something intangible between them illuminating her point. Alex kept watch on the closed door behind her. She couldn't tell Rebecca what she was feeling in case they were overheard, but she ran her thumb over Rebecca's palm and smiled at the shiver that visibly ran through her.

It was tempting to carry on the personal turn of their conversation and at least get to know Rebecca a bit better, even if she couldn't be open about why she was interested, but there was something more urgent she needed to talk to her about. She dropped Rebecca's hand and stuffed her hands in her pockets out of the way.

"Did Phoebe tell you our parents are coming to visit her at the weekend?"

"She did." Rebecca straightened in her seat.

"I'm not sure it's a great idea. It's Phoebe's call, and I'm not going to try to talk her out of it, but I don't trust them." She felt her fists balling and made her hands lie flat on the arms of her chair.

"Are you not going to be there too?"

Nope. But this wasn't about her. "They don't respect Phoebe— they don't get her wanting her independence. I just, I want you to know, so you can be on the lookout." *And prove we're right to trust you.*

"Thank you. I'll keep that in mind. I believe it's only a short visit. There's no plan for them to get involved in her care." Rebecca was in full professional mode.

But will you fight for her if they do? Alex wanted more but bit back the question. She had to tread carefully. Even if they did trust her, Rebecca was still part of the system and would stick to its rules.

Rebecca was studying her, and Alex could see a question forming in her mind and trickling to her lips. "What happened?" she finally said. "What happened to make—"

With perfect timing, Phoebe made her entrance. Alex slumped back in the chair. At some point they might have to answer Rebecca's question, to let her further in, but Alex wouldn't unless she had to. Besides, it wasn't for her to tell all. It was up to Phoebe how much her carers knew about her personal life. Alex wouldn't be passing them any extra info behind her back.

Sure, it was getting a bit murky with Rebecca, and the lines blurred at times. But she had to remember what Rebecca was to Phoebe. And what she wasn't to her.

❖

The bell rang at three p.m. on the dot. Had they sat in the car, waiting until they could be perfectly punctual? Rebecca knew from experience, that level of precision didn't come without conscious effort.

As it was her shift anyway, she hadn't needed to make any special arrangements to be there to greet Phoebe's parents. At handover they'd agreed it made sense for her to do it as Phoebe's key worker. The other staff had acted like the visit was no big deal, but she knew better.

She wasn't sure whether to take Alex's concerns about their parents seriously, given her general distrustful attitude, but there must be a reason Phoebe wasn't still with them, and why Phoebe seemed more nervous than excited in the way she flapped about as their visit approached. Rebecca got the impression she wouldn't be flinging herself into her mother's arms like she had with Willow. Phoebe clearly loved and trusted Alex's partner in a way that suggested she'd never betrayed her. Never betrayed them.

It was strange to think that Alex had been with someone that long. She didn't seem the committed type. Rebecca caught her judgement—that wasn't fair. Alex had proved her commitment to Phoebe, having gone so far as to move out there with her, so she clearly had it in her. Though wasn't she trying to make up for something? She'd practically admitted it at the meet, when she'd let slip how she hadn't been there for Phoebe before.

Rebecca attempted to push Alex and her warning from her mind as she went to answer the door. Phoebe had agreed to the visit, so she needed to treat the parents with professional curtesy.

When she opened the door, she was momentarily confused. The couple on the doorstep were well groomed and smartly dressed, in warm colours that would've looked clownish on either of the sisters. It was only when she looked into the woman's ocean eyes that she regained some certainty. She'd gazed into those bottomless pools before.

"Hello, we're Mr. and Mrs. Jennings, Phoebe's parents. She's expecting us." Mr. Jennings introduced them both, leaving his wife standing in silence slightly behind him.

"Hello, yes, she told us you were coming. I'm Rebecca, her key worker." She faltered slightly. Should she have told them that? Or was it inviting them to ask questions she shouldn't answer? She'd been telling the truth when she assured Alex there were no plans for them to get involved in Phoebe's care. One overprotective guardian was enough, and having finally earned Alex's trust, she had no desire to start the process again.

"It's good to meet you, Rebecca." Phoebe's father held out his hand and received hers in a firm shake. Her mother copied him.

"It's good to meet you too. Phoebe's upstairs in her room—let me show you up." Usually, visitors would be entertained in one of the downstairs living rooms, or the office for those who'd really come to chat to the staff, but Phoebe had wanted to keep to the safety of her own room. Rebecca would've preferred they'd been somewhere she could more discreetly keep an eye on them, but they might well want privacy, and since Alex had added all the extra furnishings, there was clearly space for them there.

The home was bustling, with nearly all the residents in as there were no day centres or colleges to attend at the weekends. Those who had gone out were more than made up for by visiting relatives. They tried to manage the number of visitors that turned up at once, but some of the parents seemed to appreciate the chance to not only see their offspring but chat to other visiting families who empathised with their situation. When they said goodbye, they could often be heard confirming when they would next visit, unofficially coordinating to bump into each other again. It was a familiar dance that seemed to be ruled by notions of English reserve, which meant they never admitted that was what they were doing.

It might be for the best that Phoebe's parents wouldn't be joining them and get drawn in. It would only encourage them to visit regularly. Rebecca deliberately didn't stop to introduce them to anyone and led them straight upstairs.

When she knocked on Phoebe's door, Phoebe didn't fling it open, instead shouting, "Come in!" Rebecca opened the door to find her standing still in the middle of the room.

"Hello, sweetheart." It was the first thing Mrs. Jennings had said since they arrived. She didn't wait for Rebecca to move aside, instead stepping around her as if she were merely part of the furniture, and striding over to Phoebe with arms outstretched.

Though she spread her arms in response and allowed herself to be embraced, Phoebe did so with noticeably less enthusiasm than for her other visitors. "Hi, Mum."

Her mother held her tight, moving one hand to stroke her head, which Phoebe rested on her shoulder. After a moment Rebecca saw Phoebe relax into it and close her eyes.

"Hello, Phoebe." It was the dad's turn to embrace her then, in a big bear hug. Phoebe squealed as he leaned back, lifting her clear off the ground.

Rebecca was obviously a fly on the wall as far as they were all concerned, and it was tempting to see how long she could get away with just standing there, silently observing. She'd promised Alex she'd keep an eye on them, but it was a promise she never should have made. She couldn't justify standing guard and was intruding on a private moment. Alex would just have to understand that there were limits to what she could and should do.

"Can I get anyone tea or coffee?" she said. Maybe once she'd prepared the drinks they would've settled in and got past the initial emotions of their reunion, and she might be able to engage in some conversation. Yes, that was a good compromise.

"That would be lovely, thank you. Tea please, white, no sugar." Mr. Jennings didn't take his eyes off his daughter.

"Same for me, please. Can I give you a hand?" Mrs. Jennings did turn, with a warm smile that seemed to boast some of Phoebe's open affection.

"It's okay, I'll get them. Phoebe?"

"Yes, tea too." Phoebe was still standing and returning her father's gaze with a look that was difficult to interpret.

"Have you forgotten your manners already, Phoebe Jennings?" His words were stern, but there was a softness to his voice that took some of the edge off.

"Tea, please."

"This place looks cosy. We didn't know what to expect. Seems like you're fully kitted out." Mrs. Jennings stood in the centre of the room and rubbed her hands together as she spoke.

"You can sit down." Phoebe pointed to the chairs, and her parents took the indicated seats. "Alex helped me get stuff and build it."

Phoebe remained standing next to her father, their heads now level. He was a fairly tall man, like his other daughter, although he had more weight to him than Alex.

"Hmm, she always was good with her hands." He rocked in the chair, as if testing its sturdiness.

Why did he have to put it like that? Rebecca tried not to imagine what Alex could do with her hands and turned away to hide any suggestive blushes, grateful for the excuse of the kitchen to head to.

"How is your sister?" Mrs. Jennings added quietly.

Rebecca paused, halfway out of the room. There was something about the way she'd said it that made her stop cold. You would think Alex was a relative of Phoebe's they barely knew, not their child too. Were they not in touch at all? As much as Rebecca wasn't close to her parents and they didn't approve of all her quote-unquote *choices*, she couldn't imagine stopping speaking to them entirely.

"She's good. She got a job here so she can stay around for a bit." Phoebe's shoulders hunched and she shuffled on the spot. Had Alex warned her not to say too much about her?

Whether she had or not, it confirmed they didn't even know the basics of their other daughter's life. Rebecca felt an ache in her chest at the thought of Alex being cast off from her family. However, that might not be the case. Alex might have been the one to turn her back on them.

She wanted to hear more but had already been stopped there for a conspicuous amount of time. Now that Alex was starting to open up to her, maybe she'd get the full story from her one day. It might be even easier to get it from Phoebe. Surely taking an interest in her family history was in line with caring for her?

As she shut the door behind her, she caught the beginning of a subject change, with Phoebe's father asking about her audition. It was likely a safer topic and one that would warm Phoebe up. Their interest in Alex didn't seem to have gone further than a polite enquiry after her health, the minimum anyone could ask of them. Despite her attempt to console herself, her heart sat heavy in her chest.

It was a relief to find Luisa in the kitchen, which would naturally stretch out the tea-making and give her the chance to refocus.

"Are you with Phoebe's parents? How is it going? What are they like? Are they as terrifying as you have been told?" Luisa started questioning her as soon as the door closed.

It also meant she wouldn't be allowed to avoid any dissection of what was happening. She had mentioned to Luisa about Alex's concerns, and Luisa agreed there must be something in them to explain their absence so far. It was the point everything always boiled down to.

"I'm just getting them some drinks. It seems to be going fine so far." Apart from the confirmation of their lack of relationship with Alex.

"Okay." Luisa looked disappointed, as if she'd been hoping for some drama to spice up their weekend. She was young enough to still act like that was a good thing, so Rebecca tried not to hold it against her. Unlike their older colleagues who really should know better.

"I'll try to keep an eye on them, but they're in Phoebe's room, so

I won't be able to do much." Rebecca took four of the nicer cups down from the cupboard and inspected them to check they were really clean.

"That does make it difficult. Unless you stand out in the corridor and place your ear to the door." Before Rebecca could protest, Luisa laughed. "I am joking with you!"

"Glad to hear it. It's understandable they want some privacy." Rebecca tried to take the moral high ground, even though the idea had occurred to her too.

"I need to get on with my duties now. Have fun. The kettle is boiled." Luisa left, laden with a tray of drinks.

Rebecca held the door open for her.

"You know where I am if you need backup," Luisa said as she passed her.

"Thank you. I'm sure it won't be needed."

She could handle the awkward family reunion and make sure she was free if Phoebe needed her after. It was unlikely she would anyway, as she seemed to prefer to take comfort in music.

Not wanting to get back too soon, Rebecca made the tea mindfully, trying to focus on each movement and sensation. The slosh of the water filling the mugs, the heat of the rising steam, the clink of the teaspoon. It was a practice she'd been taught to settle her frantic mind but didn't get round to employing very often. Most of the time she only focused afterwards. She liked having a warm cup to clasp between her hands and keep them still.

When she reached the door, she was stuck. She couldn't knock with the tray of full drinks in her hands. She could kick the door instead, but that wouldn't give a good impression. She was still considering her options when the door opened.

"I thought I heard you out there—let me take that." Mrs. Jennings reached for the tray.

"It's okay, if you can just hold the door for me..." Rebecca manoeuvred herself across the room to the desk. If she let Mrs. Jennings take it, there'd be no excuse for her to come back in.

"What are the facilities like here, for Phoebe to get food and drinks," Mr. Jennings asked as he accepted his cup.

Of course, they would ask about an area she hadn't negotiated yet. "We provide the meals, and there's a drinks trolley where they can help themselves."

"She's not cooking for herself? We did say that's something you'll need to learn. You can't feed yourself by just baking cakes." Mrs.

Jennings smiled at Phoebe over the top of her cup as Rebecca handed it to her, before facing Rebecca. "Thank you."

"We do have a kitchen upstairs for the residents' use, so they can practise their skills." It *was* intended to be used that way, though it had become more of a staff canteen. Apparently when given the option of cooking for themselves or being served, most people were happy to be waited on.

"Oh, cool. Can I do baking in there?" Phoebe piped up. Her mother gave her a look. "And cook proper food too," she added, earning herself a pat on the knee.

"Of course. I was planning to get you in there—I was just letting you settle in first." *And teaching you all the other skills no one had before.* She would've liked to point out to Mrs. Jennings that there was a lot more to independence than cooking for yourself, but it wasn't appropriate and she didn't want to add any unnecessary discomfort to the meeting. She plastered on a smile and stayed focused on Phoebe. "Depending how much you already know, we could look at college courses too."

"That sounds like a good plan," Mr. Jennings said. "As much as we enjoy Phoebe's cakes, she does have more to learn."

"I'll make sure she has plenty of opportunities," Rebecca said.

Mrs. Jennings seemed satisfied with this, and Phoebe remained cheered at the prospect. The father was harder to read. What did he want? There was Alex's warning that they didn't want Phoebe to have her independence. Was that really the case, or had they just never thought to involve Phoebe in their routine chores? They might have raised her in dependence, but that didn't mean it was intentional. You didn't have to mean harm to do harm.

What harm had the Jennings inflicted on their children to make both daughters cut off from them? They didn't seem like monsters.

Rebecca hung around for a few minutes longer, but it became clear she wasn't wanted and wasn't about to get any answers. Not yet.

Chapter Twelve

Alex wasn't sure how she'd ended up there. She sat at the back of the hall, doing her best to merge into her surroundings and not get drawn into anything. She was just there to watch, and it was a lot easier to get a clear view from the outside.

The truth was, it was because of Rebecca. Given she'd had to deal with their parents at the weekend, Alex figured she had even more making up to do. If Rebecca had brought Phoebe to the second audition herself, it would've meant going over the end of her shift again. That wasn't fair on her—she was doing enough for Phoebe. Possibly too much. Although Alex had come to trust her in some ways, and like her in more, she still didn't want Phoebe getting too dependent on her. That was how they got you, and you ended up stuck in those places. Rebecca was trying to help and did seem to actually care, but that didn't mean she wasn't doing any damage. Some folks said it's the intention that mattered, but Alex knew that was BS. You didn't have to mean harm to do harm.

So she'd found herself arguing to do something she didn't want to. Rebecca had given in quickly enough, but more because there was no good reason why Alex shouldn't take over than because she was happy about it.

There was an unspoken reason Alex wanted to bring Phoebe—this was her chance to check the drama group out and see what she was getting into. They were very different from her old crew, at least at first glance. Phoebe was the only person there with a visible disability. It made Alex uneasy, with the whiff of tokenism. Could she be a proper part of it, or was she just there to tick a diversity box? She folded her arms and sank lower in her seat. She would see.

The director had greeted Phoebe like an old friend he hadn't seen in years and was overly delighted to see. It probably wasn't about her sister—he had the classic flamboyant theatre-gay vibe. Not that she was complaining. It was a definite plus compared to the other common option of creepy, old cishet guy. At least she wouldn't have to worry about him treating Phoebe badly in that respect.

"Okay, listen up, everyone. We're going to be trying you out in the particular roles that I hope you've been practising."

He gave a dramatic pause, at which there was a chorus of confirmation. So it hadn't just been Phoebe who'd been given the chance to rehearse beforehand.

"We're going to do something a little different tonight, mix things up a bit by mixing you up." The director added a mixing mime for emphasis.

From the look on the ensemble actors' faces, they had no more idea than Alex what he meant. Phoebe seemed unbothered, though, and was watching him with that eager glint in her eye. It was good to see she'd got her spark back in time for the audition. After their parents' visit, she'd seemed cowed, more like before. As far as both she and Rebecca had reported, it had all been fine, but her mood said otherwise. To be fair, she had to remember Phoebe's emo side—she could act like it was the end of the world, but she might have just split a nail.

"I want to try you out in different combinations to see who's got that chemistry. You can act, but can you act together? We need to believe you're a team who will stand by each other no matter what!"

He made it sound like they were going to play the X-Men, not a bunch of nuns. Alex bit her lip and tried to look serious. This was important to Phoebe. And if she could find a place here, surely it was better than some day centre full of people kept hidden away from the outside world. It might be best the others didn't share her disadvantages…as long as they didn't take advantage of them.

The woman next to Phoebe had linked her arm through hers and was whispering something in her ear. Phoebe looked like she was trying to hold in a fit of giggles. Had she already teamed up with the rebel of the group? Alex didn't know how Phoebe managed to bond with people so quickly. It took her much longer to get a feel for someone and trust them enough to let them get close. Was Phoebe too trusting? But she wasn't some innocent child, even if their parents had tried to keep her that way.

The wannabes were split into small groups to practise before they got into the auditions for real. It started to dawn on Alex that this wasn't going to be quick. She'd figured it'd just be a matter of bringing her in for a quick reading, which was part of why she'd agreed to come. The hard plastic seat was already starting to bite—there was no way she could sit there all evening without her muscles cramping and setting off her damaged nerves. Maybe she could slope off without Phoebe being bothered, she seemed in the zone. It looked like all their practice hadn't been for nothing. She was shining, though it was hard for Alex to know how good she was given her own bias. And she wasn't exactly a theatre critic.

While she'd been focused on Phoebe, she'd failed to notice the director creeping up on her. By the time she spotted him homing in, she'd missed her chance to escape.

"Hi! We didn't get the chance to be properly introduced earlier. I'm Sebastian."

He held out his hand, and she had no choice but to take it.

"Alex. Phoebe's sister." She gave him a quick air kiss on either cheek, the official greeting on the scene she'd come out on. *Yep, I am one of you.*

"I don't believe I've seen you around. Are you new in town too?"

Alex paused, not wanting to get too friendly, otherwise before she knew it, she'd be made part of the crew and be lugging props around backstage. "Yeah, I came with Phoebe."

"Of course. I'm so glad Rebecca told her about our little group. I reckon she's going to fit right in."

She glanced back over at the rehearsing groups. Now they'd got down to it, he was right. Phoebe didn't stand out, at least not in a bad way.

"And thank you for bringing her back in." Sebastian gave her an over-friendly pat on the shoulder.

"No problem. I don't want to cramp her style, though, so I might take off and let her get on with it. I'll come back at the end to give her a lift home." Alex held up her keys to show her only role in all this.

"You're not in the way, don't worry. I'm sure we can find a way to put you to good use if you're bored."

Exactly what she was trying to avoid. This was Phoebe's place, not hers. Alex got to her feet and set her sights on the exit. "How long do you think you'll be?"

"I expect a good hour or two. Didn't bring a book, huh?"

"Nope, I'm afraid I came unprepared." She started to move towards the exit before he could talk her out of it. He seemed nice, but he was—hopefully—Phoebe's director, not to mention Rebecca's friend. Not someone for her to get pally with.

He seemed to have other ideas and followed her out the hall. "If you're looking for something to do around here, there's a surprising amount going on. Help yourself to flyers and check out some of our *culture*." The last word sounded like it deserved air quotes.

Alex relented and looked where he was gesturing. There was a stand full of colourful leaflets advertising various country attractions and travelling shows. "Thanks, I'll take a look."

She might as well check out the local sights and find something to do other than hang around Avebrook or the pool when she wasn't working. Apart from the poly meet, she'd not ventured far.

"Ooh, I meant to give this to Rebecca last time. It's her favourite show." Sebastian reached past Alex and pulled out one of the more lurid flyers and waved it under her nose.

It wasn't a show she'd seen, but she'd heard good things. At least, she thought she had. That stuff was more Willow's scene than hers. "Cool," she said, then had an idea and took the flyer from him. "I'll pass it on to her."

"Fabulous. It's definitely worth catching, if you fancy it yourself."

Maybe she would. She folded the leaflet carefully and slid it into the back pocket of her jeans. "I'll have a look. See you later."

Making a swift turn, she managed to get past him and out of the building. She would look at the other options later when there was no one breathing down her neck.

As she strolled around the neighbourhood, the paper in her pocket felt like it was burning a hole. Maybe she wouldn't just give it to Rebecca—maybe she'd invite her to go with her. She and Phoebe owed her a proper thank you. And it would give her and Rebecca a chance to enjoy themselves together without anyone who might question their connection watching.

When she returned, having walked as long as she could risk, the auditions seemed to be in full swing. There were three actors including Phoebe holding their own in front of the rest. A fourth seemed less with the programme. Sebastian switched them for someone else as Alex took her seat.

On her way back in, she'd grabbed a few flyers and she browsed them half-heartedly as the scene rolled on. When they finished, Sebastian called on another group but kept Phoebe on. He did the same thing the next time. Was he just giving the new woman a thorough test run? You couldn't blame him, and Phoebe seemed to be taking full advantage of the opportunity. Okay, so she was biased, but there was no question that her sister shone.

There was no denying what the others had pointed out—this was where Phoebe belonged. Unlike her, Phoebe had never had the option of going unnoticed, but thankfully she had never wanted to. The group seemed to welcome her too, without any bitchy competitiveness. They were giving Phoebe a real chance, and Alex wouldn't stand in her way.

She put down the leaflets and tried to focus on the performances. Most of the actors were significantly older than Phoebe, which might mean she didn't have too much competition. She could clearly play the part, but they could decide someone with a proven track record was a better bet. It was always a risk taking on someone new.

Occasionally something would jab her in the butt as she shuffled in her seat, unable to stay still for long. The prodding edge reminded her of another possibility. Could she ask Rebecca out without it being a big deal? To anyone, including herself? Maybe she was ready to risk it with someone new.

❖

The text came as Rebecca was nearing the end of her shift.

We've made our decision, time to make the call to Phoebe. Is she home?

She'd asked Sebastian to notify her before calling, to check it was appropriate timing. Plus, she wanted to make sure she was there for Phoebe if it was bad news and to see the look on her face if it was good. Ideally she would've been told the result of Phoebe's audition in advance, so she could prepare, but Sebastian had drawn the line there. She had to concede, Phoebe did deserve to hear her news first.

After confirming with Sebastian, she raced to Phoebe's room. As she reached the door, she heard Phoebe's mobile ring, so in her haste only briefly knocked and let herself in.

Phoebe was standing with the phone in her hand, frowning at the screen.

"Aren't you going to answer that?" Had nerves got to her at last? Was it all too much?

"It's an unknown number," Phoebe said.

Rebecca let out a light laugh in relief. She wasn't having second thoughts, just avoiding spam callers. "It might be Sebastian."

Phoebe's frown lifted and was replaced with a glint in her eyes. She showed her the screen and the number flashing up on it. "Is it him?"

"I think so. Answer it—you can hang up if it isn't." Rebecca was bouncing on her toes and couldn't wait any longer. He might give up.

"Okay." Phoebe pressed *accept* and put the phone to her ear. She was close enough that Rebecca could hear the voice coming out of it. Which was handy, but should she be able to?

"Hi, is that Phoebe?"

"Yes."

"It's Sebastian, the Wynbury Players director."

"Hi, Sebastian." Phoebe gave Rebecca a thumbs up.

"Thank you for coming to audition for us, we were really impressed. You're a talented woman."

"Thank you."

"We want to offer you the part of Sister Mary Robert, the one you read for. We think you'll be perfect."

"Oh my God, really?" Phoebe started bouncing up and down and reached out for Rebecca with her free hand. Rebecca took it, and Phoebe squeezed hard.

"Really. It's a big part with a lot of lines to learn, and some solos of course. If you want to take some time to think about it, I can send you the full script—"

"I want to do it."

"That's a definite yes?"

"Yes. Defo, yes. I can't wait to start." She looked like she would happily run over right then.

"Fabulous. I'm looking forward to working with you. Rehearsals start next week, I'll email the schedule over. Do you have an email, or shall I send it to Rebecca?"

"I have my own, send it to me. I'll text you it."

"Brilliant, thanks, Phoebe. If you text me after we hang up, I'll email you all the info. I've got to call the rest of the cast now, but I'll speak to you soon."

"Thanks. See you soon." As soon as she hung up, she flung the phone on the bed and clasped Rebecca's arms. "I got the part!"

"Congratulations, you deserve it. You're going to be amazing!" She couldn't wait to see Phoebe up onstage in her starring role. There was no doubt she'd steal the show.

"I gotta text him my email, hang on."

It was the first time she'd been aware Phoebe used email, despite her openly using a smartphone. How much did she use the internet? It wasn't something they'd talked about, but she must be used to navigating an email account at least. And she'd used her smartphone to look at film choices, without any assistance. Was she on social media too? Did she know how to stay safe online? It was another thing to add to the ever-growing list of potential issues to address.

She waited for Phoebe to finish tapping out the message before speaking. It wasn't the time to discuss internet safety. "So, are you going to celebrate?"

"Ooh, yes. I'll see when Alex has finished work. Maybe she'll take me out somewhere."

"That sounds nice." Rebecca hoped Alex would welcome Phoebe's good news. After her initial reluctance, she did seem to have come on board. She'd even done a full one-eighty and thanked her for her help. A warm glow enveloped her as she remembered Alex's change of heart.

"First, I'm gonna call Willow. I promised I would as soon as I heard."

Of course. Unlike Alex, Willow had seemed genuinely delighted at Phoebe stepping back into performing. Rebecca suspected she'd had something to do with Alex's turnaround, or at least her biting her tongue over her objection to Phoebe's initial audition. "I'm sure she'll be proud of you."

"She will be." Phoebe was already staring back at her phone, bringing up the contact.

Rebecca slipped out of the room. Her initial joy at Phoebe's triumph had been replaced by a squeezing in her chest. She hadn't known what to make of Willow when they'd met, possibly because she didn't know what she was to her. She couldn't deny, at least to herself, that there had been some jealousy there. Maybe it was simply due to the way Phoebe obviously idolised her. She couldn't blame her—Willow was the gorgeous, glamorous lesbian she'd feared she might be. But she'd also been friendly and caring. Rebecca couldn't fault her. Then there was her relationship with Alex. Rebecca had never seen Alex so happy—she'd been practically glowing. That might have had something to do with what they'd been up to beforehand. They must have had a lot of catching up to do...She shut down that train of thought.

It was all good. Phoebe was happy, Alex was happy, and Willow seemed happy too. So why was Rebecca not? She'd never been someone to resent others' happiness. She never wanted to be like that.

She needed to sort her head out. Figuring out what Alex and

Willow were to her would be a start. There was the conversation she'd put off having after finding out Alex and Drew had been out together. It had been fizzing in the back of her head, that question of what their intentions were. It was time she asked.

There was no one else in the corridor, so she slid out her phone before she found an excuse to put it off again.

Hey, I don't suppose you're free tomorrow morning for a coffee before I start work? Or we could even do lunch?

Maybe it should've waited until the end of her shift, but there was a good chance she'd wimp out if she left it until then. She knew what she needed to do, and she needed to start before the anxiety that gnawed at her brain had the chance to bully her out of it. She released the top button of her shirt and let out a long breath. She'd talk to Drew and then she'd know where they all stood.

I'm sure I can sneak out at some point. To what do I owe this unexpected pleasure?

The response brought up a ball of mixed emotions. Why did they have to ask that? What was so strange about asking to see them? It wasn't like they never saw each other midweek. Except she would usually give, and require, more notice.

There's something I wanted to talk to you about.

Just before pressing send, she added a second sentence.

Nothing to worry about x

She didn't want Drew thinking she was planning on breaking bad news.

Is it about Alex?

Rebecca stared at the message. She was right—there was something to discuss. There was no other explanation for why Drew would jump to Alex without any mention of her.

Yes.

It was all she could manage without asking questions she wanted answered in person. She needed to be able to seek reassurance in their eyes and in their arms.

Drew replied almost immediately.

Okay, I'll be there. Love you x

Her stomach churned and her eyes filled with unexplained tears.

I love you too x

She managed to tap out and send the message before running to the bathroom. She blasted the cold tap, scooping up the water with her shaking hands and splashing it on her face, over and over, desperately trying to cool the flow of adrenaline racing through her.

Did she really want to know? Could she cope with knowing? She'd always been careful to keep the different parts of her life separate, and now it felt like everything was crashing together in a way she had never anticipated. She wished she could pull it all apart again, put everyone back in their places, safe behind their lines.

She wished Alex had never come into her world, even as she wished she would find a place in it. Her head was full of contradictions. Nothing made sense.

But it would soon. She would talk to Drew the next day. She just needed to hold on until then. And stop being so melodramatic. Phoebe's theatrical tendencies must be rubbing off on her. Whatever was going on, it didn't need to be life-altering. So what if Drew had a new lover? It wasn't like she hadn't been aware of the possibility. And so what if it was the woman who'd been making her stomach flip since the moment they met?

Once she'd calmed her shaking system enough to breathe easy, she texted back and asked them to meet her as early as possible. It was time to face the truth of her situation.

❖

Alex's phone rang the minute she finished her shift, as if someone had been waiting for that moment. She was still removing her stuff from her locker but picked up as soon as she saw the name flashing on the screen.

"I got the part!" Phoebe didn't even say hello before announcing her news.

"Brilliant! Well done, Bee. I knew you would after seeing you run rings round the others at the audition." Alex didn't have to pretend to be happy about it—she could imagine Phoebe's delighted grin. And it was a relief she wasn't calling with bad news.

"I want to go celebrate!" Phoebe's excited voice crackled down the phone.

"Of course. What do you want to do?" Alex balanced her phone on her shoulder as she pulled her jacket out of her locker and attempted to shrug it on. "Wanna go eat somewhere?"

"Yes, please. And maybe we can go bowling."

"Sure, whatever you fancy. Shall I come straight over and get you?" It wasn't like she had any other plans.

"Yep, I'm starving."

"No problem. See you soon." She would make a quick pit stop to pick up a cake. It was tempting to grab a bottle too, but the home might have rules on alcohol, and she'd be driving. It would be worth checking the rules, so they would know if they were breaking them and could take care not to involve a certain someone who might not approve.

The front door was opened by the dark-haired young woman with an Eastern European accent. She was the best option, as she didn't seem to give off any of the hostility of the other staff. Unfortunately, Alex could never remember her name, if she'd ever been told it, and it seemed too late to ask. Especially as she knew hers.

"Hi Alex, come in! Ooh, what have you brought? You must be celebrating—Phoebe told me her great news."

She was unwaveringly chatty and friendly. It was impressive persistence, given the way Alex had only silently glared at her during their early encounters.

"Yep, she's stoked. I figure she's earned this." She opened the white box to reveal a chocolate mountain of sponge, icing, and chocolate curls on top.

"It looks delicious. Do not eat it all and make yourselves sick!"

"I'll tell her to save you a piece." Alex gave the woman a wink as she passed her and earned a giggle in response. There was a big rock on her ring finger that signalled an upcoming marriage, probably of the hetero-mono variety, but she seemed to enjoy Alex's mild flirting. She was careful not to take it too far, which meant resisting trying to read the tiny writing on her name badge that dangled on a lanyard right over her breasts in case her stare was misinterpreted. It was good to have more than one ally in the place. Hopefully Phoebe did know her name.

There were a few voices coming from Phoebe's room and an undercurrent of one of her more upbeat albums. Alex knocked and held the cake box open in front of her. "Congrat—"

It wasn't Phoebe who opened the door.

"Thank you. We did work hard." Rebecca smiled and stepped aside so Alex could get past her.

"She couldn't have done it without you," Alex said, gulping down the sight of Rebecca in a fluffy jumper that made you want to reach out and stroke her. She seemed to be getting cuter the longer she knew her, and her features seemed softer and warmer too. Due to the size of the box in her arms, she couldn't help brush up against her as she passed. She deliberately looked ahead at Phoebe, rather than where their bodies met. The last thing they needed was for Phoebe to spot something flickering between them.

"Yum! Thanks, sis!" Phoebe jumped up to relieve her of her chocolatey load.

"No snarfing it all before dinner."

"I'm gonna share," Phoebe said, gesturing to Rebecca and Faye, who was sitting in one of the armchairs.

"I'll get some plates." Faye also jumped up and headed out before there could be any other objections.

"So, where do you wanna go for dinner?" Alex offloaded the cake into Phoebe's outstretched arms.

Phoebe chewed her lip and looked to the door her friend had just left through. "Can Faye come?"

"I'm guessing she'll need someone with her." She looked at Rebecca, who nodded then looked at the floor. She didn't seem to be offering. Alex tried not to be disappointed—it was fair enough, it must be near the end of her shift again. "How about we just go tonight, and we can plan to go with her another time, when it's not so late."

Rebecca looked relieved at this suggestion. "That sounds like a good compromise. I'm sure we can book something in soon."

Phoebe didn't look so happy. "It feels mean leaving her behind."

"I know, Bee. You're a good friend." Alex sighed. Phoebe always wanted everyone to be happy. The problem was life didn't work that way. "How about a takeaway instead? Then she can join us."

"She'd like that. And I like takeaway. We can get lots of bits and share it."

Problem solved. Though she knew Phoebe's enthusiasm for sharing came from knowing that way she could order more. She liked to have a bit of everything. Alex was the same. *Why only sample one thing on the menu?* She nearly said it out loud but stopped herself in time as she realised Rebecca might not appreciate the insinuation at work. Not that anyone passing by was likely to guess what she was referring to or that Rebecca felt the same.

"As it's a special occasion, I'm sure it'll be okay." Rebecca piped up with her permission, not that anyone had asked for it.

Alex had forgotten about the no-meals-in-bedrooms rule. It was handy Rebecca was there and willing to vouch for them.

"I'll go tell Faye. We can have the cake for afters." Phoebe raced out before Alex could point out there was no need as she'd be back in a minute anyway and they'd still need the plates.

It did give her a moment alone with Rebecca, the first time since the audition. She took a deep breath, then attempted to look casual, leaning against the bookshelf.

"Sebastian meant to give you this. He said you're a fan." She produced the folded flyer from her back pocket. She'd been transferring it between jeans ever since, waiting for her chance.

"Oh yes, I love *Wicked*!" Rebecca's face lit up. "Have you seen it?"

"No, but I've heard good things and thought I might give it a try." Alex looked Rebecca in the eye. "Maybe we could go together?"

Rebecca glanced away, looking flustered and like she had no idea how to reply.

Was she worried about Alex asking her out at work? It didn't have to be a date. "I was thinking I could take you as a proper thank you. For all you've done for Phoebe." *And to make up for some of my arseholery.* She hoped that part went without saying, after her earlier apology.

"I…I don't think that would be appropriate." Rebecca looked down, her lips pursed.

"Oh." Had Alex completely misjudged their connection? Was Rebecca only interested in her as Phoebe's sister and didn't want to be around her from choice? It was the first time Alex had tried to arrange to see her—all their other meetings had been work related or unplanned. She needed to backtrack, save some face. "Of course, I get it."

She wasn't sure she did, but she wasn't gonna push her. What was it Willow said? *She's clearly not a path to happiness for you.* Maybe it was best they didn't spend any extra time together.

"I better go. I have paperwork to do before I can go home." Rebecca started to edge towards the door, still not looking at her, her hand agitating the neck of her jumper.

Alex thrust the flyer out towards her. "Here. You can go with someone else." Someone more *appropriate*.

Rebecca took it from her outstretched hand, as if being careful to make sure their fingers didn't make contact. "Thanks," she mumbled.

"Or you could go by yourself," Alex said, in case her earlier comment had sounded resentful. It made no difference to her who Rebecca went with if it wasn't her.

"So could you." Rebecca finally looked at her shyly, then away again as if she regretted it, and opened the door.

Had that been some kind of invitation?

"Faye's in!" Phoebe announced as she swept past Rebecca, who still had her hand on the open door.

After holding it open to allow Faye back in, who was carrying a large tray with a stack of crockery and cutlery, Rebecca slipped out of the room.

"Are you going, Becca?" Phoebe said before she disappeared out of sight.

"Yes, I'm afraid I have to. You can save me some cake. Well done again, I'm so proud of you." She spoke quickly and didn't leave room for anyone to argue before shutting the door behind her.

Neither Phoebe nor Faye seemed bothered by her departure. "So, where are we gonna order from?" Phoebe said.

"You choose." Alex's mind was not on food. She was trying to figure out what Rebecca had meant. What did she want her to do? Did she want them both to go alone to the theatre and then pretend they'd randomly bumped into each other?

She pushed away from the shelves and tried to push it from her mind. It didn't matter. She wasn't up for playing those kinds of games.

CHAPTER THIRTEEN

Rebecca fiddled with her napkin, wiping up the dribble from the teapot that she'd sprinkled over the table with her shaking hands, and tried to hold on to the fact that Drew wasn't late, she was just ridiculously early.

She'd not got much sleep the night before but must have had some as she remembered waking up several times. The image of the hurt on Alex's face when she'd rejected her haunted her. But how could she have said yes? It *was* inappropriate, though maybe she could've put it in a kinder way. And been clearer in the moments that they'd touched, suppressing her body's reckless responses, that nothing could happen between them. Even if they weren't connected through work, she could never go out with someone one of her partners was with or even interested in getting with. It was just asking for conflict, and things were complicated enough. Besides, she was closed and Drew was open, so it made sense to steer Alex in that direction.

If that's what they both wanted, of course. Alex hadn't mentioned Drew apart from that one time, and Drew hadn't mentioned Alex at all until she'd asked to talk. That didn't necessarily mean anything, as Rebecca didn't need to be involved at the start of their courtship. She'd figured out long ago that it was better if her partners waited until they were in a relationship before introducing a new partner to her, otherwise her imagination went into overdrive. She didn't need to know until she needed to know. Drew had dated around a lot more than her, and she didn't want to get attached to a new metamour until she knew they were serious. She liked to spend time with her partners' other partners, to know they were okay around each other and could all sit down together and talk things out if they needed to, or at the least support each other in an emergency. There should be no arguments about who held whose hand at the side of a hospital bed.

Would Alex ever be up for that, for hanging out as metamours? Rebecca realised she knew very little about her personal life, including how she did poly, apart from her long-term relationship with Willow. Had Alex asking her out been about Drew, about wanting to build bridges as she got closer to them? That would be a good sign. She tried to ignore the uncomfortable feeling in her chest.

Of course, there was another option. Alex could have been telling the whole truth when she said it was to thank her for helping Phoebe. Had she acted churlishly? Alex had offered her an olive branch, for whatever reason.

Where was Drew? She checked her phone. They were actually late now, albeit by one minute. They didn't usually keep her waiting. Were they nervous about telling her what was going on? No, they weren't like that—unlike her, they were never one for holding back and seemed to have no trouble telling her what was what.

She poured another cup of tea on top of the dregs of her last one, this time succeeding in slopping it into the saucer. At least she wasn't making a mess of the table for the barista to clean up. They were likely as underpaid and undervalued as people in her own profession.

A hand landed on her shoulder, making her jump and spill her tea again. At this rate very little of the much-needed caffeine would make it into her mouth.

"Hey, gorgeous." Drew appeared not to notice and drew her up into a tight squeeze.

"Hi." She breathed in their presence, then turned her head to kiss them before drawing them down into the seat next to her. She rested her head on their shoulder, still holding their hand. Would they get bored of her if they had someone as charismatic as Alex? Would they still think she was gorgeous when standing next to her?

"I'm afraid, my love, I haven't got my caffeine yet, so don't get too comfy. Do you want a top-up?"

"No, thanks." Rebecca nuzzled their shoulder and they put an arm around her. She didn't mean to be clingy, but her insecurities seemed to be getting the better of her. Sometimes she needed to let herself not be strong and give in to the need to be held. As Drew often reminded her, she was only human.

"I'll be right back, okay?"

"Don't be long." She snuggled in for another squeeze before she had to let go of them. Words could only give her so much comfort. The warmth of their embrace was another level.

While she waited for them to return, she focused on cleaning up the spilt tea, more for something to do than out of real need, as it was safely contained within the chintzy sloped saucer. It would cling to the bottom of the cup though, ready to drip down her white top if she wasn't careful. She needed more napkins. The holder across from her was empty, so she opened her bag to grab the pack of pocket tissues she always carried. She drew out a single folded sheet, then tucked them back in her bag, her hand brushing a bit of paper as she did. She pulled out the leaflet and unfolded it. The creases were almost tears from where she'd folded and unfolded it as she'd sat at home alone that morning after Ishani left for work. In the end she'd left early, before she tore it and her mind into tatters.

"Ooh, is *Wicked* coming here?" Drew plonked their tray next to hers.

"Yeah, in a couple of months." Rebecca continued to stare at the leaflet, at the mischievous smile on the face in the centre that made her think of the person who gave it to her. Who they were there to discuss.

"Cool. Isn't it your favourite show? Have you got tickets?"

"Yes. I mean, yes it's my favourite. No, I haven't got tickets." Unless Alex had already bought them. She might be cocky at times, but would she be that presumptuous?

"Well, if you need someone to go with, I'd be up for it. As long as you don't drag me to the ballet again." They fake snored. Rebecca didn't respond. "Hey, you okay, sweetheart?"

They put an arm around her and drew her back in. The leaflet fell from her hands into their lap as she let herself sink into the half hug.

"Yes. I'm just…confused." She'd chosen a sofa tucked into the back corner of the shop that was secluded enough to not worry about making anyone too uncomfortable or attracting prying eyes. Maybe she should've invited them to hers, but there were too many ways to get distracted there and not actually talk, which—as much as she didn't want to—she needed to.

"About Alex?"

Rebecca nodded into their shoulder. Drew gently nudged her upright, so she was facing them.

"I want to support you, my love, but you're gonna have to tell me what's going on." They looked her in the eye. "Did something happen between you two?"

Rebecca looked down, not sure where to start. Did that mean they weren't involved with Alex themself, or did they just want her to go first?

"It won't bother me if it did. You're the one who said you didn't want any more relationships, but you've got the right to change your mind."

Rebecca took a sip of tea to revive her suddenly dry throat. It didn't sound like Drew was after Alex—it sounded like permission for her to be. That wasn't what she'd called them there for, was it? "I haven't changed my mind. I don't want anything to change."

"There are some things even you can't control, though. Like when you meet someone and you've got that spark." They paused and nudged her gently with their elbow. "Which you two clearly do."

Was it really that obvious? Rebecca flushed. Had people at work noticed too? Oh God. "Maybe we do, but that doesn't mean we have to act on it."

Admitting that didn't have to change things. They weren't hormonal teenagers. They could control themselves and make more rational decisions. Hopefully.

"No, it doesn't. But you could." Drew lifted their cup, and the two of them sat silently for a moment, sipping their drinks, letting that sink in.

It was pretty clear what Drew was anticipating, but she still felt the need to check just in case. "Um, so you're not interested in Alex. For yourself? Just, she said you'd met up and I didn't know…"

Drew laughed, a softer, kinder laugh than their usual hoot. "Is that what you were worried about? That you'd be treading on my toes?"

Rebecca nodded sheepishly. It wasn't everything by any means, but it was part of it. She couldn't imagine dating the same person, separately, waiting for it to go wrong with one of them and make it unbearably awkward for everyone.

"I just invited her for a friendly cuppa as she's new in town and didn't know anyone."

Of course they did. She knew it was normal for them, part of their support for the community. Why had she let her mind run away with her? Maybe because it would've been simpler if it was Drew that Alex was interested in. If she was honest, she'd known that wasn't the case.

"Besides, it was clear you two were into each other from the start. She only had eyes for you at the meet. I wouldn't want to get between you."

Rebecca shifted in her seat. "I was the only person she knew there." And she had apologies to make.

"Oh, come on!" Drew laughed at full volume this time.

Rebecca remembered how Ishani had talked about it afterwards, obviously seeing the same thing. She ducked her head, hiding her face and a traitorous smile in Drew's shoulder.

"You might not be able to see how anyone could want you, but the rest of us can." They lowered their voice and took on a gentler tone, knowing the truth of it from their years with her and their own tentative start as a couple.

Rebecca couldn't believe they'd wanted her either, that they'd pick her out of the crowd. She rested her head back on their shoulder and sat silently for a moment, letting it all finally sink in.

When she eventually spoke, she did so quietly, without lifting her head. "It's not just that. I work with her, with her sister. It's a conflict of interest. And I really wasn't wanting anyone else. I love our family as it is."

"I know you didn't see this coming. But we're here now, whether you wanted it before or not. I don't know about the work part, but it's not like she's in your care herself, so surely it's not strictly forbidden. It's not like you're taking advantage of her."

It was hard to imagine anyone being able to take advantage of Alex. Rebecca picked up the flyer which had slid off Drew's lap onto the sofa. "She asked me to this."

"A date? Good on her."

Rebecca frowned. Had they put her up to it?

"What? Someone had to make the first move, and no offense, my love, but she could've turned to stone waiting for you to." Drew raised an eyebrow, daring her to disagree.

"I…" There was no point arguing, it was true. "I turned her down."

"Shit." Drew didn't seem to know what else to say. They looked almost as disappointed as Alex had. "Well, it is your choice. As long as that's what you really want."

"What if it isn't?"

It had felt wrong saying no, even as she was wrapped up in her worries about Alex and Drew. It didn't just hurt Alex's feelings, it hurt her own. It was time to own up to the fact that she wanted to say yes. She wanted Alex.

"Then you best figure it all out and tell her. Sooner rather than later—she won't hang around forever."

Which was yet another problem. Alex had been clear she wouldn't be sticking around, and Rebecca wasn't sure she could cope with a time-limited or long-distance relationship, especially since she'd got used to Alex being around so much.

"You're right. I just wish it was simpler and I knew what the right thing was to do."

"Since when were our relationships ever simple? Or any relationships, 'cause let's be clear, our mono friends have plenty of issues of their own. That doesn't mean the relationships aren't right." There was a challenge in Drew's words and tone, as if they expected an argument.

Except she could never argue with that. Relationships were complicated. People were complicated. When she'd first dipped her toe into ethical non-monogamy, she'd taken a lot of time and done a lot of research only to reach the conclusion there was no sure way. It wasn't the satisfactory one she'd been hoping for. She stirred her tea and tried to see her way through the swirling liquid.

They were jumping ahead of themselves. "It wasn't a date. When she asked me, it wasn't for a date. She said it was a thank you."

"And a chance to get to know each other better?" Drew added. "I wish I could tell you what to do, and trust me, I *really* want to tell you, but you need to figure it out, and I'm not the person you should be talking to."

"Who should I talk to?" Rebecca said. They were right—a partner was not the appropriate person to discuss a potential new partner with, but who else could she go to? Maybe she should've taken Sebastian up on his offer.

"The woman herself, of course." Drew squeezed her to them again. "Talk to Alex."

"That's one idea," Rebecca mumbled.

"But what, that would be too obvious? She likes you, and I reckon she'd much rather you talk to her than carry on rejecting her without explanation."

"What makes you think I didn't explain?"

Drew didn't justify that with a response, except for a knowing look.

"I said it was *inappropriate*."

They laughed. "That could cover a whole host of sins, mind."

What had Alex thought it meant? Surely, considering she was at work at the time, it was obvious. Surely, Alex could see how much her work meant to her? She hoped so anyway. She hoped Alex hadn't taken it as an excuse and thought she didn't want her. Because no matter how hard she tried, she couldn't stop wanting her.

❖

She's made a mistake and she knows it. Leastways, hold on x

Alex glanced at Drew's message. For about the twentieth time. What exactly had Rebecca said to them?

Assuming it was about Rebecca. Did she get her partners involved in deciding who she went out with? That did not sit right with Alex. She'd been enjoying getting to know Drew, but what if it really was just some kind of vetting process? She liked them, but if she got with Rebecca, she didn't want them involved. That was how things got messy and you ended up being pushed around, your needs coming below the group's wants. If she and Rebecca were going to get together, that was for the two of them to decide.

"Wake up, mate," the forklift driver yelled as he came rolling towards her.

She shifted out of his path before she ended up on top of his pile. The message from Drew had come three days before, and she still couldn't figure out how to reply without sounding off. Maybe leaving it at nothing was the clearest signal she could send and less rude than telling them directly to butt out. There was a slight temptation to ask them what exactly Rebecca had said, and to point out she hadn't asked her on an actual date so hadn't really been rejected. There was no need to make a big thing of it.

"Got any plans after work?"

"Huh?" Alex looked up to see another workmate, Grant—was that his name?—leaning against the shelves a few feet away.

"A few of us are going to the pub after if you want to come with." It wasn't the first time he'd made the offer. She'd been there for a couple of months, and the others had started to make more moves to include her in their social plans.

"Sorry, I said I'd go see my sister." She did appreciate them asking but had no need to get too pally. They would stop asking after a while and move on to treating her with suspicion if she didn't ever mix with them, but it wasn't like she was planning on sticking around long enough for that to matter.

Since getting her part in the local musical, Phoebe had put her to work rehearsing. It seemed a bit overboard, but it kept Phoebe happy and it was kinda fun. Especially when a certain staff member joined them, who had a surprising flair for it, as long as Phoebe didn't try to make her act as well as read. It might take Phoebe more time and effort to learn her part than other people, but the amount she was putting in, surely she'd have no trouble keeping up. Alex just hoped once rehearsals got serious, she'd be let off the hook sometimes.

"Another time, then." Grant pushed off from the shelf and slouched away. "You know, my offer still stands. Just let me know if you're interested."

"I'm still not, but will do." She knew he didn't mean to push her so tried to keep any defensiveness out of her voice. The guys at work had accepted her pretty quickly, with no real comment on her obvious queerness except to invite her into banter about famous women they wanted. They'd done it slyly at first, as if testing her, and despite her lack of interest in the kind of women they ogled, she'd joined in to show that they'd clocked her right. It was far better than them trying it on with her or quizzing her about her sex life.

She glanced back at her phone before sliding it in her pocket. Only a couple more hours, then she was free. Her stomach grumbled, even though she'd filled up in the canteen on her break and grabbed a couple of bits to munch before she got to the home. Living out of the van was getting old, and she'd started to long for a kitchen, not just a shower. Relying on the basic work canteen was not satisfying. The little camping stove she used to make coffee and noodles wasn't up to anything more. Maybe it was time she went back to the city.

It was only a couple of hours' drive, but these days she struggled even to do that distance without her beat-up limbs playing her up too badly. There was no way she could manage to drive there and back in one day to visit. She'd miss Phoebe, but her sister seemed to need her a lot less and had plenty of other support. Though there were their parents to keep an eye on. If she left, would they swoop back in and bully Phoebe into giving up the life she was starting to build? Rebecca hadn't had anything to say about them after the visit. Did she get the risk there?

Which brought her back to Rebecca and whatever was going on there. How had she managed to get herself mixed up with someone like her? Sure, she was cute and caring, but she was also rigid and closed off. It was clear there wasn't space for Alex in her life. She needed to let that fantasy go, maybe give some of the women she'd been eyeing up on OkCupid a go, women who wanted to meet someone new and who weren't involved in controlling setups that she could never consent to.

Not any more, she'd been burned enough times. Once you've been vetoed, you don't forget the pain in a hurry. It was hard enough when someone broke it off with you for their own reasons, but when it was on someone else's orders, it left you feeling like you never mattered. Drew might seem cool with her, but you could never be sure what was going on behind closed doors until you were in too deep. Besides, Drew was Rebecca's secondary—it wasn't them she'd have to worry about. They were also at risk of being cast aside.

As had become standard, Faye was with Phoebe when Alex arrived at the home three hours later. The two of them had built on their early connection and become close friends, spending most of their time at Avebrook together from what Alex could tell. She couldn't blame them—it seemed they'd found an escape from the bleakness in each other. When she knocked, laughter and frantic shushing noises could be heard before the door was unlocked.

"It's just Alex," Faye told Phoebe over her shoulder, as she opened the door.

"Hey, sis," Phoebe said, retrieving a sheet of paper that looked like it had been hastily stuffed back in its envelope.

"Hey. What you got there?" Alex nodded at what had clearly been their focus when she'd arrived.

"It's for you. From Becca."

Phoebe and Faye exchanged a look that spelled trouble.

"And you opened it?" Alex snatched the envelope from her outstretched hand.

Phoebe shifted guiltily in her seat. "No."

Alex stared her out.

"Yes. But I thought it was about me."

It was a fair guess, and why shouldn't Phoebe read anything that was written about her, but maybe not the real reason. Either way, Alex couldn't argue without telling her more than she needed to know. Usually she'd have no issue with mentioning someone she was interested in to her sister, although she didn't tend to introduce new partners in case Phoebe got too attached, but her promise to Rebecca meant she'd kept her mouth shut. Plus, she did not need Phoebe getting involved. Things were complicated enough as it was.

She opened the letter and gave it a quick once over, trying to keep her face blank due to her audience. It was only short and not too explicit for anyone who didn't know about them.

> Hi Alex,
>   I'm sorry if I seemed ungrateful the other day, it was a kind offer. You just took me by surprise when my mind was already full and confused.
>   I would like to go, but I think it would be a good idea if we talked first.

She'd given her mobile number, so there was no need to write back or try to catch her alone at work. It probably was a good idea for them to lay their cards on the table. Rebecca wasn't the only one who was confused—the mixed signals from her were getting to be too much.

Alex looked up to see Phoebe and Faye staring right at her from the matching chairs.

"Did you read it too?" Alex waved it in Faye's direction. It was bad enough Phoebe obviously had.

"I can't read."

Crap. She'd forgotten that. It was one of the reasons she'd been pulled in to run lines with Phoebe.

"Sorry, I meant…" How should she put it? She knew Phoebe understood about keeping these kinds of things on the down-low but had no idea about Faye.

"I read it to her," Phoebe said.

"Phoebe!"

"She won't tell anyone, will you, Faye?" Phoebe nudged her friend with her foot.

"Nope, no one. So, did you ask Rebecca out? Did you know she has a girlfriend already?" Faye leaned forward in her chair, her voice bubbling with the thrill of juicy gossip.

Alex groaned. She did not need this.

"I told you, she's poly. They can have more than one partner at the same time, as long as everyone is cool with it." Phoebe turned to Alex, "Is Becca poly too?"

Rebecca was gonna kill her. But it was Rebecca's own fault for leaving the note with Phoebe. She should've guessed this might happen.

"Not for me to say, Bee." She walked over and perched on the edge of the bed, careful to lower her voice. "Remember, she works here, so we should be quiet about it."

"It's a secret? That's okay, we understand, don't we, Faye?"

"Yeah, we won't say anything to anyone else. I wouldn't wanna get Becca into trouble." Faye sounded like she meant it. She probably didn't want to risk losing her from the home.

"It's not that she's doing anything wrong." She needed them to be clear that it wasn't their relationships that were the problem. "Sometimes it's just best to keep your private life private, in places like this."

She had witnessed how things got blown up when care staff stuck their noses into people's personal relationships and had already warned Phoebe to try not to let them interfere.

"We know," Phoebe said.

"Yeah, we know. I'll never tell." Faye looked at Phoebe as she made her promise.

"Anyway, I didn't ask her out. Not like that."

Phoebe laughed.

"I didn't!"

"Okay, I believe you." The grin on her face said otherwise. At least she didn't seem upset about it.

Alex really did need to talk to Rebecca now, before things got any more out of hand. She needed to make sure nobody, not Phoebe or Drew, got the wrong impression. Which meant they'd have to figure out what was right.

CHAPTER FOURTEEN

Y ou said it wrong!"
        Rebecca looked up to see Phoebe scowling at her, hand on hip.

"Sorry, I'm tired."

She was trying to focus on the script in her hands, but her mind kept wandering to the letter she'd left there three days ago.

"Okay, we can take a break. Do you need a coffee?"

"No, thank you."

Caffeine was not a good idea, given her brain was already buzzing. She needed something that would slow it down, not speed it up more. She should probably practice some mindfulness instead—it did help, when she found the time to do it, which wasn't nearly as often as she should. It ended up being another thing on her to-do list, near the bottom. And life kept happening, so she hardly ever got that far.

Phoebe's phone pinged, providing a welcome distraction. When she checked the message, a warm glow bloomed in her cheeks and a soft smile crept across her lips.

"More good news?" Rebecca couldn't contain her curiosity. Was it the message she'd read that had brought on that smile, or the person who sent it?

"It's nothing." Phoebe slid the phone back in her pocket. "If you need to go, that's okay. I can practice by myself."

The sudden dismissal was suspicious. Who was Phoebe texting that she didn't want to respond to in front of her? Could it be her sister, who still hadn't contacted Rebecca? No, Phoebe wasn't likely to avoid replying to her just because she was there. *Focus, it's not about you.*

The man in the red T-shirt surfaced hazily in her mind. She hadn't got round to asking, and Phoebe had never mentioned him. It could still be worth checking up on.

"I've been meaning to ask, how are you getting on with the others at the day centre? Have you made any friends there?"

"A couple." Phoebe shrugged and didn't meet Rebecca's eye.

If she wasn't going to offer up the information, Rebecca would have to ask directly. "What about Callum?" Was that his name?

"What about him?" Phoebe stiffened and narrowed her eyes, as if suspecting a trap.

Standing there on guard, a family resemblance was striking. Rebecca was knocked off balance. Alex hadn't looked at her like that in weeks, let alone her more open little sister.

"I was just wondering how you were getting on with him." Rebecca tugged at the bottom of her shirt, which had crumpled up while she sat in the armchair.

"Why?"

Maybe she'd hit a sore spot and they weren't getting on any more. Or she'd overestimated their interest in each other. It was just one look she'd witnessed, months before. Phoebe probably had no clue why she was suddenly asking.

Best switch to a different, less confrontational approach. "I was just wondering. He seems like a nice guy." *And looked like he was totally into you.*

Phoebe shrugged.

She clearly wasn't going to get anywhere if there was anywhere to get. There was another ping of Phoebe's phone, and they stared at each other.

Rebecca was the one to break eye contact. "I'll…I'll be getting off, then. You know how to find me if you need me."

"Yep. Bye." Phoebe had pulled out her phone again and didn't look up when Rebecca left the room.

Why had she turned so cold on her? It was like she was channelling her sister at her worst. There was an obvious explanation. Alex could've told her about Rebecca's rejection, and now she was upset with her on her sister's behalf. It had been risky leaving the note with Phoebe, but she didn't know when or if she'd see Alex again, given Alex could easily avoid her if she wanted to. It had felt inappropriate to involve Phoebe, but considering how close she was to her sister, she might well be involved anyway.

Had they looked at her note together, laughed at her confusion? Had Alex already dismissed it as a mistake, wishing she'd never asked her? Drew was right—she couldn't expect her to hang around waiting for her to figure it all out. Had she already waited too long? She couldn't imagine Alex putting herself in a position where she could get rejected a second time.

And the truth was, she still wasn't sure what she wanted or what was possible. She couldn't deny she wanted Alex, but that still didn't mean anything could happen between them. It wasn't certain what Alex wanted either, despite others' claims that it was perfectly obvious.

Her pocket vibrated. She looked around to check if there was anyone else present before she took a peek. The text message was from an unknown number. Could it be—?

"Hey, Becca!"

There went her chance to find out. She tucked the phone back out of sight. She shouldn't really have it on her at all, unless she was out with a resident, though there were no strict rules about it. Even she'd ended up following the crowd on that one, at least partly because it would've meant leaving it in the office where anyone could get to it otherwise. Even if they weren't intending to snoop, what if she forgot to put it on silent and another staff member fished it out and saw something she didn't want them to? The idea of someone like Marie getting their hands on her personal messages didn't bear thinking about.

"Hi, Faye, how are you?" Rebecca forced herself to focus on the person in front of her.

"I'm good. Are you gonna do my bath?"

Reading about wizards to Faye could be exactly what she needed. She'd read the series so many times that even in her present distracted state she should be able to manage it and be magicked away from her personal problems. "Yes, no problem."

"Great. And guess what? I've got us a different book to read." Faye ducked back into her bedroom.

Rebecca was left with her mouth open. Where had that come from? Why was Faye messing with their routine when she needed it most? *Because it's not about you.* Faye was bound to get bored eventually, it was no big deal. Or so she attempted to convince herself as her palms started to prickle and itch. Did everything have to change at once?

It was soon explained. Faye returned brandishing her new choice and handed it to Rebecca. She stifled a groan. This must be Phoebe's fault. An angsty teenage love story was *not* what she needed, even with a supernatural bent. At least the others might think it was a step up—it wasn't suitable for children from what she'd heard.

"Have you read it?"

No, but Ishani had and had not made her want to. She'd declared it a perfect example of the false choice presented in so many books and films. The heroine clearly loved both guys, whether she should have or not. Of course, if she wasn't made to choose, there would be a lot less of a story there, something Ishani said would've been a good thing.

"No, not yet." Rebecca forced a smile and tried to sound like she wasn't dreading the prospect.

"Cool. We can read it for the first time together." Faye's smile seemed a lot more genuine than her own.

Rebecca hoped it would be their first and last time. But if it made Faye happy…Maybe it wouldn't be as bad as Ishani had made out. Despite her complaints, she had read the whole series. "What time do you want to have it?"

On the plus side, Phoebe's dismissal and Faye requesting her assistance that early on in her shift meant she might actually get to leave on time.

"I don't mind, I'm not doing anything today, and I can't wait to start. Phoebe says it's really good." Faye took the book back from Rebecca and studied the cover.

"In that case, give me twenty minutes and I'll be with you."

She was tired and due a break, though she rarely took one. They didn't even have to give her one by law, as they were looking after people who needed 24-7 care, something Drew took great issue with. The problem was, if someone only had one carer, there was no one to cover breaks, and they couldn't just abandon their charge. Other times Drew was right—it was just companies taking advantage of low-paid workers. The home, though not part of some wealthy chain, did fall more into the second category.

Most of the staff got round it by taking very regular smoking breaks, Rebecca being in the minority that didn't. Some fresh air in the courtyard would be nice, if the likelihood of being interrupted wasn't so high. She could go for a walk, but she wasn't good at texting and walking at the same time. She decided to compromise and sit in her car with the windows rolled down.

When she told Luisa where she was going in case she was needed, Luisa looked concerned. Was it really that rare for her to take a break? She'd had to assure her everything was okay, she was just tired and needed a little quiet time. She managed to get out without any further questioning, just a stern instruction to look after herself.

The leather seat was cool and softened by years of use. With regular maintenance her car had been running smoothly for years, and hopefully it would continue for many more. She had no desire to trade it in for a newer, flashier model. It was comfortable and perfectly reliable.

Once she was settled, she finally retrieved her phone and opened the message.

Hey Rebecca, this is Alex.

Her heart beat a little faster. She'd told herself it might be a false alarm and just some marketing text, but it really was her.

I got your note. You're probably right, it'd be good to talk more, where we're not having to watch what we say.

That was all. It was ambiguous, but then so was the note she'd left, and she had already knocked Alex back once. It didn't mean Alex had gone off her.

Yes, it's not ideal at work. Maybe we could meet somewhere else?

Alex texted back after five heartbeats. She counted.

Sure, where?

They could meet in a coffee shop in town, but that wasn't going to be private either. Inviting Alex to her house would be too forward. What if she thought she was offering more than an open conversation? She gazed out the window. A few leaves gently blew across the car park, signalling the start of autumn…though she preferred the American term for it, which was much more descriptive. It was the start of the fall.

How about we head out into the country for a walk? I can show you some of the local beauty spots.

It would be nice to get out of town for a bit and breathe some truly fresh air. It might be just what she needed to clear her head, and clear things up with Alex.

❖

Alex waited outside the gym, taking the odd sniff of her jacket to make sure it wasn't too telling of her living situation. Somehow it had failed to cross her mind, until Rebecca had asked where she lived, that her lack of a place she could invite people to might be an issue.

She'd told Rebecca she lived nearby and that it was the easiest place to meet, which wasn't a lie exactly. She did usually park up near there, so the facilities were handy and because there was plenty of parking space around the nearby industrial estate at night, where her van didn't stand out and there weren't nosey neighbours who might show too much interest in it. A gym membership wasn't cheap, but it was a lot less than rent and bills. From the amount of people she'd come to recognise, she wasn't the only one in there every day so they shouldn't get suspicious. And it had pushed her back into an exercise routine that her body seemed grateful for, especially the swimming, which had been part of her physio but had slipped away in the months before the big move.

They'd managed to find a day when they both weren't working. Rebecca had suggested a morning before she started her late shift, but it was better not having that deadline. It was their chance to finally properly talk about what they felt for each other, and Alex didn't want her rushing off at a key moment. Or either of them feeling pressured to make a decision without having the time to think it through.

A cool breeze crept its way inside her jacket. It was definitely heading into autumn, which was going to make her current digs even less fun. She would have to find somewhere to go before it got too cold to bear. She couldn't wait to get herself a proper camper van, one that was built to be slept in and which she could use to stay wherever she pleased, but she was still saving for it. Anyway, the compact type she wanted was designed for road trips, not to live in full-time, and still relied on you using facilities elsewhere. It wouldn't be a solution if she wanted to stick around there for much longer.

By the time Rebecca pulled up, she'd zipped up her thin jacket and was pacing to keep her blood flowing. It also helped with the butterflies that had infiltrated her stomach, or maybe it was just complaining at the lack of food in it. She'd meant to grab something to eat after her swim but had run out of time so had to make do with the muffin she had left. It was a bit stale, but better than nothing. Rebecca kept the engine running as she climbed in. The warm air from the heating enveloped her as she sank into the seat.

"Morning." Rebecca smiled at her, managing to look happy and afraid at the same time, like she'd just picked up a hitchhiker and wasn't sure if they would turn out to be her new best friend or an axe murderer.

"Morning." The car made it awkward to hug, which saved the awkwardness of not knowing if she should. Instead, she returned Rebecca's smile with one that hopefully seemed more relaxed. "Thanks for driving us."

"You're welcome. It made sense as I know where I'm going, and to save petrol."

It wasn't the most welcoming response, but Alex had already clocked it took Rebecca time to relax, another reason to make sure they weren't in any rush. Going together meant they had to leave together too, unless she planned to dump her in the middle of nowhere. Could she be the one getting in with a dangerous woman? She nearly laughed out loud at the thought of Rebecca taking anyone down. But they did say it was the quiet ones.

"So, where are we heading?"

Rebecca hadn't given her any details, apart from that they were heading into the countryside, and Alex was happy to let her play tour guide. She'd take the risk on her intentions.

"There's a lovely nature park not far from here if we head straight out of town. There's not much there in the way of man-made facilities, so I bought a thermos and snacks in case we need fuelling." Rebecca definitely seemed to tend towards Girl Guide rather than murderous tendencies.

"Sounds perfect."

She was tempted to ask if there was anything to tuck into during the drive. As much as she was a city girl, she was looking forward to getting out of the small town and exploring the surroundings. Her restlessness was growing, and she was starting to feel hemmed in by the simple life she was living.

Rebecca stared straight ahead as she drove, barely glancing at her even when they stopped at traffic lights or intersections. The local radio station was playing but turned down so low she could barely hear it.

She reached for the dial and cranked it up. "That okay?"

"Yes. Feel free to change the station if you want to." Rebecca's fingers started to drum on the steering wheel in time to the music, probably without her realising it.

"I'm cool with this."

She joined in with the cheesy boyband track, singing with a mocking level of enthusiasm. Hopefully Rebecca got the mocking part.

"I didn't think this would be your cup of tea." Rebecca bore a lopsided smile. "I had you down as more alternative, like Phoebe."

"Oh, I like all sorts. It's good to have something to sing along to on a car ride. Though like her, I'd prefer to hang with the rock crowd."

"Because the clothes are cooler?"

There was a slight mocking tone to her voice, and Alex remembered the obscene T-shirt of Phoebe's she'd caught her in.

"Because the people are cooler. More open-minded and accepting of outsiders like us." There were arseholes, like there were anywhere, but they weren't the dominant majority.

Rebecca looked thoughtful. "That explains why you're happy for Phoebe to go out with them, considering how protective you are of her."

"Yep. I trust them a lot more than some concert full of obsessive model-singer fans."

"Model-singer?"

"You know, the ones who look like they were recruited more for their bland good looks than any real talent."

"And you could do better, I suppose?" There was definitely some teasing in her tone. It could have been a dig, but her lips twitched with a withheld smile.

"Nah, Phoebe's the one with the music genes—I'll leave that to her." Her sister had more than her fair share of talent, which Alex joked had been taken from her. She joined back in with the crooning man-boy.

"That's probably for the best." Rebecca laughed, then joined in with the soundtrack, quieter at first, but by the time they got to their destination she had caught up with Alex's fake enthusiasm and was smiling for real.

They pulled into an unpaved car park that was mostly empty, hidden down a small track off the winding country road. Alex spotted an old pay-and-display machine under a big sign inviting people to enjoy the beauty of nature and please not fuck it up. Not in those exact words, but that was the gist. "I'll get us a ticket."

She jumped out before Rebecca could object and fed as many coins as she could afford in the machine, buying them a few hours.

The entrance to the park was a strange wooden gate contraption. She paused when they reached it, unsure what to do and not wanting to make a fool of herself.

Rebecca took the lead, opening the catch and swinging it forward. Alex followed her, realising too late that Rebecca needed to swing it back in order to pass through.

"Er…"

"Come here out of the way." Rebecca took her hand and pulled her into the corner with her, so the gate could safely swing back in place. "You really aren't a country girl, are you?"

"Guilty." Alex held up her hands, brushing off her embarrassment and the warm flush she knew was more connected to the way their bodies had pressed together in the small space.

She regretted it when Rebecca walked on without her, ending their momentary closeness. Her disappointment was fleeting as they rounded a cluster of trees and a large lake spread before them. The low sun glittered on the calm water.

"Wow."

Rebecca turned back to her, and Alex stopped with her foot half lifted off the ground to take her next step. The wind caught Rebecca's hair, loose instead of wrapped in the tight bun she sported at work, so she looked as wild as the landscape.

"Beautiful, isn't it."

"Yes, beautiful." Alex croaked out the words, her brain short-circuiting. She cleared her throat noisily as if there was something there to blame for her strained voice.

"There's a path that goes all the way round, so we can keep it in sight." Rebecca seemed oblivious to the fact it wasn't the sparkling water Alex was referring to.

It was so quiet, away from all the usual noise of human habitation. The only sounds that reached her were the wind rustling in the leaves of the grand trees that surrounded them, and birds that made them their home calling to each other. Rebecca reached a jetty and strode onto it, where she paused leaning on the wooden support in front of her and took a deep breath.

"You can really breathe out here," she said, closing her eyes and taking another visible breath.

Alex joined her, trying not to notice the rickety nature of the platform. She loved to swim, but not in these conditions. She copied Rebecca, filling her lungs with the fresh air. It was true—it felt like she was breathing fully for the first time in a very long time. They stood there for a few moments, just breathing.

She turned towards Rebecca, who still had her eyes closed. She looked so peaceful and vibrant at the same time. She wanted to let her be, but this wasn't just a friendly walk in the country. "So, what did you want to talk about?"

Rebecca's eyes snapped open and Alex felt cruel as the furrows reappeared in her brow. "Us."

She spoke so quietly, Alex had to edge closer to hear without straining.

"What about us?" She'd already made a fool of herself and been turned down once. She wasn't going to be the one to put herself out there again.

"How we feel about each other." Rebecca took a deep breath, this time seemingly more for courage than relaxation. "I like you, Alex, and it seems, apparently, you like me."

She stopped and looked to her as if for confirmation.

"I do," she said and inched her hand along the wooden rail so it was touching Rebecca's.

"Okay." Rebecca paused again and looked across the lake. "But there's also so many reasons why we shouldn't do anything about that. I'm your sister's carer, and I know you're not planning on sticking around long."

Was that what she was worried about? That they'd get involved and then she'd bugger off?

"Maybe not. But just because I'm Solo Poly doesn't mean I don't take things seriously. I wouldn't just drop someone."

"I know. You and Willow are clearly committed to each other."

She relaxed her grip on the rail. Not everyone got that. It was good to know Rebecca did.

"Yeah. It took years for us to figure out how our relationship could work, partly as we just didn't know we had options and the standard mono model never fitted either of us. We haven't been together right from the start, you know, we actually found poly separately. We always stayed friends, though, and I'm glad we gave us another chance once we knew what we wanted."

"I...I don't know if I can give us a chance."

The words stung, even though they weren't unexpected. If Rebecca had been sure about her, she wouldn't have turned her down before. And if Alex was honest, it was the same for her and why she hadn't asked her out sooner. She was drawn to her, more than she had been to anyone in a long time. She ached to hold her and claim that they must find a way, but could they ever fit together?

"I'm not Solo, I'm not even open to more relationships." Rebecca tucked some of her windswept hair behind her ear. "Or at least that's what I thought before I met you."

Alex smiled at the confession, despite her own doubts. "Yeah, Drew told me."

"They did?" Rebecca tensed and drew back from the edge.

"Not that we were talking about you, just us—how we're poly—and obviously you came up."

"Oh, okay. Did they tell you about the hierarchy too?"

Now it was Alex's turn to tense. She looked out across the water, hoping to hide the clench of her jaw. "Yep."

"And what did you say?"

"That I don't do hierarchy, it's not fair on everyone."

Alex looked back at her and caught her wince.

"I'm not being judgy—I've been there and I've been hurt. Bad. More than once. I don't seem to learn fast."

Rebecca smiled at her reflection, but there was sadness in her eyes. "So you couldn't be with someone like me."

Alex reached over and laced her fingers through Rebecca's. "I wish I could. I want you, but I can't put myself in that place again. I won't be classed as secondary to anyone."

"What if you weren't? Classed as secondary?"

"Just getting rid of the label doesn't change everything. Or even anything." She wished it was that simple, but it wasn't.

"So I'd need to change everything." It didn't sound like a question.

She could feel Rebecca growing tenser beside her and hear her breath growing faster.

"Hey." She let go of her hand and moved to her shoulders, attempting to squeeze the tension out of them.

Rebecca didn't pull away, instead closing her eyes and seeming to invite her touch. Alex moved behind her so she could carry on rubbing her shoulders with more ease. The physical contact wasn't enough. She would have to say something to ease the tension further.

"I'm not asking you to change. I'm just telling you how it is. Like you said, there are many reasons why we don't make sense."

"So many reasons. But…I still want you."

"I want you too." She wanted to lean down and kiss the bare skin of her neck.

"I've tried not to."

"Me too." She stilled her hands but continued to stroke the tender skin of her neck with her thumbs.

If Rebecca turned around, she wouldn't be able to resist kissing her, despite all those reasons. Sure, their attraction wasn't logical, but in her experience attraction never was.

"I'm so confused." Rebecca lifted her hands to still Alex's and leaned back into her.

"Maybe we don't need to figure it out right now. We could just get to know each other more and see where we end up, not worry about what we might or might not become. Hey, once we've spent some serious time together, we may not even be interested any more." She couldn't imagine not being interested in Rebecca, but a spark, no matter how brazen, didn't necessarily grow into anything.

"You think you'll get bored of me soon?" Before Alex could respond to say she had been joking, Rebecca continued, "But what if the more time we spend together, the more we want."

"Then we can figure it out together, as we go." It was how she liked to do things, rather than trying to stick a label on at the start. "Let's not try to force this, okay? Either way."

"Either way?"

"I mean, let's not push away our feelings, and let's not push ourselves into anything that won't work for us." They still had to find a way past their conflicting relationship styles, but they were past the point of denial.

"That sounds sensible," Rebecca said, with some level of conviction.

Alex almost pointed out that it sounded it, but in reality, it wasn't so simple. It was all too easy to get swept up in a new romance and not realise you were heading in the wrong direction until it was too late. That was not what Rebecca needed to hear. Instead, she steered them towards safer territory. "*Sooo* should I buy those theatre tickets? I really do want to thank you, you know."

"Yes." Rebecca gave Alex's hands a squeeze, then let go.

"Great. It's not necessarily a date!"

Rebecca's laugh vibrated in Alex's chest where their bodies met.

Having got what was bothering them out in the open, hopefully they could just enjoy each other's company for the rest of the day and finally get to know each other outside the shadow of the home. The landscape really was beautiful, and in that moment, there was no one Alex would rather explore it with. She stepped back to walk on.

Their deal wouldn't last forever. At some point they'd have to figure out if there was a path they could take together. But not yet. At least they had their eyes open and were being honest with each other, which would hopefully be enough to stop them tripping up in the meantime.

It looked like she would need to stick around for a while longer.

CHAPTER FIFTEEN

Rebecca hesitated, fist in the air, before knocking on the door. Since Alex had confirmed Phoebe had read her note, she was not looking forward to seeing her. As Alex had also pointed out, she couldn't blame Phoebe for being curious and assuming it was to do with her.

She had done her best to hide her attraction to Alex at work. It might not be explicitly against the rules, but it still felt wrong to get involved with the guardian of one of her residents, and she strongly suspected her colleagues would agree. They didn't need another reason to ostracise her.

At least they would have a clear focus with the baking, plus an opportunity to keep her hands busy, so hopefully Phoebe would be distracted from any reflections on what was going on between her sister and her carer. Not that anything was definitely going on. Alex's idea of getting to know each other more before they made any more moves was good, though it only partially quelled the waves of confusion that lapped at her mind. And as she'd leaned against her, staring out at the dazzling lake, she'd been sure she only wanted to get closer. It'd taken all her willpower to stop herself turning around and letting their lips finally meet. That night she'd dreamed she had, and more. She forced herself back into the moment and knocked sharply. Maybe she was the one who needed the distraction.

Phoebe answered immediately. She was wearing her own apron, which read *I need a drink* above a picture of dripping fangs, and had a well-used cookbook under her arm. "Let's do this!"

"I was going to ask if you're ready, but I guess that's not necessary." She should have got set up beforehand—she hadn't anticipated Phoebe going straight in. At least she'd checked ingredients and stashed them in the upstairs kitchen earlier.

"Yep, I'm ready. Come on." Phoebe brushed past her and started heading down the corridor.

Rebecca was forced to do a little run to catch up. "What are we making?"

To start them off gently and make sure Phoebe enjoyed it, she'd suggested she bake whatever she liked for their first session.

"Muffins, to start easy."

That was a relief. She wasn't sure how well equipped they were if she wanted to do anything more fancy.

"Excellent choice. I'm looking forward to sampling your baking, after hearing how good it is."

"My dad loves my muffins. Mum says they're responsible for his big belly."

"Phoebe!" Rebecca laughed, then tried to be serious. "Not everyone is built to be slim." Phoebe's short stature meant she was never going to look like a catwalk model, and she needed to know that was okay.

"I know, but it's what she says! I'm gonna take some for him when I go visit them at the weekend."

Hang on, when had that been arranged? "You're going to their house?"

"Yeah, Dad's going to pick me up and take me over for the afternoon."

"Okay." Rebecca wanted to ask whose idea that was and whether it was what Phoebe wanted, but she seemed relaxed about it, and they'd reached the kitchen door.

They had something else to deal with first—from the noises inside, the kitchen was clearly occupied despite Rebecca having booked it out and reminded everyone at handover. She took a deep breath and inserted her key into the Yale lock.

When she opened the door, it went quiet. Marie was sitting at the table with a couple of their other colleagues. Exactly who she didn't want to come up against. Marie had raised needless objections when she had brought up using the kitchen for its intended purpose, talking about health and safety as if it was something she was usually bothered about.

"Hi," Rebecca managed to say, attempting to keep her frustration from showing.

They stared at her blankly, then went back to their conversation. She was about to try again, when Phoebe swept round her and walked right in.

"Are you baking with us?"

Phoebe's presence seemed to make more of an impression on the group, and they made no attempt to pretend she wasn't there.

"No, we'll leave you to it. Have fun," Marie said, all polite and light.

They hastily stood up and Marie led them out of the room, the smile she'd given Phoebe sliding as she passed Rebecca. At least they hadn't put up a fight and made Phoebe feel uncomfortable there. Rebecca sighed. Why couldn't anything be easy?

Phoebe didn't appear to have picked up on any tension between her carers and was busy opening all the cupboards and having a good look inside. She pulled out the odd item, building up a collection on the countertop. It didn't seem like Rebecca was needed, but negotiations had ended with her promising to be there to supervise throughout. She sat down at the table and leafed through Phoebe's cookbook. There were handwritten additions scrawled on some of the recipes, including one that said *Alex's fav!* She made a mental note.

Phoebe joined her at the table with the implements she'd collected. "I don't mind."

"Mind what?" Rebecca looked up from the book.

Had Phoebe picked up on the bad air after all? Was she trying to reassure her that she didn't mind rocking the boat and making enemies? That should not be something Phoebe had to consider. Maybe she would have to report Marie's stand to Patience.

"I don't mind you seeing Alex." Phoebe held her gaze. There was no sign of emotion on her face, to hint at any undisclosed feelings.

Rebecca was stuck between horror at the turn of the conversation and relief that the elephant in the room had been addressed. She opened and closed her mouth a few times before finding her words. "Thank you. I'm not seeing her, though, not yet anyway. There are other complications."

It wasn't right to get into it with Phoebe, but she also didn't want her thinking it was because of her that it didn't work out. If it didn't. *Don't get ahead of yourself, it's not all gone wrong yet.*

"Okay. Just, don't hurt her. She's not as tough as she likes to act." It sounded like a friendly warning.

One she probably should've anticipated, considering how close the sisters were. It really was complicated.

"I'll try my best. I don't want anyone to get hurt."

"I know. No one wants love to hurt, but it can. So just, don't hurt her."

The simplicity of that truth struck Rebecca deep inside her chest. It was never the plan, but it was what happened. She could feel tears pricking at the corners of her eyes. They were getting into very dangerous territory. Giving Phoebe reassurance was one thing, but she didn't want to end up weeping at the kitchen table about all her fears and having Phoebe mop up her tears.

She needed to lighten the mood and grasped for something to say, a paddle to guide them in a different direction. "Or will I have you to answer to?"

"You bet!" Phoebe said, with a stern expression that, combined with her style, made her appear genuinely menacing for a moment, before she lapsed into a grin. "That's still her favourite—we could make it for her."

"One day, maybe."

They would need to build up to it in more ways than one. Baking was not her speciality.

"Cool." Phoebe held out her hand for the book.

Their conversation hadn't cleared the air in the way Rebecca might have hoped. It was dawning on her that it wasn't just inappropriate, but that any relationship she had with Alex could affect her working relationship with Phoebe. Would she ever trust her again if her beloved sister did end up getting hurt? She had come so far already in her quest for independence, but she was still nowhere near ready to move on. Phoebe would need her for a while yet, to teach her new skills and fight for her right to learn them. She didn't want to do anything to jeopardise Phoebe's future.

Rebecca waited outside the shopping centre for Alex. She'd got there early in order to get some snacks for their excursion, and there had been less of a queue than she'd anticipated at the bakery. Her session with Phoebe the evening before had left her with a craving for baked goods. The scent of the warm pasties was too much to take, and she tucked into one while she waited, trying not to get stringy cheese down her chin or pastry flakes on her trousers. That last one was impossible— she'd have to get out and remove them before they got mushed into her clothes or car. Preferably before Alex got there and saw her shaking herself off like a dog.

It was tempting to go back to the same park as last time. Alex had seemed taken in by the beautiful lake, and a little routine helped calm her nerves. But she'd offered to play tour guide and show Alex around the different places Somerset had to offer. Maybe they would entice her to stay a while longer. How could anyone not fall in love with the vibrant British countryside? Soon the leaves would start to fall in earnest, and the air would turn as crisp as the leaves crunching underfoot. When she got out to flap the crumbs off, a cool breeze whipped at her.

It was a slightly odd place for them to meet. Alex had suggested it because she needed to get a new coat first and some other bits. As she must have driven there in her van, it would mean Rebecca dropping her back there too. Last time it had been the gym, which Alex said was near where she lived and the easiest place to stop, but she couldn't stop the nagging thought that she just didn't want her to know where she lived. The address on Phoebe's file was over a hundred miles away in Leicester, so clearly wasn't where she was staying at present. What was she afraid of? Did she trust her that little? Should she? Phoebe's warning flitted back to mind. *No, it doesn't mean anything.* She just needed a coat, no need to overanalyse.

Here she came. Alex exited the building and looked around the car park, spotting her and waving before she'd got half out the car. She settled back in her seat and straightened the ribboned book that she'd set on the passenger seat, then moved it into the back in case Alex sat on it. But no, then she'd have to stretch over between the seats to get it for her. She put it back where she'd started. Max's face peeped out from underneath the ribbon, judging her for her indecisiveness. Looking back up, Alex seemed to be making slow progress, as if she was in no rush to get to her. Or wait, was she limping? It was hard to tell. As she got nearer, her widening smile was what drew Rebecca's attention.

Before she could second-guess herself, she jumped out of the car to greet her. When she held out her arms, Alex didn't hesitate to lean in and wrap her up in a hug. They stayed there for a second longer than a casual greeting required, and the air felt extra cool when Alex drew back.

"Hey."

"Hey."

They smiled at each other. The breeze really was chilly, and Rebecca had taken off her bulky coat to drive, so she wrapped her arms around herself to stave off the cold.

Alex seemed to notice her slight shiver and gestured to the car. "Shall we head off, or did you want anything from the shops?"

"No, I'm good. I already got snacks." She pointed to the back seat, where she'd placed the paper bag full of pastries and cakes.

"Great." Alex walked around the passenger side and opened the door, picking up the comic book as she slid into the seat. "What's this?"

"It's the *Azura* comic, the first collection. I get kind of precious about mine, so I thought I'd get you your own copy. If you haven't already got it. And if you do want to read it." She pressed her lips closed before she rambled any more. What if Alex had only been pretending to be interested before and had just been humouring her?

"Thank you. You didn't have to." Alex flipped over the cover, revealing the bar code and price.

"I know, but I wanted to. It's just a little something—it cost a lot less than the theatre tickets. Now you don't have to wait for me to finish it before you can start."

Alex seemed the proud type who might take issue with others buying her anything, but it wasn't all one way and it didn't mean she owed her anything.

"Good point. And no, I don't already have it." Alex leaned over and gave her a peck on the cheek. "Thanks."

Rebecca could feel her cheeks growing hot. It would take just the slightest move on her part for Alex's lips to be on hers. But no, they were taking it slow. Instead, she slid her seat belt on, fumbling with the catch while Alex looked on with a gaze that implied she'd had the exact same thought. Going slow was a good thought, but harder in practice, especially after she'd already endured three months of sensual gazes in an environment where she could never act on them. With Alex in her private car, it was harder to remember why she shouldn't give in to the lust.

Time to go if they were going to avoid making out in the car like teenagers. What was it about Alex that brought out that wild side of her? Best not think about that.

"So, did you get a coat?"

"Yep, as modelled." Alex held the crisp hooded jacket out to her sides. "I figured it would come in handy, especially on our walks. I didn't bring much with me for past summer."

Because she hadn't been planning to stay around that long. But she had. The unspoken fact fizzled in the charged air between them. *Did she stay for me?* Should she?

The idea of letting Alex in no longer scared her like it had, and her closed heart was showing signs of cracking open. Maybe they could become something special. If she was willing to change more than just her closed status. Would it be so terrifying to let go of the hierarchy that had kept her safe? Because if she was honest, it had made her feel safe but more as a backup that had never had to come into play. Given how her relationships had developed, she couldn't imagine calling on it any more because that would mean pretending Drew wasn't as important to her as they had become. Maybe it was time to let go of the safety net.

"I could've borrowed something off Bee, but we don't exactly take the same size." Alex brought her back to the present and the other area of complication.

She recalled the biker jacket Phoebe wore, which she said she'd inherited from Alex, and the way she had the sleeves rolled up. Hang on, wouldn't that have been the obvious solution rather than getting a new one. "What about your old jacket Phoebe has?"

"My old leather one?" Alex closed her eyes and leaned back onto the headrest. "I suppose I could try and wrestle it off her, but it would be easier to buy a new one. Anyway, my biker days are over."

Thank God. Why anyone would put themselves at risk that way, she couldn't fathom. It was plain reckless. "I must admit, it's not something I've ever tried." *Or wanted to.*

"No? There's nothing like it. When the wind's rushing by you, it's the greatest buzz." Alex kept her eyes closed, and there was a hint of sadness to her tone. "You can leave everything behind, forget everything else."

That she could understand. The feeling of being so involved in something that everything else melted away was something she wished she could access more often. But not like that. "It does sound enticing, but I'll pass."

"Fair enough. As I said, I don't ride any more anyway."

Rebecca nearly asked why, if it was so wonderful, then remembered what Phoebe had said. Alex had been in an accident, bad enough to make her give up something she clearly loved. She kicked herself for being so quick to judge. It might not have been down to any recklessness on Alex's part—it could've easily been a larger vehicle not paying attention. An image of a van swiping the zooming bike as if it was just a pesky fly made her body tense for impact. There was a heaviness in the air, and she didn't want to bring up any more painful visions or memories, not at the start of them getting to know each other and relaxing in each other's company.

"I haven't finished reading that yet, by the way, but I'm happy to chat about it." In desperation, she orchestrated a sharp turn, back to the book in Alex's lap.

"Is it much like the TV series?" Alex seemed happy with the change of subject. "Please tell me they haven't changed Max too much."

"Seems pretty similar so far, in terms of the world building and characters, anyway. I don't think it follows the same plot, it's more of a continuation."

She'd finished watching the series first, so it was fresh in her mind. She could lend that to Alex, but it was rare. What if she lost it or disappeared without giving it back? Maybe she should invite her round to watch it. How would Alex feel about coming over with Ishani potentially being there? Would she be cool hanging out together? Hierarchy or not, their living arrangements weren't about to change, and she didn't want to be with someone who tried to avoid her nesting partner and made them both feel less comfortable in their own home.

"Cool. Don't tell me anything else—I don't like spoilers. I prefer to be kept guessing about how it's going to end." She shot Rebecca a dazzling smile.

Her line of thought vanished as she held Alex's gaze. With nothing else to say, she started the engine and tried not to fall back into it again. One page at a time. She could respect that and was in favour of enjoying what was happening as it unfolded, but she wasn't as strict about not finding out the ending. In fact, she preferred to know what she was getting into before she got too hooked.

❖

Alex dropped her phone onto the sofa next to her, not quite throwing it, but wanting to.

She'd had a bright idea for how she could stick around, but it wasn't going to work. Without her own caravan, it was far too expensive to stay at the campsite. Staying there in her van wouldn't be much better for her, and a tent would be even worse in winter. A real bed and heating were what she needed to get through it. The cramping and pain in her legs and hips was already worse than usual from sleeping on a cold mattress on the van floor. But there was no way she wanted to get tied into a rental contract as she still didn't know how long she'd be staying.

She sighed. She wanted to stick around and spend some time getting to know Rebecca, but maybe it wasn't practical. She hadn't made any promises at least. Getting to know each other didn't necessarily mean being physically near each other. If she went back to the city, they could stay in touch, even though she couldn't visit often and it was doubtful Rebecca would find the time to visit her. Would they, though? Once she was out of there, their attraction might just fade away, like some meaningless holiday flirtation.

"I don't know about you, but I need this." Drew placed the tray of steaming drinks in front of her. "Think I discovered the cause of the big queue—they've got a new person training. They looked terrified of the drinks machine, bless them."

"It does look like some hefty machinery they've got back there. You'll need a degree to operate that soon." Alex took her cup and held it between her hands to warm them. She'd woken up seriously chilled that morning.

"Yep. And I doubt they pay enough to be worth the student debt. Not that a lot of places do, part of why Becca's parents don't approve of her job choice." Drew settled into the overstuffed armchair opposite her.

"They don't?" Alex couldn't imagine any parent taking issue with Rebecca's dedicated work, but then she didn't know anything about them. So far they'd steered clear of discussing their relationships, or lack of, with their folks and Alex was happy with that. She'd got the impression Rebecca's birth family weren't a big part of her life either.

"People can be snobs, mind. Doesn't matter that most graduates I know struggled to get a decent job after Uni and ended up somewhere they could've walked straight into from school. The system's broken." Drew looked like they had a lot more they could say on the subject.

"Yeah, makes me glad I didn't bother." Not that further education was an option with her track record and the need to support herself, but it hadn't mattered. She'd always been more practical and never one for sitting at a desk all day. She'd had the best of both worlds anyway, as Willow had gone to do an arts degree and she'd been a frequent visitor to her student digs. She had fond memories of the art student parties, where being queer seemed to be not just acceptable but cool. It had never been just an experiment for them, but she didn't resent others for taking the opportunity for some exploration, even if it had led to some sticky situations. Especially while they were also figuring out the whole ethical non-monogamy thing. She was someone who learned by making mistakes, not reading about other people's.

Drew took a long drink of their coffee. "Mmm, that's better. So, what's up with you?"

"What do you mean?" She hoped they weren't asking about Rebecca.

"You look like there's something weighing on you. Other than the usual." They smirked.

She brushed off the temptation to ask what the usual was, taking their smirk as indication that it was what she wanted to avoid.

It was weird sometimes with Drew, not knowing if they were a friend or a metamour. Would it be possible for them to become both? It wasn't something she had any experience of and she was suspicious of intentions given her history of being treated like she didn't matter, but plenty of her friends had metamour-friends and swore it worked. It wasn't like Rebecca was forcing them to be friends, unless there was some background agreement she wasn't aware of at play. Which was possible. *Crap.*

"Hey, Alex, where you to?"

There was no sign they were acting on orders and they looked genuinely concerned about what was going on in her head. She had to trust that and not fuck up the one friendship she'd managed to make there.

"Just trying to figure out what to do about housing, as I'm thinking of sticking around a bit longer."

"Good to hear you're not planning on buggering off any moment, I'm getting to like having you around." Their look of concern was replaced with a bright smile. "Where are you staying now?"

"I've just been living out of my van. I wasn't planning on being here long." She shrugged and gave them a look that hopefully made it clear it wasn't a situation that needed pity.

"I never knew that! You should've said, we've got a spare room you'd be welcome to while you get sorted."

Or charity. It was exactly the kind of response she'd expected from Drew, with their role of caring for lost strays.

"Thanks, but I wouldn't want to be under your feet all the time." No matter how well you got on with someone, living with them was a big risk. She'd had (and seen) enough flat shares turn sour to prefer to live with people she wasn't that invested in, so it wasn't a big deal if it did. Not to mention how awkward it would be if things didn't work out with Rebecca. Or if they did.

"You wouldn't be. And we wouldn't get in your way, brownie's honour." Drew held up their right hand in the three-fingered salute.

"You were a brownie?" Alex nearly spit out her drink. A little

Drew in uniform, skipping along with the pack was such an offbeat image.

"I have a dark past. Don't judge me." They cocked an eyebrow, daring her to take the piss. "Anyway, I get it can be awkward staying in someone else's house, but the offer's there if you get desperate."

"Cheers." She was grateful they didn't push it and couldn't see herself seriously considering it, but had to appreciate their generosity.

"Ere, I've a thought. Bear with." Drew took out their phone and appeared to tap out a short message.

Alex sat back and drank her coffee slowly, feeling the warmth flooding her body. It was definitely getting colder out there and she really wouldn't cope in the van much longer, even with the extra sleeping bag she snuggled in under her duvet. Maybe she should consider Drew's offer, at least while she investigated other options, and not let her pride get in the way. She wouldn't need to hang around there much except to sleep.

Drew's phone buzzed and they checked it straight away. "Ideal! I've got a solution for you: my mates need someone to housesit while they go look after a sick relative, ASAP. Preferably someone who'd be happy to stay there free of charge. They're not loaded, they can't pay a pro, but they'd like someone there to keep an eye on things and feed the cat."

"I like cats." It did sound promising. Alex sat up. "How long for? And would they want me, a stranger?"

"Sure, I'd vouch for you. They trust me." They winked at her. "How long, well that's the thing. They don't know right now, it could be weeks or months."

"Of course." If they were leaving to care for someone very ill, it would depend on their recovery or the other ending. There could be no guarantees. But that wasn't a problem, as she didn't know how long she wanted to stay yet anyway.

"Are you up for it?"

"I'll have to think about it. And talk to them myself." It was tempting to jump at such an obvious solution, but there could be a catch. Things were rarely as perfect as they seemed. And having Drew vouch for her was asking a lot of them, considering how long they'd known her. She didn't want to take advantage and let them down.

"I'll give you Tiff's number. When I spoke to her yesterday, they were wanting to take off as soon as possible. She's already sorted an agreement to work remotely so doesn't have to worry about her job."

They leaned forward. "No pressure, but you'd be doing them a real favour."

No time to waste then. She'd have to decide quick or lose the chance. Drew was right, it sounded ideal. But not thinking things through was how she got herself in trouble.

CHAPTER SIXTEEN

After the success of the muffins, they'd graduated to red velvet cupcakes. It turned out that as well as singing, Phoebe had a real talent for baking or at least was so practised at it that she'd got it down to an art.

Rebecca's mother had always maintained that baking was a good way to make friends, which she'd dismissed as an anti-feminist outdated ideal. But it seemed she had a point—sharing the results of their sessions with her colleagues seemed to have more than made up for their banishment from the kitchen. She'd even heard those who were initially most resistant encouraging Phoebe with suggestions of what to make next.

The plan was to move on to cooking balanced meals, but as it made everyone happy there was no harm in carrying on with the baking alongside that. They'd agreed Faye could join in future sessions, and Rebecca was picking up some handy tips too. Would it be inappropriate to ask Phoebe to help, or at least train her, to make something for Ishani? Since she'd started hanging out with Alex outside work, she had even less time with her. It was true what they said—jealousy wasn't the biggest problem in poly relationships, time was. A sweet treat might help make it up to her. The look of surprise and joy on Ishani's face when she presented her with something she'd made just for her would be more than worth the effort. Maybe she could even contribute to their Diwali celebrations, rather than relying on her metamours as usual.

The cakes looked as good as they tasted, and she had to fight to resist taking a bite as she arranged them on a plate. Phoebe's parents were there again, following another visit to their home the last weekend. They seemed to be quickly rebuilding a bond, and Phoebe appeared much more open and happier when she greeted them in comparison to their first visit, two months before. Maybe living apart would turn out to be best for their relationship—she definitely got on better with her own family after moving out, though they'd never been close. And still weren't. In Phoebe's case, there were strong hints they had once been, including the weekly baking sessions she'd enjoyed with her mother. Rebecca would never have consented to that much interaction with hers as a teenager or young adult.

She'd offered to make them drinks as usual after escorting them to Phoebe's room, giving herself the excuse to pop in and get a better look at how things were progressing. Alex's warning had faded to a whisper, but she still caught it in some moments. The way Mr. Jennings took control and didn't seem too interested in what Phoebe had to say was a bit of a concern, but not anything out of the ordinary for an older cishet man. It was best she kept an eye on them still and build a working relationship if they were going to be a significant part of Phoebe's life again.

Nobody opened the door when she reached it with her loaded tray, but there was a temporary stilling of the voices within.

"Want a hand?" Faye popped her head out of her room.

Unlike Phoebe, Faye rarely got visitors but kept track of the comings and goings of the home. Rebecca suspected she had a better idea than her what was going on behind every door.

"No, it's okay." She attempted to balance the tray with one arm, then had second thoughts. "Actually, yes. Could you hold this a sec, please."

Faye ambled over and took the tray carefully from her, leaving Rebecca's hands free to knock. There was no answer. Should she risk intruding on a private moment by just opening it? Maybe they hadn't heard her. She knocked again. There was a shuffling of feet, then Phoebe answered. She didn't meet Rebecca's eyes. What was going on?

"Rebecca, why don't you join us a moment." Mr. Jennings was the one to invite her in.

"Of course." She looked at Phoebe again, but she still wouldn't meet her eyes and moved aside silently to let her in. "Thanks, Faye, see you later."

She took the tray back. Faye looked slightly disappointed but walked away obediently. She had plenty of practice at being dismissed, having spent most of her life in care under the charge of paid staff. Rebecca tried not to be just another impersonal carer, but she only had so much to give. It wasn't just Ishani that was being impacted by the Jennings sisters' arrival. At least Faye had gained a friend out of it.

Phoebe closed the door behind her and sat down on her bed, facing her parents who were in the armchairs opposite. "I don't know," she said.

Rebecca placed the tray on her desk. She was saved from needing to ask what was going on by Mr. Jennings.

"We were just discussing the possibility of Phoebe moving back home."

It was a good thing she'd already placed the tray, or she might have dropped it. Her chest thumped. Phoebe was considering leaving? Surely that wasn't what she wanted or needed, after all the work they'd been doing? It would be a step backwards. She swallowed, trying to keep her opinions from spilling out unwarranted.

She deliberately focused on Phoebe, not her parents. "Is that what you want to do, Phoebe?"

"I don't know." She shrugged. "I think…I need to think."

"Of course, you take your time. This isn't the kind of decision that should be rushed." Rebecca turned to the parents as she finished speaking. Were they trying to rush her?

"Certainly. We'll need to discuss all the practicalities," Mr. Jennings said, either not grasping or deliberately twisting her point.

"And all the options," she said, looking back at Phoebe.

It wasn't just about how it would work, but if it would be a good move. The parents shuffled in their seats. What had they expected her to say? Nothing? Maybe in the past she would have.

"Yes, yes. Everything needs to be taken into account. We're not suggesting going back to how things were. We're willing to negotiate and make some changes to ensure Phoebe can carry on living her life." He smiled at Rebecca, as if that was all the reassurance she needed. His smile struck a chord. It was the same type Marie gave her when she was set on something and planned to bulldoze any objections.

It sent a shiver down her spine, and she placed her palms flat on the desk to steady herself. Then it struck her that Phoebe leaving would mean Alex leaving too. Her chest tightened so much it hurt, and she had to take a moment to remember how to breathe. Could she be impartial and consider only what was best for Phoebe, and not for her? *This is why you shouldn't mix business and pleasure—it clouds your professional judgement.* She was a professional, and she must act like one.

She plastered on a calm smile and turned back to the parents. "How about we hold a meeting to discuss everything in more detail? And give Phoebe a chance to digest a bit first."

"Yes. Though if we're going to talk details there, we shouldn't wait too long." Mr. Jennings clearly had his agenda set already.

But he had a point. Phoebe needed to know her options before she could consider them properly.

"We'll come back tomorrow, talk it through then," he said.

"That should be fine by us. I'll be on duty in the afternoon if you can come then. What about you, Phoebe, would that be okay?" She was very aware Phoebe still hadn't spoken and given her consent for any meeting, let alone that soon.

"Okay." Phoebe looked down at the floor. Where was the confident, outspoken young woman she'd come to know?

Should Alex be invited? Would she ever forgive her if she wasn't, and their parents whisked Phoebe away without her knowledge? *Don't go there, focus.* Alex was her nominated next of kin. It was only right that she should be invited into any meeting where such significant developments would be discussed.

"Is there anyone else you'd like to be there?" she prompted Phoebe. Would she be justified in calling her if—

"Alex."

Rebecca breathed a sigh of relief. As Phoebe requested it, she didn't have to make the decision. Phoebe's parents seemed less impressed but didn't vocally object.

She didn't want to give them the chance to put together an objection. Alex had earned her right to be there with all she'd done for her sister. "Will you ask her, or would you like me to?"

"I can call her. After…"

After your parents are gone and won't hear Alex's reaction. Rebecca could only imagine her fierce rage. Leaving the meeting until tomorrow would hopefully give Alex time to calm down and process, as well as Phoebe.

But it did also leave their parents with the opportunity to talk Phoebe out of making the call. It was a definite risk from the look they'd shared when Phoebe had spoken her name.

"How about you send her a quick message to check she's free, and then call her later to tell her what it's about? That way we can choose a different day if she can't come tomorrow."

"Good idea." Phoebe smiled at her, the first time since she'd entered the room.

She didn't want to push her in any particular direction, but she clearly needed some guidance. Phoebe shuffled across and picked up her phone and typed a message, while Rebecca stood quietly, not wanting to carry on the conversation without her.

She leaned back slightly and her back brushed something warm. The drinks! She'd forgotten her initial purpose. She handed them out, glad to have something to do. When she was about to offer the cakes, she realised she'd not brought any side plates. "I'll be right back, just need to get something to eat these off."

It was a good excuse to leave the room and the heavy air that dominated it. She hadn't been expecting the offer at all, but maybe she should have. Alex had warned her. Had she been too naive, too trusting?

Or was she being selfish? Shouldn't she be glad Phoebe had regained her relationship with her parents, rather than worrying about losing her chance with Phoebe's sister? It was clear that she couldn't expect Alex to stick around just for her. It wasn't like there was anything serious between them or any promises had been made. Not that Alex was ever going to promise to stay by her side.

❖

Alex put the kettle on. It was the little things she'd missed most, like having water on tap and being able to boil it so quickly and easily. Drew's friends, the Hathaways, had seemed so grateful she'd stepped in that they'd practically thrown the keys at her and told her to make herself at home. Their kitchen was well-stocked and although she felt a bit guilty using up their stuff, there was no sense letting it go to waste. They could be gone for months, after all, though she didn't have to stay that long. If she wanted to leave earlier, Drew would take over cat duties or find someone else. She wouldn't be stuck there.

Steam rose from the shuddering kettle, and it clicked back off. She poured the hot water on top of a teabag and swished it around. The clear water turned dark quickly, and the teaspoon clinked against the side of the china cup. The Hathaways must be practised entertainers. Their cupboards were full of fancy crockery that looked like it was actually used, not just for display. Or for very special occasions, like her mother's. On the rare occasions she'd brought it out, everyone had been on edge in case it got damaged. Even Phoebe had eaten with *some* delicacy.

She sat herself down at the long wooden table. It had a shiny finish that betrayed its fake wooden construction. She rapped it with her knuckles—there was no depth to the sound. Still, it looked like you could host a party on it. Maybe she could invite some people round. Who, though? She didn't know the guys from work well enough, and it might be a bit weird having Drew and Rebecca over together. Or Rebecca and Phoebe. Phoebe wouldn't mind, but Rebecca was likely to be uncomfortable.

The lounge boasted a massive, curved HD television and sofas you could sink right into, perfect for movie nights. The Hathaways had said they were happy for her to have people over, including having Willow or other partners to stay, as long as she didn't wreck the place with any drunken parties. Alex had raised an eyebrow at that, not having mentioned any partners herself, but gritted her teeth. The fact they were so unbothered about it made her wonder if they were poly too. It would explain more why they were happy to leave the place to her. Another poly person was less likely to freak out if they found any evidence.

She moved through to sit on the more comfortable seats. Sure they weren't so good for her skeleton, but it was hard to relax on a firm chair. The cat, Zelda, sprang up out of apparent nothingness to curl up on her lap, and she instinctively shifted to give her room. Zelda started purring as she stroked her, the low vibration spreading into her hand, a soothing background hum. She found herself imagining there was someone else there to curl up with. She might not have nesting instincts, but she liked company to share her space, when she felt like it. It made a nice change having the run of a whole place, rather than her usual houseshares. The chance to cuddle up on the sofa with someone, with no fear of being interrupted.

When had that domestic life become her dream? But even in fantasy she couldn't imagine her cuddle buddy staying for too long. She needed space to breathe and live her life. The house would make it even easier, as long as she didn't get too used to it. When she moved back to the city, there was no way she could afford a place like that, especially while saving for her camper van. And once she got it, she and Willow had a tour of Europe planned that would take her away for months.

The route was already laid out. They'd spread out the driving and take it in turns, so she could stretch out between. They would explore during the day, then Willow would gig at night, and she would have time to do her own thing. They might not cope in the little van the whole time, but Willow reckoned she could afford the odd hotel room if they needed a change or space from each other. Navigating trips with

Willow was so much easier than with many other people, as she didn't want to live in someone else's pockets any more than Alex did. She was a free spirit, and Alex had never wanted to change that.

Usually thinking of their big trip filled her with a buzz of excitement, but there was something dulling it. Travelling for months meant leaving everyone else for months. It wouldn't be as easy as typical holidays of a week or two, which made no real difference in terms of how often she saw the other people she was close to. She'd enjoyed rebuilding her relationship with Phoebe and being able to see her so often and didn't want to go too long without seeing her again. Maybe Phoebe could go with them and see some of the world.

Her chest squeezed. Who was she kidding, it wasn't just Phoebe she was pained at the thought of being apart from for that long. When she'd suggested to Rebecca that they get to know each other more before deciding anything, she'd known her feelings were only likely to grow. Although they weren't officially together, new relationship energy was flooding her veins and threatening to take over. The extra fuel was handy, as long as she kept a grip. When she'd told Willow, Willow seemed to think she'd already lost it. Not that she'd tried to talk her out of it—Willow knew better than that. Alex could never resist a big red button or the urge to do the opposite of what she was told to flex her free will. Whatever anyone else predicted, sometimes it worked out for the best.

There was a vibration in her pocket. She fished out her phone and opened the text message from Phoebe while taking a slurp of tea, and almost spat it out. What the fuck?

The sense of relaxation vanished, and Zelda seemed to notice, springing out of her lap away from her tensed limbs. She spent the hour she waited for Phoebe's call restlessly pacing, unable to settle down to anything.

The phone call, when it finally came, didn't help. In fact, it confirmed her fears. Their parents hadn't really been respecting Phoebe's wishes—they'd just been playing nice so they could persuade her to come back. And it sounded like Phoebe had been taken in, as she was seriously thinking about it. She'd had to cut off the call to stop herself telling her how it was too plainly. It wouldn't help. Her getting angry at Phoebe would only push her more towards them. It was probably a good thing Phoebe couldn't see her clenched jaw and fists. And it wasn't Phoebe she was angry at.

The one comfort was the news that Rebecca had stood up to them and prodded Phoebe to invite her. She could just imagine their parents' response to that, but they wouldn't have wanted to show their colours in front of a professional. They'd be playing happy families and acting like they had nothing to do with their daughter wanting to leave. They'd have been gritting their teeth as hard as she was.

It was so tempting to go out to a bar for the evening, maybe even a club, and drink and dance the night away. Going in with a hangover would not be a good start, though. When she'd been in her twenties, she'd been easily able to party all night and make it through the next day with just a can of cola to revive her. Not so any more. If she was out all night, she would be no use to anyone the next day. The meeting wasn't until the afternoon, but she still couldn't risk it. She penned in her desires. Phoebe's future was at stake.

Instead, she hit the gym and managed to pass a good couple of hours there, including a swim to cool off after. She had to be cautious still, otherwise she'd pay for that the next day too, but it was enough. By the time she got home, she'd worked out enough of her rage to allow her to collapse on the sofa in front of some made-for-TV film, then get a not completely restless night's sleep with the aid of her prescription meds.

❖

Alex arrived at the home an hour early, in the hope she might get a bit of time to chat with Phoebe and Rebecca before the meeting. She needed to make sure other options were definitely on the table and that Phoebe was given the chance to consider them. Unfortunately, their parents seemed to have had the same idea. With the opposite aim, no doubt.

After she rang the bell, she heard footsteps approaching behind her. She didn't turn, not wanting to get drawn into a conversation with anyone and waste precious time she could be spending prepping Phoebe. It was their mother's voice that seeped in, giving a so-subtle tug on her heart.

It was true you couldn't choose your parents or whether you loved them, but you could choose how much you let them run your life. Their rejection of Alex's queerness had built a wall between them that had stayed up all those years and made it easy for her to slip out of their lives completely. She'd learned way back then that their parents' love wasn't unconditional. She was never going to be what they wanted her to be. Her little sister, however, had seemed more tameable. More loveable. It was no more surprising that they would fight to get Phoebe back than it was that they never fought for her.

"Hello." The familiar voice tore through her memories, but it was like greeting a stranger or a vague acquaintance at best. Just another visit where they were forced to wait and make small talk on the doorstep.

"Alex. Glad you could make it."

Her dad's contribution was even more ridiculous. She held back a snort.

"Hello," she said back to her mum with a stiff smile. She was there for Phoebe, that was all.

She was saved from any further need to talk by Rebecca opening the door. There was a flush to her cheeks that suggested she'd raced to get them, possibly after spotting them together on the security camera feed. Her smile shifted into a real one.

"Hi," said Rebecca, giving her a private smile before turning to the others. "Thank you all for coming back in. I wasn't expecting you quite yet, so I'll have to check the meeting room's free, but do come in." Her cool professionalism took over as she addressed them en masse.

It dawned on Alex with a jolt that she would have to be very careful not to give any hint of their personal involvement to their parents. They wouldn't hesitate to use it against the home, possibly even putting Rebecca's job at risk if they officially questioned her motivations. It wouldn't matter whether they really believed it was an issue—it would damage trust in Rebecca and be a handy excuse to remove Phoebe without too many questions being asked. She hadn't seen any major risk there before, but the realisation made her stone cold.

"Thanks." She gave Rebecca a nod, then waited for her to step well back before walking past. If they accidentally touched, the spark between them might be visible. "Shall we go to Phoebe's room and you can let us know when the meeting room's ready?"

It was tempting to make an excuse to hang back and speak to her alone, but she didn't want to leave their parents alone with Phoebe and give them the chance to sway her before talks officially started, even though that meant having to spend more time with them.

"Yes, of course." A brief look of confusion swept Rebecca's face, quickly enough that her parents were unlikely to have paid any notice.

If only Alex could explain and warn her of the danger, but it was too risky. She'd have to trust Rebecca wouldn't let her mask slip.

"Just let us know. Can we get some drinks sent up while we wait?"

Their father sounded like he was in a hotel or conference centre. It wasn't Rebecca's job to wait on them.

"Of course. Though if the room's free, we can get them down here and get started."

And if not, hopefully Rebecca would use it as an excuse to join them. As much as she was worried about blowing their cover, they might need her there as a buffer. Experience told her they were all unlikely to stay polite if they were left to fight over Phoebe alone.

❖

As Rebecca watched them march away, it was clear she needed backup. There was no procedure she knew of to deal with the situation even if she wasn't involved with one of the relatives.

She'd made Patience aware the day before, but had rejected her offer to join them, not wanting to make it too formal, thinking, for some reason, that she could handle it by herself. But when she'd met Alex's eyes, the cold fury in them had corrected her. There was going to be a fight, and she'd be right in the middle of it. As far as Phoebe's parents knew, she was just a member of staff with no strong attachment to their daughters. If only it were that simple.

When she entered the meeting room, Patience was already there, clearing the long table of stray paperwork. "I see your guests have arrived already. You want to start straightaway, or are they going to spend some time with Phoebe first?"

Rebecca considered the visible friction between Alex and her parents. "It's probably best we come straight in. If you're still free, I think it would be helpful for you to join us."

"Of course. Everything okay?" Patience raised an eyebrow.

Clearly not, but how much should she say? She'd not told anyone about the state of Alex's non-relationship with her parents—it wasn't like she knew for sure anyway, though there were probably plenty of rumours. "I suspect there's some…some disagreement about what will be best for Phoebe, and some…mediation may well be required."

There's likely to be a fight and I'll need your help breaking it up. Especially as she couldn't trust herself to be unbiased. She still felt sure it was the right place for Phoebe, but she couldn't be sure why she felt that way.

"Sounds like I definitely better stick around."

A lot of Patience's job seemed to involve mediation of some sort.

She often joked that her name was a sign of her biggest test, which she did her best to meet, and Rebecca suspected she wasn't entirely kidding. If anyone could keep things calm, it was her. A little weight lifted off her shoulders.

"Can I bring them in now?" The longer they left the family alone, the more hackles might rise. She almost certainly wasn't the only one who'd want to get this over with.

"Certainly. By the time you've brought them down, I'll have this place ready."

It was also a relief to have someone else handle the practical side of things, who she could trust to make sure everything was as it should be. Some of her colleagues, the ones who left the room in that state, wouldn't worry about the impression it gave. But Mr. and Mrs. Jennings would likely be looking closely at everything.

When they returned, the room was completely clear of all paperwork, apart from the framed certificates on the walls stating the assorted qualifications of the staff team. The urn had been wheeled in on a hostess trolley, with everything they needed so no one would have to leave to prepare refreshments and risk missing anything important.

"I thought it would be helpful to have our manager present, to answer any questions anyone has about practicalities."

She'd decided against giving them a choice over it and watched their reactions carefully. Thankfully Alex looked slightly relieved if anything and gave Patience a nod of recognition, possibly even approval. Mr. Jennings looked past her, as if wondering when the manager would show himself.

Patience stepped towards him and held out her hand. "Hello, I'm Patience, the manager here. I don't believe we've met."

Her smile stayed set as Mr. Jennings practically did a double take. Over his shoulder Alex clenched her jaw as if in anticipation of something objectionable.

"Ah no, we've not. I'm Mr. Jennings, Phoebe's father, and this is my wife."

He made a quick recovery, and Patience kept her professional smile going, as if she'd not noticed a thing. Not as if she was used to people looking around her for the white man who must really be in charge. Rebecca didn't know if she'd be able to take it as well in her position. Not that it was a choice. Maybe it was like the way she chose to ignore the looks she got when out with Ishani, as people struggled to take in not just their genders but Ishani's ethnicity and visible disability.

Their relationship seemed to cause some people's brains to short-circuit, without them even knowing about the non-monogamy part. People like Mr. Jennings.

Phoebe entered the room last, hanging back in the doorway as everyone finished introductions and chose their seats, looking like she'd been called into the headmaster's office for some unknown reason that surely couldn't be good. Rebecca gave her an encouraging smile and beckoned her to come in. She took a few steps, then paused again, studying the available seats.

Did even that seem like taking sides? Rebecca had been so wrapped up in her own concerns she hadn't stopped to consider how stuck Phoebe must feel, being asked to choose between her freedom and her family, her sister and her parents. She shuffled over, head down, and took the seat next to Rebecca, who was overcome by a rush of warmth that she'd chosen to have her by her side. Or maybe she just saw it as neutral territory between her sister and parents. Which it should be, but Phoebe must know it wasn't.

Rebecca risked a peek at Alex, who was watching her sister and paying no attention to Rebecca. Her stiff posture brought back earlier encounters before they'd let down their guard around each other. Maybe it wouldn't be so hard to act like there was nothing between them when she seemed so closed-off and cold.

"Let's get down to business, shall we?" Mr. Jennings took charge before Rebecca could decide how to start things. "We proposed to Phoebe that she come home to us. I think we've all learned some lessons and can find a way together now." He reached across the table to take his wife's hand, making it clear who *we* included.

And who it didn't. Alex looked like she'd taken a bite of something bitter and was attempting not to spit it out. Someone needed to step in before he made it out to be a foregone conclusion. Could she argue? Was that what Phoebe wanted? She looked at Phoebe, who was gazing down at the table and picking her nails.

"I'm pleased to hear there's been progress in your relationships. We've been impressed with how hard Phoebe's been working to prepare herself to live independently, and how quickly she's settled in and made friends here. She's a wonderful addition to our little community."

Phoebe raised her head and smiled at Patience's praise, as did Alex. It wasn't an explicit challenge to Mr. Jennings's proposal, but it was near enough and laid the groundwork.

It was Rebecca's place to back her up and show a united front.

She took her cue. "Yes, she's shown real dedication and enthusiasm in everything she's been doing. We've still got a way to go, but I'm confident that if she carries on as she is, she'll be able to move into her own flat with minimal professional support in future."

If you let her carry on.

"Yes, yes, it's been good for her to get some experience looking after herself, not just taking her mother for granted." He laughed, a short bark that contained no real humour.

No one else joined in, and Phoebe stiffened beside her. Alex looked like she was clenching her jaw so hard it might fall off.

"Is that still your long-term plan, Phoebe? To have your own place?" Rebecca turned to her, not wanting to push but needing confirmation before they could go any further. Needing to know that she really was arguing for what Phoebe wanted, not herself.

"Yes." Phoebe looked right at her as she answered, turning so she couldn't see her parents.

Rebecca could see them, though, and the shifty look they exchanged as if they had a different plan.

"Well, there's no reason you can't still have that one day if you come home. We're not going to be around forever! I'm sure your mother would appreciate you doing more around the house, and we can try not to get in your way. You wouldn't have to drop anything you've been doing." He spoke directly to Phoebe, seeming to have realised they weren't planning on supporting him.

Why would they? They were there for Phoebe. He could clearly fight his own corner. The way he put it, it sounded like Phoebe would be staying with them for as long as they wanted and needed her. What about Phoebe's wants and needs? Did she really want to go back there to help her mother keep house—and, Rebecca suspected, wait on their father? Her hands curled in her lap, hidden under the table.

"What about the musical? And my friends?" Phoebe eventually responded, her voice less sure than usual, but clear.

"We can bring you to rehearsals, or arrange something, and to see your friends. Don't worry, love." Mrs. Jennings spoke for the first time. "We're not asking you to throw it all away. We just want you back home with us, where you belong. We'll support you to carry on with whatever you want to do."

"Like you supported her before?" Alex burst in, clearly unable to sit back any longer. "It's a nice sentiment, but how can we know you've really changed."

"Let's not get personal, now. As I said, we've all learned lessons." There was a warning note to Mr. Jennings's voice that gave Rebecca the creeps.

There was no warmth to it. How could he be so dismissive of Alex while trying to cling on to his other daughter? It was like he didn't even remember Alex was his too.

"This is personal. It's Phoebe's personal life. *Her* life."

She should've guessed Alex wouldn't be pushed out that easily. She looked at Patience and sent her a silent plea. *What do we do?*

"We do need to remember that any decision is Phoebe's to make, as it's about what's best for *her*." Patience stepped up and helped bring the focus back to where it belonged. "Do you have any thoughts you would like to share, Phoebe? What do you want?"

"I want…" Phoebe trailed off, a catch to her voice that indicated she wasn't far from tears.

What she wanted was probably for everyone to get along and not play tug-of-war with her. Maybe Rebecca should call a break and give her a chance to pull herself together.

"I want my independence. I want my own life. *My* life." She smiled at her sister across the table, for a moment sounding just like her.

"We get that, we all want that." Mr. Jennings waved his hand, as if trying to sweep aside the emotion of the moment and sever the bond between the sisters. "You've made your point, sweetheart, with all this. You can come home now."

Made her point! Did they really think that was all it was? Rebecca couldn't let them throw away everything they'd worked for. She pushed herself into the fray, her fingers digging into the wood of the table. "This is her home now. Phoebe has worked so hard for her goals, and she needs to be where she'll be supported in that, not be pulled backwards."

Mr. Jennings glared at her with open hostility, all pretence of appreciation forgotten. It might have cowed her, if out of the corner of her eye she hadn't caught Alex's smile. And how she leaned back in her chair, out of her parents' eyeline, and moved her hand from her mouth in a simple sign. *Thank you.* Had she finally seen what she needed to, proof that Rebecca would stand up for her sister? That she'd fight for them?

Maybe. It wasn't certain what she was referring to. Still, Rebecca was touched by her gratitude and her use of Makaton. She hadn't known Phoebe to use the sign system, but Alex had probably learned it to support her when they were kids. She brought her hands up automatically to sign something in return, before registering that everyone was looking at her.

"It is important Phoebe continues moving forward in her plans." Patience stared at Rebecca in a way that could've been approval or a warning.

Possibly both. She must not have sounded wholly professional, but she hadn't stooped to the family's level.

"Yes." Everyone turned to Phoebe, who'd spoken without prompting for the first time since they'd entered the room. "This is my home now. I'm not a child any more—I don't want to live with my parents. I'm happy we're getting on better, but I'm not going back."

No one could argue with that. Phoebe's voice had grown certain again, and Rebecca was sure she'd made the right decision. Her parents didn't look happy, and her father's ego might have been bruised, but they didn't push back. Not there and then, anyway.

They didn't stick around much longer. Mr. Jennings left first, saying goodbye to Phoebe only and even that was frosty. Mrs. Jennings gave their youngest daughter a long hug that seemed to make up for it. After, she cradled Phoebe's face in her hand.

"My little girl, all grown up." She didn't go so far as to say she was proud, but it was in her tone.

On her way out, rushing to catch up with her husband, she placed a hand on Alex's shoulder, and Alex reached up to touch it. They exchanged a smile that contained too many different emotions for Rebecca to even attempt to understand it. Her heart recognised it, though, and squeezed so hard she had to force out her next breath.

Patience followed Mr. and Mrs. Jennings out, offering to take them to the front door.

"I should go now too, unless you want me to hang around." Alex gave Phoebe a tight hug. "Well done for standing up for yourself, Bee, you won't regret it."

"Thanks." Phoebe held on to her sister, burying her face in her chest. "It's okay, I want some no-people time."

Rebecca hoped Alex was right. Once everyone was gone, she would make sure she was there if Phoebe needed to have a meltdown. "I'll be here if you need anything."

"Thank you," Alex said. As she walked past her, she reached out and grasped Rebecca's hand. "We couldn't have done it without you."

"You're welcome. Just doing my job."

It was a lie that they both acknowledged with a smile. Would she have stood up to Mr. Jennings if Alex hadn't been on the scene? She would tell herself yes, it was clearly what was right, but the potency of Alex's hand in hers had told a different story.

CHAPTER SEVENTEEN

From the look on Alex's face, Rebecca might have made a mistake. She had picked up the bouquet from the local florist's, taking her time to select something not overly romantic and not too impersonal either. She'd gone with a rainbow assortment, which included a few roses, but few enough it wasn't like she was just giving them.

Alex stared at her from the doorway, making no move to let her in. Her hair glistened and her skin was flushed, as if she'd just stepped out of the shower. Was she just surprised to see her, or was there some other reason for her less-than-warm reception?

After the meeting the day before, Phoebe had been understandably distressed and Rebecca had done her best to comfort her. When she left, she'd calmed down and was curled up in front of a film with Faye. Hopefully she wasn't regretting her decision. Surely Alex couldn't be and had seen, once and for all, that Rebecca was on their side.

"I thought I'd bring a late housewarming gift." She held out the flowers towards Alex. "I'm not interrupting anything, am I?"

Was there someone else there? Oh God, was the state Alex was in down to something less innocent than a hot shower? Rebecca's cheeks burned. Surprising her had seemed a nice idea in theory, but she hadn't considered that possibility. Now that Alex had a house to bring women back to, maybe she was making the most of it.

"No, I just wasn't expecting you." Alex stopped and seemed to bite back something else. "Come in." She moved aside and held the door open.

Rebecca hesitated. "Are you sure? I don't want to—"

"It's fine, come in. You just caught me off guard."

It seemed more like the opposite, like she had her guard up. But the doorstep wasn't the best place to investigate why, so Rebecca walked past her into the house.

The hallway looked exactly the same as when she'd last been there visiting her friends, which was disorienting. She could hardly expect Alex to have put her stamp on the place when she was just house-sitting. Still, the sight of Tiff staring out of the photo frames lining the walls wasn't helping. She could just imagine what she'd have to say about Rebecca's current predicament. *Do you know what you're doing? How do you think this is going to end?*

"I'll put the kettle on." Alex walked past, skirting round her, heading for the kitchen.

"Wait!" Rebecca reached out and caught one of her hands, stopping her. "If you don't want me here, I'll go."

Alex laughed, a harsh, dry sound. "It's not that." She started to slip away, withdrawing her hand, then stopped. "Look, I do want you, I just wasn't expecting you to turn up here when I'd not even told you this was where I'm staying."

Ah, that should have occurred to her. "Sorry, I thought it'd be a nice surprise. Drew told me…" She realised that might be part of it. Maybe they'd crossed a line. Again.

"They told you I was staying here? And about where I was before?"

"Yes." Surely there was no real harm, unless Alex was planning on keeping her location secret from her for some reason.

"They shouldn't have. It's up to me what I tell people, especially you." Alex puffed out a long breath. "I'm not used to this, having a metamour close. *Potential* metamour."

She smiled at the term despite the context. If Alex was thinking of Drew as a metamour, *potential* metamour, then she was thinking of her as a partner. Potential partner. Unless there was something secret going on with her and Ishani…*No, don't even go there.* "They didn't mean to interfere. They didn't realise you hadn't told me. But I'll tell them you didn't appreciate it."

"I'll talk to them myself. We're friends, I want us to stay that way. Just…" Alex scrunched her lips, visibly struggling to find the right way to put it.

"Not have them involved in our relationship?" She finished for her, in case the issue might be Alex not wanting to seem like she was slagging off one of her partners in front of her.

"Potential relationship." Alex's lips resolved into a lopsided grin. "How about we start this again…Hey, Rebecca, nice to see you. To what do I owe this pleasure?"

Rebecca laughed, then held out the flowers again. "I bought you a housewarming gift."

"Thank you, they're beautiful. I better put them in some water. Why don't you come in, and I'll put the kettle on while I'm at it."

"That would be lovely." Rebecca handed her the flowers, and Alex leaned over to give her a peck on the cheek as she took them, their fingers meeting around the stems.

And then she was kissing her. Rebecca didn't know who had turned to make their lips meet, she just knew that she had wanted to kiss her like that for too long. She let go of the flowers and pulled Alex closer, craving the warmth of her body against hers. Alex obeyed, wrapping her arms around Rebecca as they savoured the kiss, slowing and deepening it as if neither of them wanted it to end.

Alex was the one to break it off, and a whimper escaped Rebecca's mouth as it was abandoned.

"I really should get these in water."

At this, Rebecca became aware of a damp patch in the middle of her back where the dripping bouquet had been pressed against her as they embraced. "Okay."

"Okay." Alex leaned in for another quick kiss.

It was tempting to pull her close to continue their embrace. Having had a taste, she was suddenly insatiable. Instead, she let Alex take her hand and walk them towards the kitchen.

"Any idea where they keep a vase in this place?"

She shook her head, too flooded with hormones to remember anything much. Which was fine, she didn't want to stop and think and let all her worries about their future back in. Alex had made it clear she didn't want to be in a relationship with someone like her, or at least someone who did relationships like her. Unless this was going to be a no-strings-attached affair, which had never been her style, she would have to make some changes. Big changes that made her heart beat even faster. Right then, she just wanted to enjoy being with Alex. Surely she'd earned that.

"Aha!" Alex grabbed a vase from on top of the tall fridge and filled it with water before popping the flowers in, still wrapped. "I'll sort them properly later." She reached for Rebecca.

Glad they were on the same page, she swiftly moved into Alex's arms and kissed her again. Alex's hand, now free, stroked her back, her face, her collarbone as they stood pressed together. She could feel her knees becoming weak. "Can we move to somewhere more comfortable?"

Alex responded with a delicious grin.

"Not there! I mean the lounge, a comfy seat…"

"I know, gorgeous, what else could you mean?"

Her eyes automatically flicked up to indicate the bedrooms upstairs. Alex's followed them. But she wouldn't go that far straightaway. Giving into their attraction that much was enough. Her lips tingled, and she was sure she must be blushing.

"I'm just teasing, come on." Alex led her through to the lounge.

They sank into the sofa together, instantly reclaiming each other's lips. Alex's arms were firm and strong, holding her close, stopping her from falling off the edge as they graduated to lying entwined together, stopping her from falling out of the moment and back into her head.

"*Sooo.*" Alex lay back with Rebecca resting on top of her. "We're doing this."

"Yes." Rebecca let herself sink into her, not able to question how right it felt.

Alex's arms tightened around her in a squeezing hug before going back to stroking up and down her body. "I'm afraid I'm not…"

She stiffened and Alex gave her a gentle kiss.

"I'm not up to much after yesterday, as in talking. And thinking."

She let out a relieved laugh. "That's okay, me neither."

It had been intense. Phoebe had looked drained after, as if standing up to her parents had taken too much out of her, and Rebecca had felt the same. By the time she got home, she was exhausted and non-verbal.

"Though it did make me realise how lucky we are to have you in our lives." Alex whispered her gratitude onto the top of Rebecca's head.

She didn't know how to reply and instead squirmed in Alex's arms, burying her face deeper into her chest, which provided a wonderful distraction. She ran her hand up Alex's T-shirt until she found the soft fabric encasing her breasts, feeling Alex's breath follow so her chest rose to meet her. She traced the edge of the bra across her right breast, seeing as well as hearing Alex's gasp as she slipped inside to stroke her nipple.

"You don't want to do that," Alex said, though she made no move to stop her.

"I don't?" She wasn't sure of much any more, but she yearned to trace every inch of her.

"Not if you want to keep your clothes on."

Alex placed a hand behind her head and pulled her into a fierce kiss. Her other hand squeezed Rebecca's butt, pressing her down onto her thigh and eliciting a moan that she released into Alex's mouth.

She did not want to keep her clothes on. But something in the back of her mind broke through, telling her to wait. If this meant something, if it was more than a brief hormonal outpouring, they could wait. "I should."

"Should what?"

"Keep my clothes on. For now. Not rush things." She let her hand rest on Alex's breast. There were things they could still enjoy staying dressed.

"So you know, I don't want you to, but agreed." Alex gently reached up under Rebecca's layers of clothing until her hands pressed on the bare skin of her back. "Judging from this, it's definitely going to be worth waiting for."

Rebecca nodded. It was all she could do. What with the sparks that trailed down her spine from Alex's hands, she could barely imagine how good they would feel elsewhere. But she could imagine enough to make her squirm against Alex's thigh that was tucked between her legs.

Alex pressed her thigh up firmer onto her, so Rebecca was riding it. Her hand drifted back to her butt, this time under her clothing, her fingers biting into the soft flesh of her buttock. Then she winced. She immediately tried to cover it with a blank expression, but Rebecca was too close to miss it.

"Are you okay?" She eased her weight off her.

"Yeah, it's just my leg." Alex let go of her and reached down to grasp it.

A flash of fur whipped between them, and Rebecca was pushed back against the sofa by a stocky tabby cat. It stood over Alex as if trying to protect her from whatever had caused her pain. Or, knowing Zelda, she was feeling left out and wanting to be the centre of attention.

"Hello, you." She gave her a pet. "I'm sorry I didn't say hello when I got here."

The cat eyed her with disdain. It was clearly going to take more than that to make up for the poor treatment. She saw Alex's smile return.

"Poor girl, you must've been heartbroken." Alex reached up and scratched Zelda's ears.

The cat purred, rubbing against Alex's hand. Rebecca felt a stab of jealousy. Towards a cat. *Oh God, I'm falling hard.*

She forced herself to sit back up, and Alex shuffled to join her upright, Zelda shifting too to stay between them. "Is your leg okay?"

"It's fine. You know, we may have an audience, but that doesn't mean we have to stop completely." Alex recaptured Rebecca's lips, stopping any more questions.

"Good," she whispered between kisses.

They shifted closer together, the cat climbing onto Alex's lap out of her way. They would have to talk, soon, but they'd earned a little indulgence.

❖

Alex ran. Leaves crunched under her pounding feet, and the sound vibrated across the still lake. Her path was clear with no one else in sight, so she picked up speed. Her feet were still adjusting to the dirt and natural debris underfoot instead of concrete, and she kept her eyes open for stray branches she'd need to dodge instead of weaving through people.

You really could breathe there. Rebecca had been right. The air by the lake seemed cleansed by its presence, as if the deep water had sucked in all the pollution. She stopped when she reached one of the wooden jetties and walked out onto it, taking in the air and the view. Memories of Rebecca tumbled into the front of her mind: Rebecca leaning into her when she'd first brought her there, Rebecca in her arms, pulling her close as if she wanted to be swallowed by their embrace...

Alex ran. She needed to stop thinking about her. Or at least, she needed to stop thinking about her like that, and take a step back. Several fast steps.

She ran, and a tornado of leaves swirled around her, released by a gust of wind that pushed her towards the water. She battled the elements and kept moving forward.

Did she really want to stay there? It was a question that had prodded her as she scrubbed herself in the shower after the standoff with their parents. They'd won. Phoebe had proved she could stand up for herself, and the staff proved they'd stand by her. As she'd washed off the bitter taint of their father's words and the tenderness of their mother's touch, she'd felt ready to move on, back to her own life that she'd been rebuilding. Phoebe wasn't the only one who'd had to fight for independence, and Alex had no intention of giving hers up. She'd put things on hold to help Phoebe, and that job was done. The longer she stayed there, the more she'd get sucked into the system and the harder it'd be for both of them to move on.

She'd reached the conclusion that it was time to go as she'd towelled her hair dry with the Hathaways' rich, deep towel. A touch of guilt had crept in. They had been so trusting when they'd handed her the keys, and though she'd made no promises to stay the whole time, leaving after a few weeks could be taking the piss. Especially as she'd be leaving Drew to take over her dumped responsibilities. Drew, who'd befriended and supported her despite clocking her attraction to their partner from the start. Which brought her to Rebecca.

Rebecca, who was clearly fighting for both her and Phoebe.

Rebecca, who'd then turned up on her doorstep, and once Alex had gotten over the intrusion of it, had wrapped herself in her arms. They'd both been too emotionally worn out by the events of the day before to fight their attraction any longer. At least they'd resisted moving past the couch. The cat had helped. She would miss the little bugger.

What had she been thinking? Clearly, she hadn't been. She'd avoided the risk of STIs, but that didn't mean it wasn't risky. Her friends back home, as well as Willow, had warned her not to go there. It was validating to hear them support her damning of hierarchies, unlike Drew, and at the same time she wished someone would've been open enough to talk about how she might negotiate a way through. Because they all knew, no matter what they said, she would go there. And she had.

She steered around a corner, leading her deeper into the bank of trees, and nearly ran straight into a dog walker. The dog leapt up at her as if it was a game, delighted to have a new friend to play with. She paused to give it a fuss, and it leapt higher in a clumsy attempt to lick her face. She swerved and laughed, apologising to the owner for running into them, as they apologised for the dog's overenthusiastic hello.

As she jogged off again, her smile remained. If she stayed in the country, maybe she could get a dog to take out exploring. She'd missed their childhood pup almost as much as she'd missed Phoebe when she left. The cat was good company when it felt like it, but it wasn't the same.

A dog wouldn't tell her off for getting involved in another romance doomed to fail. It'd just listen. That was what she needed, a friend who would listen without judgement as she ran through all the possibilities. Not seeing any of her friends in person for months made it harder to get that. In theory she could reach out to someone, rather than waiting for the moment to come up, which it never did when they weren't finding themselves huddled in the corner of a pub talking earnestly into the night while everyone else got too drunk. Group video calls weren't the same.

Would her friends ever drop their guard about Rebecca's setup, though? Or would they just be hanging on for their chance to say *I told you so*? There weren't many taboos as far as her non-monogamous, non-heteronormative crowd were concerned, but hierarchy was a big one. They were trying to protect her, like she tried to protect herself, but they couldn't stop her falling for Rebecca.

The path veered back towards the lake and another jetty. She stepped out onto it and, this time, let her memories of Rebecca join her. She was too far gone to outrun it. When she'd welcomed Rebecca into her home and into her arms the day before, she'd made her decision. They were doing this, despite their doubts and fears. The cool wind sent ripples across the water, an unstoppable pulse.

She wanted to stay and stare across the expanse until everything made sense, but the heat from her exertion was dissipating fast, and the telltale pins and needles in her leg were getting harder to ignore. There were some things she couldn't push through, and she also needed to accept her body's limitations. Running was not physio-recommended exercise, even at that gentle pace. Her days of doing whatever she felt like were over.

This wasn't something for her to figure out alone anyway. Whatever compromise she came up with would only be any good if Rebecca was willing to meet her in the middle. And there were some things she would never compromise on. It was up to Rebecca whether she'd let go of all her rules and let them be free to be together. It was up to Alex to make her boundaries clear.

She'd made a good start by being honest about her wish to have a relationship with Rebecca without her other partners interfering. Willow, or any other partner, had never had a say in who else Alex got involved with, though she would occasionally point out the warning flags as she had with Rebecca. She wouldn't be subject to a metamour's whim. Not again. Ishani was an unknown she would have to figure out. She inwardly winced as she remembered her initial assumption about Rebecca being her carer. At least she'd realised her mistake as soon as she'd seen them at the meet and hadn't said it to anyone—that would've been a deserved strike against her.

It was less clear-cut than usual because of being friends with Drew, but that didn't mean they were part of her relationship with Rebecca.

Rebecca and Drew were becoming important to her, and there must be a way to keep them both close without it getting too messy.

Her watch beeped to signal it was time to head back. If she went straightaway, she could drop in at the home before work and check on Phoebe, without bumping into Rebecca. Rebecca had been clear on keeping things quiet at work, and she needed to respect that. If anyone saw them together, it would likely give the game away, especially as Alex couldn't imagine being able to resist kissing her again.

Hopefully it wouldn't make much difference to Phoebe. As long as they were both there when she needed them, that was what mattered. She didn't need them at the same time. A pang in her chest reminded her that Phoebe didn't really seem to need her any more. Rebecca was doing a fine job supporting her. She should be glad Phoebe could do without her. They could still hang out together, for fun. Maybe they could go to a theme park or something, as a reward and release after the showdown. Phoebe might want to bring her new BFF, though, which would mean a staff member also coming. Unless…

Maybe there was a way she could help not only Phoebe enjoy a bit more freedom. If she could have a private word with Patience. She headed back to the car park, a plan forming and distracting her from any more reflections on how it had felt to finally hold Rebecca.

❖

"What are you so happy about?"

Rebecca had been humming to herself as she completed her paperwork. "Nothing."

"You love doing this?" Luisa swept her arm across the table, indicating the piles of records they were in the process of updating.

"You know me, I like getting organised." She focused on the sheet in front of her, double-checking who it belonged to. Or, more accurately, triple-checking. She was buzzing, fuelled by NRE and reminiscences of Alex's touch.

"That is true. But not even you like it so much. It is not only today—you have been bouncing and glowing for—" Luisa broke off suddenly and clutched Rebecca's arm. "Oh my God, are you…?" Her eyes flicked down to Rebecca's stomach.

"No! You know I don't want kids." How had she come to that conclusion?

Maybe it was preferable to her guessing the truth. What would

Luisa think about her getting with Alex? Even if she had already known they were poly, which she didn't as far as Rebecca was aware, could she ever approve?

"Things change." Luisa shrugged and leaned back, seeming a little disappointed. "And lesbians can have babies now. It would not be such a big thing here."

"I'm aware of that, but we still don't want any. And it's not like it would happen by accident." She lifted her pile of papers and tapped them on the table to get them in line. Had that come out as snappy? She mustn't get Luisa's back up. She was the one workmate she trusted to have her back. "I won't get married with you, so now you want us to have babies together?"

Luisa let out a tinkle of laughter. "Not yet! First marriage, then babies. My mother would never forgive me."

"Don't tell me that's why the wedding is so soon!" She hadn't taken in too much of the details of the wedding plans, but they seemed to be speeding ahead. She must've been distracted lately to not consider that before.

"No! I also would not let that happen by accident."

So she hadn't been so distracted she'd missed signs of a pregnancy. That was something. But she should pay more attention to this important time in her friend's life, even if Luisa's goals were very much not her own.

Several times during her shift, she caught herself humming and smiling for no apparent reason. She was full of nervous energy, but a different kind than usual, like she was at risk of flying, not drowning. It was probably for the best she didn't bump into Alex, in case someone saw and put two and two together, but she still felt a slight sinking feeling when she didn't visit during her shift. Not enough to bring her down completely and she sang loudly to the cheesy pop music blaring from the radio on her drive home, recalling Alex's way of giving herself over to it.

When she parked up, she spotted Drew's car outside the house. Had they made plans? She had been absent-minded but surely wouldn't have forgot that—she always looked forward to their time together. A quick check on her phone confirmed there was nothing in their shared calendar. Even if she'd neglected to add it in, wouldn't Drew have done it? Maybe they weren't visiting her, maybe they were hanging out with Ishani, though then wouldn't Ishani have put it in her calendar too?

People can see each other without pre-planning. It doesn't mean anything's wrong. It was something she might need to get more used to, as Alex struck her as the spontaneous type. Except it had been her who'd thrown Alex by turning up at her house unannounced, so maybe not. She hadn't done the exchange of calendars thing with Alex—they weren't there yet. If Alex even had one. Her style of relationships might mean she wouldn't want to get tied to a timetable or have Rebecca see what she was up to.

The house was quiet when she entered, with that edge to the silence which hinted her arrival had caused it. She removed her coat and shoes with trembling hands, then padded into the kitchen in her slippers. *Don't freak out, it's just adrenaline and imagination.*

Ishani and Drew were sitting at the kitchen table with a plate of chocolate brownies in front of them, seemingly waiting for her.

"Hi. Um, I wasn't expecting you. What's going on?" She looked between her partners, searching for a clue. Had something bad happened? Their faces were serious, their hands wrapped around nearly empty cups of tea.

It looked like an intervention.

"This is an intervention," Drew said.

Crap. If her fears weren't so often right, it would make it far easier to dismiss them. She could've asked for more information, as if she didn't already know what it was about, but didn't want to play ignorant. "You're not supposed to do this," she said meekly.

"And you're not supposed to get with someone else without telling us." As usual, Drew got straight to the point. They looked her in the eyes, unblinking.

"Why don't you sit down and join us so we can talk about it." Ishani pointed to the chair facing her.

Rebecca was about to ask if she could at least get a cup of tea first, when she noted there was a full, steaming cup by her seat. Could she just grab it and run? She had just got home from work. Surely she deserved the chance to unwind before being jumped like that? No. She sat down with a sigh.

Ishani's eyes were tinged with pink. "I don't like forcing you to talk, you know that, but I've been waiting for you to tell me what's going on with Alex for months and—"

"It hasn't been going on for months! It's only just started, and I thought we agreed we didn't need to say anything that early on." Even as she said it, she knew it wasn't true. She and Alex hadn't kissed until a few days ago, but it hadn't exactly come out of nowhere.

"Bullshit." Drew didn't hesitate to call her out.

"Drew," Ishani said in a soothing tone, playing the responsible adult in the room, "let's try and keep calm."

"I am calm, but the whole point of doing this is to get her to stop denying it." Drew turned back to Rebecca. "When was it you spoke to me about her?"

She winced. They had her there. It had been clear in their conversation that she and Alex had feelings for each other and were considering acting on them. When was that, about two months ago? She didn't answer. It seemed like a rhetorical question, and she didn't want to make things worse.

"I asked you about her after we met, do you remember? Even then it was obvious there was something between you. Everyone could see it. Yet you've said nothing to me about her since." Ishani looked down at her hands where they lay clasped on the table, seeming more hurt than angry. "And now Drew tells me you discussed Alex with them. Yet you didn't trust me for some reason."

"It's not like that, I do trust you." Rebecca wanted to take her in her arms but wasn't sure Ishani would let her touch her. Her heart sank. She'd messed up. Ishani deserved better. "I just, I didn't understand it myself, I still don't entirely, everything's changing."

"Why didn't you talk to me? I deserved to know you were considering another relationship when you'd been so clear before that you wouldn't. That big a change isn't something you should keep from me. We could figure it out together. Unless…" Ishani faltered, then finally lifted her eyes to meet Rebecca's. They were swimming with tears. "Unless you don't want me to be part of that change or your life any more."

"No!" Rebecca's own vision started to swim. This was what she'd been afraid of, that in letting Alex in she'd inadvertently push Ishani out. "I'm sorry, baby, you're right. I should've told you. I'm sorry. I do want you to be part of my life, a big part. I couldn't imagine it without you."

A tear fell from Ishani's eye, running down her cheek to her lips, which turned up in a hesitant smile. "You do? Because if you don't, I'd rather you were honest with mc so I —"

"I do, I do. I love you. I love being with you. That was never in doubt." She did go to her then, holding her to her chest and wiping away the tears that started to flow freely. She stayed holding her until they both stopped shaking. "I love you."

"Now we're getting somewhere. And it's time for these." Drew pushed the plate over towards Ishani, who stayed nestled against Rebecca.

Rebecca let her go momentarily to reach for her chair and drag it closer so she could carry on holding her. She gave her a kiss on the tracks of her tears and reached across to squeeze Drew's hand. Hopefully her love for them wasn't in question. "Thank you."

"Don't thank me. Ishani was the one who baked. Try one, they're delicious." They prodded the plate again.

She looked at it, but her stomach was too twisted to attempt one. She'd messed up so badly, and Ishani had got hurt. But what should she say? What could she say? Alex had been funny about how much Drew knew already. Would she be okay with her telling them both more? As she held Ishani's hand, her tight grip returned, it was clear there was no choice. Ishani deserved the openness and honesty they'd promised each other. That wasn't Alex's call.

"Are you and Alex together now? As in, sexually and romantically, to be clear," Drew said.

They also deserved to know that, especially as they hung out with Alex apart from her. "Yes," she said, and her stomach eased. "In a dating way. I mean we haven't—"

"We don't need to know all the details," Ishani said, putting a hand on Rebecca's chest before she could overshare, "just the basics of who you're involved with and in what way."

"And that you're being safe, of course, but I figure we can at least trust you on that." There was a hint of humour to Drew's voice and a sting.

Was she not to be trusted in other ways? A wave of anger rose up like when she'd first walked in. She'd not done anything wrong by being with Alex. They were non-monogamous, it was allowed. "It's not like I've been sneaking around behind your backs!"

She instantly regretted it as she watched her words drop hard on all their heads.

"Haven't you?" Drew shot back, then slumped in their chair. "Look, we're not saying you shouldn't be with her, just that you should be honest with us about it."

The blistering wave sank. She couldn't argue she had been. She hadn't even been honest with herself. "I'm sorry. I was confused and didn't know what was going on, or what I wanted. I wasn't deliberately hiding anything from you."

"We know." Ishani squeezed her hand.

"It's…it's complicated. You know I wasn't looking for anyone else, and she wasn't open to getting with someone in our kind of relationship."

"How do you mean?"

Ishani tensed against her, but Drew didn't look surprised.

"She's Solo Poly and anti-hierarchy." Rebecca wasn't sure how much more she needed to say. "Based on experience, she's learned it doesn't work for her."

"Yeah, she told me as much." Drew might have known, but they didn't seem entirely comfortable with the knowledge.

"What does that mean for us?" Ishani was looking down again, as if she could read the answer in the bottom of her teacup.

"It means…it means I want to try relationships without hierarchy myself. I know I was the one who wanted it at the start, but I think I want something else now." It hit Rebecca full force that it wasn't just her call to make, even though it was her idea in the first place. If Ishani didn't agree, what then? Everything could still come crashing down. Her heart sped up. Why hadn't she forced herself to speak to her earlier? Was she so afraid of what she would say?

Ishani sat quietly for a moment, visibly processing. "It sounds like this woman is a game changer." She looked up, and Rebecca saw her own fear reflected in her eyes.

That was it, wasn't it? She had been avoiding facing this because she didn't want the game to change—she liked knowing the rules—and now she was drifting without any sense of where she was or where she might end up. Her chest thumped so hard it might split open, and her palms grew sweaty.

"Hey." Drew's voice reached her as if through water. "Hey." They reached over and tilted her chin, their eyes an anchor as everything came crashing in. "Maybe that's not a bad thing."

Maybe. Rebecca wished, not for the first time since she'd sat down at the table, that she could take it all back, that she could make things how they used to be before she knew Alex existed. She'd been happy in her little bubble. But she couldn't bring herself to wish Alex hadn't come into her life. She was in too deep, and there really was no going back, wherever they ended up.

CHAPTER EIGHTEEN

Alex fiddled with the collar of her shirt. Thankfully she'd found an iron without too much rooting through the Hathaways' cupboards, something she still wasn't one hundred percent comfortable with. It was their home, not even partly hers, and going through their things felt invasive. It was the main drawback to staying in someone else's house, but at least everything she needed was already there. Having a house all to herself which she didn't have to furnish was a luxury she would miss when she went back to house-shares in the city. A friend had offered her a vacant room in their home, but being someone's lodger would be worse. At least in their run-down rentals they'd all had an equal say.

The doorbell rang and made her jump, the multiple speakers meaning it sounded like she was standing right next to it. Rebecca had insisted on driving, which meant she hadn't had to worry about clearing the van so she hadn't argued. Much. The level of insistence did send a prickle down her neck. Was Rebecca just being helpful, or was there something she was hiding? Was she hiding her?

There'd been no mention of whether Rebecca's nesting partner knew she was going out with her. Ishani had been fine with her the one time they'd met, but that was an accidental meeting and before anything developed. Had Rebecca told her about their kiss, which had led to many kisses but not much more? She wasn't sure what would be worse—if Rebecca had told Ishani everything or kept her a secret.

Rebecca stood on the doorstep with a box of fancy chocolates, tied up with a glinting bow. Her hair was down and tamed into smooth waves, and her coat was open, revealing a burgundy silk blouse that brought warmth to her pale features. Alex's body warmed in response.

"Hi. You look beautiful. Want to come in?" She held the door open, and the cool night air took the chance to creep in.

"Not for long, we'll need to leave soon to have time to park. It can get pretty hectic just before a show starts." Rebecca stepped inside.

As soon as the door closed, she reached for her and drew her into a long kiss. Rebecca's face was cold beneath her cupped hands, but her mouth was warm, and her lips grew hot beneath hers. Something sharp dug into her chest and Rebecca pulled back.

"For you." She passed Alex the chocolates which had been pressed between them, at high risk of melting.

"Thank you." There was nowhere to put them in the narrow hallway, so she took Rebecca's hand and led her into the lounge, placing them on the coffee table by the sofa.

Rebecca eyed the sofa with a slight blush, as if she was also recalling what had happened last time they were there. "We shouldn't get too comfortable."

"Probably not." She drew her back into their embrace, and Rebecca wrapped her arms tight around her as they kissed. "So, are we admitting this is a date now?"

"I think we're past the point of no return."

She couldn't be sure what emotion caused Rebecca's voice to tremble as she said this. Excitement? Fear? Happiness? A mixture of all three? She'd wondered whether the other day might be a slip, a moment of weakness while recovering from things kicking off at the home, and Rebecca would want to act like it'd never happened. She was more glad than she'd like to admit that she didn't.

They made it to the theatre as the voice on the tannoy was announcing a final call to take their seats. The usher took their tickets with a smile and pointed them to the back row of the stalls. She had read the seating plan right and got the perfect seats, with a wall at their backs rather than other people.

Rebecca paused after they held out the stubs, seeming lost in thought, and Alex had to guide her out of the doorway where a line was waiting to come in.

"Do you think Phoebe would like to volunteer here?" Rebecca gestured back at the usher and the lanyard swinging from their neck.

"I bet she would. But how about you take a break from work tonight, and we just enjoy ourselves." She nudged Rebecca with her shoulder to show she was teasing.

"Sorry. Sometimes I struggle to switch off." She gave a cute little shrug.

"I noticed." Alex flinched. It might have sounded harsher than she'd meant it. "I mean, I like that you're passionate about your work and you really care about them. But you've earned a break."

Rebecca smiled at her and it lit up her eyes. Her job was important to her, and she probably didn't get the credit she deserved. She shoved back the prickling question of whether it meant too much, and whether she did too much for her residents.

As well as being at the back, their seats were on the end of the row, so they didn't have to climb over other people to get in or out. As the lights went down, Rebecca rested her head on Alex's shoulder. She reached over and took her hand. When they'd taken Phoebe to the cinema, she'd had to fight the urge to do so. Rebecca's hand had rested on the arm between them, and it would've been so easy to reach over and lace her fingers through hers. But it would've been the wrong move and there was still so much distance between them back then. Then Rebecca had actually been working, and Alex hadn't known what she thought of her. A little voice in the back of her mind reminded her she still didn't know what Rebecca wanted or what they were to each other. She turned and planted a silent kiss on Rebecca's head. They were definitely something.

As the action started, Rebecca sat up, and all her attention seemed fixed on the stage. Her eyes shone as she watched, visibly enthralled, and her lips moved in sync with the songs. Alex found herself torn between enjoying watching the show and watching Rebecca's reaction to it. It was awesome to see her looking so happy and in the moment. Even if she didn't like the show, she'd have been glad they came.

She did like it. *Wicked* was subversive and clever, without being snobby about it. By the time they reached the interval, she was also hooked.

"What do you think?" Rebecca said, as soon as the curtain dropped.

"Loving it."

Her answer earned her an added beam to Rebecca's smile. Then people along their row started to stand and shuffle forward, so she had to move out of the way, pressing herself against the wall at the top of the aisle where they couldn't shove her. Rebecca stayed in her place, standing up and letting the seat flip up behind her, seeming in no rush to join them.

Once everyone had gone, they took their seats again and swivelled to face each other. With most people charging out to get snacks and pee, it was less busy in the auditorium than outside.

"Thanks for getting the tickets. I haven't seen it in ages," Rebecca said.

"You're welcome." She was glad she'd taken the plunge and asked her. Even though she'd got knocked back at first.

The usher had been replaced by a server with a tray of ice creams and other goodies. Rebecca studied them. "Ice cream is tempting. I need to pop to the toilet anyway."

"If you can afford it. And the queues will be massive." Alex was glad she'd resisted having a cuppa while she got ready so she didn't need to battle them.

"I'll trust you to guard it while I'm waiting." She gave Alex a quick kiss that made her wish they were back in the cinema instead. There no one batted an eyelid if you sat making out in the back row.

"I'll do my best to resist devouring it, but I can't make any promises." She spoke into Rebecca's ear and felt a tingle pass between them. Maybe it was a good thing they were somewhere they had to behave and might be able to manage a sensible conversation. There was so much she wanted to do with Rebecca other than talk, but they needed to.

She had got her to admit it was a date, which meant they were dating. Which made it harder not to face up to the gulf that still existed between their relationship styles. How long could they carry on before they had to figure out how to cross it? No matter how much she thought about it, she couldn't see any way for her to commit to another hierarchical relationship. It wasn't like she needed Rebecca to throw away her existing partners, though. There was no issue with her having a nesting partner. In some ways it was better as it meant she was less likely to want that of Alex. Different partners nourished you in different ways. But would Rebecca be willing to give up the control and false sense of safety of the structure? That was what she wanted to ask but couldn't figure out how to without it seeming like she was insulting her.

By the time Rebecca returned, her ice cream was starting to melt round the edges. She grabbed it back as soon as she sat down and tested it with her spoon. "This way, it's not too hard to eat."

Rebecca tucked in with relish, the plastic spoon easily scooping up the softened ice cream unlike Alex's, which she'd feared might break as she'd stabbed at her frozen pot. The rest of their row were filing back in, so she balanced herself on the arm, her long legs tucked down the side out of the way. Rebecca perched on her folded-up seat to let them through, continuing to pick at her ice cream and seeming unfazed by all the strangers brushing past. They'd missed any chance to talk during the break.

It would wait. Once everyone had settled, she slipped back into her own seat and slid her arm around the back of Rebecca's. She nestled into it without looking at Alex, her eyes fixed on the rising curtain. Alex made herself turn to the stage instead of gazing at her creamy lips, which her tongue darted out to lick.

The show ended with a standing ovation, which she joined. She couldn't imagine getting up there herself but pictured her sister taking her turn to soak up the applause. Could that really be her one day? Could her dream come true, despite the cards she'd been dealt? Beside her, Rebecca applauded so hard her hands must hurt. Maybe she could, with them both by her side.

They were swept up in the crowds that emptied from the theatre and flowed towards the car park. Rebecca chatted excitedly about what they'd seen, checking she had appreciated every moment. She had, and Rebecca's joy had added to it. Some things she preferred doing alone, but others were definitely improved by good company.

Once in the car, they joined the trickle leaving. It was a good thing they weren't in any rush. It also meant while they were sitting there they had no other option but to talk, with the radio hissing under the concrete layers of car park until Rebecca switched it off.

"Glad you agreed to come with me after all?" she started.

"Yes, definitely." Rebecca reached over and squeezed her knee as they sat in the stalled queue, before resting her hands back on the wheel. "Glad you asked me?"

"Of course." Just not at first but her ego had taken worse hits. And it was time to put herself out there again. "Now we're doing this, us, we need to talk more."

"I know." Rebecca's hands visibly tightened on the steering wheel. "I've been thinking…I want to do this, to give us a shot."

"Good, so do I." She took a breath before the next part. "I've not changed my mind, you know. I'm still not up for getting into a hierarchy-style relationship. I need to know I'm not gonna get pushed aside on someone else's orders."

"You won't. Ishani isn't like that. She's always been less into the structure than me, and over time we've got less strict with it anyway.

I can't remember the last time it actually influenced anything. Until now." Rebecca let out a long breath. "It was me who asked for it, at the start, and it seemed to work."

"But now?"

"But now I'm ready to take the plunge and try something else. For you." Her last two words were almost a whisper.

Alex let this sink in. *For you.* Should she really be asking Rebecca to make that big a move when she couldn't be sure if they had a future? She'd never been one for making false promises. "As long as you're sure that's what you want, and everyone's okay with it."

Rebecca's mouth twitched. "It was a surprise to them, coming from me, but Ishani and Drew are happy to let the hierarchy part go. To be honest, they wanted to before now, but I'd been unsure about getting rid of that safety net."

"So no vetoes? Including pocket ones, like if someone changes their mind?" Many couples didn't admit to having the right to say no to each other's partners, but she'd found they still did it in an underhanded way by asking for a break from poly, which happened to mean dumping the new person or some other insidious demand. Which was kinda worse, as you didn't see it coming. Or she didn't, anyway.

"No vetoes of any kind." Rebecca sounded sure of that at least. "I was wondering, do you fancy joining us for Diwali? Ishani usually spends some time with her family of origin before heading back to let her hair down with us. Her other partners will be there too."

The invitation caught her off guard. It sounded like a big deal and more of an involvement than she was ready for. Or might ever want. She got the chosen family thing, but she'd never made metamours part of hers.

"Drew will be there, so you'll know someone other than me." Rebecca seemed to have misinterpreted her hesitation.

"Thanks, but I'll give it a miss. Big polycule gatherings aren't really my thing." She tried to let her down gently. It wasn't personal.

"Oh, okay." Rebecca tried to smile, but it didn't stick.

They finally made it out of the underground car park, and Rebecca reached for the radio dial. Music burst out as if it had been waiting to be freed from the underground cavern. She didn't say anything else, either upset at Alex's refusal or just focused on the busy traffic as she navigated her way out of the town centre.

Alex didn't want to ask. It was better to let some things lie rather than dive into a conversation that wouldn't leave anyone feeling good.

She shifted her chair back so she could stretch out and massage her legs, focusing on the physical aches rather than the twinge of guilt. Rebecca had compromised and changed her whole relationship structure for her. Did that mean it was her turn to figure out what she was willing to give?

❖

"I can't do it!" Phoebe dropped into a chair.

Before Rebecca could decide what to say to reassure her, Faye jumped in.

"Yes, you can—you did it last week."

"That was last week." Phoebe's voice was muffled as she slid down in her chair and retreated into her hoodie.

It was hardly surprising she wasn't her usual self after the events of the weekend. Rebecca had hoped standing up to her parents would have left her feeling more confident, but it seemed to have done the opposite. "You've had a tough time. Why not take it easy this week and come back to it when you're feeling better."

Phoebe grunted.

"Yeah. You nailed it before, you just need to rest." Faye sat next to her and squeezed Phoebe's hand.

There was still a month to go until the show opened, so she had time to take a break, especially considering how hard she'd worked so far. Rebecca's jaw clenched. It would be awful if her parents' move sent her off course now and messed up this opportunity. Maybe it had been too soon, maybe she should've given her more time to settle in, maybe she should've kept a closer eye on—

"Okay. But not all week. I've got rehearsal on Friday." Phoebe was clinging to Faye's hand as if she was lost.

Rebecca didn't know if she'd had any contact with her parents since the meeting. She hadn't wanted to talk about it, and Rebecca hadn't pushed her. The recollection of the look Alex and their mother shared when they said goodbye still made Rebecca's chest ache. She prayed Phoebe would be able to avoid that level of estrangement.

"How about that bowling trip? Throwing some heavy balls around might help," Faye suggested.

Phoebe snorted. "Good plan. I'll have to check when Alex is free this week."

"She's got Wednesday and Thursday off, as she's working the weekend shift," Rebecca said.

"How do you know that?" Faye sounded annoyed Rebecca knew something she didn't.

Or she'd just given herself away.

"They've been hanging out." A smile brought some energy back to Phoebe's expression, and she peeked out of her hoodie to exchange a knowing look with Faye.

What had Alex said to her? And what had she said to Faye?

Rebecca's face grew hot. "So, is Alex going to take you? Is anyone else going?" She hated to bring it up, but it gave her an out and nothing had changed in terms of Faye needing support. No outing had been organised through her, and there'd been nothing in the notes or handover.

"Once she's done her training, she can take us by herself, but we have to wait until then if we want to go without staff," Phoebe told Faye.

"Oh yeah. Never mind, it can wait."

What training was this? Rebecca wanted to ask but didn't want to make a fool of herself. They probably thought she already knew. What was Alex up to, and why hadn't she told her? She started to feel uncomfortable in her skin and scratched discreetly at her neck. What plan had the three of them hatched so that they wouldn't have to put up with her tagging along when they went out?

"Not that we don't want you to come. We just know you're busy." Phoebe seemed to have picked up on this last worry.

"Of course. Unfortunately, I can't support Faye to go out as much as we'd like, so it's good if she has other options."

That was what was important. If Alex was taking steps to help Faye get out and enjoy herself more, surely she should encourage that. *But why didn't she tell me?*

"That's what we thought." Faye beamed at her. "This way I can go out with my friends without bugging you."

That was that, then. Rebecca couldn't argue, though she wondered if Faye had taken into account that Alex might not be sticking around much longer.

Or had that changed? Alex had taken on the house-sitting job, which showed some level of commitment to staying, but it was only short term. She could take off as soon as Tiff and Nish got back. If she didn't have anywhere else to stay, how could she stick around? Winter was fast approaching, and she'd need a warm home.

For a moment she pondered the possibility of offering their guest room. Would Ishani go for that? Would Alex? The idea of living with them both was a nice daydream. They all worked different hours so wouldn't be under each other's feet all the time. Ishani might appreciate the company when Rebecca worked late. But no—Alex was Solo and didn't even like Drew's involvement, and they were friends. She wouldn't live with them unless she had no option, and Rebecca didn't want it to be for that reason.

She looked up to see Phoebe and Faye studying her with concerned expressions. Had they been waiting for her to say something? Did they think they'd upset her?

"Yes, that all makes sense." She tried to make her face blank, nothing for them to question or worry about.

"When is the training?" Faye asked.

Damn. She hadn't managed to dodge it without making it obvious she didn't know anything about it. "I'm not sure. I'll have to check."

Which gave her a legitimate reason to ask Alex what was going on. It must be some type of epilepsy training, if the purpose was to support Faye. Had she managed to talk Patience into training her to give emergency medication? It wouldn't be completely unprecedented, as family members did join that type of training to facilitate safe visits. And Faye's family of origin had given her up decades ago, so there was no one to challenge Alex's place. Their absence was seen as no big deal for someone of Faye's generation who had been placed in institutional care for so long they might not remember anything else, but it still made Rebecca's chest squeeze when it came up. Maybe Faye and Alex had more than Phoebe in common and had bonded over the unspoken void of their missing families.

"I don't think they had a date yet. I'll text her and see." Phoebe pulled out her phone and started tapping away.

Which was her opportunity gone. Maybe she could ask Patience instead? Or hope it came up. Though she wasn't convinced she could discuss Alex with her manager without Patience getting suspicious. Should her manager know about them? What would she think, if Rebecca confessed she was not just non-monogamous but had started a relationship with one of their residents' relatives? If it was a relationship.

How could she be expected to tell anyone when she didn't even know how to define it?

"I'll leave you to rest now. Let me know if you need anything." She plastered her professional goodbye smile on as she spoke, then nodded farewell to Faye.

"I'll see you later. We need to carry on—it's getting good," Faye said.

It took a few beats to realise Faye was talking about her bath time book. "Of course. I'll come by when I've finished my other jobs."

As she walked out, the two friends started to discuss the loaned book. Maybe Phoebe or Alex could read it to Faye, then she wouldn't be needed for that either. *No, don't be silly.* They might be able to accompany her bowling, but not in the bath. She could see if it was available on audiobook, though Faye didn't have a device she could download it onto. Should she have? Was that a chance for independence Rebecca had neglected? No, that didn't take away from the fact that Faye needed someone to keep an eye on her and ensure she was safe. An audiobook couldn't do that. Maybe one day technology would take over more of her job, but for now she was still needed.

After closing the door behind her, she checked no one was about, then slipped her phone out of her pocket. A message from Alex was waiting for her. Despite Faye's revelation, it still set off a fluttering in her chest and a flashback to their kiss. Kisses.

Just so you know, I'm not avoiding you exactly, but I'm trying not to bump into you at work. It'd be difficult not to show how much I want you, and I'm guessing it'd be inappropriate for me to snog you in front of everyone there.

She let out a relieved laugh. She had been nervous about what would happen when they next saw each other there and whether she could avoid crossing paths without causing offence. The next time she saw Alex, she wanted it to be somewhere they could carry on what they'd started. At least they were on the same page on that.

She ignored the little voice that was still agitating about what Alex had been planning behind her back. It wasn't about her. Surely she could trust Alex to tell her anything she needed to know.

CHAPTER NINETEEN

F rom Willow." Alex handed Phoebe the extravagant bouquet. "She's gutted she couldn't be here, but she couldn't get out of work."

"I know, she said. Lots of times." Phoebe took the flowers with a smile. "They're recording tonight, so I said I'd send her it."

"Great, she'll love that. We're so proud of you." Alex drew Phoebe into a squishy hug.

"I need to get ready," Phoebe mumbled into her shoulder. "And you need to get your seats before the good ones go."

"More flowers! Somebody's popular." Sebastian sidled into the room.

There was already a makeshift vase of roses on the table in front of her.

"Who are they from?" Alex asked her.

Phoebe's eyes flicked over her shoulder to where Rebecca stood in the doorway. Alex had forgotten she was there. That wasn't it—more importantly, she'd forgotten who she was. Since they'd taken the plunge and were definitely dating, she'd not been thinking of Rebecca as her sister's carer.

Sorry, she signed, her fist on her chest hidden from Rebecca's view.

"I better find something to put these in. And you better let my new star get ready." Sebastian broke the silence with only a raised eyebrow at their secret communication and started to sweep Alex and Rebecca out of the room. He placed a kiss somewhere near Rebecca's cheek before leaving them, with a stage whisper of, "I'll talk to *you* later," and a very indiscreet glance at Alex.

Rebecca returned his kiss with a blush. After he had waltzed down the corridor, she groaned. "You do realise he's going to give me the third degree about us. Maybe we should skip the after-party."

"No way! We promised Bee we'd be there. And we have nothing to hide." Alex leaned over and gave her a proper kiss on the lips.

"True." Rebecca took a shuddering breath, as if to summon courage. "Except at work."

"What they don't know won't hurt them."

Rebecca hadn't told her colleagues about them, and she didn't blame her. They were doing nothing wrong, but some people might not see it that way, and it was none of their business.

Rebecca looked less sure but laced her fingers through Alex's. "Let's go find our seats."

They managed to grab a couple right in the middle of the tiered stalls. It wouldn't have been Alex's first choice usually, but she wanted to have a good view. A decent crowd was filtering into the small theatre, including what looked like some of the college students from the campus they were on. They'd better behave themselves. Hopefully they'd hold off drinking until the end of the Saturday night performance.

"Luisa said it was really good—she was impressed by how professional they all were." Rebecca spoke in a low voice as people settled in around them.

"Who?" It was the final night, so some people would've already seen it, though Phoebe had urged them to wait until then to see their best performance.

"Luisa. From the home. She brought Faye on the first night, she couldn't wait."

"Ah right. Yeah, Phoebe said she'd come." It was handy someone else had stepped up so Faye could come without them. She'd wondered if they should offer, but then they couldn't have come together—that would've been too weird for Faye. It sucked that Willow couldn't make it at all, but it had meant they could make it a date. Willow had been a bit funny about that, and if she didn't know her better, she'd say she was jealous. None of Alex's exes had much to do with Phoebe, so it was the first time anyone else had got close to Willow's role as honorary sister. It seemed to have shaken her.

There was nothing to worry about though—the bond she'd formed with Phoebe wouldn't be easily broken. They'd been through too much together. When Alex hadn't been there, Willow had. She had been the one to call out their parents and bring Alex back to help Phoebe get out of the prison their home had morphed into. Neither of them would ever forget that.

"Do you think she's nervous? She didn't seem it, but you know her better than me." Rebecca was fidgeting in her seat, as if she was the one that had something to be nervous about.

Alex squeezed her hand. "She's fine, she's a pro." Phoebe had taken to being back onstage like a tropical fish released back into the ocean from a tiny tank. There was no doubt she was loving every minute of it.

"Who do you think sent those other flowers?" Rebecca wasn't looking at her. Her eyes were fixed on the stage as if she feared she might miss a moment, and she spoke out of the side of her mouth.

"Er…" She thought fast. "Could be our mother—she was coming to the matinee this afternoon." She had checked they wouldn't bump into her parents and had been surprised to find out that she was coming alone. Maybe she was finally stepping out of their father's shadow and respecting Phoebe's wishes. Alex tried not to hold too tightly to the glimmer of hope, hope for Phoebe's relationship with their mother and maybe even her own.

"Yes, of course." Rebecca squeezed her hand.

Before she could ask any more awkward questions, an announcement boomed out, ordering them to take their seats because the show was about to start.

The voices and rustling around them died down as everyone prepared for the curtains to open. Alex looked over at Rebecca. She really did seem to care about Phoebe. And for her, or she wouldn't take the risk with her work that meant so much. A flicker of guilt tickled her shoulders.

All their rehearsing meant she knew some parts of the show off by heart, but the bits Phoebe wasn't in weren't so familiar. She tried not to make comparisons between the play and the film, or between Phoebe and the other actors. Most were decent, with a few dodgy extras who'd been allowed a line or two. Phoebe clearly belonged with the more talented leads. Alex knew it before she stepped onstage, and the rest of the audience knew it as soon as she did. She showed no nerves, except those that belonged to the character she played, and her comic timing was perfect. But it was when it was time for her first solo that Alex sat up, tensed in anticipation. If she was on form, this was where she would rise above the rest.

She blew them away. Alex felt the room still and everyone snap to attention as Phoebe's voice flowed through them. She shimmered before her eyes as Alex tried not to make a fool out of herself by crying. She'd really done it, all that work had got her where she wanted to be, with an audience drinking in her every note. When she finished, they broke into applause, and Phoebe broke character for a moment as she beamed her thanks.

Behind them someone said over the applause, "Oh my God, she's amazing."

Alex turned to Rebecca and saw she'd not managed to hold back—tears ran down her cheeks. She brushed one away with a finger and Rebecca turned towards her. The temptation to kiss her rose again, and Alex had to turn away quickly so she didn't miss the rest of the show.

Rebecca wrapped herself around Alex's arm and kissed her cheek. "Later," she whispered.

The show rolled on, with Phoebe and the leading lady keeping up the energy and making up for the less confident players. She looked like she was having the time of her life up there, and Alex even found herself wondering if she'd enjoy it too. Best leave it to the professionals, though. It ended with a standing ovation, and Alex cheered herself hoarse as Phoebe soaked it up, looking like she might burst with pride, a feeling Alex shared. Beside her, Rebecca whooped just as enthusiastically, and she realised it wasn't just Phoebe that was happier than she'd seemed in a long time. Alex hadn't felt so happy in so long either.

❖

The after-party was in another building on the college campus. Tables were arranged along the edge of the hall with student volunteers standing guard and acting as servers. It took a few minutes to spot Phoebe in the crowd of performers and supporters. The man by her side was familiar from some of her photos. Alex waited until he'd moved away before they went over.

"You were awesome, Bee. Well done." She gave her another massive hug, and Phoebe squeezed back.

"You stole the show!" Rebecca added and gave her a quick squeeze after Alex released her.

"Thanks for coming," Phoebe said, with a smile that lit up her whole face.

"Wouldn't miss it for the world." Alex reached over to ruffle her hair, but Phoebe jumped out of the way, almost knocking the drink out of Sebastian's hand who had come up behind her.

"Almost! You would not be my favourite person any more if you'd ruined this shirt." He placed a hand to his breast protectively.

Phoebe laughed. "Good thing I missed."

"Too right. I'm already plotting what to do with you next. I've got big plans for you, girl." Sebastian turned to Rebecca. "Thanks so much for introducing us. Though you are still in my bad books for holding out on me."

Rebecca squirmed. "There was nothing to tell."

"Uh-huh, looks like it." He turned to Alex. "So, you're the one who's been putting a bounce in her step."

"Guilty." She put her arm around Rebecca's waist.

"I knew you were into her from the start. They've been trying to pretend for ages nothing was going on." Phoebe rolled her eyes.

"They're clearly not as good actors as you. But they look so cute together, so we'll forgive them."

Sebastian didn't seem to have any issues with them dating, apart from Rebecca not having told him. It was nice to not have to be a secret everywhere. It was hard enough at the home, where she had to avoid Rebecca in case the heat between them was visible.

"Where can we get a drink around here?" She still wanted to change the subject from them.

"Allow me to show you the way." Sebastian linked his arm through Rebecca's and guided them towards the drinks table. Alex saw him whisper something in her ear that brought colour to her cheeks, but there was too much chatter around them for her to hear exactly what.

As they moved towards the makeshift bar, the guy she'd recognised earlier passed them. That was him, wasn't it? For a moment Alex wished Rebecca wasn't with her so she could question him, but Phoebe would not be impressed. She should let her enjoy her triumph. They could talk men later.

❖

"Do you think we've been here long enough?" Rebecca squeezed Alex's hand, keeping her voice low, though it was unlikely anyone would hear them among all the chatter. It was getting louder as families filtered off and the creatives started to celebrate in earnest.

"If you want to leave, then yes. Bee won't mind or probably even notice us sloping off."

Phoebe was constantly surrounded by people and holding her own, the adrenaline from her final performance apparently still flowing. The only other person Rebecca knew there was Sebastian, and he was also fully occupied. Nobody would mind them leaving.

"Good. We've stayed a respectable amount of time."

"You're still worried about appearing respectable." Alex raised an eyebrow and stroked her arm.

The light touch sent shivers through her. "Only in public."

"In that case, we should definitely get you out of here." Alex raised her hand to her lips and kissed it.

Rebecca laughed at the chivalrous gesture. "You're driving."

"Yep. The question is, where am I driving you to?" Alex looked deep into her eyes. It seemed to be a serious question.

It was. Rebecca had sworn not to rush things, but they'd waited so long before they'd acted on their feelings that it felt like they'd been together a lot longer than the single month since their first kiss. They'd waited enough. "You could take me back to yours."

A broad smile lit up Alex's face. "Are you sure? How much have you had to drink?"

"I'm sure." She actually was. "And just one glass of wine."

"Good, I wouldn't want to take advantage of you. Not in that way anyway." Alex took her hand and started to move towards the exit.

"We should say goodbye. And what about Phoebe, how will she get home?" Rebecca stopped, resisting the tug of Alex.

"Same way she got here, there's plenty of drivers in the group, she doesn't need us." Alex didn't seem at all concerned but did look around then change direction. "She's over there."

Phoebe was standing in the midst of a group Rebecca recognised from the show. The man standing by her side seemed vaguely familiar too, though she hadn't seen him onstage and couldn't recall where she had. Conversation was in full swing, and Phoebe was clutching a wine glass. Should she be drinking alcohol? Rebecca knew it wasn't her responsibility, she wasn't on duty, but…no, Phoebe wasn't on any medication it could mess with. It was her choice.

Alex strode up to the group and tapped Phoebe on the shoulder. She whispered something in her ear and Phoebe turned to give her a big hug.

"You did good, enjoy the rest of your night," Alex told her at full volume after they released each other.

"And you enjoy yours." Phoebe looked at Rebecca not at all subtly and dug her sister in the ribs.

Rebecca did not know what to say and realised she was standing with her mouth slightly open as she tried to figure out an appropriate response. But there was nothing appropriate about the situation. And there didn't need to be. Like Alex, Phoebe could act different outside of their roles at the home, though she never seemed to hold back much when she was there.

"Night!" Alex called to the group en masse, as she led her away. "You were all awesome."

A chorus of gratitude and goodbyes followed them out of the hall. She couldn't see Sebastian, but there was no need to seek him out, especially as he'd likely be even less discreet than Phoebe.

The drive back was full of anticipation, the air in the van static with it. Rebecca wished she could reach over and touch Alex. She seemed too far away in the driver's seat after being pressed together in the small theatre and sticking to each other's sides at the after-party. It was cold without her close warmth.

However, it wasn't the movies, and Alex was driving a manual. She'd never understood how anyone could get up to anything in a moving vehicle. If you really needed each other right then, surely you could pull over? Or was the danger the point of it, how they got their kicks?

She didn't need any element of danger to want Alex, or maybe there was already enough there. Her job, her family. *No, it'll be okay.* It was easier to reassure herself after her heart-to-heart with Drew and Ishani. Despite how she'd messed up at the start, they wanted to stick with her and thought it could work. She gazed at Alex. *This could work.*

"You know, it's pretty hard to concentrate on the road with you staring at me." Alex caught her eye in the mirror.

"Sorry." Rebecca looked down. Her hands twisted in her lap, and she watched them as if they didn't belong to her.

"I'm joking! Well, partly. The main distraction is you being with me at all." Alex took her hand off the gear stick and laid it briefly over Rebecca's twisting hands.

Maybe she did get it. When Alex let go and moved her hand back to the wheel, she wished she'd moved it somewhere else.

"If you're that desperate, I do still have a mattress in the back."

Without thinking, she twisted round to look but couldn't see the contents through the small window that separated them from it.

"Joking still. Well, partly." Alex winked. "Before we get to that, I meant to tell you I got my results after I went to the sexual health clinic a couple of weeks ago, and they all came back negative. I can forward you them if you like."

Alex had mentioned she was going beforehand, in a matter-of-fact way. It'd been reassuring to know she was considering safer sex and preparing to be with her. It'd prompted Rebecca to do the same. She'd not been with anyone new since Drew, but they'd had newer partners, and she wanted to be able to give Alex the same reassurance.

"Ditto. Shall I email you?" It was best practice and it gave her something to do with her hands as they neared Alex's temporary home.

When they finally entered the house, Rebecca shivered and pulled her coat tighter instead of taking it off.

"Let me put the heating and the kettle on." Alex rushed into the kitchen, followed by the sound of switches being clicked and the reassuring rumble of a boiler, then the kettle.

She jumped as Alex suddenly appeared by her side, holding a fleece throw she'd detoured through the living room to grab.

"May I?" Alex placed her hands to the neck of her coat, grazing the delicate skin of her throat.

Rebecca managed a nod and unwrapped her arms from around her so Alex could remove it. There was a moment of chill that sent shivers through her before Alex replaced it by wrapping the soft throw around her.

"Come here." She tugged at it, pulling her into her arms.

Rebecca pressed against her, wrapping them up together. She kissed Alex, her lips warm and surprisingly sweet, and Alex slipped her arms around her waist. Their kiss grew fiercer, and Alex's hands started to roam over her chest.

"I don't think we need the tea," she gasped into Alex's mouth.

Alex chuckled. "You're right. This is a better way to get warm."

"Though we…we could do with more blankets." Rebecca deliberately looked up the stairs before recapturing Alex's lips, not wanting to be apart from them for any longer than necessary.

Alex broke off and looked at her, tilting her chin with her hand. Rebecca could feel Alex's arousal in the way she pulled at her clothes and pushed against her, but something was making her hold off.

"Are you sure this is what you want?"

Was it somehow not clear in the way her body surrendered to her touch? "I'm sure. I want you." Her voice was steady despite her breathing, heavy with her need for Alex. But what if it wasn't *her* desire that was in doubt. Her breath hitched. "Do you want me?"

"Yes. Always." Alex kissed her again, even more fiercely than before, as if she was finally letting go and letting their passion play out. She tugged at Rebecca's layers of clothing and slid her hands underneath to stroke her skin.

Rebecca gasped as Alex's light touch laid sparks and reached down to do the same, the throw dropping to the floor around them, its artificial heat no longer needed. Alex's T-shirt was harder to free, trapped under a thick leather belt, but she didn't want to pull back to look at what she was doing.

But her need made her clumsy, so Alex parted her hands and finished the task herself. Rebecca reached for the button of her jeans, desperate for access to her body that she'd been craving for so long, but Alex removed her hands again. "Upstairs. While I can still walk."

They stumbled up the stairs together and into the guest room, immediately falling on the double bed that took up most of the floor space. Alex rolled on top of her, slipping her thigh between Rebecca's legs as her hands slipped back under her clothes, leaving trails of heat as she explored her stomach and chest. Rebecca arched towards her as her hand reached her bra, teasing her through the fabric. She unclasped it so Alex's hand could slip under it to her breasts and moaned when her thumb grazed her nipple, breaking away from Alex's lips to gasp for air.

Alex was gazing down at her with a hungry look. She balanced on one elbow, giving Rebecca a clear view of her, her hardness and softness coming together in her strong, curvy body. Muscles tensed under her tight long-sleeved tee, which was stretched even tighter over her chest. Rebecca reached up to pull it off, but Alex moved away.

"Wait." She stood up and went over to the small dresser in the corner and flicked on a lamp, then switched off the main light, casting them in a dull glow. Soft shadows danced over her as she moved back to the bed, seeming more in her element with them covering her. She drew Rebecca up, kissing her again, then swept back the covers so they could tumble inside.

This time she let Rebecca tug off her top, so she was finally able to explore her pulsing skin, trailing her hands over this new terrain. She kissed the tender flesh where her breasts strained against her bra, looking up at Alex as she reached for the catch to release them, and their hands met as she fumbled. Alex didn't stop her. She helped steady her shaking hands and removed her bra completely. Rebecca slid down to take her erect nipple in her mouth, Alex's gasps spurring her on. She wanted to taste every inch of her and kissed a meandering trail down her stomach, until tough denim stood in her way.

Alex pulled her back up. "I want you here where I can see you." She stroked Rebecca's face, planting light kisses across her jawline. When she reached Rebecca's pouting lip, she nipped it.

The sharp spasm caused by her teeth only encouraged her. She grasped Alex's breasts and Alex rocked against her.

Their kiss was broken by Alex pulling off her many layers so they were pressed skin to skin. Rebecca melted into her, and there was no doubt that it was how they were supposed to be, connected in the flesh. They reached for each other's waists simultaneously and shrugged off their trousers, trying not to break contact for a moment. She could feel the dampness of Alex's underwear on her thigh where she rubbed against her and reached down to find its source. Her fingers were coated in juices as soon as she slipped inside the final layer of clothing, and Alex's hard clit seemed to seek her touch. When she stroked it, she felt as well as heard Alex's moans of pleasure.

"Oh, baby, don't stop." Alex urged her on with her words and body, grinding against her.

Rebecca took her nipple back in her mouth, sucking it as she made her strokes longer and harder, moving towards Alex's opening. She didn't just want to be under her, she wanted to be inside her. The deep groan Alex let out as she slipped into her assured her she felt the same.

Between them they wrenched off the last scrap of cotton so she was free to ride Rebecca and let her deeper inside. From her tensing muscles Rebecca knew Alex wouldn't last long, but she couldn't slow down, she needed to bring her over the edge. She found Alex's swollen clit again with her thumb and gazed at her as she rode her, all shields down, finally, completely, letting her in. When she cried out with a final spasm, Rebecca didn't want to stop, she wanted to keep them in that moment for as long as possible. She left her hand between them, pressed lightly against Alex's warmth so she continued to shudder until eventually she collapsed on top of her.

Rebecca wrapped her arms around her as Alex got her breathing back under control.

"Just give me a moment," Alex gasped.

"I'm okay, you enjoy it." Rebecca kissed her softly.

"Really?"

Alex leaned on one elbow and slid her other arm down to Rebecca's own soaking underwear. She jerked against her involuntarily, and Alex let out a dirty laugh.

"Just as long as you don't fall asleep on me," Rebecca said. There was no way she could sleep until she'd taken her release.

"No risk of that"—Alex's words came out in short bursts as she flopped back down against Rebecca—"not now I know how good this feels."

It did feel too good to stop. And there was only a very quiet voice inside Rebecca's head that questioned if it was too good to be true.

CHAPTER TWENTY

Rebecca woke alone, as usual. Except she wasn't in her own bed. The glorious floating feeling from the night before quickly started to fade.

She's probably just got up to make tea. She strained for any sounds of human activity in the house, but there was nothing.

There was a warm-looking hoodie hanging on the back of the door. She braced herself then slipped out from under the warm duvet and ran for it. The soft fabric enveloped her, thankfully hanging below her butt as she knew her underwear would not be wearable. The memory of Alex removing it brought some of the floating feeling back. She had been so attentive and passionate as she'd explored her body and wrapped her in her arms to sleep when they were finally both spent. When she'd woken partway through the night, they'd reached for each other again, slower, less frenzied, making love.

Was that what it was, love? Her heart raced, but she wasn't sure if it was that or fear at the thought that things had moved that fast. How did Alex feel? She wouldn't ask her and put her on the spot straight after their first night together, but she did want to find her.

She opened the bedroom door and listened. Still no sign of where Alex was or what she was up to. *She's probably curled up with a cuppa downstairs, not wanting to disturb me.* Then why hadn't she come back when she heard her get up? Rebecca shook herself. It wasn't like she expected her to be at her beck and call, just…She was very aware of her nakedness under the hoodie and how naked they'd been with each other.

The wooden stairs were cold and clammy under her bare feet. She should've found some slippers, but it didn't feel right going through Alex's things without her permission. Or Tiff's and Nish's. She got the impression Alex travelled light, and it was unlikely she'd have any to spare. After all, she hadn't been planning on sticking around.

When she reached the bottom of the stairs, she paused and listened again. Nothing. She passed through each empty room just in case, but there was no Alex and no note saying she'd just popped out. Except there wouldn't be, would there? This wasn't an old movie. Alex had her mobile phone number and would've texted instead. Rebecca raced back upstairs and found her phone lying in her discarded clothes.

There were no messages from Alex. But there were several missed calls from the home and a garbled voicemail from Luisa urging her to stay calm but call her as soon as she got it. Which of course had the opposite effect. Her heart pounded painfully as if it might break right through its tight case.

She found the fleece throw on the floor and tried not to recall how Alex had wrapped it around her as she wrapped it around her waist and sat back on the bed, her jiggling legs testing the stretchy fabric.

"Hello. Becca?" Luisa answered after five rings.

"Luisa, what's happened?" There wasn't time for pleasantries—she had to know what was wrong. Something must have happened to prompt the flurry of calls and the cryptic message.

"It's Phoebe."

The line went quiet. Had it cut out? It wasn't like Luisa to hold back.

"She's gone."

"Gone!" A violent wave of nausea rose up and her head started spinning. "Gone, as in…" She couldn't bring herself to say it.

"Gone as in gone away. Left in the night."

Rebecca let out a sigh of relief before the implications of it set in. "She's run away?"

"Yes, after her show last night. She never came home. Except no one noticed until this morning. They didn't realise she should've come back. The night staff said they thought she must've gone home with her sister instead as it was late."

"She didn't," Rebecca said, before realising there was no good explanation for how she knew that.

"We know." Thankfully Luisa didn't seem to have picked up on the slip. "They spoke to her this morning."

So they'd called Alex. That explained her disappearance. She must have charged off to help find her, Phoebe's personal knight in shining armour. But it didn't explain why she hadn't woken Rebecca. Surely, she could've helped.

"As you would expect, she was not happy. I am glad I did not have to make that call."

"Of course she wasn't. Her sister, who we're supposed to be caring for, has disappeared." Rebecca couldn't believe Luisa was making out Alex was the bad guy for being upset. How could she not be? Would she ever forgive them if something happened to Phoebe? Would she ever forgive her?

"Of course, of course. She is right to be angry. I did not mean to—"

"I know. Sorry. I'm just in shock." She mustn't take it out on her. It wasn't her fault. Luisa wasn't the one responsible for Phoebe. She was.

"We do not think anything bad happened. We looked in her room, and it looks like she packed some things."

"She planned this? But why?" Phoebe had seemed to be settling in and happy there. Rebecca folded her body up tighter to try to stop herself shaking. It didn't make sense. Unless... "You should speak to Faye. If she planned it, she might have told her."

"That is what I said. Faye had told them she did not know anything, but in the end she confessed to me when I explained we were worried about her friend and she would not get in trouble."

"Confessed what?" Rebecca's head was still spinning, and she leaned forward to rest it on her knees. It didn't help, but it felt less likely to fall off there.

"There is a man." Luisa let out a loud sigh. "Of course. It is always a man. It seems she has run away with him."

Rebecca groaned. "Callum," she whispered, more a statement than question, the name returning to her unbidden.

"Yes. From the day centre. You knew about him?" Luisa hissed this last part.

"No! I mean, I guessed there might be something there, but I didn't think it was serious. I asked her a while back, and she denied there was anything to tell." Phoebe hadn't just hidden her relationship from her, she'd lied to her face. A heavy weight took over the thumping in her chest.

"Patience talked to his parents, and they are on their way in for a meeting. He was living with them and is also gone. They don't know why—all was fine with him, or that is what they say. Phoebe's sister is coming too."

"What time?" Rebecca jumped up and started desperately looking round for something decent to wear.

"About an hour. Can you get here? They have not said you have to be in it, but I think it would be…a good idea for you to be here."

To defend herself. But how could she?

Or to take the fall for it? Yes, someone would be expected to take the blame. "Okay," she croaked, her eyes filling with tears. "I'll be there."

"I will be here. You do not have to manage it alone. Come find me when you get here."

Her friend's kindness just made it worse. The tears started to fall. "Will do. See you soon." She hung up before the first loud sob escaped her.

Phoebe was gone. It was her fault—she should've paid more attention to what she was up to instead of getting distracted by her charming sister, who would surely agree, and then she would be gone too. Rebecca fought the urge to collapse to the ground and give in to the full weight of her emotions. *Pull yourself together.*

Taking a deep, shuddering breath she strode over to Alex's bag, which still seemed to hold all her clothes despite the presence of the wardrobe it was leaning against, then had second thoughts. Even if she found something suitable for an important work meeting there, she couldn't risk anyone recognising it as Alex's. And Alex was likely to be angry enough without her striding in wearing her best clothes. Thankfully, Tiff was about the same size as her. Surely she'd understand her borrowing something given the situation. She tried not to think about how exactly she would explain the situation to her.

❖

By the time Rebecca arrived at the home, it was packed with staff. They must've called everyone, not just her. She'd sat in the car, taking in the overflowing car park, daring herself to get out and ring the bell. In the end she'd texted Luisa to say she was there, and she met her at the door. She'd needed her support as she'd walked down the corridor with all eyes on her, Marie and her cronies going quiet as she'd passed but continuing to judge with their eyes. Rebecca bowed her head and tried to stay focused. This wasn't about her; it was about Phoebe. It didn't matter what they thought of her as long as Phoebe was safe.

"Patience is with the boyfriend's parents. They are very upset. The mum was crying when they got here, and the dad looked like he wanted to."

It was clear Luisa was trying to be helpful by filling her in, but it just made it worse. At least Patience was there to take charge of the situation. If anyone could calm everyone down and find a solution, it was her. That was a small relief, but not enough weight off to breathe easily.

"Alex was here but did not stay long. She said she would be back for the meeting. I think she did not want to meet with his parents. She said she would be better off looking for them, but Patience pushed her to come."

That added up. Rebecca suspected Alex would prefer not to be there, given the recent fight with her own parents. Oh God, their parents. "Are Phoebe's parents coming in? Have they been called?"

That would be all she needed. This was the evidence they wanted to show the home wasn't the right place for Phoebe and that she needed to be back under their control.

"No, Alex is her emergency contact, and she asked us not to. And now we know she has run off with her boyfriend, not anything bad has happened." Luisa gave her a quick squeeze with one arm round her shoulders. "I am sure she is okay. Stupid maybe, but okay."

"Luisa! You shouldn't call her that."

"She ran off with her boyfriend after only knowing each other not a year. That is a stupid move." Luisa shrugged.

Rebecca couldn't argue with that. At a better time she might have argued about ableist language, but there were more immediate issues to think about. "Do we know where they've gone?"

"No, not as far as I know. They say Alex asked not to call the police either."

The mention of the authorities made Rebecca freeze. It was really that serious. Would social services be called in? Safeguarding? Her head swam with the implications.

"We will find them. She is right, it will not be necessary. Don't panic!" Luisa gave her one last squeeze. "I offered to be on call for refreshments for the meeting and will hang around in case you need me."

"Thank you." Rebecca faced the meeting room door. There were faint voices coming from behind it, too quiet to identify. Had Alex joined them yet? There was only one way to know. She took a few deep breaths and knocked.

"Come in," Patience called.

She took another breath and pushed the door open.

"Ah, Rebecca, thank you for coming in on your day off."

An unfamiliar couple were sitting at the long table with Patience, their faces pale and drawn.

"This is Rebecca, Phoebe's key worker." Patience spoke to the couple in her most calm yet authoritative voice. "Rebecca, this is Mr. and Mrs. Oliver, Callum's parents."

They looked at each other, normal small talk out of reach. Rebecca was trapped by the haunted look in their eyes.

"Did you...did you know about them?" Mrs. Oliver finally broke the silence.

"No. Well, I suspected"—she took on board the warning look Patience shot her—"something, at one point. But no."

There was another knock at the door. She froze, knowing who it must be. How could she face Alex? Her lover, who had run out after their first night together, on learning she'd failed her sister.

Patience shot her another look, this time more concerned. "Will you see who that is please, Rebecca."

"Of course." There was no choice. It took her a couple of goes to twist the handle as it slipped in her sweaty grip. Thankfully, Tiff's jacket was slightly too long on her, and she was able to use it to cover her palm.

It was her. Alex was dressed in her usual jeans, but with a smart sweater Rebecca didn't recognise. Had she raided the Hathaways' wardrobe too? Neither of them attempted direct eye contact, and Alex seemed to look right past her to the people beyond. This wasn't the passionate woman who'd slept in her arms. Her walls were visibly raised again, the guard back at her post.

"Alex, thank you for coming back and meeting with us all. This is Phoebe's sister." Patience seemed to have decided it was best she handle the introductions and stay in charge.

Which was fine by Rebecca. Her throat had squeezed so tight she wasn't sure she could speak even if she could think what to say. Breathing was hard enough.

"I just...I just don't understand why he didn't tell us. We've always been close, there's never been a need for secrets. We wouldn't have had a problem with it, quite the opposite. He's seemed so happy lately, I said, didn't I, I said, if I didn't know better, I'd think he was in love." Mrs. Oliver looked to her husband as if for confirmation.

He nodded and squeezed her hand. "We wouldn't have stood in the way of his happiness."

But would you have taken them seriously? The mother's words had pierced Rebecca's fear-fogged brain. Had she thought she knew better because of his learning disability? Had they thought him incapable of love because he was autistic? Maybe Callum had his reasons for not telling them.

"Did Phoebe tell you about their relationship?"

This time it was Alex that Mrs. Oliver put on the spot.

Rebecca stiffened and wished she could close her eyes and ears to not hear the answer, which in the pit of her stomach she knew was coming. But her eyes were drawn to Alex. Who nodded.

A slight groan escaped her lips. It wasn't only Phoebe who had lied to her. No wonder Alex hadn't woken her when she got the news. She would've had to admit it. A flame of fury licked at her. Maybe Alex hadn't run out on her after their night together because she didn't trust her to help, leaving her cold and alone to deal with this news. It was Alex, the lover who she'd taken a chance on, who couldn't be trusted.

"Then why…why not tell us?"

Mrs. Oliver clearly couldn't get past that earlier betrayal, even in the face of this bigger one. Rebecca understood. She couldn't fathom why Phoebe and Alex had completely hidden it from her, either.

Alex stared at Mrs. Oliver as if trying to read her soul. She opened her mouth, then closed it.

"Children do hide things from their parents, even as grown-ups and without good reason. I know I can be the last to know about my children's private lives," Patience said, filling the gap where Alex's reply should have been. It was a kinder response than Alex probably would have given, given her relationship with her parents.

"I guess you're right," Mr. Oliver said. "But surely that doesn't explain them running away. Why they would feel the need to do that."

"No, it doesn't." Patience turned to Alex. "Do you have any idea why they chose that route?"

It was a surprising move. Patience had saved Alex from answering earlier, but maybe she'd just been giving her a chance to choose her words carefully. A sensible call. Thinking before she spoke was not Alex's strong point.

"Our parents…our parents didn't feel the same way." Alex looked down at the table as she spoke, as if about to read a story. "Phoebe had a boyfriend she was really serious about before. They were in love. They met in her local drama group. When our parents found out they weren't just rehearsing together, they hit the roof. Accused him of being a predator and threatened to call the police on him if he didn't stay away. So he did. Bee was heartbroken."

"When was this?" Rebecca asked, the pieces starting to fall into place.

"A while ago. I wasn't around, but when I found out, I came back as soon as I could and promised to get her out of there, and that it wouldn't happen again." Alex's fingers curled on the table, preparing for a fight.

"So, if I understand correctly, that's why she moved here?" Patience had made the same link as Rebecca.

"Yes. They'd come down hard on her, deciding she had to be chaperoned everywhere and pushing her to drop out of her group in case he was there, or anyone else who might take advantage of their little girl."

"It doesn't sound like he was taking advantage," Mr. Oliver interjected. "They were both adults, I take it, both consenting?"

Alex nodded with force. "Definitely. From what she and Willow told me, they had a lot in common and were good together."

"We're sorry Phoebe went through all that." Mrs. Oliver did look truly sorry, her red eyes lined again with tears. "I don't know your parents and shouldn't judge, but that wasn't fair on her. She should be free to love like anyone else."

"Thank you." Alex shifted in her chair. "I'm sorry they kept it secret from you. Phoebe was scared you'd react like our parents did…"

The end of her sentence went unspoken. Phoebe must've warned Callum not to tell.

Tears prickled at Rebecca's eyes and grief for what Phoebe had been through overrode her earlier feelings of betrayal. Of course she wouldn't trust them after that.

"We understand." Mr. Oliver offered Alex a sympathetic smile. "But you need to understand, we're not like that. If you tell us where they are, we won't force them apart. We'll support them if they want to be together. We just want them to be happy *and* safe."

The betrayal crashed back down on Rebecca, even weightier than before. How had she not guessed it too? There was only one explanation for why Alex hadn't damned them all to hell for losing her sister and called the police herself. She knew where they were.

All eyes were on Alex then, even Rebecca's despite the pain it caused her to look at the lover who, it turned out, had never trusted her. The room was so quiet everyone must have been holding their breath.

"Okay," Alex said. "But let me call her first, give them a chance to come back of their own free will before anyone goes after them."

"But what if they go somewhere else when they know we know?" There was a panicky edge to Mrs. Oliver's voice, and her eyes darted between the faces around her.

"They won't. I'll explain. She trusts me." Alex laid her hands flat on the table, back straight, the picture of control.

"But can we trust you?" Rebecca felt everyone turn to her as she said it, the accusation burning her lips on the way out, but it was only Alex's jolt she saw.

What did she expect, that Rebecca would just roll over and say she totally understood too why they'd shut her out? A bolt of anger flashed through her. She'd risked everything for Alex—her family, her job— and yet she was willing to just throw her under the bus like this. Had she wanted her to take the blame? Was that the plan after all?

"Yes, you can. I've told you everything now, even though it's not my story to tell. If I was planning on helping her run again, I wouldn't have told you." The calm was gone from Alex's posture as quickly as it had taken hold, her hands curling.

"She has a point. What if Phoebe isn't happy you've told us and still doesn't want to risk it?" Mr. Oliver wasn't so easily persuaded either.

"Worst case scenario, I can see where she's used her credit card if I log in to her account." Alex seemed satisfied she was right, then her expression became shifty as she most likely realised what else she'd just admitted to.

"Credit card?" Patience rubbed at her forehead, the strain of the situation starting to bleed through even her professional composure. What time had she been called in to sort out the mess they'd found themselves in? She didn't look like she'd had enough sleep.

Alex sat back, some of her righteous indignation fading. "It's in my name as it'd be hard for her to get credit without any income and so I can pay it off. Our parents didn't give her access to money either. She needed something." She crossed her arms and stared ahead, as if challenging anyone to argue with her reasoning.

But it didn't excuse her not telling them. How much more had the sisters kept hidden? Rebecca fought to stay in work mode and focus on what was important. Phoebe was safe. She glared at Alex across the table, a gap which seemed too wide to bridge. *Phoebe's safe, that's all that matters.*

There was no further questioning of Alex's plan, and Rebecca was too shaken up to say anything more. Patience called a break after it was agreed they would let Alex call Phoebe.

Rebecca rose from the table with relief and went to leave.

"Rebecca, can you show Alex to somewhere quiet where she can make her call?" Patience caught her before she managed to reach the door.

No. She did not want to face her, let alone be in a room with her unaccompanied. But it was her job. She couldn't say no without revealing her own betrayal. She choked out a, "Yes, of course," and left without turning to see if Alex was following.

"Rebecca." Alex's voice opened the stab wound in her back.

She unlocked the door to the small office and checked no one was inside, then held it open for Alex.

"Rebecca, please. This isn't about—"

"You can make your call in here. Please don't touch anything. I'll let Luisa know where you are, and she can help if you need anything."

"Becca." Alex reached out to touch her.

Rebecca jumped back. She couldn't, she just couldn't.

Instead, she rushed out to the courtyard, craving the fresh air, and collapsed on the smokers' stoop. After firing off a quick text to Luisa, she let the full weight of everything overtake her. She rested her head on her knees, her body too heavy to hold upright.

The door creaked open and footsteps headed down towards her. Had Alex followed her? The last thing Rebecca wanted was to have it out with her there, but if she pushed her—

"Mind if I join you?"

Marie's polite tone made her sit up in surprise. She was waving an unlit cigarette in front of her, holding the lighter close as if waiting for permission.

"Sure," Rebecca mumbled. It was Marie's territory, and she never thought she'd be glad to see her most antagonistic colleague, but at least she wasn't Alex.

"This is all a right mess, isn't it." Marie didn't wait for a response. "Is it true the sister knows where she is, knew all along?"

Rebecca nodded.

"For God's sake. At least she's safe, though, that's the main thing." Marie patted Rebecca's arm.

She nodded again. Yes, that was what mattered.

"It's not your fault, love. You couldn't have known—they were obviously set on secrecy." Marie's voice was softer than she'd ever heard it, at least when speaking to her.

"Thank you." Rebecca felt the tears begin to slide down her cheeks.

"Hey, none of that. It's all okay." She slid her arm around Rebecca's shaking shoulders. "Look, I know we don't always see eye to eye, but we want the same thing at the end of the day. For them to be safe and well."

Was that what Rebecca wanted? Or had she wanted something more for Phoebe? Maybe that was where she'd gone wrong.

Even if Marie meant it when she said she didn't blame her, she didn't know the full story and the lines Rebecca had crossed. She didn't know that she wasn't crying about losing Phoebe. Phoebe would be okay, though she'd have all her work cut out earning back their trust. She was crying at losing Alex. She'd thought they'd had something real, but Alex had been playing her. And whatever her game had been, Rebecca had lost.

CHAPTER TWENTY-ONE

P romise?" Phoebe's voice cracked, or maybe it was just the poor signal making it crackle.

"You know I can't." Alex closed her eyes and kneaded the sockets. She'd not had much sleep and hadn't been able to relax since she got Phoebe's first message that morning. "They seemed legit, like they meant it."

"Do you trust them?"

"I don't know them, Bee!" Alex paused and tried to breathe through her frustration. Phoebe had dropped her right in it, and although she would do anything for her sister, she wished she hadn't left her behind to clean up her mess. "But they seem to care and not want to break you two up. They could see you make Callum happy."

Phoebe's smile was almost audible. "They said that?"

"Yep. They want you to be happy. We all do. You can come back and it'll be okay."

It wouldn't be that simple really, and Phoebe would have to deal with at least some of the fallout. But they could talk about that more once she was back.

The line became muffled, like it was smothered in fabric, and two indistinct voices spoke in the background. Alex hoped Callum would see sense and help talk Phoebe round. His parents made it sound like he had a happy home to come back to, though that could just be for appearances' sake. Their own parents had been known to put on a show. Callum was the only one who could really know if it was true.

"Callum thinks we can trust them. And he misses them already and wants to go home." Phoebe didn't sound entirely happy about that, as if it was a rejection of her.

"And does he still want to be with you?" Alex had to ask. She didn't want to give any false reassurances if she could help it.

"Do you still want to be with me?" Phoebe's voice was quieter as she spoke away from the handset.

The loud "Yes!" Alex heard in the distance made her smile.

"He says yes." Phoebe sounded immediately perkier. "We'll come back as long as we can come back together."

"Deal." Alex let out a giant sigh of relief. *Thank fuck for that.* She didn't know what would've happened if she couldn't persuade Phoebe herself, but it wouldn't have been good. "I'll come get you."

"What about Becca? Will she come too?" When Alex didn't reply immediately, she added, "Is she angry with us?"

"No, not angry. She's…" Alex tried not to picture Rebecca's devastated face as she'd learned all they'd kept from her. Her chest ached. "To be honest, she looked…heartbroken."

She hadn't wanted to admit it, but she couldn't ignore Rebecca's pain. Pain she'd helped cause.

"Oh."

Silence. Neither of them seemed to know what to say or do about that.

"I'm sorry. I didn't mean to hurt her."

"I know. Neither did I. But she's done so much for you, I guess she's got a right to be upset." As much as Alex wanted to make out it was an overreaction, they had to give her that.

"Is she upset with you too? I can tell her it wasn't your fault, you didn't know we were going—"

"It's okay, Bee. Thanks."

Rebecca probably wouldn't want to talk to either of them for a while.

"Okay."

"Seriously, it's not your problem. It's up to me to sort out my relationship with her." If they still had one. It was so early, and it seemed such a big blow to Rebecca that they might not get past it. She had to be realistic—she might have to walk away. The ache in her chest swelled.

"Fine, I won't talk to her about you." Phoebe sounded reluctant, but at least she'd agreed.

"Thanks. So, when shall I come pick you up?"

Alex steered them back to the point of the call. Hopefully it wasn't too late for Phoebe and Callum to sort out the mess they'd created, even if it was too late for her and Rebecca.

More muffled talking. "We're ready when you are. Callum says he'll call his parents now and tell them."

"Great."

That took some extra weight off, not having to play go-between for Callum and his parents too. They'd seemed grateful she'd told them all that had happened but likely still weren't her biggest fans given her part in the betrayal. Who knew if they'd forgiven her for not telling them straightaway and understood why she had waited, unsure if she could trust them.

"Will you tell Becca?"

That would depend on if she agreed to talk to her. "I'll try. If not, I'll tell Patience and make sure the home knows."

"Thanks, sis. You're the best. Love you."

"Love you too."

Alex sighed as she hung up. No matter what shit Phoebe pulled, it remained true. It was doubtful there was anything her little sister could do that would make her turn on her. A pang shot across her chest. She couldn't blame Phoebe for how she'd treated Rebecca. Phoebe hadn't needed to swear her to secrecy. She'd never intended to tell her.

When she'd got the message that morning, she'd been careful not to disturb Rebecca and get her involved. She'd told herself it was for Rebecca's sake because there was no professional excuse she could give for why she'd been with her. Deep down she knew that couldn't be the whole reason, but it was all she could admit to at the time, even to herself. Phoebe wasn't the only one who had messed up. She'd been forced to tell Phoebe's story to help her. Maybe in order to sort things with Rebecca, she'd have to tell her own too.

There was a knock on the door, followed swiftly by it opening and Luisa's head appearing.

"Is everything okay? Do you need anything?"

At least she knew her name now and had a friendly staff member she could speak to other than Rebecca. "Yes. Phoebe and Callum agreed to come back, together. I've said I'll pick them up soon."

"That is brilliant news! So much relief. I shall tell Patience." Luisa looked like she was considering hugging her.

Alex kept her arms stiffly by her sides. "Thanks. Um, do you know where Rebecca is? I want to tell her myself."

She hadn't decided how much she would tell her, but she owed her that.

"Of course. I think she went outside for some air, in the courtyard. I will take you." Luisa held the door wide open.

"Thanks." Alex stepped out and waited for Luisa to lock up behind her.

They walked through the corridors in silence. Thankfully Luisa didn't attempt to fill it with small talk. Alex tried to put together what she would say to Rebecca, different options, different stories jostling in her mind along with their possible different endings. How much should she offer her? How much would she want to know? Would it make any difference anyway?

"She is here," Luisa said, looking out of the window next to the door that led to the courtyard. She opened the door. "Rebecca, Phoebe's sister would like to speak to you."

Through the window, Alex saw Rebecca look up, a dozen different emotions passing swiftly across her face. Then she was distracted by the woman next to her turning around, her arm still round Rebecca's shoulders. Wasn't that the arsehole she'd butted heads with and who gave her the coldest welcome? She hadn't realised she and Rebecca were friends. But why wouldn't they be—Rebecca was one of them. So why would she offer her anything, let alone everything? *Because she's different. She has to be.*

Luisa stayed with her as Rebecca rose and shuffled towards them, clearly against her will.

"Yes?" Rebecca said, as if a single word was all she was willing to grant her. She didn't even look at her.

"Can I talk to you? Please?" Alex tried to ignore the spectators.

"Okay."

"In private?" There was no way she could tell her anything there. They couldn't talk about *them*. She was trying to keep her promise to keep things quiet there at least.

Rebecca shifted and stared at her own shuffling feet. It seemed to be a no.

She wouldn't force her. If Rebecca needed space, she could give her it. The arsehole had followed her and was giving Alex daggers over her shoulder. Fuck it. She could give her all the space in the world.

"Are you okay? Do you want me to handle this?" Luisa put a hand on Rebecca's shoulder and looked at her with concern.

"No. I mean, yes, I'm okay. I can deal with it myself." Rebecca finally looked at Alex. "We'll be in the office if anyone needs me."

All her resolve to walk away dissolved with that glimmer of an opening. But the office didn't seem like a place they could really talk. Surely any other staff could walk in on them.

"What about Phoebe's room—we'll be out of the way there." It seemed fitting too, being where they'd first met all those months ago. It could end where it began.

"Good idea," Luisa said.

Rebecca looked like she wanted to raise an objection, possibly on Phoebe's behalf, but decided it wasn't worth it. "Fine."

They walked upstairs, Rebecca leading the way and keeping her back to Alex. She unlocked Phoebe's door and entered but didn't sit down, just moved out of the doorway so Alex could come in.

Alex closed the door behind them, then collapsed into one of the armchairs. Part of her just wanted to lay her head back and sleep, but she didn't know when or if she'd get the chance to speak to Rebecca again.

"Is Phoebe coming back?" Rebecca got straight to the point.

"Yes. I'm gonna go get them."

Some of the stiffness left Rebecca and she sank into the other armchair. "Thank God for that."

"I didn't know you believed in God." Alex attempted a jokey tone, but anything they both said had too much weight to it.

"I don't."

She took a breath. "I'm sorry you got dragged into all this. It's nothing to do with you."

"Evidently." The hurt in Rebecca's voice was palpable.

She winced. "I didn't mean it like that! I meant, it wasn't your fault, it wasn't anything you did or didn't do. Like I said in the meeting, it was because of Phoebe's past."

Rebecca picked at something not visible on her shirt. "I understand. But I thought I'd earned her trust." Her voice faded to a whisper. "And yours."

"It wasn't for me to tell you about her personal life. She's got a right to privacy." Even if she did it all over again, she wouldn't betray Phoebe's confidence. What could Rebecca expect? She'd known and loved Phoebe all her life and had only known Rebecca for six months. She brushed aside the thought of how long she'd loved her. Okay, she'd fallen for her, but was it love? And it wasn't about them. "You're her paid carer."

"Not her friend?" Rebecca's voice rose back up, sounding fuelled with anger. "You think I don't know that? I may have ignored professional boundaries for *you*, but that's different. Or I thought it was."

"It was! It is." Alex tried to take Rebecca's hand but she pulled away. "I know we betrayed your trust, but she's my little sister. I had no real choice. I swore I'd stand by her."

"Maybe. Maybe before it came to this, but you helped her run away and left me to deal with the consequences. That's another level. You left me, alone, after last night." Rebecca finally looked at her. There were tears in her eyes, bloodshot eyes that were clearly not strangers to tears that day.

Tears she'd caused with her cold-heartedness. "I didn't want to, but—"

"Then why did you?" There was no denying the angry tone to Rebecca's voice, and she seemed to let go of the last of her professional front. "You had a choice, don't pretend you didn't. You're Ms. Independent. You always do what you want to do."

It was a solid punch in the gut. "That's what you think of me, that I just do whatever I want and don't care about others? I thought you got it." Her jaw clenched shut. Maybe they'd both been deceived.

"And I thought you cared about me. How could you just leave me like that? Why didn't you let me in?"

"What, and give away that we were together? You were the one that didn't want anyone here to know," Alex shot back before she could think.

"So it's my own fault for having boundaries?" Rebecca wrapped her arms around herself.

They stared at each other. Checkmate. Someone had to back down or they would never move on. Alex's hands curled around the arms of the chair.

"No," she said. "No, it's not your fault. It was a hopeless situation. I didn't know what I could do except what Phoebe asked."

"She asked you to leave me without saying a word?"

"Funnily enough, I didn't tell her you were in my bed. We don't tell each other everything."

A flicker of what might have become a smile crossed Rebecca's face. "That's probably for the best."

They sat in silence again, this time with less charge in the air. Rebecca had dark circles under her eyes and deep lines in her face, looking as knackered as Alex felt. She wished she could kiss them away but didn't dare try to touch her again. She tried to see her as just

Phoebe's carer instead, to take away some of the emotion of it all, but she couldn't. Even picturing the arsehole's arm around her couldn't make her see Rebecca as anything less than her lover.

"I still don't see why you couldn't tell me. You must've known it would come out sooner rather than later. Even if you didn't tell me exactly where they were, you could've at least told me she was safe. Or did you think I didn't care?"

"I know you care. It's your job, you're a carer." Alex focused on where they were: a care home, not a real one.

"That's not the same thing and you know it. I really care about Phoebe. I've gone above and beyond over and over again. Why did you think I'd do that? It's definitely not for the pay."

There were other reasons care workers did it, and not all noble ones. Alex's clawing hands curled into fists. "Some people do it because they enjoy the control, because they like having others dependent on them. You're not all selfless angels, that's what I know. You get hold of people and don't let them go."

"You really think that's what drives me?" The anger had faded and the naked hurt was back in Rebecca's eyes.

Alex stared across the room at the red button on the wall. What would happen if she pressed it? Who would come? Would they lay hands on her without giving her a chance? Would they—The memories, the resentment, the suffocation crowded in on her. "It's not about you."

She closed her eyes, fought to let the traumatic scenes pass and not just run. Run from that place, with its reek of the institutions that assaulted her every time she stepped through its doors. Run from Rebecca, who maybe really did care, and who she owed. Because it was true, it wasn't about her, but she was one of *them*. One of the professionals who treated you like shit on their shoes that they couldn't wait to wipe clean, or worse, a vulnerable child they needed to protect from the big bad world. Who didn't listen but assumed they knew how to make you better even when they made you worse.

"Then what is it about? Phoebe's never been in care before, has she? Or is that something else you've kept from us? Or who...?" Rebecca's eyes flicked over her face, searching for the answer to her unfinished question.

Who did they hurt?

"No, Phoebe hasn't. But I have."

Me. They hurt *me.* Alex gazed at the button on the wall and this time let it draw her back.

"I had a motorbike crash, a bad one. It took a long time to get back on my feet. Literally. I was in a chair for a while." She reached down to stroke her crushed legs.

"You had to be cared for while you recovered?" Rebecca prompted, clearly thinking she understood.

"No. Yes. It wasn't that simple. I…" She paused to breathe again and allow herself a glimpse of her current surroundings. "I took it bad, didn't do well with being suddenly dependent. I'd always looked after myself. Then my life just stopped. It got to me. I became down, really down. Post-traumatic stress or something like that, not just from the accident, which was horrific, but from that time stuck there with just the pain. When I was ready to leave the hospital physically, they weren't happy I was ready mentally, so they moved me to the psych ward instead."

Rebecca reached over and took her hand, granting her an anchor to the present. She held it tight.

"But you don't get better there, not really. They just drug you up and leave you not knowing how to tie your own shoelaces. And accuse you of acting up if you show any emotions and focus on annihilating your quote-unquote *bad behaviour*. Eventually they agreed it wasn't doing me much good staying there, and a social worker arranged for me to go into supported accommodation instead, while I was still recovering physically and mentally. That wasn't much better.

"I had my own space, but they resented my desire to get my own life back, rather than trying to help me. It was supposed to be a temporary thing, but I soon learned most of the other people had been in the system for years, back and forth between those places and hospital, and there was no sign of them leaving. They didn't even seem to want to. They'd become so institutionalised they didn't know there was any other way to be. I reckon it was the fear of becoming like them that got me fighting." Alex reached up to wipe something wet from her cheek. She hadn't realised she was crying. She always tried not to think of the lost souls she'd left behind. Like the souls who were shuffling around the home below them.

Rebecca moved closer to her, pulling her chair forward so their knees touched. She took Alex's other hand and kissed away the tear stains. "I'm so sorry."

"You see now…" Alex's voice was becoming hoarse, and she feared an avalanche might follow those first tears. "You see why I didn't want Bee coming here and getting sucked into that. You see why—"

"You couldn't trust me?" Rebecca finished for her, saving her from having to spell out the brutal truth.

"Do you think you can forgive me?" She had to know if her truth was enough. Rebecca's sympathetic response didn't mean it was all okay. It wasn't sympathy she wanted from her.

"I don't think..." Rebecca looked down at their clasped hands, as if considering her words carefully. "I don't think that's really the question, do you? The real question is, can you ever trust me?"

Alex leaned towards her, cupped their hands between them, and pressed her forehead to hers. "I want to."

"But?" Rebecca whispered.

"But it's not easy. When I see you here, I remember you're one of them. One of the people who were supposed to help but did more harm instead. And I do know you're not like that, but it's not easy to shake off the past. Coming here with Phoebe, it's brought it back up." She let their hands drop to her lap but kept her head leaned on Rebecca's, eyes closed.

"Why didn't you tell me before?" Rebecca squeezed her hands. "Oh. Because you didn't trust me."

"It's not just that. I didn't want you thinking that was why I wanted to stay independent. I was Solo Poly before all that, it's not because of what happened, but"—she couldn't pretend nothing had changed—"it's made it even more important. Now I know what it means to lose my freedom completely."

"I understand. I...I don't know what it's like to be trapped in that way, but I know what it's like to be trapped in my own dark thoughts. It's not the same thing, but my anxiety, sometimes it's hard to see the way out. It's not as bad as it used to be. I've learned to manage it a lot better, with the help of therapy. And sometimes medication. Some things, they don't ever go away completely, but you learn to live with them."

"You're right. I am learning. This is the first time I've got into a new close relationship since, one that seems like it could be a long-term connection. I've been focused on getting my life back and then helping Phoebe get hers."

"Do you think you're ready?" Rebecca pulled back and gave her a searching look.

Alex forced herself not to retreat from her gaze. Rebecca was right, this was on her. Could she let her in, truly, completely? She had started to the night before, but when the time had come, she'd still turned off the lights and hid her scars. The physical ones that had changed the shape of her legs, and the jagged traces in her mind.

"I'll leave you to think." Rebecca leaned over and planted a gentle kiss on her cheek as she got up to leave.

As Alex watched her walk away, it hit her that if she didn't take this chance, she might never move on and learn to trust again.

"Come with me," she called after her, before the vulnerability got too much and she closed down again. "Come with me to get Phoebe?"

Rebecca turned back, a shy smile lightening her weary face. "Will Phoebe be happy about that?"

"She asked if you would. She's worried you're pissed off with her. With us."

"I hope you told her I am." Rebecca's broadening smile contradicted her words.

"You can tell her yourself if you come. Please? We can talk more on the way." She didn't need to think more by herself. She'd done enough of that.

"Okay. Though can we stop by mine, so I can take a shower and get dressed?"

Rebecca tugged at her shirt, which Alex realised probably didn't belong to her. Maybe they'd had the same thoughts when they'd rushed to join the fray.

"I'm sure we can manage that."

As tempting as it was to join her and try to revive some of their intimacy from the night before, she might grab a nap while Rebecca got herself ready. The day had held too many confrontations and emotions, and she needed to let it all float away.

Chapter Twenty-two

Rebecca's heart pounded as she knocked. Even after a long sleep, she was still dizzy from all the revelations of the day before. It was tempting to put it off, but she had to face the consequences.

"Come in," Patience called.

She stepped inside the office. It was really a glorified broom cupboard, with only just enough space for the two chairs facing Patience's desk. It served its purpose, giving Patience a place to retreat and get some peace from the bustling home. Plus meet with people privately when needed. Rebecca was glad of the privacy. As hard as it was to face Patience, it would be far worse with her colleagues around.

"Hi, Rebecca." Patience smiled, though it didn't quite reach her eyes and the bags hanging under them. It didn't look like she'd managed to get much rest, and her strong shoulders drooped. She folded her hands on the desk in front of her. Too formal. "How are you today?"

"Fine, thank you. How are you?" She heard the tremor in her voice and cleared her throat as if that was the problem. She didn't want to drop any more emotional baggage on her boss—she was carrying more than enough.

"Fine, now everything's been resolved. Thank you for coming in on your day off yesterday to help." Patience lifted her mug and gestured to another on Rebecca's side of the desk. "Do join me. I imagine you could do with the extra caffeine too."

Rebecca let out a shaky laugh and reached for the second mug. "You could say that. And I'm glad I was called in, though I'm not sure how much help I was in the end."

Hadn't she only antagonised Alex in their meeting rather than make any useful contribution? She took a sip of the hot coffee to distract herself from the recollection. It was just past scalding and left a heated trail down her throat.

"It was helpful to have you there, given the cooperative relationship you've built with Alex. We needed someone she trusted and who might help her open up. I had my suspicions that she was holding out on us."

Rebecca spluttered at the word *relationship*, midway through a bigger slurp. Patience offered a glass of water, which she refused, then waited until she'd finished coughing and had taken another silent sip of her coffee.

"Callum's parents were comforted to know you were going with her to collect Phoebe and Callum. I'm not sure they'd have agreed with the plan if not. Alex might have come clean in the meeting, but they weren't sure whether to trust her that far, and I'm not sure Alex would've let anyone else go with her."

Rebecca had to bite back the desire to defend Alex. Now that she knew her past, it was easier to understand her misguided actions. But she couldn't tell Patience, as much as she wanted to let out a stream of excuses and explanations. Like Alex would say, it wasn't her story to tell. Instead, she nodded and blocked her mouth with the cup.

"Have you checked in with Phoebe today? How is she doing?"

"No, I came straight here. But Alex said she's fine and not about to make any other rash decisions." She looked down into her mug as she spoke, anticipating the next question.

"You've spoken to Alex today?"

On the desk in front of them was Phoebe's file, now double the size from when she arrived six months before. No, triple. Quadruple? Rebecca studied it rather than her manager. "Yes. We've…we've become involved, outside of work. It wasn't planned, nothing happened here, and I didn't want to do anything to compromise Phoebe's care, but things developed and we've been seeing each other."

"Seeing each other? As in dating? Are you in a relationship with her?" Patience didn't sound entirely surprised.

Rebecca risked looking up at her. How could she describe it, when she didn't know exactly where they were heading? Did that matter? Did anyone ever really know? "Yes." She wasn't planning to say any more but realised she needed to. "We're polyamorous, Ishani and I, and Alex. We have multiple loving relationships at the same time."

"Oh, I know what polyamory is." Patience let out a chuckle. "I'm glad to hear Ishani's still in the picture too. You've clearly got a good thing going there. It's true what they say—it's always the quiet ones."

She chuckled again and settled back in her seat, hands wrapped around her own mug. There was no radiator in the cupboard-office.

Rebecca leaned back in her own chair, allowing some tension to leave her torso, thankful she didn't have to explain any further or defend her relationship style. Maybe it wasn't such a big deal.

"Of course, this does leave us with a bit of a conflict of interest as far as Phoebe's concerned."

She'd relaxed too soon. She couldn't deny it—she'd known they would reach that point one day. "I understand. I had that concern too."

"You've technically not broken any rules, so it's not a disciplinary matter. But it doesn't seem appropriate for you to be so involved in Phoebe's care."

Rebecca put her cup down as her hands started shaking at the word *disciplinary*. "Of course."

"That can be easily remedied. If we're in agreement, we can quietly shift Phoebe over to somebody else. No need to make a big announcement."

Thank God. Although she hated the idea of handing Phoebe's plans over, at least no one would be given the chance to question her keeping her job, and she would be around to monitor things. It was the best outcome she could've hoped for, and it might not have a negative impact on Phoebe, depending on who she was reassigned to. It wasn't her call, but maybe she could nudge her towards someone who would do a decent job.

"Can I suggest Luisa? She's built a good working relationship with Phoebe already." And Alex. She'd noted she was less edgy around Luisa than the others, possibly because Luisa gave her more of a chance. Luisa was not someone to be put off by an initial cold exterior. She'd squeezed past her own defences and seemed to be making good work of Alex's.

"I was thinking the same thing. Yes, as long as Luisa's on board and doesn't think she's too much trouble after yesterday, that will work."

"It was Luisa who got the truth out of Faye." Her friend deserved credit for being the one to find out what happened.

"Which is why I thought of her. She clearly has a good understanding of those two."

Those two. Would they take Faye away from her as well? Maybe they should, given how she hung around Phoebe and Alex. Rebecca had to be responsible about it. "Do…do you want her to take both of them?"

"No, no. I don't see any need." Patience brushed off the suggestion with a wave. "And we wouldn't want to risk Faye stopping bathing."

They allowed themselves a smile at that. Rebecca looked into Patience's eyes for the first time since she'd entered and saw no sign of judgement or distrust.

It was nice to know she was still needed. The mention of Faye brought up Alex's story of the institutionalised people she'd met. She'd seen Phoebe as a special case who had the chance of a more independent life, but seeing the way Faye had started to explore the wider world under her friend's wing…maybe she should rethink that. Maybe Faye could do more than she'd ever been given credit for. Maybe she wanted more, but no one had asked her and she didn't know to ask. Rebecca let the nauseating guilt roll over her and tried to hold on to the spark of hope and excitement that came with it. There was a chance of a bigger, bolder life for Faye too, and she could help her build it.

"That will assist with my other plan too, by lightening your caseload. The events leading up to yesterday have proved that we need to rethink how we approach the residents' sexuality and relationships."

Rebecca's heart froze. She'd promised Phoebe they wouldn't try to stop her relationship. Had she made a promise they wouldn't keep? Why had Phoebe had to act so…dramatically? *She's a drama queen*, Alex's voice reminded her. Maybe it would've always ended that way, no matter what she'd done.

"Clearly it wasn't what we wanted to happen, but it has given us an opening. It shows sticking our heads in the sand isn't a viable strategy. We need to embrace the reality of caring for all our residents' needs. Do you see, we can use this as evidence of the need to start delivering sex and relationship education like you've suggested before and build it into their care plans. We need them to know they can talk to us, and we'll respect their desires." Patience lowered her voice and spoke more urgently, inviting Rebecca into her confidence.

"Really?" She didn't know what else to say.

"Really. This is our opportunity, and we need to take it. No more patiently chipping away at old values and assumptions—we're shaking things up." Patience gave her a broad smile and a twinkle returned to her eyes. "We need to move with the times, and traditional care homes aren't what people with learning disabilities are looking for any more, if they ever were. We need to become more like supported accommodation, supporting them to live their own lives. There may well be some resistance from certain quarters, but if we work together, I believe we can push forward. Are you with me?"

"Yes." Rebecca surprised herself with her quick agreement. "What do you need me to do?"

She gripped the edge of the desk, ready to jump into action. Patience was right, they had to take their chance. It wasn't just Faye who deserved more from them, they all did. Phoebe had shaken things up and given them the opportunity to decide how they wanted to reset. Just like Alex had shaken up another part of her world, and it was coming together again in a different order. It was time to move forward.

"I want to put you in charge of this project. As I said, without all the work you've been putting in with Phoebe, you'll have more time for other concerns. I could do with your assistance updating other aspects of our approach too, including making our care plans more truly personalised, which is something you've been leading the way on." Patience gestured to Phoebe's expanded file.

"Thank you. I have ideas. I've done some research already into who can provide training, including well-respected charities. I want to do more, but I don't want to give up the hands-on care side of things completely."

It was why she'd never put herself forward for management training or roles—she went into care because she wanted to provide direct care. Partly why, anyway. Her heart started racing at the thought of the extra responsibility, and she had to remind herself to breathe. This was what she'd been fighting for, and she might finally have the chance to put her plans into action.

"I know, which is why we'll leave you with the rest of your key residents for now. If it becomes too much, we can move more people over, but to start with you can carry on with most of your other duties. As long as you promise to tell me if it gets too much. Don't think I'm not aware of all the extra hours you've been doing."

Rebecca felt the heat rising in her cheeks with embarrassment and pride. Patience was trusting her. She would show her it wasn't a mistake.

"I will, I promise. I've already assured Ishani I'll start leaving on time." It was a compromise they'd reached to ensure they got to spend time together, especially with a new lover on the scene.

"Good. If we need to increase your hours, it'd be better for you to come in earlier in the day while I'm here anyway." Patience pulled a notebook in front of her and took up a pen. "Now, tell me your ideas. Where shall we start?"

Wouldn't it be better to go away and prepare for that discussion? Rebecca opened her mouth to say she needed time, then shut it again. How many years had she been preparing, debating, researching, campaigning for exactly this opportunity? She was as ready as she'd ever be, and this was just the start. She opened her mouth again and told her manager what they needed to do.

❖

Alex gripped the pen tighter and printed her name before she could change her mind.

"And last one." The letting agent flipped to the final page of the contract.

She scrawled her signature on the line where he pointed and completed her details. After she printed the final letter she hovered over the ink, wondering if she was making a big mistake. But it was only twelve months—that was nothing in the course of her life. And it was what she needed. She put the pen down and let the paperwork be removed.

"Excellent. Here are your keys. The landlord will deal with any issues directly. You have his details." The letting agent put the papers in his briefcase and left, pausing briefly to shake Grant's hand on his way out.

It seemed her workmate had come through on his offer to find her a decent rental. He'd even done the introductions and vouched for her, so they hadn't been bothered about formal references.

"See, I told you, it's lush. Wouldn't get a place like this in Leicester for half the price, mind." Grant walked over to her with a wide grin and slapped her on the back. "My uncle will look after you too—you don't need to worry about a dodgy landlord."

That wasn't actually something she'd been worried about. She'd dealt with enough useless landlords over the years to know how to live with it. Better them than a prying one who kept too close an eye on their investment. "Long as he lets me, I'll take care of the place. He won't need to worry about any dodgy tenants either."

"Ha! That's all good then. You see, that's why he likes to rent to someone we know, not some random students who won't respect the place or the neighbours." He rubbed his hands together. "I better leave you in peace and let you unpack. Let me know if you need a hand, yeah?"

"Will do." Alex clapped him on the shoulder, the closest he'd get to a hug. "Thanks for setting me up with this place. It's great, really. See you at work."

Once she was left alone, she sat down on the faux-leather sofa to survey the flat. The living area was open plan, with a kitchen along one wall and a large table separating it from the lounge. It was smaller than the Hathaways' place, but plenty big enough for her and to have people round. The location was just right too. Being in Ampchester, it was still close to Phoebe's home but not right on the doorstep. The furniture was minimal, which left space to make it her own. Phoebe wouldn't need much persuading to make another trip to flat-pack heaven, and maybe this time she would let Rebecca join them. After all, she was a big part of the reason Alex had committed to stay. For the length of a rental agreement at least. After that, she'd see where they ended up. Having her own place was a promise of continued independence as well as sticking around.

Her phone buzzed. It was Drew, checking in to see if she was all sorted and demanding photos. It was followed by a message from Rebecca, checking if she was still okay to join them later. Within the same chat. Another compromise and one that meant she didn't have to wonder what information was being shared between them. It was all out in the open where everyone could see. She had to admit, Rebecca was right. It was easier for times like this than messaging them separately or trusting the right amount of info was passed on. As long as they didn't overuse it.

She fired off a response to their group chat, including a shot of her standing in the middle of the living space. She could give them a tour in person soon enough.

There was still plenty of time to make it back to the Hathaways' and pack her stuff before she headed over to Rebecca's. They weren't coming back for another couple of weeks anyway, but she was impatient to start making the flat her own. Grant had even said she was welcome to redecorate the place, as long as it wasn't anything too out there that could put off future renters. Which was fine, she wasn't about to go all psychedelic on the walls. Though she might have to contend with Willow, who loved an opportunity to let loose her creativity and had already bagsied painting duties. Along with Phoebe, of course. She'd have to closely supervise so she didn't end up living on a stage set.

At least Willow hadn't taken any issue with Alex deciding to stay there. In fact, she'd seemed happy about it, as it meant being able to see Phoebe more often and involved Alex having her own private flat. Hotels weren't anything more than a short-term solution, and when Willow had a decent break from touring, it'd be a nice place for them to relax together with no time limits. And it made impromptu visits a lot easier.

It would be a good bolthole for Phoebe too, if she was feeling too penned in at the home. Though it seemed like she'd have plenty of chances to get out of there. After her success in the recent show, there'd be plenty more offers to follow. They'd already announced auditions for the next one, and Phoebe had her eye on a leading role. Rebecca had mentioned something about singing lessons too, to refine her talent. She didn't see how Phoebe needed that, but maybe she'd enjoy it, and it'd keep her out of trouble.

If Phoebe started working at the theatre, she'd be kept busy anyway by the sounds of it. Maybe she could swing by the home on her way back that night to make sure she was all sorted for her interview. Despite being for a voluntary position, it sounded like a full-on process. It'd be good practice for Phoebe either way, and she'd be there to help commiserate if it didn't go well. The role did sound perfect for her, with free seats to the shows making up for the lack of pay in Phoebe's eyes. There was talk it could lead to a paid position. Not that you could count on that, and she'd made sure Phoebe understood there were no promises.

Her phone buzzed again. Phoebe was fretting over choosing interview clothes and had sent a few pics of different combinations. She was really not the right person to ask. Luisa had taken her clothes shopping to find something, and they'd returned with various work style outfits. It'd seemed a bit much to get all the clothes in advance—she didn't wanna know how much they'd spent—but Luisa had pointed out they'd be looking for other roles if she didn't get this one.

Since Phoebe's flit, they'd drawn up detailed plans to help her move forward with her life, including starting to look at getting into work. Formal volunteering was a step in that direction, even if it didn't lead directly to a job. Their desire to help Phoebe become financially independent was reassuring. When Rebecca had stepped down as Phoebe's key worker, even though she'd had no choice now they were openly together, Alex had worried her replacement might not be as dedicated to Phoebe's cause. Thankfully Rebecca had nominated the only other member of staff there that Alex had come to trust to have her sister's best interests at heart. Luisa was as safe a pair of hands as they could hope for.

She was also the only member of staff, apart from the manager, who knew about Alex and Rebecca, not because she was Phoebe's key worker, but because she was Rebecca's friend. It did help that they didn't have to worry about someone who'd question Rebecca's role in Phoebe's life outside the home. Phoebe could cover their tracks if needed, she'd proved she knew how to keep something under wraps, but it was better if she didn't have to. They had to be careful not to teach Phoebe that relationships should always be shadowed in secrecy and lies.

She studied the photos. Her little sister looked surprisingly respectable in all of them, even with her dyed hair. She really was all grown up. So, what did that make her? Birthdays had never bothered her, but seeing Phoebe as a fully-fledged adult made her feel suddenly old. She shook off the ridiculous dread that came in. She was only midway through her life, if that, and she had a lot more living to do. There was one outfit that was a clear winner: the cut of the shirt had an edge that made it seem more Phoebe than the others. She only needed to conform so much.

In the end, she'd just had time to feed Zelda and get changed before leaving the Hathaways' place again. She'd miss the little fluff ball. Maybe she could get a pet of her own, something that'd cope in a flat and moving around. And that wouldn't mind her leaving it to stop out with someone. Cats were good for that—they didn't seem to give a shit how much you were there, as long as they got fed. She didn't want to be forced to return to the flat every night.

There was a space on the drive waiting for her when she arrived at Rebecca's, with Rebecca's car parked on the street alongside the bungalow. She'd never actually been inside, only picked Rebecca up, except for the day of Phoebe's escape when she'd been too knackered to take in her surroundings. It looked like it'd been extended, with a wide porch in a slightly different style to the main building. Alex walked up the shallow ramp that led to it. Before she could ring the bell, the door opened and Rebecca stood there with a smile that flickered with excitement or nerves. Probably both.

"You came!" She pulled Alex inside by the hand. As soon as she closed the door behind her, she planted a short but sensual kiss on her lips. "Thank you."

"My pleasure," Alex murmured and drew her back for a longer kiss. Heat rushed through her as they pressed together.

Rebecca pulled away with a show of reluctance. "You should come in properly."

"Or we could stay here and draw this out as long as possible." She was only half joking. Snogging Rebecca on the porch was definitely better than meeting the family. Sure, she had already met them but not as Rebecca's newest lover.

"Tempting, but they're waiting. And there'll be plenty of opportunity for this"—she leaned in for another kiss—"when you take me back to your flat."

"Deal." Alex ran her hand lightly down Rebecca's side and smiled at her shiver.

They parted long enough for Alex to remove her winter garb. Then Rebecca took her hand again and drew her into the house. "Shall I give you the tour first, or shall we join the others for a cuppa?"

There was no point delaying the main purpose of her visit. She wasn't concerned about whether the house itself was happy with her being there. "A cuppa sounds good."

"Great." Rebecca's smile assured her that was the answer she'd wanted. "It means a lot, you doing this for me."

"You mean a lot to me."

She gazed into Rebecca's eyes and didn't need her to say it to know she felt the same.

"Here goes." Rebecca gripped her hand tighter and led her through the spacious living room into the attached kitchen.

There was a round table laden with cakes and steaming cups, which Drew and Ishani were already sitting around. They looked up as Rebecca and Alex entered.

"When you said Kitchen Table Poly, I didn't think you meant it literally," she said, the picturesque scene having thrown her.

The others' laughter seemed to release any tension that had been in the room. Rebecca pulled out a chair and gestured for her to take a seat.

There was only a tiny flash of fear of what she might be letting herself in for, nothing more than a tickle. She looked at her friend sitting across from her, their open smile and raised eyebrow daring her not to feel welcome. It was the first time she'd gotten that close to a metamour, even accidentally as it had been with Drew. The strange truth was that it wasn't Rebecca who was the real game changer. Sure, she wanted to be Rebecca's partner, but it was Drew who made her want to join their family. She hadn't imagined herself ever being in that position, but now she was. She took her seat.

By her side, Rebecca did the same. Alex laid her hands on the table, showing she had nothing to hide, and Rebecca took hold of one. She turned towards Rebecca and saw her eyes brimming with affection. Home had never been one place to Alex, it was wherever her heart was, and it looked like she had found herself another home.

❖

Rebecca had been in two minds about whether to suggest they all stay for a family meal or whether to savour some alone time with Alex in her new place. In the end, she'd decided not to push her luck—everyone had got on well and seemed relaxed together, and it was best to leave while they were all still feeling good about it. Plus it was important she take the time to make sure Alex understood how much the effort she'd made with Rebecca's other partners meant to her. Family dinners could come later.

"Did I pass?" Alex flung herself down on the sofa as soon as they got back and eyed Rebecca as she closed the door behind them.

"I thought you were going to give me the grand tour?" Rebecca looked around the flat as she removed her shoes, curious to see the place where she would hopefully be spending a lot of time in future.

"Bathroom's through there, and the bedroom's in the back." Alex gestured vaguely behind her. "I'll show you properly shortly." She stretched out her arms towards Rebecca.

"Or you could do it now." Rebecca walked over into Alex's arms and stood above her, leaning on the sofa as she bent over to give her a seductive kiss. After the afternoon with her newly expanded polycule, she was buzzing with affection and desire.

"Tempting." Alex kissed her again, matching her intensity. "But first, you need to answer my question."

She'd assumed it was rhetorical, or a joke to release any leftover tension, and that Alex didn't need that kind of reassurance. She was only starting to uncover Alex's vulnerable side. They'd come straight back to Alex's flat, so she hadn't had a chance to catch up with her other partners on how they felt. But she'd seen how they treated Alex, and the couple of messages they'd sent since meant she could be pretty sure. "Not that it was a test, but you excelled. They loved you."

"*They* love me?" Alex looked up at her with a cautious smile.

Which was when it occurred to Rebecca that it wasn't a word she'd used to describe her own feelings yet, at least not out loud, so it wasn't the best choice. Sometimes she got so caught up in her own head it was hard to remember what she had said or just thought. Surely Alex knew how she felt, even if she hadn't spoken those three words. Or were they both waiting for the other to be the one who said it first?

She knelt on the sofa, resting lightly on Alex's lap, and took her hands. She'd waited long enough. "*I* love you."

She couldn't help dropping her gaze at the last moment, focusing on their joined hands as she waited for a reply.

Alex extricated one of her hands and gently tilted Rebecca's chin so she was looking at her. "I love you too. Thank you for inviting me into your family."

With relief, Rebecca sank down further on the sofa and into Alex's arms. Alex held her close and didn't make her explain the happy tears brimming in her eyes. She'd have been lying if she'd pretended not to have had any fears about how the big introduction would go, or how deep Alex's feelings for her ran. Knowing that everyone she loved was happy with how things had turned out and wanted to stay with her was all she could have wished for. She hadn't imagined finding more love in her life, but she was glad she hadn't shut herself off from the possibility in the end. Whatever the future held, she wouldn't regret letting Alex into her life and into her heart.

About the Author

Kit Meredith (they/them) lives in the middle of England with their furbabies and too many craft materials. They have worked in health and social care from a young age and are passionate about improving the system using their experience on both sides of the assessment chart.

They're an extroverted introvert who enjoys connecting with people through the arts, including running local community groups focusing on queer storytelling. Neurodivergent, polyamorous, sapphic, and non-binary, they relish writing about characters who also live and love queerly.

They have had short stories published in various anthologies under other pen names. This is their first novel.

You can find out more about them and connect with them via their website, https://kitmeredithauthor.wordpress.com/.

Books Available From Bold Strokes Books

A Calculated Risk by Cari Hunter. Detective Jo Shaw doesn't need complications, but the stabbing of a young woman brings plenty of those, and Jo will have to risk everything if she's going to make it through the case alive. (978-1-63679-477-8)

An Independent Woman by Kit Meredith. Alex and Rebecca's attraction won't stop smoldering, despite their reluctance to act on it and incompatible poly relationship styles. (978-1-63679-553-9)

Cherish by Kris Bryant. Josie and Olivia cherish the time spent together, but when the summer ends and their temporary romance melts into the real deal, reality gets complicated. (978-1-63679-567-6)

Cold Case Heat by Mary P. Burns. Sydney Hansen receives a threat in a very cold murder case that sends her to the police for help, where she finds more than justice with Detective Gale Sterling. (978-1-63679-374-0)

Proximity by Jordan Meadows. Joan really likes Ellie, but being alone with her could turn deadly unless she can keep her dangerous powers under control. (978-1-63679-476-1)

Sweet Spot by Kimberly Cooper Griffin. Pro surfer Shia Turning will have to take a chance if she wants to find the sweet spot. (978-1-63679-418-1)

The Haunting of Oak Springs by Crin Claxton. Ghosts and the past haunt the supernatural detective in a race to save the lesbians of Oak Springs farm. (978-1-63679-432-7)

Transitory by J.M. Redmann. The cops blow it off as a customer surprised by what was under the dress, but PI Micky Knight knows they're wrong—she either makes it her case or lets a murderer go free to kill again. (978-1-63679-251-4)

Unexpectedly Yours by Toni Logan. A private resort on a tropical island, a feisty old chief, and a kleptomaniac pet pig bring Suzanne and Allie together for unexpected love. (978-1-63679-160-9)

Crush by Ana Hartnett Reichardt. Josie Sanchez worked for years for the opportunity to create her own wine label, and nothing will stand in her way. Not even Mac, the owner's annoyingly beautiful niece Josie's forced to hire as her harvest intern. (978-1-63679-330-6)

Decadence by Ronica Black, Renee Roman & Piper Jordan. You are cordially invited to Decadence, Las Vegas's most talked about invitation-only Masquerade Ball. Come for the entertainment and stay for the erotic indulgence. We guarantee it'll be a party that lives up to its name. (978-1-63679-361-0)

Gimmicks and Glamour by Lauren Melissa Ellzey. Ashly has learned to hide her Sight, but as she speeds toward high school graduation she must protect the classmates she claims to hate from an evil that no one else sees. (978-1-63679-401-3)

Heart of Stone by Sam Ledel. Princess Keeva Glantor meets Maeve, a gorgon forced to live alone thanks to a decades-old lie, and together the two women battle forces they formerly thought to be good in the hopes of leading lives they can finally call their own. (978-1-63679-407-5)

Peaches and Cream by Georgia Beers. Adley Purcell is living her dreams owning Get the Scoop ice cream shop until national dessert chain Sweet Heaven opens less than two blocks away and Adley has to compete with the far too heavenly Sabrina James. (978-1-63679-412-9)

The Only Fish in the Sea by Angie Williams. Will love overcome years of bitter rivalry for the daughters of two crab fishing families in this queer modern-day spin on Romeo and Juliet? (978-1-63679-444-0)

Wildflower by Cathleen Collins. When a plane crash leaves eleven-year-old Lily Andrews stranded in the vast wilderness of Arkansas, will she be able to overcome the odds and make it back to civilization and the one person who holds the key to her future? (978-1-63679-621-5)

Witch Finder by Sheri Lewis Wohl. Tasmin, the Keeper of the Book of Darkness, is in terrible danger, and as a Witch Finder, Morrigan must protect her and the secrets she guards even if it costs Morrigan her life. (978-1-63679-335-1)